POOR GIRLS

CLARE WHITFIELD

HEAD of ZEUS

An Aries Book

First published in the UK in 2024 by Head of Zeus,
part of Bloomsbury Publishing Plc

9 7 5 3 1 2 4 6 8

A catalogue record for this book is available from the British Library.

ISBN (HB): 9781837930869
ISBN (Goldsboro HB): 9781035916368
ISBN (XTPB): 9781837930876
ISBN (E): 9781837930845

Printed and bound in Great Britain by
CPI Group (UK) Ltd, Croydon CR0 4YY

Head of Zeus
First Floor East
5–8 Hardwick Street
London EC1R 4RG

WWW.HEADOFZEUS.COM

This fictional story is inspired by the real women in The Forty Elephants, as led by Queen Alice Diamond.

To the young!
May you laugh at our mistakes
but never repeat them.

PROLOGUE

SERVE, STEAL OR STARVE.

Choose one, or all three, but these are your only choices.

Starving has its obvious disadvantages. Serve? Then choose your master wisely. As a woman in England, 1922, be sure to seek out a benign ruler. But should you opt to steal, you could live like a queen – until you get caught, that is.

The mighty British Empire is in shock and mourning, crippled by debt and inflation, turgid with grief as the Great War turned unimaginable horrors into reality. When giant monsters of machinery tore their way across Europe, grinding men into dust. Now it is over, those of us still standing are angry and divided. Different generations may as well be alien to each other and are to be regarded with suspicion and fear. Rich and poor women, lost sons, brothers and fathers. But the old grey men who led the country from ivory towers ordered us to return to the ways of before. The wealthy clutched their pearls and retreated to their familiar customs.

But the young had seen what war had to offer. Then came the deadly Spanish flu, inflation, food shortages, unemployment, poverty. The children had run out of fear in the schoolyard. We were starving and lustful, cavalier to those who held their own mortality so sacrosanct. We were on fire! We would deny ourselves nothing, because tomorrow, who knew what horror those silly old fools would bring upon us.

We were never destined to have anything, that was a given, so you know what we did? We took it anyway.

3rd March 1911

Mrs Mackridge,

Today your youngest, Eleanor, received four strikes of the cane. Even during punishment, she maintained a resolute defiance and professed a wish to not be a young lady when she grows up!

The reason for today's punishment is that Eleanor was seen wilfully exposing her bloomers by hanging upside down from a tree alongside a boy at playtime.

As we have discussed on prior occasions, Eleanor is a capable young girl. Perhaps even one of the brightest in the class, but she has within her a rebellious streak that must be tamed. While Eleanor clearly understands the rules, she insists on questioning each and every one, defying them, especially if she thinks this will gain herself attention. Eleanor has shown time and time again that she remains unable, or unwilling, to show restraint when it comes to indulging her sense of mischief. She is never satisfied and always restless. I fear her boisterous appetite for adventure may inevitably cause her a mischief. She lacks self-discipline and I, for one, would welcome a discussion on how to control these troublesome aspects of her character, as the girl seems impervious to the cane.

Frankly, I fear for Eleanor's future. I do not believe her to be a wicked girl, but when she comes of age and must enter into service, I fear such qualities will inevitably lead her to a troubled existence.

Yours sincerely,
Miss V. Williams, Schoolmistress

CHAPTER ONE

Brighton, England, October 1922

IT WAS COMING UP TO THE END OF HER FIRST BUSY Friday shift at the Grand Hotel. Eleanor had been stitched up with the busiest section of sixteen tables – a baptism of fire for amusement. Sixteen unfamiliar tables in an unfamiliar restaurant that she must wait on dressed up in the fussiest, most old-fashioned uniform, with corset, lace collar, puffed sleeves and frilly cap. To top it all, it was itchy. She felt like a right pillock, but the wages were better, so one must suffer for the greater good.

The Victorian Terrace at the Grand Hotel had a veranda facing the seafront. The Terrace specialised in high teas, freshly baked cakes, finger sandwiches and scones – that sort of thing. It was much posher than her previous employer, the Lyons Tearoom, but that was due to be shut down with a new one opening up on James Street, so it seemed a good time to move on. Eleanor had been a waitress since being let go from the munitions factory, as all the girls had when the war ended. She was a pretty good waitress, fast on her feet, good memory and fit, having built up calves of rock and feet that could walk over broken glass. The Victorian Terrace restaurant, however, was tricky. It had many shady nooks and crannies and, being new, she was still trying to find the most efficient rotation of the floor, depending on how many covers were on. Table two had only just sat down and were looking at the menu. Table four could likely do with more drinks and table eleven had asked for the bill. A noisy little boy with what appeared to be his mother and grandmother sat on table eight. The table had become cluttered and needed to be cleared before something ended up on the floor, but Eleanor had a tray full of dirty glassware and empty soda bottles to get rid of.

'Eleanor,' Miss Larson, the manager, snapped, 'Table two are waiting to order.'

'They said they needed more time, Miss Larson.' Eleanor emptied the tray of glass as Miss Larson watched, arms folded. She liked to stay pinned to the cash register, much like a prison warden, with her set of keys on a long full skirt that didn't suit her.

'They look bored if you ask me.'

'Yes, Miss Larson.' *Three bags full, Miss Larson. Think of the money, Eleanor.*

'Leave those and get back there.'

'Yes, Miss Larson,' she said again, sounding like a flipping parrot.

Eleanor spun on her heels and glided over to table two, taking her notepad out of the impractically small apron and a pencil out of her hair. She'd already been told off once for keeping her pencil there and hoped Miss Larson hadn't caught her doing it again. The hard-faced woman was all over her. She struck Eleanor as one of those tough birds that had thrived during the war. Had a demanding job, wore trousers, commanded respect and now found herself back wearing ridiculous skirts and serving her betters. It is a universal truth that all managers are bastards when you first start, trying to sniff out a bad attitude or a cut corner. The staff at Lyons had been more friendly whereas the staff at the Grand were stuffed kippers, but the clientele was much classier and the tips better. *Think of the tips, think of the tips*.

The Grand may be the most luxurious hotel in Brighton, but it didn't stop it being infamous for dirty weekenders. It is a somewhat lesser-known fact that the well-to-do are the most badly behaved. If you had a mind for people watching, you could see all sorts of odd pairs checking in under false names. They might be married, but not necessarily to each other. It could be an effort to keep a poker face when a mismatched pair with an obvious gap in age or status appeared, with many young ladies, and a few men, being of the professional variety. This reputation meant privileged young men could be predatory in their behaviour, especially when it came to working-class girls. Not that this was anything new to Eleanor. She was no innocent. There couldn't be one left in the country after the last few years.

Eleanor took table two's order and didn't even realise she was smiling to herself until she caught the eye of a dark gentleman smiling back as if her smile were for him. Eleanor let her face fall and looked away. The man was sat alone at a table for two in a shady little nook by the window, not in her section. A shame, for it had not escaped her attention how attractive he was. He was half obscured by a meddlesome marble pillar, and when she did catch sight of him, he gazed out to sea, which only added to the intrigue of the mysterious well-groomed gentleman. Eleanor made her way back to Miss Larson at the register and stole a peek at the man on her way. Her eyes crawled from high-polished shoes to head as he sat facing the blustery ocean. It was October and wet and windy, but there was something romantic about the wind whipping up a hoolie as the waves crashed onto the pebbled shoreline – as long as Eleanor was indoors. The man was mid-twenties with glossy black hair parted on one side. Dark suit, wool, white shirt and burgundy tie, gold tie pin and cufflinks. But he did hold his teacup with a pinkie sticking out with a signet ring – a little on the gaudy side. He must be a new money man, or a black marketeer.

'Waitress!' called the grandmother on table eight, pulling Eleanor from her mindless trance. She rushed over. 'Clear this table, we can barely move. Such small tables you have.'

'They do it intentionally, Mother, so they can cram more people in, like sardines,' said the younger woman – by the resemblance, she assumed, the older woman's daughter.

'Of course, madam,' Eleanor said, 'I'll fetch a tray.' If only walking wasn't so impossible in this bloody skirt; it was like wearing a Christmas tree.

King George V had been on the throne since 1910 but the uniform was stuck in the 1890s, when Victoria was still kicking. It was on purpose, of course: everything about the Grand was designed to pander to the nostalgia held by the upper classes for all things from the last century. It was even affectionately called *palace by the sea*.

Eleanor snatched up a tray from the bar and flew back to the table as the boy managed to knock off a piece of

Victoria sponge cake, china smashing, well-heeled heads stopping to sneer at the disruption.

'Heavens! This is exactly what I feared,' prevailed the grandmother.

'I shall clear it, madam, it'll only take a moment.'

Miss Larson marched over with a dustpan and brush. Eleanor was on the floor on her knees, scooping chunks of broken cake from the floor when she felt a hard whack on her behind and kneeled bolt upright, nearly banging her head on the table. Grinning and with a wet bottom lip, the little boy brandished a dessert spoon covered in cream, which Eleanor had to assume was now on the back of her skirt. Little sod must have been at least eight – old enough to know better.

'If you'd done your job properly in the first place,' asserted the grandmother, looking down her hawk-like nose, 'none of this would have happened.' She had the ice-cold smile of the impenetrably wealthy.

Eleanor didn't say a word, as expected. She kept her eyes to the floor and wiped away streaks of jam, flicked buttercream off her fingers into the dustpan and got to her feet.

'Is there anything else I can do, madam?'

'The bill, right away.'

'Of course.'

Eleanor asked Miss Larson to ring up the bill, made a prompt return to the table and had taken a few steps when the grandmother called her back.

'What's this?' she asked, pointing at the bill.

'I'm sorry, madam?'

'You've had the cheek to charge us for the cake that

ended up on the floor. Take it off, I shan't be paying for your mistakes.' She slapped the slip down on the silver salver and pushed it towards her. To her daughter she said, 'Honestly, you have to watch these girls nowadays.'

In a bit of a panic, Eleanor ran back to Miss Larson, feeling herself getting hot under all the layers.

'Miss Larson, table eight has said I need to take the Victoria sponge off, what should I do?'

'Take it off, can't have an unhappy customer, can we?'

'Right, oh, it's just that when I was at the Lyons...'

'It'll come off your wages.'

'...what?'

'And the crockery. Here, there you are, I've rung it up for you.' Miss Larson thrust the new bill at her, so she had to reach up under her chin to take it. Wonderful: third shift and already docked wages.

She'd spent so long fussing with table eight that the others had been neglected and three were waving at her. The grandmother had gone to the ladies, and it was the mother who settled the bill. As Eleanor accepted the salver, the mother kept a firm grip until Eleanor looked her in the face.

'Keep the change,' she said, with a frigid smile. A pleasant surprise, she hadn't expected to get one.

'Thank you very much, miss.'

'Mother can be a bit of an old stickler about service, but you should be careful, what do you expect to happen if you offer your behind to the sky like that? Boys will be boys.'

The woman dragged her handsy little son towards where her mother was being helped into a lavender coat. The two women dressed nearly identically: long skirts, high neck blouses, matching wide brim hats. The little goblin looked back, grinning at Eleanor.

'Waitress! Can we have service, please?' a table called. Lord, what she would give to be back in the Lyons. *Think of the money, think of the money, think of the money.*

Eleanor drew breath and masked herself with the face of the willing to please. On her way to the table, she was disappointed to find the mysterious dark gentleman had disappeared and was surprised by her reaction. It was boredom, not that she wasn't busy, but the tasks were so incredibly dull, it was nice to have a daydream. Sometimes she wanted to scream and would look for glimmers of excitement in silly places. All in the hope that one day, if she kept bloody looking, something might happen.

CHAPTER TWO

AT THE END OF HER SHIFT, ELEANOR MADE POLITE small talk with the other staff. The clattering of the kitchen echoed around the gloomy passageway behind the swing doors of the restaurant.

'Don't worry, love,' said one waitress, 'Larson is like that to everyone when they start. She's taken it hard, the war ending.'

'She can get in the queue,' said Eleanor.

'Tell me about it. Munitionette?'

'Light & Co. on Circus Street.'

'I was at St James's Street. We made all the dope for the planes. What about you?'

'Started on shells and worked up to pyrotechnics.'

'A canary, eh?' The girls in pyro got called canaries because of the yellow that stained their skin. The colour became almost a badge of honour.

'Larson was driving ambulances in France, as far to the front as they dare. She's er... one to clean the cage out, if you know what I mean.' Eleanor looked mystified.

'She likes girls.'

'Oh! Right.'

'Apparently, she had a girlfriend in France and now she's stuck back in this shithole like the rest of us. I'd feel for her, if she wasn't such a cow.' The waitress offered a cigarette. 'Welcome to the Grand.'

'Thank you,' said Eleanor, taking a cigarette, and desperate to get that uniform off.

It was ten past four when she left the staff entrance and hopped over the road to the blue railings overlooking the beach. Above was a boiling grey sky and the sea was choppy, but there were still determined day-trippers braving the weather nibbling on whelks wrapped in yesterday's newspaper.

On a clear day she could see past the big fish market all the way to the Palace Pier. To the right was the famous West Pier with the concert hall. Eleanor rested on the railings and took out the gifted cigarette, stuck it in her mouth and patted down the pockets of her coat to find she didn't have any matches. She let out a groan and tipped her head to the sky, only to be startled by the grind of a lighter to her ear. It was the dark gentleman with the pinkie finger. Eleanor lit her cigarette as the man shielded the flame with his hands.

'Thank you.'

'Tough day?' he asked.

'Not really.'

'You don't strike me as the delicate type.'

'You can tell that, can you?' she said, raising an eyebrow.

'Something I consider myself good at picking up on.'

'Do you read palms and all?' The man smiled but didn't respond.

His woollen coat was heavy and expensive. As was the midnight blue suit and white shirt. She could have sworn the burgundy tie was silk, and the gold tie pin had a ruby in it. Probably fake – his accent was working-class London.

'So, if a man should find himself in Brighton,' he said, 'where should he go to find good company?' *Here we go.*

Eleanor took a long drag and exhaled. Men hit on girls like her all the time. Even so, this one wasn't unattractive, and she wished she didn't look like she'd worked a full shift. She'd taken her bun out and her long hair was flying about, growing curlier and curlier in the sea air, making knots to swear about later.

'It depends what kind of company a man is looking for,' said Eleanor. 'I think we cater for all tastes; you'll have to give me some idea of what it is that interests you, it's best to be specific.'

The men that came skulking for girls like her weren't usually this well dressed, nor did they smell this good: leather and musk, with a citrus hint. They tended to be escaped boarding school boys who in a few years would be pounding the halls of Westminster; either that or miserable middle-aged men. This one was neither: five foot six or seven with black brogues that gleamed and gold rings on his fingers. His cufflinks twinkled, as if they might have diamonds. Someone must have done rather well out of the war. She hoped he couldn't tell she was taking everything in; compared to him she must have looked poor, skinny and pale – *cheap to acquire.*

'Are you a Brighton girl?'

'I am. You?'

'Elephant and Castle, London. Do you know it?'

She shook her head. Her father's family hailed from Clapham, but her parents had moved before Eleanor and her older sister were born.

'What brings you here?'

'Business, but I'm off home tomorrow.'

'And you want recommendations?'

'And good company.' The man's cocksure way was grating, but also intriguing.

'Are you always this confident?'

'I don't like wasting time. It's a luxury none of us have.'

He leaned with his back to the railings, as Eleanor smoked her cigarette.

'I'll tell you what,' he said, stepping up his game, 'why don't you meet me later? You choose a place for dinner, and I'll pick up the bill. What do you say?'

'Why should I?'

'Because I'm a wonderful chap.'

'What's so wonderful about you?'

'I won't be around long enough to disappoint you.'

That made her laugh, which the bloke took as a win. Eleanor was tempted. She shouldn't, his confidence was offensive, but then again, she had to admit she quite admired his cheek.

'Did you know that during the Somme you could hear the cannons from this very spot.'

'It's exactly that kind of local expertise I'm looking for, combined with good looks and charm.'

'One out of three isn't bad, I suppose,' whipped back Eleanor.

'Don't be hard on yourself, you've at least two.' He did it again, made her laugh.

'While I am grateful for the invitation,' she said, exhaling smoke, 'I'm not sure I'm free.'

'Well, I have nothing to do but spend money and time. I will make you laugh, pay the bill and all you have to do is bring yourself, as much or as little as you want. I'll tell you what, I'll swing by this spot at seven. If you are here, great. If not, I'll take a lonely meal in my hotel room wondering what might have been. It was a pleasure meeting you.' He held out his hand and she shook it. Then he stuck his hands in the pockets of his expensive coat, turned and walked back along the promenade.

'Thank you for the light!' she shouted, and he turned back.

'You're welcome, what's your name?'

'Eleanor. Yours?'

'Come back at seven and find out.'

Good looking, definitely. Cocky, yes. Yet tempting. The man dressed well but was as common as she was. Perhaps he had done well for himself. It's a pity she'd become so cynical so young, her mother often said. But not so cynical that she wasn't tempted to turn up to see what would happen.

CHAPTER THREE

As soon as the mysterious gentleman was far enough away, Eleanor picked up her bicycle from where it leaned against the railings and swung a leg over in the most unladylike fashion. The bike had belonged to her brother-in-law, Paul, from when he'd had the use of two good legs. A fat lot of good it did him now he'd been sent flying by a bomb. Lucky for him he'd been sprinting away from the gas so spared his lungs, but he now walked with a limp, and had begrudgingly given the bike to her. Eleanor was dead chuffed it was a boy's bike, a *Coventry Royal Humber Roadster*, but the seat was stuck for a man of five feet and seven inches. No one could shift it and several blokes had tried. Eleanor managed a good five feet three inches in the morning, and so to stop, she had to brake and fall to one side.

She rode off towards home, a fifteen-minute ride. Up North Laine, past The Level playing fields full of grubby little kids, past Union Road and onto Elm Grove. She stood on the pedals to take the final thigh-burning yards uphill to see if she could do it, up to the house they rented from her mother's boss, Mr Bright. The family had moved in after Dad went to war and rented it for a very fair price.

Mr Bright ran the upmarket grocers at 23 Western Road in the city and was quite the aspirational businessman. Specialising in selling groceries and imported goods to wealthy day trippers and second homers from London, strange creatures with a taste for the exotic, such as gherkins in jars. Her mother had met Mr Bright when she found God after Dad had joined up, but it had to be a Catholic God, because the Church of England wasn't a real church, she said. It was made up so Henry VIII could get a divorce and therefore godless. Mum and Mr Bright had become friends in the choir, then he'd gone and offered her a job after they all lost theirs at the munitions factory. Mr Bright said Mum brought an authentic air of elegance to his shop on account of her being French. Mr Bright had lived in the house with his brother until he'd left for London but said that the house was too big for one bachelor and moved into the flat above his shop. Eleanor and Stephanie, her older sister, liked to joke behind Mum's back that Mr Bright must have been devastated when their dad made it back alive – well, what was left of him – because it was obvious to anyone with a pair of working eyes that Mr Bright fancied their mother.

It was a lovely house, much better than the rooms they'd had before. On a row of terraces, close to shops and school. It was small but had all the modern conveniences. A kitchen, scullery, front parlour and three bedrooms, and an off room with a bath, flushing lavatory outside, gas lighting, a copper water heater and a coal-fired range. At first, it had been only the three women, but add to those two husbands, and now twins, since Steph and her husband Paul had two six-month-old boys. It was getting rather crowded.

Eleanor hopped off, pushed the bike up the garden path and left it down the side of the house. On opening the front door, she was blasted by the smell of cooking and babies crying. She took her coat off and hung it up on the rack of raincoats Mr Bright had left behind. Eleanor hated living among other people's things and having to tiptoe around, fearful of damaging something; it was like living in a flipping museum. She didn't understand why he couldn't pack up his stuff. There were still Oxford shoes by the door, stuffed with brown paper from when they'd last been shined up. Eleanor couldn't help but find it intrusive, as if they all needed reminding that nothing belonged to them.

Eleanor poked her head into the front parlour with the old upright piano they'd been sworn off touching. There were Steph and Paul walking circles around the table, each with a red-faced baby in their arms, bobbing up and down. Not that it was helping – both were screaming their heads off.

'What have you done to those poor boys?' asked Eleanor.

'You have a go,' said Paul, thrusting one screaming child towards her.

'Oh, Michael! What has Daddy done to you!?' mocked Eleanor, then to Paul, 'I'm not good with kids, you know that.'

'Yeah, so it turns out, neither are we.'

'Paul, they're teething, they're bound to fuss.' Stephanie looked tired and worn. 'Mum's cooking and Dad is out back, having a fag.'

'Do you blame him?'

'No, I flipping don't,' said Steph. 'I'd be out in a flash if I could palm this one off.' As if Eleanor might take the hint.

'Not bloody likely,' said Eleanor. 'Nice try though.' She skipped off.

'I'll remember this when it's the other way round!' Steph shouted.

Sliding in stockinged feet, Eleanor skated into the scullery over the wooden floor. This was where the whole family lived and ate. It had dark green wallpaper, with Mr Bright's family's pictures on the wall, a fender, curtains and high-back chairs. A rag rug lay in front of the fire made of offcuts of serge and tweed. Cups hung from hooks on shelves. Off from the scullery was a cubby hole for the sink. They'd not had modern conveniences in their old place in Sun Street, only the three rooms rotting from the inside for eight shillings a week. No indoor plumbing, and a seasonal chorus line of pests – ants in summer, rats in winter.

Her mother was sat in a high-back chair peeling potatoes with a big bucket at her feet, elbows on knees. Eleanor crept up and gripped her on both shoulders.

'Aïe! Oh, la vache!' Mum cried out, dropping the knife, and a potato went rolling across the floor, Eleanor scooped it up and dropped it into the pan of water by the bucket, as her mother retrieved the knife.

'Can you not say hello, like a normal girl?' She thrust her cheek out, and Eleanor gave her a kiss on one and then the other. 'How was it today?'

'Better,' said Eleanor, if only to make her mother happy.

It was very obvious what appealed to Mr Bright, and others, too. Emilie was forty-six now and somehow still seemed youthful, despite grey strands above her ears. She still wore her dark hair long and had a slender build and bright blue eyes. When men looked on her heart-shaped face and round eyes staring up at them, you could practically watch them drift away. But mother often said what came out of an Englishman's mouth was incomprehensible, or as she said, *they use many words but say nuffink.*

Eleanor sat at the table, hungry, and opened the cupboard above to see only a tin of lychees, Bovril, John West tinned sardines and herrings.

'What's for dinner?' she asked.

'*La boeuf au pif.*'

'Beef?'

'*Oui*, Mr Bright has given each of us a piece of braising steak as trade has been so good. We will have meat with dinner today, I will make a crusted mash…'

Eleanor suffered a flash of the evening that lay ahead of her if she should spurn the mysterious man and his invitation. It was the same as the one the day before and likely the ones coming forever after. They would eat, Paul would complain that he was still hungry, the babies would take turns to cry, laugh or break wind – most certainly vomit. Stephanie and Paul would bicker. Her mother would make conversation with her father as he twitched involuntarily or drifted off to his netherworld.

William 'Bill' Mackridge had been wounded on 8th October 1916 at the Battle of the Somme where he was hit in the groin by exploding artillery. Already riddled with lice and lungs scorched by gas. He still wore a back brace, and aside from the trembling, headaches, tinnitus, absolutely no concentration, inability to remember much and occasional confusion – he was tickety-boo. He'd been treated at Rouen then transferred by hospital ship to Netley Military Hospital in Southampton. Eleanor shuddered when she remembered the first time they'd been able to visit him during the months he was there. How the Southampton waters had turned black with all the ships carrying wounded soldiers arriving. How her mother had told her and Steph he'd been hurt, but not warned them how badly; likely she knew no better herself. How the hospital had been full of twitching electric monsters, scars deep as trenches across their faces, missing parts, smiling freaks of deformed men, and how she'd been frightened of them.

'Can you save mine, I'm going out,' said Eleanor.

'Oh, where? And who with?'

'Maureen, we're off to the pictures.' There were no plans with Maureen, but her mother would never know.

'I thought Maureen was engaged.'

'Does that mean she can't go to the pictures?'

Her mother's round eyes adopted a heavy-lidded stare.

'How old is he?'

'Why must you always suspect I am up to mischief, *Maman*?'

'Because I was young once and we are too alike.'

'We're going to see *Bleak House*, if you must know.'

'*Bien sûr*, I will keep a plate for you.'

'Thank you, Mummy.' Eleanor leapt up and planted another kiss on her mother as she muttered in French.

Eleanor slipped out the back door. The lav was down a few steps to the right and she knocked on the door.

'It's open,' her dad called.

She pushed open the door to the lavatory filled with spiderwebs and there was her old dad sat smoking with a hand on one knee. He had his shoulders up around his ears the way he always did. Eleanor squeezed in beside him, stuck an arm through his and rested her head on his shoulder. Before the war he'd been twice the size he was now, and Eleanor could have slept on those shoulders comfortably. The man was knocking fifty and while the war, or his part in it, had lasted less than a year, it had added decades to his body. He offered his cigarette; Eleanor took it.

'You'll never guess what,' he said.

'What?'

'Four jewellers smashed and grabbed today. Proper job, all at the same time.'

'Really? What were you doing up The Lanes?'

'Delivery,' he said. He worked as a middle-aged barrow boy at the market stalls as and when he could get work. 'The police turned up about the same time I did. Bunch of useless fannies. Proper gangsters they reckon: pinstripe suits and flashy cars.' She handed the roll-up back.

'What are gangsters doing in Brighton?'

'Maybe they fancied the sea air.'

'I'm off out. Catch you later.'

'Right-o, love. You watch yourself.'

'Don't let Paul eat the meat from my dinner.' Eleanor shut him back inside the lavatory.

Eleanor snuck past the others in the front parlour singing, 'My Old Man Said Follow the Van'. Mum, Paul and Stephanie were dancing around the table, trying to stop the babies crying to no avail.

Her bedroom had a single brass bed pushed up against the corner of the room, overlapping the sash window at the front of the house. This was crucial, since it meant she could pull herself in through the window when she snuck out at night. Stephanie had taught her this – it was bloody difficult to miss your sister as she climbed over you as you slept.

The wallpaper was a tight pattern of flowers, red on cream. There was a small dressing table in the other corner with a rotating mirror. Beneath was a ceramic pitcher and wash bowl, and a chamber pot on the floor. A washing line ran from wall to wall above the bed, for drying underwear. Eleanor's room was messy, with books, hairbrushes, creams and empty soda bottles, but her most treasured possession was a big poster of exotic birds on a blossom tree of pink flowers. Her dad told her it was Oriental. Eleanor didn't know or care – she'd bought it at the market. The sky behind the birds was such a luminous blue, exotic and beautiful.

The Grand dictated female waiting staff wear a chemise, corset and petticoat. Stockings must be cotton lisle or wool. Eleanor exhaled as she took it all off and let her ribs expand. She hated corsets and this one had cost ten shillings. Before the war it would have cost only six but now she had to purchase something she hated at near twice the price. She opened her drawers and unfolded her best pink chiffon chemise with blue chiffon bows. Light and soft, it had been worth her skin turning yellow with the TNT. The money had let her buy pretty things, but now such pretty things were out of reach, again.

Both Steph and Eleanor plucked their eyebrows to within an inch of their lives and pencilled them back in. The sisters shared makeup, although Steph hadn't been one to wear much of late, so it lived in Eleanor's room.

Being pale was the fashion – as pale as possible, though the trick was not to end up looking like a cue ball. A little cold cream to even out the skin tone and a fine white powder to set. For the eyeshadow, the colour must go all the way up to the brow and match the main colour of whatever dress she would wear; Eleanor picked deep purple. Next was the black cake mascara – a little spit got it wet enough – and she never bothered with her nails, never had, having left school and gone straight to the factory at fourteen. The heart-shaped 'Cupid's bow' lip was the shape to have. She picked a dark red to make her mouth look as small and round as possible. For scent, she snuck into her mother's bedroom and stole the oil she made from crushing peonies. Steph appeared at her bedroom door, arms folded.

'You're wearing my stockings, aren't you?' asked Steph.

'I vow, if I damage them, I will buy you new ones.'

'You may as well wear them. Not like I'll be needing them for the next eighteen years. I'll likely never go out again, and when I do, I'll be grey and portly.'

'Give over.'

'I wonder how England will be when the boys are eighteen. That would make it 1938, it might be a different place by then, I hope.'

'What's given you the gloom?'

'Nothing, I'm envious, that's all. I'd like a night off but all I would do is sleep, truth be told. Tonight, no doubt Mum and Dad will be in bed before me and Paul, but I will lock the door by ten o'clock. And don't forget to bloody well take my stockings off before you climb in that window.'

'Of course.'

'*Bleak House*, my arse. You be careful, whoever he is. You don't want to end up like me, do you?' Steph disappeared back downstairs to her wailing babies.

25

CHAPTER FOUR

ELEANOR WAITED AT THE SPOT WHERE SHE'D MET THE man that afternoon. She smoked one cigarette after the other, worrying if she'd worn too much makeup, especially if she found herself stood up. What a waste, and humiliating.

She'd first started sneaking out at fourteen once she'd started earning her own money. Being a munitionette meant she'd never had to go into domestic service, unlike Steph and her mother. Most girls in service had abandoned their positions to take up factory shift work. Who wouldn't want a shift start and end time, decent pay, defined working conditions, being trained up on all sorts of things to do with machinery and explosives? There was singing in the choir, football, fundraising for the boys at the front. They even made a tapestry to fundraise to buy kits to send to soldiers on the front line, with cocaine, sweets and snuff. With all those fathers absent, curfews were practically impossible to impose. After shifts they would go canoodling in the park with young soldiers, trying to hide in the dark from the elderly women hired to patrol the parks and break up any young couples about to slip into 'regrettable moral degeneracy'. At the factory Eleanor learned all about men and their bits, and male appliances, the prophylactics they gave to soldiers, and how many came back with venereal disease. The older girls loved telling horror stories to all the young girls.

'They're at it all the time with French and Belgian whores, you know. They queue outside the brothels, waiting for the women to turn the light on and send up a good cheer when it does – my brother told me. You get a good look down there first when his flies come undone, you can't trust them. If you see anything funny or it smells a bit off, you bloody well run.' It was lucky it hadn't put a whole generation of girls off boys altogether.

Eleanor heard all about pessaries, sponges and douching. Rubber caps and raspberry leaf tea. Laxatives, gin, hot baths and if all else fails, violent exercise. Some girls even swore by Lysol disinfectant douches. Lost in thought, Eleanor didn't hear the car crawl up alongside her.

'Been here long?' The interruption made her jump.

There was that handsome smile, the hand covered in gold rings over the car door, rubies glinting. He'd only turned up driving a bloody great big motor. Shiny black, with a cream roof and a little silver statue on the front. And huge wheels, fat ones; she'd never seen such a car – well, only at the pictures.

'You do know you're on the wrong side of the road,' she said, as he pulled the car to a stop.

'You best get in then,' he said, 'I'd rather not get arrested.'

Eleanor hesitated. Was hopping into a man's car the wisest thing to do? But it was a nice car, and she'd never been in one before.

'You didn't tell me your name,' she said. 'Surely I should know a man's name if I'm to get in his car.'

'John Noon. Now you know, come on, get in.' Sod it, she threw the cigarette onto the ground, ran around and jumped into the passenger seat.

'You may want to hold on, Eleanor, this baby can go fifty miles an hour. Are you ready?'

'Always.'

When he slammed his foot down, the car hurtled forward and swerved across the road. Eleanor yelped, pinned to her seat. They flew past the aquarium, Volk's electric railway and the ladies' bathing tents, and headed out eastwards.

'Fast, huh?' John's eyes darted about, hands fixed on the steering wheel. 'Is there somewhere I can park it? A nice area where it will be safe.'

'If you slow down, you can turn into Royal Crescent, here.' She pointed across the windscreen.

They turned into a crescent-shaped row of beautiful Regency houses over four floors with glorious views of the Channel. These houses were not for the general Brighton population, of course, but London gentry that liked to take in regular doses of sea air. They parked the car and the sound of each door slamming heightened Eleanor's nerves. Was this a little odd? Not that she'd ever been out with a man with an actual car before.

'Your car should be quite safe here. Is it new?'

'I'll let you in on a little secret,' he said, bending towards her ear. 'It's not mine.'

'Oh?' Eleanor stopped walking.

John laughed, slapped her on the back, grabbed her arm and pulled her along. 'I didn't steal it or anything. It belongs to my aunt.'

'Heavens! What does your aunt do?' Eleanor did not take to being manhandled.

'She's the Queen of London.' He lit two cigarettes and gave her one.

'Your aunt is Queen Mary?'

'No, Mary is the Queen of England, but my aunt Alice, she is the Queen of *London*. She's not my blood aunt, she's my big sister's friend, our families grew up together.'

'And she lets you borrow her car? That seems… generous.'

'Yeah, she's good like that. My sister, Chrissie, she loves a bit of shopping, she does.' He grinned. 'They all do.'

They walked onto the main road and back up towards the piers where John spotted the Volk's electric railway station.

'What's that?' He pointed like an over-excited child, as Eleanor explained it was a small car train that ran along the seafront.

'Let's get the next one.' He jumped on the spot, a giddy schoolboy, then sprinted ahead. 'Come on, we're going to miss it!'

Where was the seductive flirt from this afternoon? Eleanor wasn't much impressed.

When the next car came, John paid, and they sat huddled with the other passengers. This wasn't the elegant evening she had entertained fantasies of, and dinner had better not be a bag of chips. They bumbled along, the close confines not conducive to chatter until the aquarium came into view.

'We should get off here,' said Eleanor, and they joined others shuffling off into the dusk.

'How come you speak like that, a bit posh like – when you say "off" you say *awf*.'

'Blame Mrs Williams. She was a dragon of an old schoolmistress who was forever giving me the cane. She was determined if nothing else we should leave speaking the King's English. She'd train us like mynah birds. For *often*, she made us say *awfan*, and careful not to pronounce the 'T', because this is the way our betters speak. Bloody stupid if you ask me, as if sitting in a draughty old house saying, 'isn't this *awfully cewld*,' is any use when you've not got two brass farthings to rub...'

John had stopped listening and become excited again, absorbed by the illuminated pier.

'What is that?!' he shouted.

'That's the Palace Pier,' she said. 'Surely you've seen a pier before?'

'Not like that one!' John ran ahead, leaving her to follow. Eleanor took a deep breath and trudged behind.

She had used an awful lot of makeup and risked her sister's silk stockings for what might be another unremarkable two-minute knee-trembler under that flipping pier. She had half a mind to make a run for it. The man was loud, his brash ways made her cringe, and he seemed to have no consciousness of his volume.

The wooden boards shook with stamping feet and John tried the planks for his weight, as if he thought he may fall through. Yellow bulbs flashed to the ring of ear-splitting bells, vendors shouted and kids ran past the coconut stalls, fortune tellers and queues for whelks and warm beer, as the sea thrashed underfoot.

'You can see the water between the gaps!' he said.

Eleanor rolled her eyes and didn't hide it. In her mind she was already stuffing the stockings into her pockets. They strolled on, once she'd convinced him off the pier, but every time she pointed at a restaurant she knew to be of middling quality, he would pull away.

'Not for me, it's too bright in there.'

Four or five places she suggested, none being right, but the final straw was when he tried to take her into a dingy pub. The only women who went in places like that were wives chasing errant husbands, drunks and drug-addicted prostitutes, so her mother told her.

'You were wrong,' she said, pulling her arm free from him. 'You *were* around long enough to disappoint me.' Eleanor marched off towards the bus stop. John grabbed her by the elbow.

'Don't you put your hands on me! I will scream so loud your ears will bleed!' John released his grip. Then, leaping into her path, he held up his hands to stop her advance.

'Please don't scream! What did I do?'

'Are you mad?'

'Not officially,' he said, trying to be glib.

'You told me you wanted company for dinner, and so far, you've dragged me halfway out of the city to park your aunt's flipping car, the pier where I've been a thousand times, and then tried to take me into a dirty old man's boozer! You must take me for some floozy who can be bought and paid for with beer! I may be poor, Mr Noon, and we may be in Brighton, but I am not that bloody desperate. You can take your pint and stick it up your bloody arse where I hope it breaks into a million pieces and you spend years picking it back out. Now get out of my way.'

She pushed past, leaving John bewildered on the pavement where he burst out laughing. She turned around to see the man bent over, laughing maniacally, but this enraged her even more.

'Urgh, you're nothing but a common pig in a good suit!' she shouted, then carried on, stewing with rage. She was too easily tempted by novelties and had allowed a man to make a fool of her. It was her own fault. John – a man with bundles of audacity and no shame – came chasing after her again.

'Oh, Lord, leave me alone!'

'I think we may have misunderstood each other,' he said.

'Oh, I disagree, I think I understand perfectly.' Eleanor went to push past, but he kept getting in the way, and he was still amused by the whole thing.

'Stop! I only want to talk. Give me one more chance,' he said in between trying not to laugh. 'Did you know your nostrils flare when you're angry?'

'You have exactly ten seconds and it better include an apology.'

'I'm sorry,' said John. 'I had no idea you would feel that way about pubs. For the record, my sister and her friends are in pubs in Southwark all the time. Pubs, clubs, bars... restaurants, it's all the same.'

'Not in Brighton they're not.'

'And I have every intention of taking you to dinner... let's go now. At my hotel there's a fancy restaurant downstairs, proper stuff, seafood and champagne. Come on. This may come as a surprise, but I am known for my charm.'

'You could have fooled me.'

'Can we start again?'

'I'm not having dinner in your room, if that's what you're thinking, like some tart you can hire for a couple of shillings.'

'In the restaurant, downstairs, with witnesses and plenty of people to hear you scream, in case you want to threaten to do that again.'

'I will if I have to.'

'I don't doubt it.'

She considered a moment, unsure why, but in reality, Eleanor was more distressed at the idea of having to go home than letting this farce play out further and see what might happen.

'All right, but you are on thin ice, Mr Noon,' she spat. 'Now, where is this restaurant?'

'The Grand – where I'm staying.'

'I can't go there! I'm a waitress, I'll be fired.'

'Don't be daft, no one will notice. We'll be in the restaurant downstairs; you work in the other one.'

'If someone should recognise me, I could lose my job.'

'Trust me, they won't be looking for you. You look completely different out of uniform anyway. Pretend to be someone else, that's what I do.'

Against her better judgement, she found herself being convinced by him once again. They got all the way to the entrance of the Grand before Eleanor balked.

'I can't go in. It's madness.'

'Come on, I bet you've never been to dinner inside, have you? What's the worst that could happen?'

This had been Eleanor's issue since birth. Any offering of adventure, however small or cavalier, held such an allure that she often found herself tempted into stupid things. There was forever a little dancing devil pulling on her innards, ringing bells, telling her to hell with it.

'I can order what I like?' she asked.

'I demand you order the most expensive item on the menu, whatever it is – I don't care.'

'Champagne?'

'I'd be offended if you didn't.' He stepped up onto the stairs to the entrance and held out his hand. 'Come on, don't run out on me now.'

'Only dinner.' And she took his hand.

'We'll see,' he said, flashing a grin.

'Thin ice, Mr Noon!'

'It was a joke! I can't help myself.'

At the entrance, she clung on to John's arm. She shouldn't be inside the Grand among this clientele and she could feel it leaking from every pore.

'What is it?' he asked.

'I don't belong here,' she whispered. 'I have a tatty old dress and it's so bloody posh.'

'Remember who you are, Eleanor.'

'And who is that?'

'Where are we?' he asked.

'The Grand, in Brighton. East Sussex, England, is this… neurosis?'

'Tonight, you are the Duchess of Sussex.'

'You *are* a lunatic.'

'Possibly,' he said. John tipped Eleanor's chin up. 'There we are. There's that face again, the one that told me to stick a pint up my arse. Now, come along, Duchess, that champagne won't drink itself.'

CHAPTER FIVE

WHEN ELEANOR WOKE THE NEXT MORNING, IT WAS AS if she were waking on a heavenly cloud drifting through the sky. Stretched out on a huge bed with the softest mattress, she lay like a snow angel and her fingers couldn't find the edges, nor John beside her. She sat up; the sun was screaming into the room and the curtains had been drawn. She shielded her eyes as flashes of the night before came like bullets behind the eyelids.

They had ordered champagne and seafood: prawns, lobster, samphire and a second course of pork and peaches. The Eton mess had exploded, and pieces had flown across the room as they howled, blind drunk, at the table. Oh Lord, there was much to be embarrassed about. She had told John her sister had a shotgun wedding, and her father was a frail old man with shellshock, and her mother worked for a man who was in love with her. Eleanor fell back on the pillow and groaned. She also vaguely remembered doing impressions, one of her schoolmistresses, of her mother...

and of her boss at the factory – and of the Queen! How wretched she felt, but where was John?

The last memory she had was of John dragging her out of the hotel and down to the beach and walking on pebbles, full of champagne, like negotiating a floor of snooker balls. They had tripped over in the dark and wandered towards the crashing sea. Shoes had been thrown and John had rolled up his trousers and taken his socks off. He'd bent over and told her to jump on his back and she had tried several times before he had grabbed her under the knees. Then, as he stumbled towards the sea, she had slowly slid down his back. The freezing cold water stopped them laughing and she had screamed when the cold splashed them. John had lost his balance and sent them both in and the shock had sobered them up. They then carried their shoes back through the hotel, shivering, Eleanor clutching on to John's hand past the staff, as they trod up the stairs with wet feet to his suite overlooking the seafront. Her sister's dress was soaked, and the stockings? She had no idea what had happened to those but suspected they had come to a tragic end when John had removed them with his teeth. Eleanor removed the pillow from her face and, clutching sheets to her naked chest, saw her clothes dotted about the floor. Good grief – what time was it?

'John?' said Eleanor, throwing her legs out of the bed. It was so high her feet didn't touch the carpet.

He might have answered but she couldn't hear over the roar of cars outside the hotel. Then came three hard bangs on the door, and the furious whisper of a woman from the other side.

'Mr Rogers! Mr Rogers! The police are here!'

John came tearing out of the bathroom, half shaved but dressed. He opened the door and in slithered a dark-haired chambermaid.

'There's so many of them,' she said. 'They're all out at the front!'

John ran over to the windows and turned ash grey. He put his hands into his black hair, stumbling backwards. Eleanor sat up, covering her modesty (what was left of it), now awake and in panic. The waiter the night before had called John Mr Rogers, and she had meant to ask but had promptly forgotten when another bottle of champagne arrived.

'Why are the police here? Are they here for you?' asked Eleanor.

The next few minutes passed in the worst type of terror. John screamed at her to collect her things, no time for dressing. Naked, Eleanor ran about the room, scooping up her clothes in front of the chambermaid.

'Polly, get rid of her!'

'But what about you?' said the chambermaid.

Even in her nakedness, clutching her bundle, Eleanor noticed the earnest affection in the chambermaid's voice.

'Don't worry about me, sweetheart, I'll go the same way I came in, sort of.' The chambermaid and John stole a passionate kiss as Eleanor watched with hair standing in all directions. Mr Rogers was a fast worker.

John had hold of Eleanor's, or rather Stephanie's black wool coat with the fur trim and was shoving it into her arms and pushing her out of the door, buttocks first. Eleanor squealed as she was about to be thrust naked into the corridor, but John silenced her with a hand over her mouth.

'Polly will help you.'

Tiny Polly grabbed Eleanor, yanking her backwards as John slammed the door in her face. Eleanor dared not look behind, expecting shocked patrons. Polly pushed her again, and she was thrown into a cupboard and the door was shut behind them. The cupboard turned out to be a linen room with shelves of crisp cotton bedsheets. Four knees shook as booted feet thundered down the corridor on the other side of the door. Eleanor thought she might be sick. Men barked, then came another stampede. *He's gone out the window! Get him!* Polly put a trembling finger up to her own lips, then slowly opened the door a crack. As she stuck her head out, she nearly lost it when a herd of policemen ran past, but she dodged out of the way and closed the door again.

'Get dressed, I'll get you out,' Polly whispered.

'How?'

'Laundry room.'

'My clothes are soaking wet.'

Polly's nose scrunched up. 'Wet? But how... urgh.'

Polly grabbed a long blue overcoat from a hook on the door, the type worn by housekeeping staff, and threw it at Eleanor.

'Must be your lucky day, put this on.'

When they emerged from the cupboard, Polly led the way with a laundry trolley between them, Eleanor's clothes thrown in. She wore the long blue overcoat and a cap with her hair back and her eyes down.

The journey via the lift with the laundry trolley was agonisingly slow as a torrent of chaos blazed through the hotel: policemen everywhere, uniform and plain clothes. Both women adopted the glaze of the servant: soulless, empty, hoping to render themselves invisible. Sweet freedom was in reach when they entered the sweat and steam of the laundry rooms. Polly told Eleanor to grab her clothes out of the trolley and opened double doors onto an alleyway. A dank exit encased by tall, dark, soot-covered buildings, sodden newspapers and old crates rotting in heaps, topped with the smell of rats' piss.

'Go to the end and right, it will take you under a building and you'll come out on Cannon Street.'

'Right.'

'I'm going to need that back.' Polly nodded at the overcoat.

'What? How am I...'

'Hurry up, the longer you fuss, the more likely someone will see you,' said Polly, arms folded.

'Fuss, you say?' spat Eleanor. The girl was enjoying this.

'I did.' Polly smirked.

Eleanor unbuttoned the blue overcoat and took it off, naked in her shoes, then threw it at Polly, who could barely stop her smile from spreading. She put her black woollen coat over the top, and bundled her wet dress, chemise and what remained of her sister's stockings into her pockets and put on her cloche hat to flatten her hair. Wrapping her arms around herself, she thrust her chin in the air; she couldn't possibly be less of a duchess at that moment.

'Thank you, Polly.'

'You're welcome, I never did catch your name.'

'Probably best,' said Eleanor, and with as much dignity as she could muster, she walked along the dirty, stinking alley.

Given the fragility of her accoutrements, she decided she would walk home, pulling her coat about her as tight as she could, every button fastened.

It wasn't until she started up the hill to her house that the full enormity of what had happened sunk in, and she wasn't out of the woods yet. It was coming up to seven o'clock in the morning, and she had yet to get back into the house. She made a mad dash up the garden path. This part would be interesting.

She climbed up the side of the porch, thanks to the trelliswork, heaved herself up onto the porch roof, maintaining most of her decency. As she clambered up, she couldn't be sure how much of her derrière she had displayed to poor old Mr Spooner, the wheelchair-bound veteran across the street who had already been wheeled out into the garden to take his morning air, blanket across his knees. He had been that way for as long as they'd lived there, sat by the big window, looking out, or in the garden. Eleanor had no clue how compos mentis the man was, having never heard him speak, and she didn't have the desire to find out now. On her knees, she levered her bedroom window open and – seconds away from sanctuary – glanced back at Mr Spooner, staring as always with his mouth agape. Then, to her horror, Mr Spooner slowly shook his head in disgust. Shuddering, she crawled into her bedroom, as Steph nearly finished her off by bursting in.

'I thought I heard you,' said Steph. 'Good God! You are the devil's spawn, Eleanor Mackridge. You don't know how lucky you are. Dad is at market and Mum left early… If she had caught you like that, oh, I dread to think.'

Steph carried Michael and Robert, fat babies digging into

the top of each hip. Michael stared with saucer eyes and Robert chewed on his fist, dribbling.

'Please, Steph, believe it or not, I've been through enough today already. What is it they used to call them – the vapours? I think I have them.'

'Paul found your dinner and all the meat's gone out of it.'

'That is the least of my concerns.'

'Oh, how you stink! How much have you drunk? Why are you so determined to get into trouble?'

'I'm not.'

'Could have fooled me.' Steph heaved each baby a little higher so she could sit down on Eleanor's bed. 'Haven't you got work?'

'Not until later, my shift starts at two, thank God. I'm going to bed.'

'You'll have the house to yourself, I've got to go and look after Paul's little sisters. His brother who usually does has a new job, as a horse slaughterer.'

'Lovely.'

'Oh, sod it! Tell me everything!' Steph's eyes glowed.

'Later, I promise.'

'What about my stockings…?'

Eleanor pulled out the remnants from her pocket and her sister's face dropped then curled to a point.

'I knew it! I should never have let you wear them!' she hissed.

'I'm going to buy you new ones, it's an oath, a vow, practically etched in stone, but first let me sleep.'

'You make sure you do.' Steph heaved herself up with the babes and made for the door. Before she left, she looked back. 'Icarus, you are, you fly too close to the bloody sun.'

She left the door open, and it took all of Eleanor's energy to kick it shut.

Safe in her bedroom, she let out a breath and collapsed onto her bed. She pulled out the rest of her clothes from her pockets and thew them on the floor. But when the pockets were empty, she felt a strange weight about the coat. She held the breast and shook it. Something rattled in the hem. Stuffing her hands back inside the right-hand pocket she found a hole, one that her whole hand fit through. She stuck her hand in and found a lump of something hard bundled in the hem. She wrestled it free and out into the light.

'Oh shit!' Eleanor said aloud. In her hands was a tangled pile of jewellery: diamonds and emeralds. Her face grew hot as the diamonds flashed so brightly. When she blinked, she saw stars.

CHAPTER SIX

WE LIKE TO THINK OF OURSELVES AS A NOBLE, rational country, educated and civilised. The truth is we are childish brats, driven by greed and desire.

Eleanor had been naïve. The fake name, Mr Rogers, the robberies in The Lanes, the fancy car parked out of sight. She had been a useful distraction and now, unwittingly, she had become part of a crime. She could slap her own face for being such a fool! How could she not have seen it all unfolding in front of her? It all made sense now, and yet she wasn't regretful. There was a part of her that found it exciting to have been with a real live criminal. A man who had the balls to go and get what he wanted without doffing caps and seeking permission. She must have studied those diamonds for hours, wearing all the bracelets, holding her arms up to see the light bounce like white sparks of fire. There was a brooch with diamonds and emeralds, the gems set in the shape of a spade on a pack of playing cards. Another was in the shape of a bow, diamonds and black onyx. The remaining three pieces were bracelets, the real deal. One was a solid-link chain studded with diamonds, the second with round ones and rectangular onyx. The last was Eleanor's favourite – the most beautiful and decadent thing she'd ever seen. This one had diamonds of all shapes and sizes set together with three huge emeralds and a tassel of stones from the clasp. How did they make such things!?

Terrified one of the staff from that night might recognise her at work, Eleanor learned another lesson – and that is that the vast majority of people can't see what's in front of them. They say they never forget a face, but the same face without makeup, a different setting? John – or Mr Rogers or whoever he really was – was right. It's easy to become an entirely new person. One only needs audacity, and John had that in droves.

Eleanor was back serving scones to old ladies in her prim corseted uniform below the knee, hidden in plain sight in the very hotel the police hunted the mysterious Mr Rogers; it was the best disguise she could have worn. She knew he would come back for the jewellery and all she could do was wait, like a spiritualist at a séance, for him or someone to come and make their presence known. Periodically her insides would turn over, a tombola where the only prizes were a sudden rush of thrill or fear. The merest noise or clatter made her startle, and yet she couldn't stop thinking about John.

In the first week of November, the Grand was gearing up for Guy Fawkes night and the fireworks display. One lunchtime at the Terrace, not more than a week after the burglaries, the hotel was very busy. The weather had been settled for the last few days, and bright, if cold. Eleanor was looking forward to a season of generously good tips right up until Christmas.

Miss Larson left Eleanor alone now she had witnessed her work ethic. Another girl had started and her eye for persecution was fixed purely on the freshest meat. The poor girl trembled under the scrutiny. Eleanor quickly learned that the way to get the best of Miss Larson was to ask her about her time during the war. Her eyes would brighten, her arms would unfold and wave about, and she could prove herself a witty storyteller with her recollections as an ambulance driver. Otherwise, the Grand remained stuffy and pretentious; it thrived on offering a door to a past era missed by relatively few in number, disproportionate in wealth.

Eleanor took a sweep of the tables in her section but did a double take when she saw a woman at the same table where she had first laid eyes on John. She was dressed in a navy-blue velvet jacket and skirt. The rich colour contrasted with her skin and complimented the purple feathers on the band of her hat, paired with dark lipstick. Her hair was cut to the jawline with a slight wave. This glamorous creature with fashionable clothes must have felt Eleanor's gaze and looked up. Eleanor turned away and went to the kitchen to check on her orders but couldn't resist peeking at the woman. Perhaps she was an actress from London or New York? When she came back out, she approached the woman, hoping to get a closer look. 'Good afternoon, madam, something to drink?' She took out her notepad and pencil. The woman smelled of roses and wore a necklace with a pear-shaped diamond.

'Pretty, isn't it?' she said, reaching up to hold the diamond between her fingers.

'I'm sorry, madam, I didn't mean…'

'It's quite all right, I bought it. A pleasure, buying gifts for yourself, don't you agree?'

Eleanor smiled politely. 'Yes, I should think so.'

'I'll have some tea, and the finger sandwiches.'

'Shan't be long, madam.'

She was English, not American, but Eleanor still couldn't place her and was sure she knew that face. When she returned to pour the tea, the lady cupped her chin in one hand, and gazing up at Eleanor, whispered, 'Tell me, have you tried them on?'

Eleanor's arm shook and she forgot she was pouring until the tea spilled over the tablecloth.

'I'm sorry, madam.' Eleanor slammed the pot down as the lady sat back and watched her panic.

Eleanor grabbed at napkins, blotting the wet cloth where it had turned a golden brown. Miss Larson marched over with a change of tablecloth.

'What's wrong with you, Eleanor?' she hissed.

'I'm sorry, Miss Larson.'

'Honestly,' said the lady, 'it was my fault. I'm afraid I distracted your waitress.'

Miss Larson and Eleanor switched tablecloths, moving china and silverware with the serious pretentiousness of a military operation.

'There, good as new, thank you very much,' said the lady, amused by the austere way they had gone about such a trivial matter.

When the table was set, the tea poured, and the sandwiches

placed on the table, Miss Larson left after several grovelling apologies and the lady attempted to speak to Eleanor again.

'I think I should fancy shopping after this. Where would you recommend, Eleanor? Johnny said you know your way about.' The woman pursed her lips to the bone-china cup, peering up from underneath her black eyelashes. It was the dark eyes that gave her away, and the cheekbones casting shadows a person could shelter under. She was John's sister.

'What am I to do?' whispered Eleanor.

'You're to come to London, week on Monday. Bring everything.'

'I could give them to you, after work, you could meet me...'

'No. You must deliver them to us.' Her accent wasn't as coarse as John's. She didn't have the affected vowels of the aristocracy, but it didn't howl working class.

'But I have to work...'

'Then swap your shift. I'm sure you'll find a way.'

'What happens if I don't?'

The lady laughed. 'Then a different kind of person will come, and they might not be the type so inclined to take responsibility for spilled tea.'

'Where?'

'Elephant and Castle station.'

'The Underground?'

'Bakerloo line entrance and be there at midday, a week on Monday – wait inside.'

Eleanor nodded and, stricken with nerves, went straight to a table of young men waving for service. There were five in states of standing, chairs scraping. One was holding out a crisp note for her, but as she reached to take it, he snatched it back and the group roared with laughter.

'Only teasing,' he said, then he threw it up into the air. 'You need it more than me.'

Eleanor waited for the note to land, rather than grasp at it like a dancing bear. Despite wanting to throw it in his face, the man was right, she did need it. She would have to swallow the insult and take it – but not in front of them. She waited until they had left and picked it up.

Chrissie, that was it. That was what John had called his big sister, she remembered now. She slipped the note into her apron, hoping no one saw, only to catch John's sister again, lighting another cigarette. When she blew smoke out, she stared Eleanor dead in the eyes, her head tilted with an expression between pity and threat.

CHAPTER SEVEN

THE BEST LIES ARE TOLD WITH LIGHTNESS AND flippancy, which was exactly the approach Eleanor took when she dashed out of the house, shouting over a shoulder that she was off to visit an old friend in London. Everyone was rushing to work; even if they had wanted to enquire about this trip, they had other demands on their time.

Her mother was usually front of the queue in terms of who Eleanor had to be scared of, but carrying diamonds on behalf of a gang of professional criminals had pushed even her down the line. The whole train journey she'd sat paralysed, desperately willing the whole transaction to be over so she could scuttle home.

Elephant & Castle sat between Kennington and Borough stations if you travelled by London Underground. Eleanor waited in the Bakerloo entrance as instructed, a looming square building with oxblood faience blocks in the modern British style. Inside the tiled walls felt like a cross between an asylum and the public baths and smelled about the same. Soot, oil, rats, and the odour of many bodies thrust together with no light or air. The rumbling of the trains underfoot kept reminding her that hell raged below and beckoned. What on earth was she doing delivering stolen goods to *criminals*? She'd fussed about her outfit and had settled on one of her sister's high-neck blouses and a dusty blue skirt that was too long to be fashionable. Her long hair was plaited, and she wore a blue beret.

Having thought long and hard about how to bring the jewellery up to London, she had used an old rag doll she'd kept since she was a girl, cut it open and dragged the stuffing out to place the pieces inside before stuffing it back up with old newspaper. The doll was now inside her coat, trapped under her arm, which she hadn't moved since she had left the house. She took shallow breaths, waiting, thinking, worrying and spinning in a slow circle with her eyes peeled.

'There she is…' A voice made her spin round – it was John, swaggering towards her, the cloud of his cologne hitting her in the face like a fist. 'I almost didn't recognise you with your clothes on,' he leaned in for a kiss and Eleanor flinched.

'Don't you try that on me. Last time I saw you, I was being thrown out of a hotel room with my arse for the world to see,' she spat. 'Why are you here?'

'Chrissie sent me, she's outside.' John grinned. 'Don't be like that, I was looking forward to seeing you.'

'You and the chambermaid seemed friendly.'

'What can I say? I like to make friends.' He adjusted his tie in the imaginary mirror above her head. 'I'm a charming young man.' Then he whispered, 'We had fun though, didn't we?' *Urgh, he was maddening.* 'I tell you what, that electric train turned out proper handy, hopped straight on one, got back to my car in no time. Nice little tip that, much appreciated.'

Eleanor was not amused. 'That girl had me strip naked in an alleyway like some mangy old cat. And I had to walk all the way home with only my coat and nothing underneath.'

'You shouldn't tell me such things.'

'I don't say it to excite you.' She looked about to make sure no one could hear. 'I had to climb in my bedroom window in broad daylight and almost killed the old veteran living opposite. Lord knows what I flashed at him.'

'Oh, give over, you weren't shy the night before.'

'That's called bad judgement, and champagne. Imagine my horror when I get home to find the crown jewels in my coat! Why did you do that to me?'

'See, this is where women are different,' he said, sticking his hands in his pocket of his dark suit. As before, a handmade shirt, white, but this time he'd opted for a kingfisher-blue silk tie. 'Why did I do it to *you*... that's what a woman would say. I didn't do it to *you*, don't take it so personal. I had to make some hasty decisions. Sorry about your coat, mind.'

'Nothing I can't fix.' Despite very much wanting to slap him across that handsome face, she could feel her rage subsiding against her will.

'Come on,' he said, offering her an arm, 'best not keep Chrissie waiting.'

'Where are you taking me?' she said, taking his arm, careful to keep the rag doll close with her elbow.

'Lunch, we're not savages.'

Parked on the road outside was a black Daimler, a fancy enclosed car. John opened the door and Eleanor climbed in the back as John got in the other side beside her. In the front passenger seat was Chrissie. In the driver's seat was a young woman with a flat cap, in chequered trousers, shirt, waistcoat and tie – like a boy, but very much a girl. Her hair was cropped short. Chrissie turned from the passenger seat as if greeting an old friend.

'Eleanor! I'm so glad you could come to our manor. I hope the journey wasn't too bad?'

'It was very good, thank you.' While the journey itself had been fine, her stomach had been whirling like a dervish and most of the way she'd felt nauseous, speculating that she might be robbed along the way, or perhaps murdered when she got there, but she wasn't going to tell them that.

'Lovely.' Then, addressing the tomrig, 'The Criterion please, Jay.'

Chrissie nestled in a thick grey and black fur stole with a bottle-green wool suit and a green hat with fuchsia feathers. She looked a million dollars. Again, Eleanor couldn't help but admire her clothes. The car pulled away and they headed over the Thames.

'Do you know London, Eleanor?' asked Chrissie.

'Not well, my father's family come from Clapham.'

'Ah, south Londoners, like us. What's his name?'

'Mackridge, but my grandmother was a Lewis, but me and my sister were born in Brighton.'

'Just the two girls?'

'There were two boys before us in Clapham, but they died as babies. It's why they moved down to the coast – they thought it would be cleaner.'

Eleanor saw London flying past as her eyes tried to grab on to something. It was as if everything was crammed into every space, filled; buildings were bigger and taller, with bright lights and billboards in between fancy old structures. The roads were busier here, horses and carts, trams, motor vehicles, and the roads were wide, and policemen blew whistles, waving their arms around trying to direct chaos. London is a lie or rather, everything that exists in London cannot help but lie. As it flies past it looks gleaming, bright and flamboyant, but every single thing or person, upon closer inspection, falls rather short of the first impression. Its magic is in chaos and can cast a spell on the naïve. Once one is used to the parts that are designed to bombard human eyes, it's the rubbish piling up, the gaunt-looking girls and the men with fists covered in scabs and bruises that come leaping forward. Eleanor was still in the bedazzled stage.

They passed Trafalgar Square with its great grey lions and fountain covered in flapping pigeons. Down Pall Mall and onto Piccadilly Circus, a mad circus, and pulled up outside a tall red-brick building with big white letters across the front: *The Criterion*.

Everyone got out except the driver, who Chrissie sent away. Chrissie took off her gloves and climbed the stairs as the others followed.

'I've made a booking for luncheon,' she said over her shoulder. 'I do hope you're hungry, anything you don't eat, I'm sure Johnny will finish off.'

'You know me,' said John.

'Indeed, I do. How well do you know John, Eleanor?' Chrissie stopped at the door. The restaurant doorman was holding it open for them, but Chrissie ignored him. She was too busy regarding Eleanor with an expression that told her she knew exactly how well. Eleanor turned scarlet, glanced at John, who shook his head as if he couldn't believe what his sister had said, then Chrissie burst out laughing.

'Oh, you two! Stop blushing, I'm only teasing,' and she finally walked through the door being held open.

'Ladies first,' said John, letting Eleanor go ahead of him.

'I think we've established I'm not one of those,' she snapped, and followed as John sloped behind scratching his chin.

'Lovely to have you back, Mrs Chambers,' said the man on the front desk. 'Have you been keeping well?'

'I have, thank you, Charles.'

The waiters were dressed in full regalia, bow ties and white gloves. Inside was an assault of glitz: hard marble, crystal chandeliers, gold handles. Staff rushed about as if the King were waiting. They were led through a glass door into more shining corridors, light bouncing off glass and crystal. She had expected a little more discretion, but Chrissie and John acted like landed gentry.

'Your coat, madam?' Yet another man emerged, unsmiling, butler like, trying to take Eleanor out of her coat.

Chrissie was being helped out of hers, but Eleanor clung on, clasping it together at the neck. She could hardly take it off or else the world would see the rag doll.

'Oh no, thank you, I'll keep mine.' The man raised his eyebrows and John and Chrissie regarded her odd behaviour.

'I'm... cold. I've had a bit of a sniffle,' said Eleanor, immediately regretting the choice of words that made her sound like an old Edwardian lady.

They set off on another journey to their table and Chrissie entertained them on the way.

'It's a wonderful venue. There's an Italian roof garden

and they serve until two in the morning. There is dancing, comedians, musicians, acrobats... all the latest acts.'

When they entered the restaurant, the lighting was set to a perennial dusk. Louche-looking men and boyish women dressed in silk clinked glasses. Gamine girls, Eleanor's own age, lounged, smoking and drinking freely. Women laughed and threw their heads back. Men leaned in to light cigarettes and steal kisses at the table. Eleanor was shocked – she'd never seen such behaviour.

'Lunch here is a set menu at 3/6.' Eleanor had to stop herself from gasping. She wasn't even sure she had the total sum in her purse.

'My treat, my love.' Chrissie touched her arm, and Eleanor exhaled, her ribs sore where she gripped the rag doll.

They sat in a rounded booth in the white and gold East Room, with lurid painted wall panels depicting scenes of writhing bodies that Eleanor didn't know what to make of. Opulent and designed to shock, tiling, endless marble and the very rude murals. The carpets – yes, carpets, with all these dirty feet – furniture and curtains were a soft palette of greys and pinks, like a spoiled girl's dream, indulgent and fussy. The glassware was thick crystal, silver cutlery and heavy white linens. At least being a waitress, she knew her way around cutlery. At the front of the restaurant a jazz band perched high over them in a fabricated gilded cage. The musicians were all Black men, and no one seemed to pay any attention. In Brighton, when they'd had Indian soldiers at the hospital, people had come from miles around to catch sight of them. The factory foreman had even given the girls a stern lecture on the dangers of being seduced by exotic men.

'They have the best musicians,' said Chrissie. She sat opposite Eleanor while John slouched next to his sister, unbuttoning his jacket, eyes dancing about the room.

Eleanor's gaze drifted up to the ceiling of gold mosaic, then she saw couples disappearing into the shadows behind pillars at the edge of the room to continue conversations away from their tables. A waiter approached and Chrissie told him they would all be having the set menu.

'You seem nervous, Eleanor,' said Chrissie. 'Would you like a drink?'

'Oh no. Water is fine for me, thank you.'

Mr Rogers, Mrs Chambers, Chrissie, John Noon, who were these people?

Another waiter approached, this time a snooty one with a narrow face and hair swept back like a member of Prussian aristocracy. He peered down on Eleanor as if she were a fly, and she took her hands off the linen and put them on her lap, then realised they were waiting for something.

'What is it?' asked Eleanor.

'This is the part where you hand over the goods. Our man will take them,' Chrissie whispered.

'Oh,' said Eleanor, and she took the rag doll from where it had been welded to her side under her coat. The realisation slipped over John and Chrissie's faces about why she had acted so keen to keep her coat with her, as Eleanor placed the doll on the tray.

'I... it's inside the doll.'

'Original, I like it,' said Chrissie.

'I told you,' said John, nudging his sister.

The waiter resigned himself to touching the old toy, deftly covered it with napkins and whisked himself and the tray away.

'You hear such terrible stories about people being robbed and...'

'It's absolutely fine, Karl there is a good, dear friend. Despite his rather frosty appearance he really can be quite the card, can't he, Johnny?'

'He's got a sense of humour, I'll give him that.'

'That and his boyfriend is one of the best fences this side of the river.'

'Boyfriend?' said a stunned Eleanor. She didn't know what a fence was but hadn't got that far yet.

'Yes, my dear, it is 1922 – the posh boys are all at it. I think it was all those years, hunkered down on the Western Front.'

'It's not for everyone,' said John, rolling his eyes.

'Prince George is at it with everyone, and everything, so they say.'

'Really?' Eleanor had come up on the train and found herself in an entirely different world.

'You know what,' said Chrissie, taking a cigarette out and offering them one each, as John reached for his lighter. 'You should cut your hair. It's the fashion now. Long hair is rather, Edwardian. Yes, you should do that. The plaits make you look like a milkmaid.' *Ouch.*

Lunch was served. Trays of sandwiches, tea and small fancy French cakes. Everything was small and delicate, and struck Eleanor as an underwhelming fuss, but it was obvious people didn't come for the food.

'Here, before I forget,' said Chrissie, 'I'd like to reimburse you for your train fare. Such a long way.' She slipped paper money over on the table.

'Thank you, that's very kind,' said Eleanor.

'John tells me you live with your parents.'

'Yes, my parents and my sister, her husband and her two twin boys. It's a bit crowded. My dad hasn't been well since the war – full of shrapnel, bad lungs. He has that shellshock, and can't earn like he used to.'

'And your mother?'

'My mum works in a fancy grocer, selling gherkins and pickles and cheese that smells like feet.'

'And you?'

'I don't mean to be rude but why do you ask? I've delivered the jewellery, does the man need to check it or will someone be after me? Because I swear on my life it's all there.' Eleanor thought she had politely prattled along enough.

'I see, cut to the chase, shall we,' said Chrissie.

'I'm no gangster's moll,' said Eleanor. They both found this most amusing and laughed at her expense, then leaned forward with elbows on the table as if the real conversation could begin.

'This has nothing to do with John. Men... oh dear. They drink too much, fight too much, forever corralled by their egos, this imaginary sense of themselves which they promote to hysterical proportions. The poor things are delusional.'

'Thanks, I love you too,' said John. Chrissie ignored him.

'And don't you find they expect praise for the most minor of effort? Men are exhausting. We love them, but it's not good business to work with them. This has nothing to do with being anyone's *moll*.'

'It's a matriarchy,' said John, as if he'd recently learned the word and wanted to use it.

'Women have slower tempers and clearer heads – most of the time. We're used to having to think our way out of things.'

'Shoot the women first, I say,' said John.

'Be quiet, Johnny,' snapped Chrissie. John sat back, put in his place, and called the waiter for another whisky.

'I'm not sure I understand,' asked Eleanor. 'What is it you do?'

'We do what the ruling classes do, except we don't have the convenience of setting the laws in our favour.'

'You're thieves, aren't you?' Eleanor whispered the word. 'Why are you interested in me?' They both shifted in their seats, so this was the bad news.

'A few girls have been arrested recently and some of the charges are going to stick. They're going to spend some time in the Holly.'

'The Holly?'

'Holloway Prison, north of the River Thames.' Eleanor looked suitably horrified. She imagined a dungeon from the medieval era, people screaming as they are flogged.

'If you have the right connections, prison really isn't so bad.'

'Have... you been in... prison?'

'Yes, more than once, but not for a few years. I've got rather a lot better at what I do.'

'Oh.' Eleanor couldn't imagine a creature so sophisticated or elegant being inside a prison. She thought it would be full of mad women or sorry creatures who'd drowned their babies at birth.

'The sentences are short, in and out these days. Now it's one month, two months – that's if our lawyer can't get us off, which he very often does.'

'Luckily, the police are bumbling idiots,' John confirmed.

'And so, we find ourselves... short staffed,' Chrissie continued. 'We work hard, stay organised and reap big rewards. We live very good lives, Eleanor, and earn a lot of money. We don't believe in much more than having a good time and acquiring some beautiful things along the way. We all just about got through the last five years by the skin of our teeth so we're making hay while the sun shines. Girls like us have no way of working our way to a life worth having in this country, the rich have no intention of sharing. We take what we want when we have need of it – like winners throughout history.'

'That's what my mum says, about history. We are ruled by the thugs from the past.' Eleanor was listening and spinning her glass in her fingers.

'Your mother sounds very forward thinking,' said Chrissie.

'She's French.'

'Do you speak French?'

'Yes, not that it did us any favours at school.'

'Well, the things that don't do you any favours as a child are often the things that set you apart as an adult.'

'I'm not sure it's been useful...'

'Look, we are not in the business of cruelty. Our business exists to relieve already ludicrously rich businesses of luxurious goods – and they don't lose either. It's all covered by insurance. They put their losses into next year's retail prices, so no one loses out.'

'But it is theft.'

'No one gets hurt – unless they get in our way.'

'I'm no grass.'

'Good, then you should fit in.'

'Who said I want to fit in?'

'Dear Eleanor, you may not know it yet, but the yearning for excitement leaks from you. I can practically smell it from here.'

'I don't know what you mean.' Christ. Was it that obvious that she was desperate for adventure?

'You do know that the years laid out in front of you have been decided already without your consent. You're a bright girl, I'm sure you've figured it out. Let's see, you'll continue working as a waitress until you either marry or your waist expands in line with your feet and the Grand let you go. You'll take a position in domestic service and, if you are lucky, get to go to church on a Sunday. Quite frankly, what I'm offering you now is the only real choice you may ever have. If you are good at it, you'll make more money in a month than your poor old dad has made in the last ten years.'

Eleanor knew what Chrissie said was true. Every word of it. And the money, it was no small temptress. Places like this, the air was practically rippling with the sense that anything could happen. Opportunity and adventure. That didn't come knocking in Brighton.

'In the past we've only recruited from our own, but we've grown to the point it is hindering the expansion of a profitable enterprise,' said Chrissie, tapping another cigarette on the back of the holder. 'Like all businesses, we must adapt. That means more girls, different ones, with other talents.'

'I thought you might be worth a punt,' said John.

'So that's why you had me deliver the jewellery,' realised Eleanor.

'You'll want to think about all this, I'm sure. I wanted to give you this, something to help you.' Chrissie took the pear-shaped diamond she had round her neck.

'Oh, no, I can't accept that!'

'I insist. Call it your commission for delivering Johnny's mislaid package on account of him being an idiot led by his cock. I want you to have it.'

Chrissie held it out and Eleanor watched as the pear swung from side to side. Her mother had held a necklace over her sister's stomach, saying it would tell whether she would have a boy or a girl, and she wondered if by the way it swung it was speaking to her now.

'Thank you,' said Eleanor, and watched her own grasping hand reach up and catch the necklace as it fell into her palm.

'If you should need to talk, come and find me,' said Chrissie.

'Wait, where?'

'The Duke of Clarence, The Cut. On a Sunday, be there from lunch. Ask for Dolly Chambers. I'll write it down.'

John reached into his inside suit pocket and took out a pen for Chrissie to write on the back of a card and slip it across the table. The number written in fresh ink smudged under her thumb. It smelled of peonies. Eleanor had a place to find her, her scent in her nose, a diamond in her hand and money in her pocket – it was going to be hard to forget. The woman certainly knew how to charm. Better than her brother.

★

After lunch, Chrissie returned to her car and John walked Eleanor back to the station. When they said goodbye, Eleanor had to ask one last thing.

'Is this a trick?' As if he'd tell her if it was.

'There is no trick. None of this works if we play games with each other. I told her you have a streak of mischief. I see it in my aunt and Chrissie and the others. It's why you seek out distractions with men like me. Catch you later, must dash.'

John flew up the steps to daylight and left Eleanor standing, convincing herself she had yet to decide.

CHAPTER EIGHT

THAT WEEKEND AFTER THE TRIP TO LONDON ELEANOR was still in a daze, wrestling with the proposal. It was an absurd idea, but Chrissie was right, what other choices were there? She could struggle and live the same little insignificant life she had now or... take a leap and see what was on the other side. It was fear of the law and mixing with dangerous people that put her off. But Chrissie didn't seem like a monster. Imagine, choosing to become a criminal of all things! Outrageous! Eleanor was from a good home, her parents law abiding, aside from the odd bit of pilfering, but everyone did that, that was *normal*.

When Eleanor and her sister were small, they would run with others in packs through the market, picking at fruit and vegetable stalls. Mum would send them to look for coal on the beach with the other children, and they'd pinch it from yards. If there weren't any broken biscuits at the shop, it wasn't unknown for Mum to knock some off with a hip so they could be bought cheaper, and everyone went scrumping, stealing apples from farmers' fields. *Everyone.*

A bigger boy from school had shown Eleanor how to lay a halfpenny on the train tracks, then lie on their bellies by the side and wait for a train to flatten it into a penny for vending machines and meters. Eleanor learned early there was no real order in the world, no matter how much grown-ups pretended there was.

There was progress, apparently, but never for them. Eleanor was in a class born to serve, clean, be invisible. She wasn't meant to *become* anything. All she needed was one more little push, and it didn't take long for that to happen.

Back at the Grand, Eleanor was pandering to an Edwardian dame – and this one had her running up and down like a pony at a gymkhana. Nothing was good enough: the tea was cold, her table was draughty, the chair wobbled. At one point she had called her a *useless girl*. It was water off a duck's back most days. She was clearing tables when the old grey bird started clicking her fingers. This time, the cake was stale.

'Sorry, madam, I shall replace it at once.' The cake had been baked that morning – everything had.

Eleanor had no sooner replaced it, but this one was too dry. Old birds often behaved this way. Those who served knew it to be the vice of the diminishing older woman. Eleanor tried to reassure the lady she was mistaken, but she tore into her.

'Such insolence. I did not ask *you* for an opinion, be quiet. Look at you, glaring at me, who do you think you are?'

'Madam, what would you have me do?' Eleanor strained to retain her cool. 'Perhaps you might prefer to see the menu again, we have many cakes...'

'Bring it to me and watch your tone when you speak

to me.' Eleanor, like all staff at the Grand, had cultured a voice devoid of anything, least of all tone. But her carefully constructed mask was slipping.

She fetched the menu and set it down in front of the tutting woman. Back at the counter to ring up the bill for another table, Miss Larson hovered over her.

'What was that all about?'

'The cake is stale or the table wobbles – she's one of those. I changed it, it's dry apparently, and now she wants to see the menu again. You know these old birds, complaining is the only thing that brings them joy.'

'Well get a lid on it, it's a waste of good cake. What does she mean stale? They're all fresh!'

A glance saw the old lady boring holes into Eleanor from across the restaurant – the woman was out for blood. Miss Larson whispered into her ear. 'You've got orders waiting, and the kitchen's been chasing.'

'Yes, Miss Larson.' *Yes Miss Larson. Yes Miss Larson.* Parrot. Idiot. Fool.

Eleanor pushed palms first through the swing door to the corridor leading to the kitchen and was at once swallowed into the cool shadows of the windowless tunnel. She was back in the restaurant at the Criterion. Chrissie's perfume – peonies – floated on the air, women with short hair, dark lips and bare shoulders, laughing men lighting cigarettes. The American jazz band floating in a cage and twinkling crystal. She shook the vision from her mind and pushed the left-hand swing door into the clatter of the kitchen.

'Where've you been?' said the chef. 'These have been sat for ages.'

'I'm here now.'

Piling the plates up her arms, she smiled at the other waitress as she passed, also dashing into the kitchen. She turned backwards and bent over to push the door open with her bottom. The old bird was waving again. This was working out to be a terrible shift. She stopped by the tables still waiting, apologised and promised their dishes were on their way. There were huffs but they didn't make a fuss, and now on to the old dame.

'Yes, madam, is there anything else I can get you?'

'Another fork,' she thrust her fork up at Eleanor. 'This one is dirty.'

Feeling heat rise to the surface of her skin, she took the fork. There was no mark or dirt, not that could be seen by the naked working-class eye. In a moment of lapsed judgement, Eleanor spun to a newly set table, picked up a fork and tapped the woman on the shoulder to let her know she was replacing it. The old dame erupted.

'Don't touch me! Never, ever hand me anything with your bare hands and you certainly never touch a lady!' The woman recoiled from her as if Eleanor were a leper.

Eleanor straightened, bit the inside of her cheek, and set the fork down gently, but as she stepped away, fuming, the woman hissed at her, 'You young girls, is it ignorance or laziness? Perhaps both. I would wager you were one of those army lot, weren't you?' Eleanor looked over her shoulder, her body followed. 'You have that mannish arrogance. How you strut about with your chin in the air, wanting people to look at you. A few years in service would teach you how to behave.'

The other tables were watching the spectacle. Everyone loves a good show, even Miss Larson. The other waitress had stopped taking an order because her table was too busy staring. Eleanor felt reckless. The frustration of remaining meek and deferential in the face of nothing other than bullying for sport was too much. Eleanor stepped back to the woman, put both knuckles on the table and bent until her face was inches away from the old woman's.

'What you mean is, a few years in service would teach me how to *crawl*,' she said.

The woman, shocked by such defiance, couldn't speak; only her chin wobbled. Eleanor picked up the teapot and checked its temperature with her hand.

'Ah, you'll never guess, this one is cold now too – which means it won't burn when I do this.' She held up the teapot and poured the liquid all over the table, over the cake, linens, cutlery and splashing onto the woman's lap. Audible gasps were heard in canon around the Victorian Terrace.

'I shall have you fired!' said the woman, lips trembling.

'I'll save you the bother. I quit!'

Eleanor tore off her apron, threw it on the table and stormed off, not even stopping as she unpinned her cap and threw it behind her. The other waitress's mouth hung open, her face a mixture of awe and shock. Not even Miss Larson dared utter a word as Eleanor swung the door on her way out.

Back home, Mother was sat in the kitchen with the radio on.

'Eleanor, I was not expecting you back at this hour.'

'Is Steph in?'

'Yes. Did something happen?'

'Nothing, everything is fine.'

Eleanor went upstairs to her bedroom, took the pear-drop diamond out from where she'd hidden it among her underwear, and held it so tight she could feel it digging into her palm as she forced the tears that threatened to spill over back inside. Tears never did any good anyway. When she looked up out of the window there was mad old Mr Spooner sat in his wheelchair, shouting at pigeons on the grass. Then Steph came in.

'Mum said you came back in a mood.' Eleanor shoved the pendant inside her pocket. There was no way she could explain that, not even to Steph.

'I quit the Grand.' Steph's face was a picture – mouth dropped at least four feet, hands to her cheeks.

'Are you mad?' Steph looked to make sure no one had crept up the landing and shut the door, then fell on her bed. 'What happened?'

Eleanor huffed. 'I'm not quite sure. Some old bird really got under my girdle. She said I could do with a few years in service.'

'Stuck up cow. It's because they can't get servants – they call it the servant problem in the papers. No one wants to do it – and they wonder why.'

'You were in service, was it that bad?'

Steph screwed up her face. 'Up before six every day to clean the grates, set fires in every room, take up everyone's morning tea, scrub the steps and cook breakfast – all before I could have mine. Mrs Hammond used to weigh out my food like she oversaw national rationing. Working at the factory was bloody heaven compared: shifts, pay, friends, canteen, sports and games. Have you told Mum?'

'Not yet. Do you think she'll take it badly?' Eleanor still felt the fear of being scolded.

'You never know, she might not be so bad,' offered Steph.

Stephanie was wrong. Their mother took the news of Eleanor being unemployed very badly.

'You did what?! How could you do such a thing! Quit! Have you lost your mind? Bah!'

The woman leapt up from her chair and paced, throwing her hands up then storming the other way, muttering to herself in French and shouting in English.

'Ah, Eleanor, *être dans la galère*.' Which is something about getting oneself into a mess. 'How can you let one person rattle you so?' Eleanor drew breath to answer, but she didn't get the chance. '*Non!* Do not answer. I am afraid of what you will say.'

'What?'

'I'm afraid you will sound like your father. And then? Then I will have to kill you myself!'

Eleanor wasn't sure how she felt about what she'd done at all. At the time it had felt liberating – freeing! Now she wondered if she had lost her mind. Either way, it was too late, but she knew what she would do. She would be taking the train to London after all – to find Chrissie.

CHAPTER NINE

THE FIRST SUNDAY AFTER QUITTING HER JOB, ELEANOR was on the train to London. In turns she felt sick and then excited. She convinced herself this was simply a trip to enquire more about an opportunity. But she had to admit she held an irrational desire to be among people like John and Chrissie. Why wouldn't she? They were exciting and glamorous. Eleanor had told them she was visiting her friend again and, thankfully, Mr Bright had left an old street map of London on the bureau in the front parlour. Eleanor had memorised the walk from Waterloo station to the Duke of Clarence pub on a road called The Cut.

The Cut made sense when she found it; it was a broad open stretch of road and a busy commercial thoroughfare linking Waterloo and Southwark stations. The road was littered with market stalls, as many as the law would allow, and police patrols made sure only licensed proprietors were hawking. She saw the odd vendor packing up and scarpering when a peeler was on the approach. It was a bustling bazaar for working-class businesses and the self-educated entrepreneur: tailoring, garages, spirit merchants, wire workers – everything from spot welders to lampshade frame makers. You could buy anything you ever needed and a whole load of junk you never should, all under the shadow of the railway tracks. If the thunderous rumble of the trains felt unsettling, it became unnoticeable, even comforting, in a shockingly brief amount of time. Among the locals were commuters, like factory-made men, nondescript and bowler hatted with uniform moustaches and starched collars. This new kind of man with soft skin, white from indoor work, hands dry from shuffling paper, carrying nothing heavier than an umbrella and a veneer of superiority.

The Duke of Clarence was an unremarkable building with small windows veiled with lace fringes. She pushed on the double doors and slithered inside hoping not to draw much attention. It was a proper boozer, the type Eleanor had recoiled from when John had attempted to drag her inside, with yellowing walls of anaglypta, the colour spreading like a stain across the ceiling, discoloured by years of nicotine. Dark wood panelling and bottle-green leather stools. It was dim and dingy, aside from the brass bar with drip trays and bottles hooked up to optics against a big mirror. A smattering of men like gargoyles lined the bar with their backs to the door. There was an upright piano stood against a wall and a picture of the King above it. From inside, the windows were flecked with soot and streaked, and the nets brown.

Eleanor approached the bar and stood between two men nursing pints. Flat caps, bent shoulders, brown wrinkled hands and split nails. It was not the Criterion restaurant, that was for sure, and Eleanor couldn't envisage Chrissie or

John coming in here. These people were ordinary, in tatty old clothes repaired over and over, like her own. Eleanor took out the card Chrissie had written on and ran her thumbs over the handwriting; it *was* the right place. The barwoman padded over without smiling, arms like legs of uncooked ham and a faded tattoo on one forearm. As Eleanor asked for Dolly Chambers, cackling old ladies roared from a table and the barwoman strained to hear. Eleanor stood up on the footrail and tried again, louder.

'I'm looking for Mrs Dolly Chambers!' and the bar fell silent. She didn't have to look to know everyone was staring at her.

'Does she know you?' asked the barwoman.

'Yes. It's Eleanor, from Brighton. She said I could find her here.'

'Wait here,' said the woman, disappearing through a door behind the bar.

So, she waited, trying not to catch the eyes she knew were creeping all over her, narrated with whispers. She could only stick her chin up in the air and pretend to be a duchess.

The barwoman re-emerged from another door sectioned off with panelling and frosted glass. She ushered Eleanor over, through the door to a corridor that led to another room – from which she could hear women's voices talking all at once.

'Go on, they're in there,' said the barwoman. Eleanor took a few steps, and the woman went back to the bar and shut her in the corridor alone. She felt her heart quicken and she had to force herself to rap on the glass window of the door.

'Come in!' a voice sang out.

Eleanor crept into a room like *The Last Supper*, with women flanking every spot, in some sort of meeting. A dark and feathered version of the Women's Institute with furs and heels, rows of kohl-lined eyes waiting to inspect a specimen. Eleanor began to perspire under the attention of the most serious women she had ever seen, a whole range of plumage and age. Waved hair set in partings, hats in the latest fashion, bright lipsticks, pearls and twinkling gems. Intense flowery perfume fought with cigarettes. Whippet-like blondes and voluptuous brunettes, all dressed like a million dollars in the latest wool suits and pencil skirts. Each and every one had a good bloody look, hitching an elbow over the back of a chair, or leaning forward.

'Is this Frenchie?' said one, the accent not matching the sophisticated outfit.

'Come on in, you. Come a bit closer, we don't bite,' said another, and they cackled.

'Let her be, you lot. You are mean!' said Chrissie, who sprang up, black feathers around her shoulders and magenta on her lips, and Eleanor let out a sigh of relief.

One of the older ladies pushed an empty chair across the floor with a heeled foot.

'*Voulez-vous avec une seat.*'

'Even I know that don't sound right,' shouted a woman, younger with blonde waves. 'Chrissie, does she speak English?'

Chrissie tutted. 'Of course she speaks bloody English, she *is* English. Her mother is French, and Eleanor's a friend of Johnny's.' A collective groan and smirks swept the table – it seemed John had a reputation and Eleanor had been another conquest. *Embarrassing.*

'What did I say then?' asked the one who had tried to speak French.

'You said... you asked me, *would I want with a chair*,' said Eleanor, and the room erupted into laughter, the older lady giggling hardest of all.

'Not sure what Frenchmen you've been knocking boots with, Ada, but I shan't be looking at your chairs the same way.' And they all hooted, except for Chrissie, who led Eleanor back out into the corridor and closed the door on the squawking birds.

'Shall we have a chat,' said Chrissie. It wasn't a question.

Chrissie lit a cigarette, offered one to Eleanor, who refused – she didn't want her to see her hands shaking.

'I didn't expect to see you again,' said Chrissie.

'I needed time to think,' said Eleanor, now made even more nervous by Chrissie's coolness.

'I thought you were happy being a waitress.'

'I quit.'

'Oh dear, and now you want to reconsider.'

'Reconsider?! I didn't say no,' said Eleanor. She hadn't been sure about any of this, and now it felt as if the opportunity might be slipping away, making her desperate. 'You said I could have time to think, and I have. You wrote this place down on the card, you remember?' She took out the card, but Chrissie didn't so much as glance at it.

'We're thieves, do you remember?'

'I'm sorry if I was a little wary before, but I was nervous. Truth is, Chrissie, I need money, real money, and... I left school at fourteen, went straight to the factory and I was bloody good at it, and now... Waitressing is never going to pay enough and what else is there? I don't have the money for education and my parents don't have any. I thought about what you said and it's true, there are no choices for me. I am a hard worker, and I was one of the brightest in my class, and I'm quick to learn, and reliable.'

'You quit your job. Doesn't sound very reliable to me.'

'That was different, I meant to quit that.'

Chrissie eyeballed Eleanor, not throwing the same easy charm on her now, and drew on her cigarette. 'There are the girls you must meet first.'

'What girls?'

'Come on, we're making a house call.'

Chrissie clipped on her high heels back through the pub and out onto The Cut with Eleanor scampering behind like a puppy.

CHAPTER TEN

THIS TIME CHRISSIE DROVE THEM IN A CAR, WHICH impressed Eleanor, although she couldn't tell you why. But there was something captivating about a glamorous woman a little older than herself driving her own car like they did in the pictures, and it swelled her sense of awe. Imagine buying your own diamonds, furs and cars! She was intrigued. She thought Chrissie so beautiful she had to stop herself from staring. Studying her, from the flowers in her hat to the rings on her fingers, and here she was, driving a car, answering, apparently, to no one. The journey was less than a mile and, on the way, they passed a ragtag group of faded men. Pale-faced ghosts carrying placards with scrawled words: *a fair day's work for a fair day's pay.*

'It's a hunger march,' said Chrissie. 'They've been springing up all over, so they say on the radio. This one started in Poplar and is marching to Westminster, but I'm not sure what for. Nothing ever changes, and it never will. The lies stay the same, except now they broadcast them on the radio. I'll let you into a little secret, Eleanor, and save you the time it took me to learn it. No man or woman who's made something of themselves in this country ever did it playing by the rules. We may be thieves, but so are the government. The police are hired thugs to keep their riches safe from the rest of us. Be under no illusion, the arrangement is by design. Still, hard not to feel for the poor old boys.'

Eleanor didn't know what to say. In every face she saw her dad. A man who held himself to the standards he believed everyone should aspire to – loyalty, honesty, decency. *Stupid, stupid man.* Who could have known the industrial-scale plans for slaughter hatched in backrooms by men who would never face them.

They parked on Elliot's Row. One side was lined with Victorian terraces, but these looked timid when faced with the block opposite running near the length of the road. The housing development, Hayles Buildings, resembled a city wall.

Eleanor looked up to where the building touched the sky and it seemed to look back down on her, sending her giddy. Separated into blocks, each had five floors split into flats. Children played outside and women sat about the communal entrances on every block. It was stern-faced, as if designed by a schoolmistress, prison warden and hospital matron. With regimented flat-faced fronts and parapets in sandy and rust-coloured bricks.

Eleanor fell in behind Chrissie and they entered one block, weaving their way through the women sat on the walls, leaning, smoking and gossiping. Inside it was more hospital with low-spirited sterile corridors. People milling about, children up and down stairs, their squeals echoing.

They walked up the stairs before stopping on the third floor at flat number thirty-four. Chrissie brought her knuckles to the door, hesitated and looked to Eleanor.

'If you are serious, you'll need to be all in. I'm taking quite the risk with you. It's an experiment, and not everyone thinks it's a good idea. You'll need to win a few over. But if you do, you'll have friends, sisters... in the truest sense.' Eleanor nodded. 'If you're having doubts, let's not waste time – you can leave right now. But I mean it, Eleanor. Once you're in, there's no going back.'

'No, I... I'll be all in. I'm serious, deadly.' Eleanor wasn't sure what she was agreeing to exactly, but Chrissie's ambivalence towards her had ignited an urgency. That and the fact she had no job to go back to.

'Good!' Chrissie knocked on the door, waited a minute, but no one answered.

Chrissie balled up a fist and thumped the door again, making it shake, and gave a kick for good measure. After a few seconds they heard the padding of footsteps – someone was coming. The door creaked open and in the slither of a gap, a young woman with platinum blonde curls appeared. Bizarrely, she wore a bejewelled headband with a crooked ostrich feather and had a scarf tied across her eyes.

'What?' said the girl, pouting and resting her forehead in the gap between the doors.

'Good afternoon, have we interrupted a game of blind man's buff?' said Chrissie.

The girl pulled the scarf down to reveal makeup-smeared eyes, round and green.

'Chrissie!' the girl exclaimed, pleased to see her, but quickly taken by an open-mouthed yawn. 'I didn't know you were coming… Lily has my eye mask and won't give it back. I'm forced to tie myself up, always a pity.'

Another voice from inside: 'I gave it back!'

The girl's round, childlike eyes wandered to Eleanor and retracted like a reptile assessing its prey. 'Who is that?' she pointed a long finger through the gap.

'That, Effie, is Eleanor. I've brought her here to meet you all. Eleanor, this is Effie, and inside somewhere, once we are invited in, we should find Lilian and Charlotte.'

'Righto,' said Effie, stepping back and letting the door swing open. 'Won't you come in, it's a bit of a mess.'

Effie sashayed ahead of them through a dark and narrow corridor. Chrissie entered, followed by Eleanor, stepping gingerly over the threshold with shoes all over the floor, skirting sideways for the great number of fur coats on hooks on the wall. It was surreal, a block of social housing with its shadowy corridors and inside this flat an abundance of fur coats. Effie turned left and they passed a tall black-haired girl standing in a doorway. Exotic with dark eyes, straight hair cut to the chin with a blunt fridge, in a silk kimono – silk. It was decorated with pink flamingos and was ocean blue like the poster on Eleanor's bedroom wall. She hoped it was an omen.

'Eleanor, meet Lilian,' said Chrissie.

'Call me Lily,' said the black-haired girl, who didn't smile. Eleanor felt an idiot with her sappy grin.

Before they made it into the kitchen, they passed another room and another girl. This one was friendlier, with chestnut wavy brown hair and small features, leaning against the doorframe in only a slip of a nightie.

'And this is Charlotte,' explained Chrissie.

'I'm Charlie, nice to meet you.' At least this one smiled back.

The women all fell in behind Eleanor and they ended up in the kitchen, led by Effie, who still had the headband with its bent ostrich feather and a see-through nightdress; when she leaned up against the stove, Eleanor could see practically everything, but Effie didn't seem to care.

'Is someone going to offer us a cup of tea?' Chrissie snapped.

Effie tutted, shoved a cigarette in her mouth and put the kettle on the hob.

'This is Eleanor,' started Chrissie. 'She's from Brighton and we will be giving her a trial run. All being well, I thought she could work in your cell.'

There were gasps about the room.

'Why?' said Effie.

'We work as a three. What if four changes everything?' asked Lily. Charlie looked between them all in shock.

'Which is why I used the word *trial*. She has to be trained up first, but she'll be staying here with you.'

Staying? Was Chrissie implying Eleanor would have to move in here, and live with these girls? Eleanor's stomach did a loop. It made sense to move to London, but how on earth was she going to spin this at home to her mother? It was all happening very fast.

'What!? Where? We haven't got any rooms left, Effie's already in what should be the parlour,' said Charlie. 'I'm not sharing.'

'I'm not sharing neither,' said Lily, folding her arms.

'Which is why I'm going to suggest Eleanor share with Effie, since she has the largest room.'

'Urghhh! I knew it!' said Effie. 'Make the tea, share your bedroom.' She turned to Eleanor and pointed at her with a spoon. 'I'm telling you what right now, you better not snore.'

'I don't think I do,' said Eleanor.

Eleanor was reeling. She'd been so keen not to miss out on the 'opportunity' being offered that she'd not thought through the immediate implications, as usual, and now she was in a tailspin of panic. Moving to London? Living with strangers? But she couldn't let Chrissie see her trepidation or else whatever was being offered would be retracted. She had to maintain a veneer of absolute calm and commitment. It would be all right, she told herself. These were things done by adventurous people, of course it would feel strange.

'Your rent will go down, split four ways instead of three,' said Chrissie. 'That's a good thing.'

'Yeah, and when she don't work out, I'll get my bedroom back and the rent will go back up.' Effie threw sugar lumps in the cups. 'Do you want one?' she asked Eleanor.

'No, thanks.'

Effie lifted the kettle as it started whistling, slammed it down onto a cool ring, and stirred the tea as if she were ringing a cow bell, plonking a cup down by each woman as Chrissie spoke.

'Effie's mother was one of the Forties – very good at it too.'

'Yeah, shame she was a bitch,' said Effie, blowing on her cup of tea.

'The Forties?' asked Eleanor, to a round of audible offence taken at her ignorance of who she was in the presence of.

'It's our name – the *Forty Elephants*. Lily here, her mother and aunt were in the Forties before her, and Charlie, her family for generations, the Forties and the Elephants...'

'...that'll be the boys – the Elephant Gang,' said Lily.

'Charlie's father went all religious and moved them away to Southend, but she came back to us,' explained Chrissie. 'You see we all grew up in Lambeth.'

'We don't do outsiders,' said Effie.

'You can't trust them,' said Charlie.

Eleanor knew better than to argue. They were poking at her, to see if she bit. At that moment she was worrying more about what she was going to tell her mother.

'Right!' said Chrissie, clicking her fingers, and the girls seemed to stiffen. 'Chop chop – make yourselves decent and I'll buy breakfast.'

CHAPTER ELEVEN

A MAD DASH, WITH CLOTHES FLYING AND BARE LIMBS racing erupted as the girls got dressed. Eleanor found herself sat quietly observing the chaos with Chrissie in the kitchen, hands on her lap, feeling overwhelmed and petrified of revealing anything. The girls appeared presentable in minutes. A transformation given largely to the vibrancy of youth, fashionable clothes and makeup. Even if they did give themselves away as mudlarks as soon as they opened their mouths. The five women clattered down the stairwells, screaming kids parting like the Red Sea for Moses, and spilled out onto the street to stares and whistles. They trotted in a high-heeled pack around the corner to the Victory Coffee House and Dining Room. Bare brickwork was painted with giant white letters for the passengers passing on trains: *liver & bacon, saltfish & bloaters, gammon & eggs.*

Inside was a humid little café in one narrow room that echoed with the sound of a dripping tap. The soot and grime of Lambeth blocked out by steamed-up windows and the walls plastered with hand-scrawled price lists:

pies, teacakes and cold meats. Crammed at a wonky table, sticky with grease, Eleanor made a mental note not to put her elbows down. She sipped a cup of black tea, as did Chrissie, as Charlie, Lily and Effie gobbled up eggs, bacon and fried bread. Shovelling in handfuls of soggy bread, lips smacking over greasy chins. If her mother had been present, there would be clipped ears at such terrible manners. Charlie and Effie talked with their mouths full while Lily was more restrained. She seemed more interested in sizing Eleanor up.

'How does she know Johnny anyway?' Lily asked Chrissie, as if Eleanor were not there.

'She helped him out when he got in a spot of bother,' said Chrissie, reapplying her lipstick with a compact.

'I bet she did,' said Effie, soggy bread spinning in her mouth.

'Haven't we all,' smirked Charlie, smacking her lips.

'It's like national service,' said Effie, and all three giggled. Luckily, Eleanor was far too distracted by the eating to feel offended, and she was getting the picture that John's exploits were well documented.

Chrissie snapped her compact shut. 'Eleanor will be on probation, the same as everyone else when they start. When she's being trained, you girls carry on working as a three until she's done. Then you will need to train her how to work with you. I'm sure you all have your own tricks to teach her. In the meantime, she has to live with you. I'm trusting you to look out for her.' The last part landed to more sighs and groans.

'Will I be paid while I'm... training?' asked Eleanor. She had no savings and had left her job already. How could she be expected to survive if she didn't get paid as she was learning.

'Straight to it – I told you!' shouted Charlie. 'I've got a pound on you – said you'd work out all right.'

'And me,' said Effie. 'Even though you look a bit...'

'You've put bets on her already? When?' interrupted Chrissie.

'When we were getting ready,' said Lily. 'I was the one who bet against.' Addressing Eleanor, 'It's nothing personal, someone had to.'

'You will be given money,' said Chrissie. 'But it won't be what you can earn when you're in a cell, and these girls are good earners. You'll start with the retired girls who will teach you the basics. After that, it's up to you.'

'I think it's risky,' said Lily.

'Look a bit what?' Eleanor asked Effie. But everyone had forgotten Effie's half-finished sentence. 'You said, *even though I look a bit...* You didn't finish.'

'Like a social worker, or a charity person. One of those posh girls who runs about trying to rescue everyone even though no one bloody asked. Charlie said you looked prim and proper, but I said those are the ones you want to watch, they generally turn out to be filth.' Eleanor was mortified, social worker or *filth*?

'How do we know she's not stupid?' said Lily, still talking to Chrissie.

'Look!' Eleanor said, feeling compelled to defend herself and, forgetting about the greasy table, placing her arms, and sleeves, down. 'Lily, why don't you ask me? I'm right here, and no, I'm not stupid,' and to Effie, 'I'm not prim and proper or filth, thank you very much.'

'As much as I could strangle these two,' Lily leaned in, 'we work well together. We take our work seriously, and we don't get caught. I've got no plans of doing bird...'

'...again,' added Effie.

Lily carried on, 'Yeah, we have bigger balls than most blokes, but you've got to have something going on up here.' She pointed at her temple with a long-nailed finger.

Eleanor leaned back, arms folded. 'I worked on explosives. Do you think they'd let me handle TNT if I didn't have any brains? What did you do during the war?'

'Lil was in borstal,' said Effie.

'You were there too, and you still eat like a pig. Borstal didn't teach you anything,' snapped Lily.

'Only stuff I wanted to learn,' said Effie.

'This squabbling is... irritating,' said Chrissie. 'Sort it out between yourselves, you're all big girls.'

Eleanor had heard stories about borstal. A handful of girls from around Sun Street had ended up there. They were from bad homes, or runaways who took up with soldiers gone rogue. Or that's what she'd *heard*. Their crimes were minor – stealing change from an employer, not having ID – but they always ended up with bastard children and from then on were considered deviant, far worse than the boys. *Disturbed.* Boys could steal cars, and it was considered *spirit challenged in the wrong direction*. Disturbed girls were promiscuous and that was an abomination – wicked girls must be controlled. There were an awful lot of people who made a good living out of worrying what goes on in a girl's bloomers.

The door to the café opened and in strode four labourers, young enough to still have the shoulders and looks that would abandon them in a few years, along with their teeth. Charlotte pulled her cloche down over her face.

'Another of your conquests, Charlotte?' asked Chrissie. Even Lily cracked a smile.

'Perhaps,' said Charlie, trying to disappear into her tea.

'What was wrong with him?' asked Effie.

'Nada in the larda,' said Charlie, and they giggled. Eleanor didn't understand, so Charlie whispered across the table. 'He had a skinny little cock.' And she wiggled her pinkie finger.

'On that note, are we done? Good,' said Chrissie, standing up, chair scraping across the floor. 'I've got business to get to. You girls get to know each other, plan for Eleanor moving in.' She waved her hands over the girls as if she didn't want to be bothered with the minutiae. 'And I expect to see you lot at Ada's later. Eleanor, you best work on the story you're going to tell your mother. If you're serious, I expect you up here this week.'

Oh God. How on earth was she going to tell a convincing fantasy that would satisfy her mother? She felt as if she were being swept away at sea, it was all moving rapidly. She had so many questions but was intimidated into silence, bamboozled. And yet, at the same time, she wanted in on whatever this was. She would have to find a way of explaining it to her family that made them comfortable – a lie but not too elaborate.

Chrissie paid on her way out and marched off with the troops behind.

'Take care, my lovelies!' shouted the woman behind the counter, with a voice that suggested she gargled with oil and glass.

CHAPTER TWELVE

ELEANOR WAITED UNTIL AFTER DINNER BEFORE ASKING for everyone's attention. Every single family member, including the twins, gathered in the scullery. Ashen faces told her they were anticipating something shocking. The last time this happened, Steph announced she was expecting.

Her mother wiped her hands on a tea towel and perched on the arm of the chair her father sat on. Steph and Paul were on another with a bairn on a knee each. Eleanor stood like a child forced to sing at Christmas.

'I have a new job, and... it's in London!' No one moved an eyelash. 'Isn't that good news?! And you shall be free of me too. Think how tidy the house shall be!'

'London!' said Steph.

'Where?' said her mother, arms folded, tea towel in the grip of a fist.

Dad seemed to be slowly pondering on the news. Paul was waiting to see who he should take his cue from.

'A new job, eh?' said Paul, pitching for the good news band. 'So, when do you start?'

'I'm moving up Wednesday and I start the day after.' Eleanor forced a nervous smile as she dropped each little bomb.

'*Cette semaine!? Non!* Bill, did you hear this?' But Bill didn't seem to understand what reaction his wife expected.

'Bill, your daughter moving to London, alone!' Steph looked as if she might cry, their dad simply shrugged.

'Emilie, we go where the work is,' her dad offered.

Her mother threw questions like tennis balls, demanding to know every detail, but Eleanor had anticipated this.

'Where is this job, doing what?' spat her mother.

'The Savoy, in the Strand. Waitress in a formal dining room.'

Paul and Dad amiably nodded along as Steph seemed bereft, casting her eyes down in despair, making Eleanor feel guilty. Then Mother started waving her hands as if expressing herself in two languages wasn't enough and she must also mime her rage.

'Bill! This is what we have raised. We move out of London for our children, and they move back, eh! To squalor, disease and deviants. We achieve nothing. What are the wages, eh?'

'Better than the Grand.'

'How much?'

'More when I've passed probation. Perhaps more than ten pounds a week with tips.' Her only benchmark had been the wages at the factory, which she now flung about with no clue as to how accurate the true figure was. 'My friend works there and introduced me to the manageress who interviewed me and offered me a job on the spot. I spoke about the Grand – it is the finest in Brighton. She knew of it, but the Savoy is grander!' Eleanor's face had become unnaturally animated, as if she were Mary Pickford.

'Does this manageress know you were fired?' asked her mother.

'I quit, there's a difference.'

'Did you tell her the difference?'

'She asked me about etiquette and service, things only a proper waitress would know, and offered me a trial and I said yes. I thought you would be pleased.'

'You still haven't told me the wages,' her mother spat.

'I have, it depends on the shifts and if I pass probation.'

'*Pas spécifique*. You are hiding something, or you don't know. Bill, are you listening? We have raised an idiot.'

'No, I do, it's going to be less while I am on probation but if I pass, then I'll be on more.'

'Give me numbers!'

'And I can share accommodation with other girls. They have room...'

'What girls?'

'Girls from the Savoy.'

'Do they not have accommodation for staff at this palace?'

'They have a charming little flat in Lambeth.'

'Lambeth!?' Her mother threw the tea towel at Eleanor. She let it hit her in the face and fall to the floor.

'I'll share a bedroom, but I can send more money home. I told you I would get a better job, and I have.'

'Well done,' nodded Paul, clapping and quickly stopping as no one joined in. 'Good for you!' He nodded, as Steph glared at her husband for picking the wrong side.

'Good job, love,' said her dad.

★

Things had settled down into monosyllabic conversation by
the Tuesday when it appeared Eleanor was adamant about
going through with it. Steph would miss her, she said, but
understood, and even her mother softened.

On Tuesday night before she was to leave, Eleanor
struggled to sleep. She had finally dropped off and didn't
hear her mother creep into her bedroom. Eleanor woke to
her arm being patted and her mother sat on the side of her
bed.

'Mum? What is it?' Eleanor sat up, squinting eyes on her
mother in her nightgown, plait over a shoulder.

Her mother lit a candle by her bedside, and then came
a flash of silver as she brandished what appeared to be a
sword.

'Good God! What is that?'

'Shush, you will wake up the house,' said her mother. 'It
is my machete; I want you to have it.'

Her mother had a huge blade out of its leather sheath.
Eleanor had no idea her mother even had a machete and
was unsettled by how she admired it now, her eyes glinting
with pride.

'Where on earth did you get that?'

'My great aunt used to be a nun in Senegal. When I came
of age for service she gave it to me for my protection. Now
I give it to you.' Mum handed her the gleaming knife. 'She
was a nurse in the colonies and had to protect herself from
men.'

'Which men?' asked Eleanor.

'All of them. My aunt told me, should my master get lost

in his own house and find himself in my bedroom, I was to swing at him, and he will not get lost again. Thankfully, I never had to use it. It is a *coup-coup machete*. Listen, I know you must have your own life and despite how I feel about that, I understand. You must have your dreams. I left my family at fifteen. I love you, Eleanor, and despite your attempts there is nothing you can do to change that. Please take the machete, for me.'

Her mother lay the sheath down on her bed as Eleanor held the blade, kissed her on the forehead and left. It took a while for Eleanor to get back to sleep after that.

Promising to be back in a fortnight, and waving a teary Steph goodbye, Eleanor travelled to London the next morning. Needless to say, that particular visit never happened. Although she did write letters of pure fiction about her new life at the Savoy, how wonderful everything was, how well-mannered and polite her flatmates were.

Some people get homesick. Steph had when she'd gone to Bournemouth for her honeymoon, and Eleanor could not understand. How could a person miss something they wanted to escape from? Not out of rejection, but for an appetite for the new and exciting? Why was it perfectly natural for a boy to dream of adventure and yet for a girl to have such fantasies was to reveal herself as naïve and worse, *immoral*. Such a girl was inviting the world to abuse her. A nice girl would be grateful to be settled in whatever wallpapered tomb she had been given. Objects do not long for experiences – they are there to give pleasure to those that regard them. Girls are possessions to be guarded and admired. But for Eleanor, being her own master was a feverish dream. Imagine not answering to anyone!

CHAPTER THIRTEEN

IT WAS NOT LONG AFTER LUNCH O'CLOCK WHEN ELEANOR arrived at Hayles Buildings. She stepped through women's legs as they sat smoking on the stairs – they'd parted for Chrissie, but not her. Children ran about. Men loitered near an open door to a flat on the first floor, speaking a language she didn't recognise. They called after her, but Eleanor ignored them. Men in packs were always like this. Eleanor was anxious and already thinking of some further elaborate story if she were to turn around and run back home. In truth, she couldn't really believe she was doing this. She'd always been accused of being cavalier, but this was a leap into the unknown. *What was she thinking?*

At flat thirty-four, Eleanor rapped on the door. Within seconds it was ripped open and there was Lily dressed soberly in a black wool suit with a bulky jacket and long skirt – not quite as fashionable as last time. She let Eleanor in and kicked her own shoes off down the hall.

'Good timing, we've only just got back, come in.' Eleanor

stepped inside and shimmied past the coats, and Lily shut the door.

'The walls are paper thin here,' Lil explained, 'and it's a bugger for mould. The windows steam up something rotten, but it's nice other than that. Good electrics, wash houses on every floor – you'll want to clean the bath before you get in, of course. Some of the tenants can be ropey but they won't mess with us. Where's your stuff?'

'This is it,' said Eleanor, lifting a puny suitcase.

'Oh.'

Feeling awkward, Eleanor followed Lily to Effie's bedroom, into what should have been the parlour. Like cats come to regard a stranger, Lily and Charlie followed. Effie slumped on her double bed with brass finials, pillows with girlish frills. Charlie lay across the foot of her bed. Lily knocked a pile of clothes onto the floor to sit on a stool by a dressing table.

'Wasn't sure you'd come back,' Effie admitted.

There was only a double bed, and the room, aside from the odd piece of furniture, was an explosion of lamé, crêpe, silk, satin and chiffon. On the floor, on every piece of furniture. Where there weren't clothes there were hats, scarves, purses and hair pieces.

'You can take whatever space you can find in that dresser and shove the clothes over in the wardrobe. There are coat hangers around, somewhere,' said Effie.

'Found one.' Lily retrieved one from under her bottom and offered it to Eleanor.

'Thank you,' said Eleanor, taking the hanger and wishing very much they'd all leave her be for five minutes. This was worse scrutiny than under Miss Larson. Having convinced herself this was the adventure to embark on, she suddenly felt full of self-doubt and wanted to cry. She switched her attention to the wardrobe to hide her face between the doors, hoping they would all go away so she could get a grip. *You will be fine.* Things are always strange in the beginning. The factory had been strange too, and she had ended up loving it, although that had been entirely legal.

'Oh! I have a note for you!' shouted Charlie, leaping up and skipping off like a deer.

'We will have to see about a bed. Tonight it will be top and toe, I'm afraid,' grunted Effie.

Eleanor wasn't thrilled about the prospect of sharing either. She opened her little suitcase and started to take things out as Charlie returned and thrust an envelope at her.

'Here, from Chrissie,' she said, and sat back on Effie's bed. Charlie seemed the most welcoming – whereas Effie seemed sullen and Lily wary. When Eleanor started with TNT, an older girl had told her the way to steady nerves was to forget she was dealing with explosives and to fixate on each little task in isolation. Make progress, inch by inch. Eleanor forced her attention now on unpacking her meagre possessions.

'Is that all you've got?' asked Effie.

'I've left a lot back home,' she lied.

'You must be poor?' said Effie.

'Excuse me? I'm not *poor*, I'm ordinary.'

'Ordinary is poor,' added Effie, like a child.

'Effie, you can't say that, it's rude,' said Lily.

'But it's true,' Effie protested.

'Then think it inside your head and be polite. But she is right, Eleanor, you can't go working in those, not with us,' said Lily. 'You'll have to borrow some of our clothes until you buy your own.'

Eleanor's pride was stung and she found herself becoming upset just when she thought she was controlling herself. There were so many sequins about the room, twinkling like little stars, no wonder they thought her a dreary raincloud. Perhaps she was out of her depth, her ambitions too high for her abilities. What was she doing here? Was it a temperament problem? What if all she was good for was domestic service? *Inch by inch, girl! Task in hand!*

Eleanor opened the envelope and found a note telling her to be outside the Duke of Clarence pub at nine o'clock the next morning. The Two Anns would be training her. Then she found a second piece of paper outlining the rules all girls must abide by – by Queen Alice's decree. *The Hoisters' Code*, which had been written like the Ten Commandments, each one starting with *Thou Shalt*, made the rules seem so grave she trembled with fear at somehow breaking one before she'd even begun. There was also a crisp new one-pound note: *buy the girls a drink, make friends.* She clasped the paper note and remembered why she was here: *money.* Not only for herself, but for those she'd left behind. She read through them quickly, put it all back in the envelope and stuffed it into her pocket.

The novelty of watching Eleanor unpack having worn off, Effie and Lily deserted them, leaving her and Charlie.

'Did you have to pass a probation?' Eleanor asked, making the most of the opportunity to bond. Charlie was reading a romantic novel called *The Sheikh*. With a swooning white woman being ravaged by a dark-skinned Arab man against a desert backdrop on the cover.

'Sort of. I already knew how to lift. Me, Lily and Effie knocked about these streets when we were little. My dad moved us all to Southend, but I ran away when I was thirteen, drifted back here. For a while I was rolling.'

'All these words – hoisters, lift, rolling – how will I ever understand what's going on?'

'You'll get used to it, fast as you like.'

'What's rolling?'

'Well,' said Charlie, snapping the book shut and sitting up. 'You go out and let a man think you're up for it, have them buy you drinks thinking they're on a promise. Then right before you have to go through with it, you run off with the money. I ended up in Soho with all the other runaways. I thought I was lucky when two women took me in. They were lovely at first, really looked after me. They were older and had beaten-up faces, broken fingers and noses all smashed in from years of work, and men, so I was the bait. By day we would go shopping, lifting what we could, and by night, they'd fill me with brandy and send me out, bait and trap. It didn't always work, mind. Sometimes I had to do it. It's all well and good being clever but men are stronger. It's most unfair. Then I bumped into Lily and she told Alice. It was Alice who helped me get away from those nasty old witches. Trust me, they didn't dare touch me after she dealt with them!'

'Who is Alice?' asked Eleanor. 'John called her his aunt. And Chrissie works for her, so she's the boss, isn't she?'

'Yes, we call her Queen but she's an angel, is Alice Diamond. One for girls like us. Alice tells us you don't need to be stronger than a man if you run in packs, it's why we work in cells. Alice is like the patron saint of lady hoisters!' Charlie laughed. 'We're all off out tonight, will you come?'

'Oh, I best not.'

'Only one,' pleaded Charlie. 'It *is* your first night.'

'I'll need a clear head tomorrow; it says in Alice's rules.'

'I think you should come for one. You won't even have to buy. I've never bought myself a drink at Murray's. It's what God invented boys for.'

'They didn't teach that at Sunday school.'

Effie reappeared, having been in the bath, in a dressing gown made of tissue, for as much modesty as it gave her.

'What's going on?' asked Effie.

'She says she won't come out,' said Charlie.

'Now who is rude! It won't be a late one. We're working tomorrow, and some drinkiepoos might make it easier for us to sleep naked in the same bed.'

'Naked! Why would we be naked?' gasped Eleanor.

'I always sleep naked.'

'Perhaps you could make an exception.'

'Urgh... Prude.'

Lily had been to the wash house too and stood in the door of the bedroom in a negligée, brushing her teeth. The girls had no boundaries for decency or ladylike manners.

'What's this? Not coming out? It's only for one,' said Lily.

'Oh, all right, but only one.'

Eleanor waited for a welcome response, but there was a pregnant silence. All three girls stared at her. Poised, she regarded them with confused wariness.

'What? I said I'd come,' said Eleanor.

As if a starter gun had gone off, Effie and Lily lunged at her and grabbed her arms. Eleanor screamed.

'Stop your wailing, no one will come! You should hear the screaming here at night!'

'Charlie! The scissors!' shouted Effie, as Eleanor pulled and protested.

Lily and Effie pushed Eleanor to the dressing table and forced her to sit down on the stool at the mirror.

'What are you doing to me!?' Eleanor said, trying to extract herself from all the hands.

'It's for your own good,' said Lily.

Charlie handed scissors to Effie as she grabbed a handful of Eleanor's long brown hair.

'Don't you dare cut my hair!' Eleanor tried to cover her hair with her hands. 'I'll look like a boy!'

'I'd rather look like a boy than a Salvationist,' said Lily. 'You can't be seen with us like that.'

'Or one of those sickly women drowning in paintings,' said Effie. 'I should know, I was an artist's muse. Now, if you stay still, I'll only cut to the chin.'

Lily peeled Eleanor's hands off her hair and put them on her lap. Eleanor shut her eyes as she was forced to listen to the slicing of the blades through her hair. One minute she'd got hold of her emotions, and now they were butchering her hair. When Effie had finished, Eleanor opened her eyes and was shocked by what she saw.

Her long dark hair was in a chin-length bob, parted on one side so half an eye was obscured. The unkempt ends were in a frizzy heap on the floor. It made her face heart shaped – like her mother. Her neck was slimmer, and slender shoulders had appeared from nowhere.

'Oh my! I was worried I'd look like a boy,' said Eleanor.

'See?' said Effie. 'You look like that French actress, *Renée*

Adorée: pouty but regal, as if your shit don't stink. Me and Lil were talking, and we think we should call you Nell, it's short for Eleanor and more stylish. A new name and new hair. What do you think?'

Eleanor was so taken with her own reflection she didn't respond. Who was this intriguing young woman? *Nell?* The idea of pretending to be a new person, Nell, might help her overcome her jumbled feelings. Nell could be a new character, whatever Eleanor needed her to be. And she had to admit to herself, in terms of the hair, she rather liked it.

CHAPTER FOURTEEN

THE FOUR YOUNG WOMEN PREPARED FOR A NIGHT OUT. Clothes torn from hangers, cheeks pinched, eyebrows plucked and drawn back in. Scarlet Cupid's bows.

Nell borrowed a dress from Charlie as they were similar: flat chested, slight and average height. Effie was reed thin and tall. Lilian tall, but shorter than Effie, and voluptuous with a cleavage a regiment could rest on. When Nell slipped off her dress and stood in her tatty underwear, Effie winced.

'Best wear none. No man wants to see that,' said Effie.

'Are all your clothes... lifted?' Nell asked, beginning to understand Effie's bluntness as childish blundering, rather than malicious.

'No, and never! You never keep what you lift.'

'You can't risk getting caught with it – the peelers use it as evidence,' added Lily, admiring her dress in Effie's long mirror. She wore a black velvet and gold lamé dress, a knot of pearls at her cleavage.

Lily pulled up the dress to fix her suspenders and Nell saw a little tattoo on her thigh.

'It's a swallow,' she said, catching Nell looking by the reflection in the mirror. 'Before you ask,' Lily said, grinning, 'I don't.' It took Nell a second to get what she was hinting at.

'I do,' said Charlie, appearing sweet and flirtatious in a jade-green dress. *Good God, were they talking about...? Surely not.* Nell blushed.

'How can you!?' squealed Effie, drawing kohl around her eyes. 'It looks like a wrinkly old mole. All that wiry hair and that horrible flappy bit. I could gag thinking about it.'

'Effie always makes a beeline for Jewish men,' said Lily.

'And it's boring, makes my mouth ache.' Effie wore a silver and blue chiffon dress slashed near to the navel with too much chiffon to be ladylike.

'That's because you're not doing it right,' said Charlie.

'It's faster than doing it by hand,' said Lily. 'What about you, Nell?'

'Er... me?'

'What do you prefer, hand or mouth?' asked Charlie.

It was quite a reach for Nell to assume the role of blushing ingénue and yet that's how the girls were making her feel with their lack of inhibition.

'Depends on who it is.'

The freedom with which these girls prattled about such private matters made Nell shrink. She felt like a little girl! They chatted about such delicate subjects the way housewives complained of the price of potatoes.

Nell was resembling a flapper in a short black dress of chiffon and velvet, practically backless. It was the most expensive thing she'd ever worn. From *Atelier Bachroitz*, whoever that was – sounded posh anyway.

First stop was a music hall over the river in Leicester Square. Nell wore one of the furs from the hall. The girls skipped the queue and the men on the door ushered them in and up to a private box on the upper circle. Effie retrieved a bottle of champagne from inside her coat. They cheered and shared the warm bottle, passing it between them and smoking. From the box, Nell looked down on the people below packed in like billy goats, raucous and loud. It was so much better watching from a box. The first comedian was booed off with a shoe thrown at his head. Then came Russian acrobats, and a banjo player who was pelted with drinks. Once the champagne was gone, the girls grew restless.

'Let's go to Murray's,' said Effie. They went outside, hailed a cab and were off to Beak Street.

So much for one drink, but Nell had never been in a private box, let alone swigged champagne from the bottle in a fur coat hanging off her bare shoulders. The day before may as well have been a different world. Her head was spinning – she didn't even have the same hair! Wrapped up in the moment, the champagne deadening the scream of her nerves, she rather got carried away. Chrissie had specifically instructed her to *make friends*. That's what she was doing.

Murray's was a cabaret club and looked nothing special from the outside. But once inside, it was a party palace with one agenda: pleasure! At the top of the grand staircase sweeping down to a vast dancefloor, Lily offered Nell her arm as they descended into an underworld, and with each step Nell felt her heart bursting. This was where she wanted to be. She had always felt there was something out there where she would belong, but hadn't known where to find it, or what *it* was. But this? The jazz band played its heart-thumping rhythms, making her own heart quicken until the drumbeats felt as if they were fighting to come out of her body. *This was it!* The ceiling was miles away with glittering chandeliers. Painted Chinese ladies sat near naked in giant glass oysters on the stage. The dancefloor was dominated by one very good-looking couple doing the Venetian furlana. It *was* a different world, one of fun, freedom, jazz and America. Why would anyone not want this?

The dowdy British newspapers complained of anything American coming over here and corrupting the youth, and called jazz a 'dangerous craze'. Nell had heard about the dances but didn't know any. The tango, the shimmy, the Missouri walk, the vampire, and the evillest of all: the Charleston. The papers said that in nightclubs men and women, Black and white, *openly mingled* in hedonistic settings. Not for decent girls, but then neither was walking home in the dark, drinking in pubs, smoking, mixing with men or, quite frankly, doing anything that didn't involve staying at home and quivering behind the curtains. Her mother would be in bits if she knew where she was.

'The hair does suit you,' a man's voice whispered into her ear from behind. It was John, wearing a satisfied grin. The others were being drooled over by men with slick hair, sharp suits and collars, all carbon copies of John's style.

'Here, I know you are partial.' John handed her a flute of champagne.

'I'm still not over the last hangover.'

'Best cure is to get back on it, you know.'

'I have an early start tomorrow.'

'I hear you're having pillow fights with Effie. I'm always

available if you fancy a rematch. I'm glad you made it to the party.'

'What party?'

'Doesn't this look like a party?' John held arms out wide, drink in one hand, cigar in the other. He bent down to kiss her below the ear, and whispered, 'Better than waiting tables, right?' Nell felt something put into her hand by her side.

'A welcome gift,' he said as she looked at a little tightly wrapped envelope. 'A little pick-me-up. Everyone loves Murray's, some for the dancing, some for the showgirls, but everyone loves cocaine.'

Christ! Cocaine? Nell thought it was medicine for soldiers, and knew that some men had gone mad with addiction.

When she showed the packet to Effie, she dragged her to the ladies, into a cubicle, locked the door and showed Nell how to snort it in lines, and sniff it back, then wait for its magic to bring a wondrous sensation all over. Nell liked the feeling of cocaine very much, and all those stupid fears had been banished, at least for one night.

They made it back home sometime after four in the morning. The birds were up, singing. Effie and Nell lay top to toe in their shared bed. Nell was horribly regretful and unable to sleep.

'Are you asleep?' Effie asked.

'I can't stop thinking about home.' Nell propped herself up on one elbow. 'What about your home? Your mum was in the Forty Elephants too, right?'

'She was even queen for a bit, years ago. She was always banging on about it.'

'Where is she now, and your dad?'

'She's still about. She moved to Streatham. I see my little brothers and sisters in the street sometimes, but I don't *see* her if you know what I mean. We don't get on. Nor my dad, I only met him once.'

'Once? How come?' Effie sat up and the two women were like teenagers whispering after lights out.

'Mum always told me my dad was on holiday, but he was banged up in Wandsworth. He was a bond fraudster. I met him the one time in Wootton Street, where we lived. He'd just got out and had nowhere to go, so he came to see Mum. She had to point me out to him, show him which one was his. He didn't seem interested; then why would he be?' Effie shrugged.

'Where is he now? Do you know?'

'Last I heard, he was arrested in New York. My mum was up in court a few times but always got off. I could never understand why she had so many bloody kids, because she didn't seem to like them. When I was thirteen, I left with a bloke. He turned out to be a big bully, so I left him and worked in the clubs, seeing what I could get away with. I went hoisting too. I'd been taught as a kid; it was the family trade – the only thing worthwhile my mum taught me. Then completely out of the blue this old man with a long grey beard stopped me in the street. Proper posh fella with a cane and a big ruby on his little finger. Wore a velvet smoking jacket! He told me I had the most beautiful neck he had ever seen and asked to see my feet in the middle of the street. Look!' Effie stuck one skinny foot out from under the blankets, shining alabaster in the moonlight. Nell giggled; she had such long toes.

'He said I could stay with him in Covent Garden. I didn't need asking twice. He named me Euphemia, Effie for short. He had me dress up in costumes and wigs and pose. He was a painter, and I was his muse in residence. I couldn't believe my luck. I mean, he was a pervert, but kind with it.'

'He couldn't be that kind, Effie, more like a creepy old man. What's your real name?'

'Ethel,' she said. 'But don't call me Ethel, or I'll slap you. Anyway, I was still shopping and got arrested, then sent to borstal. That's where I ran into Lil again. After we both got out, we joined the Forty Elephants. I have my own career now. No rolling, no "come on, girl", no bloke telling me how to sit or what to wear. Can I tell you something?'

'Of course.' No wonder the girls seemed wary of new people. It appeared the girls had had terrible experiences. By comparison Nell had been cossetted.

'We are good at this game, Nell, hoisting. Really good, and you could be too. But you have to work at it and remember.'

'Remember what?'

'Think like a man and do what a man would do.'

'All right. I'll try. I'm not sure how though?'

'I'll teach you, but mainly, you must always put yourself first. Alice always says you're no good for helping anyone else if you're weak.'

'Hmm, I guess that does make sense.' Nell assumed people all thought the same way, but she didn't want to extend the conversation now, except for one last question.

'If you don't know where your mum lives, where is home?'

'This is home, silly. My girls and this flat. You're in it, you daft brush.'

CHAPTER FIFTEEN

A T TEN PAST NINE, NELL WAITED OUTSIDE THE PUB BY the wall, smoking one cigarette after another, feeling dreadful, bleak. And as if to mock her new image, her neck was freezing. It was a brisk November morning, and the frost hadn't quite disappeared. Nell thoroughly regretted her behaviour the night before. She was praying for mercy and bargaining on future good behaviour when she saw two little old ladies shuffling towards her, arm in arm. She could have sworn they had been in the pub when she'd come to find Chrissie.

'This must be her,' said the paler one. Frizzy white hair poking out from under a grey bucket hat.

Nell threw down her cigarette. The darker one had a tawny complexion with curly dark hair peppered with grey swirls and came right up close to Nell's face, as if she were going to sniff her.

'Morning,' said Nell, inserting a hand between them, if only to encourage a little distance. 'I'm Nell.'

'Nell it is,' said the darker one, squinting. 'Lovely to meet you, Nell. I'm Ann, and so is she.'

'We are the Two Anns,' said the paler one.

From nowhere she flicked out a cut-throat razor and held it up to Nell's face. Nell pushed her head back as far into the wall as she could, but there was nowhere to go.

'First things first: are you a grass?' asked pale Ann, closing one side of escape with her stout body.

'No! I am not!' Nell pleaded, conscious of the silver blade at her soft cheek.

'Do you have balls?' asked dark Ann.

'Erm, yes?' said Nell, hoping they referred to the brass and metaphorical variety.

Dark Ann's face broke into a wide grin. She stepped back and slipped the razor back into her pocket. Nell could exhale, losing a couple of inches in height.

'Work on that poker face, my darling. You're not used to this, are you?'

'Not exactly,' whimpered Nell, her voice shakier than she'd have liked.

Pale Ann approached the pub door and started banging and shouting through the letterbox. People walked past them, but not one paid any attention. Nell wasn't sure what she had expected – perhaps two versions of Chrissie. But these ladies were rougher, and their clothes worn. No jewellery on fingers or even a hint of lipstick. They were no different from any other old ladies, aside from the razor to the face, that is. Nell's overburdened mind ran about in frantic circles. Was this the sophisticated network that Chrissie and John had sold her? Nell had a sudden fear she was much like the excitable young boys who had joined up at the start of the war. Waved off by weeping mothers and full of tales of glory, only to be trampled on, buried somewhere in the mud.

'Maureen, open up! It's bloody freezing.'

The keys clanged in the door and, despite grumbling, the bar lady let them come in from the cold. What they were going to do in a pub was beyond Nell. The women ushered her inside. The first class was to be of the sitting variety. The Two Anns explained how they had met, and despite best efforts, had reached their seventies.

'1862 we were renting in the same brothel...' barked dark Ann as if delivering a sermon. 'We were being robbed every other night, then we met each other and worked a way off the merry-go-round...'

'...two halves of the same coin, aren't we, Ann?'

'...indeed we are, Ann.'

Dark Ann was the daughter of a West Indian fencing instructor, a skilled man with a respectable position, and her mother was native English. She had even grown up in a house on mansion grounds in Surrey. But when her father suddenly died, her family's prospects were destroyed. They lost their home and were soon destitute. Ann began to run with a gang and her mother washed her hands of her, and she eventually made her way to London at thirteen. Pale Ann had less auspicious beginnings but had also run away at thirteen. It was meant to be, for, as soon as the girls found each other, they were thick as thieves, quite literally.

'What's funny is neither of us thought we'd make old bones, and yet here we are!' said pale Ann. Then dark Ann laid down the basics.

'The Forties work Tuesday to Saturday. Saturday night, let your hair down. Sunday is rest. Monday is planning day, meetings take place to discuss who has been nicking what, what blags are on, who is doing bird, who is up in court and planning the rota. You won't be involved in that; your cell will pick up your rota from Chrissie. They change weekly. You will know nothing about what any other cells are up to. You don't need to know, only Alice and her close associates, such as Chrissie, will be aware of the wider operation.' Monday was the quietest day for shopping (as they called work) – too many staff, not enough customers.

'...clear heads for work!' said pale Ann, pointing in Nell's face with a yellow fingernail. 'I could smell you twenty yards away this morning, and when Ann pulled that razor out, you took half an hour to notice.'

Dark Ann added, 'I could have carved you a new smile, my love. Be a shame to ruin such a pretty face.'

As they talked, more elderly folk dribbled through the doors. Nell didn't understand, it was hours before serving was legal.

'It's coal,' explained pale Ann. 'Or lack of. There's never enough coal when you're old. Maureen lets us in.'

'You girls don't even know you're born,' said dark Ann. 'See her over there?'

Ann pointed at a geriatric woman sat at a table. Frail, knitting by the window. She wore a head scarf in a knot under her chin and her spotted hands worked furiously with knitting needles.

Dark Ann leaned in, 'That's Nana Gregg. She's been in prison ten times, bless her, escaped four. Birthed thirteen and four of them are inside. Hard as nails, that old dear.

The old girls are made of something else, I'll tell you. Get arrested back then, it was hard labour, whippings, beatings – not you young ones. It's all sewing and laundry these days. You've got it easy, my love! This is the golden age for thievery – make the bloody most of it. If you don't, that'd be the real crime.'

The mention of a golden age gave Nell the feeling it was a temporary state; rather than boosting her confidence, she could only think that golden ages had a habit of ending and implied a sense of urgency. Not good for the nerves.

'Toffs won't ever do right by us,' spat pale Ann. 'They'll shell out for reform schools all right, borstal, or prison, but only because their mates make money out of the contracts.'

'Charlie said I should ask you about The Code. I've read the rules,' said Nell.

'Them's the Queen's rules. You have to abide by them or… at least not get caught breaking them.' Pale Ann winked. 'Especially the one about stealing other people's men. So undignified. Discipline is one, punctuality is another.'

'You can't blame the Queen if a job goes wrong, these things happen in war,' said dark Ann.

'War?' asked Nell.

'The war our own government wages against us, their people. They barely let us scrape by while stealing everything for themselves. Oh, and all Forties pay a subscription to the Queen, for if and when you get into trouble…'

'…that will buy you a defence, it's like insurance,' said pale Ann.

'What about Queen Alice, when will I meet her?' Nell was desperate to see the big woman, and a little scared.

The old birds exchanged looks and dark Ann leaned in. 'I'm sure you will at some point, but don't get too ahead of yourself, my darling. Alice keeps her circle small, and I don't blame her. The Forty Elephants have been around for years, used to be called the Forty Thieves; but then Queen Alice has always had an eye for opportunity and she's made business bigger than it's ever been. Alice won't suffer men interfering and she doesn't take shit from anyone. She's strong and good with her fists, like her dad. That girl can knock a punch that sends most men flying across a room. One of a kind she is. This is *her* Lambeth – we just live in it.'

The women talked about Alice as if she were a goddess. The oldest of eight, they told Nell, she wore diamonds on every finger, and she was smart as a whip, and sober. Unlike her best friend and second in command, Maggie Hughes, who was as short as Alice was tall, and as big a drinker as Alice was not.

'A word of warning about Maggie Hughes and her sisters, the Hill girls. They might look small and pretty, but they are wild with quick tempers. Don't ever step on Maggie's feet. I saw that once happen by accident – went stark raving. Within a second the poor girl that done it had her face sliced open.' Nell struggled to control her expression. She'd felt bold as brass only the night before and now quivered at the thought of being arrested, attacked and felt totally out of her depth.

'That's enough sitting,' said pale Ann. 'Up we get, nervous Nelly, we're off for a walk.'

'Nervous?' said Nell, becoming defensive. 'Whatever gave you that idea?'

Both Anns doubled up laughing and looked down at the table where Nell's hands had been clutching on, her white knuckles gripping the edge. Once she let go she had pins and needles in her hands.

CHAPTER SIXTEEN

NEXT LESSON WAS GEOGRAPHY. LIVING IN LAMBETH AND south of the Thames, Westminster and Waterloo Bridges were the nearest way over the water. The journey was lined with seedy hotels, often fronts for brothels. Once over the river, Nell was in prime hunting ground: the West End, and that thoroughly modern gift to hoisters – the department store.

The Anns explained how Debenham & Freebody had been the first big shop of the self-serve variety and Bon Marché followed. Selfridges on Oxford Street had hundreds of sections and even looked like a palace, especially when you'd crawled out from the grime of Southwark. That month, British archaeologist Howard Carter and his benefactor Lord Carnarvon opened Tutankhamun's tomb in Egypt and everything had turned gold, quite literally – London had gone Ancient Egypt mad. Shop windows were decorated with hieroglyphics, gold-covered chariots and alabaster props. Fashion channelled the regal charisma of

Queen Cleopatra and Queen Nefertiti. Department stores actually resembled tombs of treasure waiting to be looted.

With the department store, any lowly poor girl could touch luxury previously only within reach of the privileged. Never before had a commercial destination been designed to seduce a woman. Perfume, music, colour palettes. For many, going up West was as good as being in a movie, or a dream. Shopping was a passionate, all-consuming love affair for women with dull and monotonous lives. But, as with all addictions, the euphoria never lasts, the disease is progressive. But it certainly made the drab reality of a mediocre husband grunting on top of you after making his dinner for the thousandth time a little more bearable. Liberty, Whiteley's, Harrods, Bourne & Hollingsworth, all tempting whores – they were practically asking for it. The defeated god of love had handed the baton to the god of almighty profit. He ensured shop assistants were on hand and goods were stacked high: silks, furs, shawls, gloves, parasols, ribbons, cotton, hats, you name it, it was there for the taking.

'If they didn't want us to take it, then why make it so easy?' as dark Ann said.

They walked down Oxford Street and the Strand, Nell in the middle, not even tall but towering above the short ladies. Pale Ann explained operations.

'Cells in four, or five, hit several stores at the same time. Big targets are furs, jewellery and silks. You'll be shown how to lift these things. Girls work as a team, signal to each other, cover and go. They drop the goods off at the car, and those goods will be driven to safe houses back in Elephant

& Castle. Goods are split or divvied up and delivered to fences, tailors or jewellers all over London.'

'Fences?' asked Nell.

'They handle stolen goods. But you don't need to worry about that. You deliver the goods and get paid.'

'How much are we talking, roughly?' asked Nell, desperate for a figure.

'It depends on how good your cell is, could be up to thirty pounds a week.'

'Thirty pounds!?' Nell gulped, stopping on the spot. 'In a week! Is that true?'

Both Anns smiled. They each took an arm each side of Nell and shuffled her onwards.

'Oh yes, my love, more if you get very good at it. Make as much as you can while you're young, that's all I'll say.'

Areas were divided into districts, and cells would be assigned on a rota, which made the routine unpredictable but orderly. Rotas were picked up once a week on a Monday. No one changed the rota; you got what you were given. You were not to know or even ask about any of the other cells' rotas or districts. This stopped grasses or leaks giving the police a heads-up. *Accidents of war* or getting nicked – whatever you wanted to call it – was a hazard of the job. But it seemed a good thing they didn't have to handle the goods for long and could offload onto these fences.

If Nell had to choose between her former wage of seven pounds a year or a chance of making thirty in a single week, the risk had to be worth it.

What Nell could do with that kind of money. She could save! And send lots home. Her mother wouldn't have to worry about Dad not working, and he could rest up. She would need to tell some tall stories about fancy tips from exotic guests at the Savoy. Life would surely be wonderful on thirty pounds a week. Why, she could not imagine a single problem a person would have in life if they were on that sort of money. The fear of rotting in prison, the shame of being branded a thief, the risk, all of it faded at the prospect of making thirty pounds a week! She wouldn't do it forever, obviously. Long enough to make money and get out before she got caught. Other women were doing it, why couldn't she?

'Do you think Alice is the first woman to run a business of women?' asked pale Ann.

Nell shook her head. She had to assume others had tried, but she'd never heard of any.

'Course not. We can't blame men for this; we women let ourselves down. I'll bet you ten bob every time a woman's business goes tits up it's because of a bloody man having to come first! And we let them!'

Dark Ann jumped in. 'The Forty Elephants doesn't want those girls. Alice wants ones with fire in their bellies, not wedding veils in their eyes. Let them chase the fairy tale because I'll tell you something for nothing, sweetheart – that's what it is. No prince is coming to save you.'

By mid-afternoon it seemed the day had come to a natural conclusion. Nell's head was still banging from the night before. But the Anns had one last task for her, bringing Nell's fright lurching to the foreground again.

'First test, my love,' said dark Ann.

'What, now?! I can't. I'm not ready,' Nell protested.

'No one is ever ready. Now's the perfect time. Don't worry, we've saved the easy job for you,' said pale Ann.

Nell was to play decoy in a little trick. She was to enter a small boutique down a quiet street, peruse through racks of dresses and pick something with a pattern. Then make a great show of taking it to the front of the shop, close to the door, in order to see the pattern in daylight.

Nell steeled herself as she entered the shop. She tried to appear relaxed despite being anything but as she flicked through the racks of dresses. Pale Ann came in without her hat, but now she wore a beret and had taken off her coat. Nell cast her eyes down for fear of one of the shop assistants spotting her looking at pale Ann. In swaggered dark Ann, bowling through the doors – a most conspicuous entrance. Dark Ann was overcome with a hacking cough, only she didn't cover her mouth, spluttering everywhere. Dark Ann coughed into her hands and touched clothes in front of a wincing clientele. A young shop assistant appeared flustered and looked towards the cash register to the other assistants for guidance.

The coughing was Nell's cue. *I can do this. It's easy. Task in hand. Task in hand!* She picked a lurid blouse and bowled towards the doors, knees trembling, heart thumping, despite not really doing anything at all.

'Miss! Miss! May I help you!?' The flustered shop assistant took the opportunity to abandon dark Ann. As instructed, Nell acted the dolt, which came quite naturally given the circumstances.

'Oh, I'm so sorry, I was only trying to see the pattern properly in this ghastly light. It's a little gloomy today, don't you think? Good heavens! Silly me! I do hope you didn't think I was going to steal it.' Nell giggled like a silly little goose, stumbling over an entirely new character, drawing on the varied but well-heeled clientele she'd served at the Grand.

'Oh no, madam, of course not! Here let me hold it up for you by the doors,' said the shop assistant, much more comfortable in the company of someone who appeared to be *normal*, a respectable middle-class English lady.

Dark Ann knocked hats off a stand and attracted the attentions of an austere male manager. Two male assistants and the manager formed a collective around her, sweeping up the fallen hats from the floor, dusting them off and placing them back, ushering dark Ann out of the shop.

'Time for you to leave, madam, there's nothing for you, here,' said the manager.

'Well, that's bloody charming, ain't it!' shouted dark Ann, to the gawps and gasps of ladies in the boutique.

Pale Ann was long gone. Nell thanked the shop assistant, and after a few minutes put the blouse back and left. She was absolutely bubbling over with excitement at the minor part she'd played in what had been, thus far, her grandest heist. She met the Two Anns, as planned, down a side street.

'What d'ya get, Ann?' asked dark Ann.

'A few bits and bobs, Ann. Not too shabby,' said pale Ann.

'With my complexion I attract attention,' explained dark Ann to Nell. 'Which is why I act the fool.'

'And with my complexion,' said pale Ann, 'and my age, I may as well be a bloody ghost. May as well makes the most of it! That's your first day done, my darling. Now who fancies a little steak and kidney pie and a look-see at what I fetched. Oh, before I forget; here, this is for you.' Ann thrust into Nell's hand a piece of paper with an address for her training the next day.

'You pay attention tomorrow. There's nothing those girls can't get in a pair of bloomers – and lay off the booze,' said dark Ann, pointing in Nell's face.

Nell went back to the flat utterly exhausted, every nerve rung out, her stomach having lurched between terror and delight several times over. Every time she closed her eyes, all she could see were the shining golden shop windows – it was beautiful.

That night, even with Effie snoring naked next to her, all she could hear was a little voice somewhere whispering, *thirty pounds a week!*

CHAPTER SEVENTEEN

THE ADDRESS ON THE PIECE OF PAPER WAS FOR A SHOE factory called Freeman, Hardy & Willis on the corner of Newington Butts and St George's Road. A sign above the door on the six-storey block said, 'Rabbit's Shoe Factory – Established 1846'.

Nell pushed open double doors and stepped into an empty warehouse where a bearded man in a dirty vest and leather apron appeared, wiping his hands with a cloth.

'I'm looking for Maggie,' Nell said, fearful of being in the wrong place. Trepidation in her voice.

The man didn't speak but pointed to another door in the far corner. Nell hurried towards it as he leered. *What was this place?* Through the door was a storeroom, and in it were three women, older than her mother, well dressed, in white blouses and long woollen skirts, makeup and hair set. Their discussion stopped abruptly as Nell entered and they glared at her. Around the perimeter were full rails of the latest fashions, handbags, scarves and rolls of coloured fabrics. It must be a sorting room for stolen goods, as the Two Anns had mentioned. Such places were all over Southwark.

'Nell?' said the most elegantly suited of the three. Nell nodded. 'Chop chop, over here. I'm Maggie, and these two are Phoebe and Sarah.'

Phoebe and Sarah were to measure Nell up for a pair of special bloomers. Nell took off her coat and hitched up her skirt as the two women kneeled on the floor, sticking pins into her, bickering over inches.

'I was your size once,' sighed Phoebe, who blamed having three daughters, and said girls stole your looks and left you with nothing. 'And your tits go south.'

'Like two eggs dribbling down a wall!' said Sarah, and both broke out laughing. With her skirt up, Nell was reminded of one of the many times she was caned as a naughty schoolgirl for showing her bloomers to the boys in the playground. How her mother had near died of shame. Thoughts of her family came like a shallow stabbing pain between the ribs and Nell forced them to the back of her mind. Sentimentality would not help her focus on her new job. Such emotions wouldn't help her at all.

The third woman who seemed in charge was Maggie Springate, who, as she explained, was now a semi-retired hoister. Maggie was famed for her magic bloomers, so Phoebe and Sarah said. A serious dame, she was to tutor Nell in basic technique. Nell knew it was important to impress her; she was thoroughly intimidated but determined to learn what she could, the same way as she had at the munitions factory.

'The bloomers are silk because you get more in. Get yourself a big coat, the heavy fabric will hide any hard lines once your bloomers are full,' said Maggie.

'Maggie could fit an elephant down hers – she's one of the best,' added Sarah.

Inside the bloomers would be webbing, from which Nell would have to practise how to hang goods from hooks. She would need to make slits in her own dresses and coats, and fix belts with hooks on. Shoes could be hollowed at the heels and filled with wax to stick tomfoolery inside. A *bit of tom, tomfoolery* – thieves' slang for jewellery.

'If you get good at it,' said Maggie, 'you can steal to order – get yourself some regular clients and they'll tell you what they want.'

'Clients? Like who?' asked Nell.

'Toffs,' said Maggie.

'Toffs? But if they're toffs, can't they simply buy?'

Maggie cackled and Nell saw a flash of a gold tooth. Sarah and Phoebe chuckled along and shook their heads.

'Toffs hate spending their money, sweetheart. That's how they stay so bloody rich. You will learn,' Maggie said, patting her on the cheek like an old school matron.

Nell was too intimidated by Maggie to ask more questions. The woman was polite enough but had a hard presence about her. One you certainly didn't mess with. Nell was back on the adrenaline rollercoaster. Dreaming of thirty pounds a week the night before and the next day wondering what on earth was she getting herself into? Trying to reassure herself that this wasn't a doomed mission to prison. If her mother had near died of shame when she'd brandished her knickers as a mere girl, how on earth would she react on hearing her youngest daughter was a criminal. A thief, no less. A more pressing fear: how was she ever going to walk in stuffed bloomers?

After being measured up, Maggie showed her the basic tricks of the trade. Everything was a variation on a theme. Maggie showed Nell how to signal to another girl which dresses to hoist. How to slide the dress to one side as the other girl – in this example, Nell – approached the rail.

'Now watch,' said Maggie, as Phoebe and Sarah sat observing the lesson. 'The first girl waves for assistance to occupy the shop girl. Remember, they ain't paid nothing at all, most couldn't care less if things go missing. Sometimes, the shop girl might even be an old schoolfriend or a niece of a neighbour – my point is, they don't want to stir things up in their community, so often they'll ignore hoisters. It's all about how you carry yourself – you can't look frightened. To steal a whole fur coat is a real skill. You have to pack it right down to your knees and be able to walk out without looking as if you've shit yourself.'

Maggie showed her how to roll a fur up and tuck it between her legs. Nell tried wearing a pair of Maggie's old bloomers she'd brought along, but rolling the fur coat up tight enough was beyond her weedy little hands. It kept bouncing open or coming out at the sides. Nell was sweating with the frustration and pressure to get it right, but it seemed hopeless.

'How is this possible?' she whined.

'Ask Lil – she is a master at rolling a fur, that girl. You need to practise and stick at it, don't give up. Give it a rest for now, carrying on and getting yourself worked up won't help. Let's talk distraction.'

'What kind of distraction?'

'These are the signals and tricks you work out in your cell. If a friend was in a spot of bother, I'd often drop something into the bag of the most stuck-up posh type in there. A real hoity toity. Then have another girl accuse her of thieving and those old birds are guaranteed to make the biggest fuss if stopped. While that kerfuffle is going on, we're all buggering off.'

The afternoon went on, with reiterations of decoy tricks, signals, rotations, rolling and dropping – it was exhausting. Nell was told to pick up her bloomers on Sunday, ready for the next stage, working in her cell, for real this time, in the department stores! When Maggie told her, Nell's face tingled with terror. *What? Was that the training?* Chrissie had made it sound as if she was going to be graduating from proper training, over time. Like school or the factory. Not a couple of scrappy days practising tricks she was very obviously useless at. It was as good as being thrown to the wolves. *Had Chrissie said as much, or had Nell conjured that assumption all by herself?*

'Believe in yourself, my darling,' said Maggie, as the blood drained from Nell's face. 'Audacity, shamelessness and, if confronted, bloody outrage. Blame the shopgirl, blame the other customer, blame the weather, everyone but yourself. And for God's sake remember to breathe. I had one girl who fainted from holding her breath.'

'What happened to her?'

'She got kicked out. Some just don't have *it*. You'll be fine, my darling.'

'How do you know?' asked Nell, eyes wide, hoping

Maggie had seen some spark of potential and was about to offer reassurance.

'I don't, my lovely, I'm only trying to make you feel better. God bless, now off you pop. And remember! Practise!'

And like that she was back outside, trudging home suffering from a headache and a terribly dry mouth. All she could think about was how difficult it was to roll a fur up and how simple Maggie made it look. This hurt Nell's ego; it made her angry. Nell had not found much difficult to learn up until this very point. As a girl her teacher had told her this natural ability spoiled her attitude. She found things *too easy*, and if she found anything hard, she lost interest. But that was not going to happen here.

Nell marched home, hands in pockets, eyes on pavement. She wanted to get home and crack on with more practice, starting with those furs in the hall. There really was no other choice, she *had* to make this work. The other women were doing it, so it must be possible. Remember, thirty flipping pounds a week. There was no way she was going home with her tail between her legs. Not now.

CHAPTER EIGHTEEN

On Sunday, Nell picked up her special bloomers and went straight home to practise, unable to tell if what she felt was crippling fear or excited anticipation. It was the run up to Christmas and the West End would be a shopping frenzy. By rights, the girls told her, pickings should be easy.

Their bedroom was Selfridges, and Nell would practise the signals and tricks as the three others sat giving critique, shouting direction. Taking turns to play shop assistants or customers. The criticism was merciless and whatever unconscious confidence she'd awarded herself had evaporated.

'Stop looking so bloody scared,' said Charlie. 'The staff will pick up on it, they'll be all over you.'

'I look frightened?'

'A trembling rabbit!'

'You've got to believe you belong there.' This was Effie. 'If you knock something on the floor, it was their fault for putting it in your way. Ladies never apologise because they're never wrong.'

But when it came to smuggling a fur in her bloomers, Nell was hopeless.

'You can't squat like that!' Lily shouted when she tried to stuff her bloomers with a badly rolled coat. 'You can't risk rolling anything thicker than crêpe at this point, because it's so obvious.'

'Was I squatting?' Nell was unravelling. What if she didn't have *it*? At this rate, she'd be in prison by the end of the week! No matter what the Anns had said about prison these days being soft, Nell could practically hear the clinking of chains and torturous screams from the Tower of London. If she were sent to prison, that would make her a *convicted criminal*. Her family would no doubt disown her. She would die alone, in poverty and misery, an old maid. And to have been such a rubbish criminal at that! The prospect was too humiliating to bear.

'Your rolling isn't bad for a beginner, but when you're stuffing it down your bloomers, it looks like you're going to take a shit right there on the floor,' said Lil.

'Or give birth!' said Charlie. All burst out laughing, aside from Nell, who wanted to cry. Instead, she threw a tantrum.

'That's it! I can't do it! I'm never going to be able to do it! What if I get caught on the first day? It'll be so shameful.' Nell flopped down on the bed.

'You won't. We won't let it happen,' said Lily.

'You would win that bet though. Wasn't it a pound against me?' asked Nell.

'I'd rather be wrong and lose a pound than see you

arrested on the first day – I'm not evil. Now come on, keep going.'

Their district that first week was the northern end of Oxford Street and the small radius around it. They didn't get the prime retail estate assigned – the rota was made up in isolation by Alice and her most trusted lieutenants – because of the burden of a new girl. Nell felt herself to be a burden keenly. It was a horrible feeling, and Nell knew it wouldn't be long before her lack of technique would be discussed if she couldn't improve. All she wanted to do was practise.

'Going at it like that is only going to make things worse, give yourself a break or you'll make silly mistakes going over and over. It's like a sickness! You really are thinking too much. Feel natural,' said Effie.

'Well, it's not bloody natural!' snapped Nell. 'I'll simply have to keep going until I crack it.'

'Look at me,' said Effie, pulling Nell's arms off the mock rack that had taken up residence in their bedroom. 'Technique is important, but what I know is that confidence will get you most of the way. You act like you belong there, show people what they expect to see from a middle-class lady, and I promise, it'll be easy. Look, people are stupid. They only see what they want to see and they're lazy too. No one gets paid enough to care that much. I'm telling you, Nell. It's balls, not brains. Big old brass balls. Now you better grow some.'

The night before the first day, they went to the pub for a quiet drink. Rota memorised; district confirmed. Even seeing the rota Nell had felt on the cusp of withering into a pile of ashes. The routines, tricks and signals were agreed. Nell was stuck in her own world, rehearsing the techniques in her head. She wanted to run home to Brighton, get into her nightgown, eat her mother's food, bicker with Steph and crawl into bed. Instead she was here, in Lambeth. In a pub with a bunch of people she barely knew, criminals, getting herself involved in something she barely understood. *What the hell was she doing?*

'Evening, Duchess, fancy seeing you.' John sauntered over to where she sat on a stool by the bar nursing a gin. The others were drinking with a crowd of Forty Elephants, mingling with the men from the Elephant Gang, and a group of locals.

Curiously, with everything being so strange to her – digs, job, people, clothes… even hair – John represented the nearest thing to the familiarity of home.

'I don't think I'm cutting it, John,' Nell confessed. 'Lil says I look like I'm taking a shit when stuffing a fur in my bloomers.'

John chuckled and regarded Nell with an odd, almost smug expression. If she had been in a better frame of mind, Nell might have challenged him, but she was vulnerable and didn't have the fight in her.

'Do you know how many times I've heard that from a new girl before?' he said.

'You have?' Nell also wondered how many of these girls he had slept with.

'Come in here all grim faced, as if they're going over the top in the morning. I'll put money on it you'll do all right. You know why?'

'Why?'

'I've got an eye for talent, me. And you, Duchess, I have the utmost confidence in.'

'Oh? How come?' Nell was willing to abandon any pride in exchange for some hot air.

'Don't take this the wrong way but you look stuck up,' he said. That was not what she was expecting.

'I'm not stuck up!'

'You can't help it; you look like a real prim and proper sort. It's the nose, sticks up a bit.'

Nell gasped at the remark and touched her nose. 'It's my mother's nose. You can blame her for making me look snooty.'

'You have this air about you,' he said, lighting a cigarette and straightening his jacket. 'Arrogant. That's it. Arrogant, like a real Duchess. Stop fretting and play the part. You have to have the brass—'

'Balls, I know. Effie told me.'

'Fuck me. Effie and me in agreement? I suppose even the sun shines on a dog's arse once in a while. Why don't you come back to mine. I'll take your mind off it.'

Under normal circumstances Nell would have told him to jog on, but she found herself spending the evening in John's bed. She promised it would be the last time. John was the closest connection she had to home, and therefore the most familiar comfort.

They hit the West End on Tuesday morning and started in a small independent boutique. Nell was to play decoy and distract the shop assistants. She was relieved at first; it was an easy enough role. But Nell became more desperate, and frustration grew as she was simply avoiding the real test and wanted it over with. Much like a condemned man may wish to get to the gallows sooner rather than later. The wait worse than the consequences. They worked their way up their district to Whiteley's during lunch, Nell still playing decoy much the same as she'd done with the Two Anns. Lily targeted furs, Charlie and Effie dropped dresses and whatever else they could into their bloomers. When they had finished, they met the car parked on a corner, dropped their rolled-up parcels into the open top Velux driven by a youth from the Elephant Gang, no older than sixteen, a mere boy. The threat of getting the first real job out of the way was tormenting Nell.

'I can't go the whole day being decoy. Let me try lifting,' said Nell to Lil as they were dropping off in the car after Whiteley's. Lil studied her face for signs of mettle. Nell stared right back, willing Lil to let her try.

'All right. Small and light fabrics, and certainly no furs!'

'Thank you!' said Nell. She wanted this first job done.

They entered John Lewis on Oxford Street. This time it would be Charlie and Effie who occupied the frazzled shop assistants. Lily was rolling furs and Nell was on the crêpe de Chines, silks and cotton – items that she could take on the hanger, roll and slip without much effort into her bloomers. She thought of the hoity toity rudest ladies of the Grand, and found herself adopting a manner, sneering down her supposedly prim-and-proper nose. Catching the eye of the shop assistant, she looked straight through the girl as if she weren't there. That's what a lady would do, and it worked! The girl didn't pay her another look.

Getting goods in her bloomers was one thing. Walking in full bloomers was another matter, which is why they wore conservative clothes when working, for the coverage and bulky fabrics. Nell stuck her chin in the air, handbag over a bent arm, and walked, slowly but purposely, towards the door. Her heart thumped in a syncopated rhythm with all the goods in her knickers, moving and shuffling about. Her whole body trembled; the door seemed like the gates to heaven, with blinding daylight on the other side. Her instinct was to get out as fast as possible, but that is not what a lady would do. A lady would meander, stop by the door to peruse one last item before snootily dismissing it and exiting. As she stepped over the threshold, Effie covered from the back. No one stopped her, or screamed, or whistled, or wrestled her to the floor. The whole experience was almost... *underwhelming.*

Nell raced back to the car, this time bursting with pride. She removed the flimsy, meagre takings from her bloomers and dropped them into the car with the exploding heart of a Viking warrior. She did it! Thank God that was done! The first hill ever climbed is the biggest mountain. It really hadn't been difficult at all! Her cheeks soon hurt from grinning.

And the girls were pleased too. Charlie was squealing the way she did, hopping on tiptoes.

'You did it! First trick down.'

'Good job, Nelly. You'll only get better from here on,' said Lily, dark eyes beaming.

'I told you,' said Effie. 'It's all about confidence.'

Nell floated back to the flat on a cloud. Blissful and elated. High on the ecstasy of getting away with something. She wanted nothing more than to get dressed up, put on makeup, and go out and prolong the feeling of euphoria. Suddenly the lifestyle of partying and dressing up in their spare hours made perfect sense. A girl runs on blood and nerves all day, gets away with it, of course she wants to let off steam.

Nothing would ever beat that first thrill of stealing ever again. Nell knew she would spend the rest of her days chasing that high. That exhilaration was better than anything – champagne, sex, cocaine – you name it. Nothing could ever come close to the thrill of getting away with it.

CHAPTER NINETEEN

ALTOGETHER THEY WERE A WELL-BALANCED SET OF four: strategic, tactical, cautious, and occasionally, a little crazy. Lil analysed every outcome and had to plan ahead. Charlie and Effie were extroverted by nature and reacted in the moment. Lil and Nell were less spontaneous but had an ability to see the bigger picture.

The girls must have fed back to Chrissie because after two weeks of probationary trial, she was officially a member of the Forty Elephants. There wasn't a certificate or passing-out ceremony or anything like that. Although she'd half expected there would be. More a pat on the back and a drink in the pub. Nell was pleased, and relieved, but she had to be amused by her own gullibility. The way proper official-sounding words had been used, like *training, probation, cells* and *codes*. Chrissie had made it all seem much more sophisticated than it was in reality. There was no avoiding the fact that it was a risky operation, but Nell wasn't about to complain because of the money – that was very real, and there was lots of it.

Effie was a curious combination of ingénue and femme fatale. She wandered about the flat naked, and men in the nightclubs found she looked good on an arm – but Effie also picked her nose, no matter how much everyone shouted at her to stop doing so.

Nell called Lily the Bluestocking because she could debate any subject, and switch sides too. She had nicknamed Charlie the Honey Pot because she was all things sweet and a man trap. Full of tricks she'd learned from her past, Charlie carried Fisherman's Friend cough sweets – for protection, not sore throats.

'If the way to a man's heart is through his stomach,' Charlie would say, 'then the way to his fear is through his rear. Stick one of these up his bottom and he'll soon know about it.'

The four fell fast into a set routine, which they rehearsed at home: *the ringer, penny weighting, the decoy*. All were theatrical variations on tricks as old as the hills.

Charlie would enter a small family-owned jewellery shop, preferably manned by a young male assistant, and ask in her exuberant way to try on a number of rings. Playing the giggling nymph, she would dazzle the young man, beguile him, make him blush and stammer. Then Effie would enter, under a different guise, and do the same. Soon, he would have difficulty keeping track of the rings being tried on and taken out, distracted by the pretty women. Charlie would swap one with a cheap replica. Then she would fix the genuine jewellery under the counter with chewing gum. Effie would do the same.

Lily, Nell, or together as a pair of housewives chatting gaily, would enter under separate cover and run their gloved hands under the counter trim, find the rings stuck there in the gum, slip them into a pocket and be gone. Effie and Charlie would leave with nothing aside from the knowledge that the shy male assistant would be thinking of them for a while yet, most likely alone at night with Mrs Palm and her five lovely daughters. It could be hours or days before the theft was discovered. The four women split all earnings equally, according to the Hoisters' Code set down by Alice Diamond herself. A woman Nell had yet to even set eyes on.

The fur coat switch was a classic. All four would enter a department store at peak trading, lunch hour, before payday on a Friday, but pretend to be four women shopping separately. Effie would wear a loose-fitting coat as Lily tried on a fur coat. Effie would take her coat off and hide it in the racks; underneath, she would already be wearing a cheap fur that resembled the target fur. Charlie and Nell would occupy the shop assistant or assistants, both asking for help at the same time – being demanding and wanting different things, making them work hard. Lil would put on the discarded loose coat to cover the fur she had tried on and leave the shop. When Effie would try to leave, she'd be stopped and searched, and found to be wearing the inferior fur. Confusion would abound; shop assistants would fluster, grow hot with fear of consequences and start running about on the spot like headless chickens.

In between distracting the staff, Charlie and Nell would be stuffing their bloomers with ribbons, silk scarves and gloves. They would leave separately as the staff were still panicking.

Most store detectives in the big department stores were men and loath to search a lady. Manhandling a woman was tantamount to an infringement on her husband or father's property. Any true gentleman witnessing a violation would be morally inclined to intervene and validate his own masculinity. It was no small risk to the reputation of the department store if a detective should make a mistake, and for the clientele to learn that a lower-class man, a *brute*, had mistakenly molested a respectable lady.

Females were victims by grace of their sex. Sickness, swooning, fainting, crying – or being dazzlingly seductive. Whatever you have, use it. It's only natural that a man uses his fists if provoked, why shouldn't women use tears, whatever works? *N'est-ce pas?*

Nell made more in those first few weeks than her old wage would earn her in a year. She was rich! The week after, they made double. Nell sent a small amount home under the premise of having received some very generous tips. The rest she blew on going out, clothes, drinking and clubs.

She had found her purpose. The Two Anns said they wanted girls with fire in the belly – and Nell's was well and truly blazing.

CHAPTER TWENTY

HAVING NOT VISITED HOME, NELL HAD COMPENSATED with a few hastily written letters. All things were well, and she would come back as soon as she'd worked long enough to earn holiday. A week before Christmas, Nell scheduled a telephone call from the post office to her mother.

'Allo? Eleanor! Can you hear me?' her mother shouted down the mouthpiece as if they were talking on two cans and a piece of string.

'*Ouais, Maman,* you don't have to shout. I can hear you. Are you all well? How is Dad these days?'

Nell was hit with rapid-fire questions, all shouted down the line.

'Yes,' Nell said, 'yes, work is going well. I'm enjoying it. Yes, there is a bit of mould, but we are dealing with it. No, my chest is fine. No, I don't have a cough. We will deal with the mould. It's really not that bad. Yes, I am eating. How are you?'

'I am calling from the shop, Eleanor. Mr Bright has

bought a telephone! It is a candlestick with a horn! I am speaking on it right now! Isn't science wonderful?'

'A telephone, why, he must be doing well.'

'Yes, and he is opening another shop, in Hove…' Even after all these years being in *Angleterre*, her mum refused to pronounce 'H's, and for some reason it was annoying Nell. '…and he wants me to be the manageress! I'm going to get a raise.'

'Ah, congratulations. How is Dad? And Steph and the boys?'

'They are good! Dad, the same, always the same, but listen, this must be costing a fortune so we must be quick. When are you coming home for Christmas? Mr Bright has given us a goose to have for dinner.'

'Isn't Mr Bright the perfect Father Christmas? All he needs is a beard.'

'Pardon?'

'*De rien, Maman*, I'm being silly. I miss you all and tell Steph she needs to schedule a call with me too.' Nell drew breath and spat the next bit out, 'But I can't come home this Christmas. I promise I will come back in the new year, as soon as I can. I haven't been at the hotel long enough, so other girls have the holiday.' Her mother's disappointment was palpable, but as a working-class woman, she understood the constant priority to earn money.

'Oh, really? Not a chance? Not even for one day? Ah, Eleanor, it will not be the same. We will be missing you. Pah, I understand, and I wanted to say thank you for the money you sent. It is very much appreciated, my bright star. Ah, I have to go, I might cry on the customers.'

'I'm sorry, *Maman*, I do love you, and I miss you all. I must go now or else I will cry too. I will send more money, and I will be back soon, I promise.'

'You will call again?'

'*Bien sûr.*' Nell put the receiver down.

Nell wiped her eyes and shook her armour back on. What was going on with Mr Bright? Giving her mother a shop to run and a flipping goose to boot. What was he playing at?

If the lies came easy, then hoisting came easier. It was as if a mist had cleared and now the way forward seemed brightly lit. Silver bullets, epiphanies, and all those mythical things. If Nell had need of something, she took it. How could it be wrong?

The girls didn't even get their own coal. When they wanted some, they would open the door of the flat and shout at the little buggers running around the stairwells.

'Oi! Which one of you lot wants to earn a few bob?'

They would be only too eager to fetch some. The kids loved running errands for the Forties, who paid over what was fair to get them full of gratitude. The children remembered generosity, but not as much as their parents, especially mothers. No one in the block bothered them, not even the dirty old men who would steal devouring glances at bare legs and bow lips. Everyone knew who they were and that meant they were left alone. They also had male protectors by association – the Elephant Gang.

Effie and Nell discussed getting another bed, but decided against it as it would take up too much room.

'Nelly, do you like doing *it* with John? You disappear to his often enough.'

'It's all right. He puts the effort in. You know, I used to think it was a big disappointment, boring. It was exciting right up until they shoved it in, and then like someone having a fit.'

'Or being knocked over by a giant fish gasping for air!' Effie giggled.

'Every man should do press-ups over a mirror to see how stupid they look.' Nell snickered. 'It's a crying shame you don't know what a man is like in bed until you let them have a go. If only they came with references.' That was actually quite a good idea.

'I can't read,' said Effie.

'Really? No matter, I could read them to you.'

'I can read a bit – I'm not stupid – I just never learned properly. I did learn a bit at borstal.'

'Oh?'

'Yeah, there was a proper butch girl called Gemma Bennet. Some of the girls in there were nasty. Gemma was hard as nails – but kind with it. She taught me how to read by limericks.'

'Limericks? How?'

'You learn the limerick by speaking aloud and then practise writing the words out and work out what word is what. Then Gemma would write another, and I had to guess the words. I'm not so good at reading but I do know a lot of limericks, see: *There was a young lady called Alice, who used dynamite for a phallus. They found her vagina in North Carolina, and her arsehole in Buckingham Palace.*

I can read all those words fine. Just don't tell Alice I said that.'

They both burst out laughing, until cackles fell into sighs, but Nell wanted to know more about their mysterious leader.

'Tell me about Alice, is she scary?'

'She's tall, and big with it, but always looks the business.' Effie sat up, cross legged. 'Big furs and heels and diamonds on every finger. Like a movie star, and she's clever – like a fox! When she laughs, she is loud. A proper boom! And she can dance too, which you'd never think for someone on the big side but... you will meet her.'

'When?'

'Soon, I'm sure. They'll call a big meeting or there'll be a party. She likes to keep her distance – she's smart. Sends the orders down through others, like Chrissie does to us.'

'What if she doesn't like me?' Nell asked.

'As long as you're earning, keep your mouth shut, stay out of trouble – what's not to like!?'

Then, as Nell was drifting off, Effie started up again, startling her awake.

'Nelly, do you believe in God?'

'I don't know,' Nell mumbled.

'I worry sometimes.'

'You? Worry. I didn't think you knew how.'

'I worry how things always go bad in the end.' Effie was off on one. 'Like Jesus, he sounded like a good bloke, feeding the five thousand and what not, giving out fish and helping lepers.'

'Where did you get all this?'

'Borstal, but what I'm saying is, everything ends up a racket. That's all we are, a kind of racket, don't you think? Like church, school, government, borstal, prison, everything. I do think Jesus would approve of us though, cos we are poor taking from the rich and he was always up for that, wasn't he?'

'I'm fairly sure that was Robin Hood, but I'm going to assume Jesus would approve too. We should go to sleep, lie down.'

'Nelly, one last thing?'

'What?'

'What we've got going, it's good and I worry it'll go bad somehow and end. Then I'd be alone again. I have nightmares about it. Will you promise not to leave me.' This was possibly the most emotion Effie had ever displayed; Nell had to roll over and look at her, albeit in the dark.

'No, it won't, we won't let it go bad. And no, I won't leave you all alone.'

'Do you promise? We *are* a family, aren't we?' Nell supposed they were family after such an intense but short time, working together, sleeping together.

'Of course, we are sisters. Now please, shut the fuck up and go to sleep.'

'Night then.'

CHAPTER TWENTY-ONE

ON CHRISTMAS DAY, NELL AND THE CELL WERE TO go for dinner at Chrissie's house. They were not requested, per se, but instructed, in a spirit of familial expectation. Like any good visitor to a new culture, Nell must learn the customs; they were a cell, thus Chrissie the matriarch.

Practically everyone associated with the Forty Elephants lived in or around Lambeth, and it would have been fair to assume with all the money flooding in they'd live in fancy houses, but they lived in ordinary council terraces or social housing flats developed this side of the century. The modest exterior perhaps felt like the safety of camouflage to the treasure trove that might be found inside – if you knew where to look, that is. Loose floorboards might be lifted to reveal boxes of jewellery or cash. Attics might be stuffed full of designer clothes.

The men of the Elephant Gang splurged on expensive cars and sharp suits. Property or investments, things rich people do – not so much. Money was like water; when it flowed, it was common sense (if there is such a thing) to spend it and have fun. You never knew when the taps might turn off and you'd have to do a runner. There was the habit of squirrelling cash away or investing in jewellery and wearing it – like one might have invested in gold teeth in the last century. It made sense to carry wealth in your mouth – if someone wanted to take it, they'd have to catch you first, then prise your jaw open.

Chrissie lived in a two up and two down and managed to pack in twelve people around two tables buttressed together, at different heights, for dinner. Nell's cell, Chrissie and her husband, Ed, who dealt in bent motors, and his elderly parents. Another cell of four girls, two of whom were called Florrie, a Maggie and a Constance, and a couple of lovely old dears who Nell assumed were relatives of some sort.

Ed and Chrissie performed like a magic act, with Chrissie pulling the feast out of a top hat and Ed entertaining folks with old stories, ensuring glasses were kept topped up. Nell watched how they would squeeze past each other in a doorway and Ed, already tipsy, would try to block her and steal kisses. Chrissie would scold him for his wandering hands and getting in the way as she juggled blazing hot plates of food as he played his frisky soldier act. It was like being at home with her old dad, before the war, not so much the one that they lived with now. That made Nell sad.

All the guests huddled round, passing plates, knocking knees and elbows; criminals, conmen and thieves celebrating the birth of Christ. Chrissie cooked the biggest turkey and a whole mountain of roast potatoes, but it was strange not being at home. It would be too far to call, say she missed home, because truth be told she didn't. Nell wished to have her family here, in London and enjoying the spoils with her. One day maybe she'd earn enough to stop and do something legitimate and make that a reality.

All day long people came and went. In the afternoon John and his mates came crawling in, half cut. John carried a sack of presents and emptied them under the tree straight onto the floor, and several children, belonging to guests or neighbours, Nell assumed, flew at them like flies round you know what.

'This one is for you, Nelly girl,' and everyone cooed and awed, as if she were his sweetheart. Nell turned bright red as he set down a square-shaped present on the table.

'Go on, open it,' said Lil, kicking Nell under the table.

Nell peeled off the paper – which was yesterday's news-paper, like a bag of chips – and inside was a grey metal box.

'What the bloody hell is that?' said Effie, screwing her nose up, disappointed on Nell's behalf.

'Effie! It's Christmas! Language!' shouted Chrissie.

Effie grabbed the box out of Nell's hands. 'It's a flipping safe,' she said. 'Why give her this?'

'I won it in a card game from some bloke who'd done a job in a block of apartments – some legal bloke, he reckoned. Can't open it, I think it might be empty – reminded me of you, Effie,' he said, biting off the end of a cigar.

'Piss off,' said Effie. 'Could have got her something decent.'

'Cheeky bugger,' Nell said, thoroughly relieved it wasn't a proper present. She didn't want to feel an obligation to anyone, least of all a man.

'Johnny, don't you think you're a bit old to act like a brat?' said Chrissie, hands on hips.

'It was a joke and besides, what do you get a girl who can get whatever she wants herself?' John shrugged.

Nell gave it a rattle. 'It's not empty – sounds like there's paper inside. How do I get it open?'

'Lady Jay,' said Chrissie, 'my driver, she's turning into a fine little screwsman, that girl. Very talented. I'll let her know you want to speak to her.'

News was shared that there was to be a party at the 43 Club in the week between Christmas and New Year. The 43 was a favourite of the Forty Elephants – all would be expected. Then a roll call of old stories was shared, primarily a reel of the infamous Maggie Hughes highlights. Ed held court, telling them all about Maggie's last trial. Nell was all ears, desperate to learn more about the higher ups, especially Alice.

'When Alice and Maggie were up at the Old Bailey,' he said, 'the old bill tried to trump up more charges against them, all made-up bollocks. The peelers aren't above making shit up, but the brief, Mr Hardy, managed to get rid of the fictional charges. You can't trust them. Sodding peelers. Corrupt as we are.'

Chrissie chimed in, 'Tell them what they said about Maggie and Alice, what ridiculous things they came up with, Ed.'

'They said that Maggie and Alice ran a "network of cunning thieves",' said Ed, leaning in, hands on table, as if he was telling an old ghost story. 'They called Alice "The Queen of Misrule".'

Everyone loved Ed's theatrical retellings of near misses and fights, trials and how Alice had punched a policeman and knocked him spark out, and now they called her Diamond Alice.

The stories were fun, but Nell felt more nervous each time she heard of the women's aptitude for violence. It wasn't a moral standpoint – she understood the need to fight when cornered – but she didn't know in herself if she had the ability to act the same way if the time should come. The fear turned into butterflies, a tangled ball of pure wool in her belly.

That night, as they lay in bed, Nell asked Effie about something else that played on her mind.

'If the law are onto Alice and Maggie, what chance do we have of *not* getting caught? Surely it's only a matter of time?'

'Oh, Nelly, the police don't know who we are,' said Effie. 'The problem with Maggie and Alice is that they've been at it for years. Everyone knows what they look like, so it's harder for them. Plus, they both stick out like sore thumbs. Alice is as tall as a beanpole and Maggie is tiny. We're different. You'll turn yourself grey, you will.' Effie was snoring within minutes and all Nell could do was lie there, *thinking*.

Since she'd joined up, Nell had exhausted herself trying to fit in. She had watched herself get louder, become more gregarious. Acting the clown and dominating the space, the way men did – behaving with abandon. And she'd seen how other women in their presence shrank and made themselves smaller to avoid confrontation. Exactly the type of behaviour Nell had been raised to think bad manners.

Nell could certainly act the part, but she didn't know if she had the guts inside, *to be violent.*

CHAPTER TWENTY-TWO

NIGHTCLUB QUEEN KATE MEYRICK, OR 'MA' AS SHE was affectionately called, was regularly shutting down her clubs, only to reopen under different names because the police were waging war on the nightclub scene, as ordered by the Home Secretary.

Her nightclub, Dalton's, in Leicester Square had to close despite a guest list including the King of Denmark. Raided on grounds that *women present were known to police –* police speak for prostitutes. The private gentlemen's clubs got away with exactly the same carry on without being raided, but their clientele were carefully selected from the right class, with the right opinions. Ma, on the other hand, opened her establishments to everyone, from royalty to rascals – come as you are. That wasn't how things were meant to be done. Thus, she had to be shut down. The fear of political radicals organising in such places seemed to set the government's teeth on edge.

That night there was to be a gala event with a dancing competition from ten o'clock to six in the morning. Costume was key, and Nell's cell dressed up as movie stars. Effie was, of course, Marlene Dietrich, in a man's tuxedo with dickie bow and top hat. Charlie was Greta Garbo, in black fur and dark lipstick, and an irritating impression in a terrible accent of curious origin, somewhere between German and Welsh. Lily went as Gloria Swanson from *The Great Moment*, dressed as an exotic Russian gypsy in bangles and clattering jewellery. Nell was Renée Adorée, the French ingénue, *bien sûr*. She wrapped her hair in a scarf and wore a chiffon top with bell sleeves and a skirt slashed to the thigh.

As they left the flat, Charlie bizarrely ran ahead. When they caught up with her outside, she introduced them to her latest purchase with a ta-da: a black Ford. The girls stood on the pavement with several locals who had gathered to poke the vehicle – mostly men, thumbs in pockets, bending down to inspect it as if they knew what they were looking at. There was a dent in the driver's side door and huge scratches. Charlie sat in the car, tooting the horn.

'Do you like it?' she shouted out of the open window.

'Where did you get it?' Nell asked, looking at the deep scratches that had eviscerated the black paint work.

'I bought it from Lady Diana Manners. I met her at the 43 and she was saying how she wanted rid because she drove it into a ditch and it had put her right off it.'

'She put it in a ditch?'

'That's why she sold it to me for buttons, but it works fine.'

'Do you know how to work it?' asked Lily, who rattled as she walked – coins lined a headscarf that she'd wrapped around her hips. Several men had stopped gawping at the car to stare at her cleavage.

'Lady Diana showed me the pedals and how to start it up and switch it off. She said the rest is easy – a learn as you go sort of thing.'

'Coming from a woman who rolled it into a ditch,' said Nell.

'I'm sure you need a licence or classes,' added Lil.

'Yes, yes, I'll get to that in good time,' said Charlie, waving away their concerns. 'Come, on, let's go.' She tooted the horn again and they resigned themselves to getting in.

Nell and Lil claimed the back seats; Effie was in the passenger seat, next to Charlie.

'Why do you keep doing that?' asked Effie.

'Doing what?'

'Fingering the wheel like that, it's creepy.'

'It's the sense of freedom! Think, Effie! We can go where we want, when we want. Isn't it exciting?'

'We could go where we wanted before...' said Effie.

'This is different. Righto, let's see, right, that's it. I shall take all three of you battered old Cinderellas to the ball.'

There was much mechanical crunching that didn't sound good. As Charlie pulled away, the car stuttered from the pavement. The men on the street laughed, kids heckled. Nell threw coins out of the window to get rid of the little blighters as Lily shut her eyes and dug her nails into the seat. Effie remained unfazed, and they made it to the club alive.

Ma was on the door to greet everyone personally, on the lookout for undercover police who would enjoy her nightclubs and, when it suited, order the raids and fabricate what was necessary to shut her down.

Inside it was heaving. The Café Royal crowd had arrived – the nation's bright young things. Youth whose every sigh must be considered, whose every whimsical thought the whole country must pay attention to, while other narratives less auspicious simply never registered in the zeitgeist. Most were affable enough, curiously eager to mix with the lower classes. Like wasps at a picnic, they had no skin in the game. If it all went wrong, they could retreat to family money. Much more fun were the characters of exiled European royalty and celebrities of the entertainment world. Prince Christopher of Greece was a pleasant bespectacled man who played the piano. Various dukes and old nobility would turn out to indulge in the atmosphere of the modern and bohemian.

Such people may fuck each other and go to the same parties, but they didn't trust each other – much like the eternal relationship between men and women. We have the old criminally rich and the new criminally rich. Both think the other undeserving and inferior. Both were obsessed with having more and wondering how those with less seemed happier. The only thing that gave them periodic relief from such despair was the sensation of winning, more and more, and for that, others must *lose*. In among the princes, publishers, stage stars and exiled princes, were the Forty Elephants and men of the Elephant Gang. The prettiest hostesses were on hand to help people learn the latest dances, but Nell avoided dancing like the plague.

In the ladies' cloakroom, Nell was fixing her lipstick when a giant of a woman in a luxurious fur and tight cloche stood beside her at the mirror to do the same. Nell stole glances, her heart began racing. She couldn't be sure, but she suspected she had somehow found herself, purely by chance, stood next to Alice Diamond.

The woman was nearly six feet in heels with large fair eyes, heavy eyelids that gave her an audacious pride, and straight light brown hair cut at the chin. Nell looked like a mere child beside her. It had to be Queen Alice, surely? Nell practically quivered in her presence, intimidated and yet feeling compelled to introduce herself.

'Excuse me, are you Alice?' The words stumbled out.

The woman peered down at Nell, considering her as a cat might consider a fly. She snapped her lipstick shut and turned to the insect, one arm on a hip.

'Oh, I'm sorry,' Nell blurted on. 'I should explain. I know Chrissie. I come from Brighton and... You see...' Nell whispered the next part, a cringe-inducing moment that would torture her for years to come whenever the memory danced across her mind. 'I'm in the Forty Elephants too! Chrissie...' Nell began to babble and realised her cheeks were turning red and she had no way of stopping them glowing like tomatoes. At that moment, even as she was speaking, Nell very much wanted to punch herself in the face.

'I know.' The woman put her lipstick in her clutch bag and gave a bemused smile. 'I can see why Chrissie liked you,' said Alice.

'Oh, thank you!' Nell surmised some story of her ethic had been passed along and swelled up with pride.

'It's your nose.'

'My nose?' Nell tried to look at it and went cross-eyed.

'It sticks up.'

'Oh. Yes, I have heard that before.' Nell touched her own nose as if to find out.

Alice stepped forward using her towering height to enforce her sense of power. 'You have the kind of face that cracks under a man's fist, but yours hasn't been cracked, yet.' She didn't smile.

For a moment Nell panicked, unable to think of anything to say. Alice, sensing the girl's anxiety, explained further.

'When our men beat their wives, they don't give a shit who sees the damage. But middle- and upper-class men like to hide their sins. They only hit where it doesn't show. People see your delicate little nose and think, *what a lovely respectable young lady*. It's a good idea bringing pretty girls like you in – ours sometimes give it away. Chrissie says you can speak French too. Do you dance?'

'French I can do. Dancing I can't.'

'Shame. Catch you later.' And just like that, the conversation was over. Alice threw her handbag over her shoulder and sauntered out of the cloakroom. Nell could relax, although she had a terrible fear she'd come across as a simpleton and had so wanted to make a good first impression on Alice. It had been a monumental meeting for Nell, but she had the feeling for Alice, not so much. The woman would probably forget about her entirely, despite the nose.

Alice Diamond did indeed know how to move on her feet and won the Charleston prize that night. Nell couldn't help observing Alice and her entourage from a safe distance. Like a closely guarded regiment of the most important women that you dare not get caught staring at. Of course, there was Alice, dominating by height and sheer presence. She used up space freely with her arms and when she laughed, which she did often, the woman roared. Head back, mouth wide open, shoulders back, free and bold. Not shrunken up like an invisible little woman born to serve. Nell spotted little Maggie Hughes, who practically kicked the door in, entering to cheers and applause. The core lieutenants from the Forty Elephants flanked both women like bodyguards dressed as starlets. Nell stole snatched glances from a safe distance.

Maggie Hughes, the infamous firebrand, was barely five feet tall. Mid-twenties and with round cheeks that earned her nickname: Babyface. Maggie favoured a fashionable Tam O'Shanter, a Scottish bonnet. She was surrounded by her sisters, Allie and Dollie. There were Alice's younger sisters, Louisa and Maggie. Charlie narrated the scene to Nell like it was a Renaissance painting, explaining who was who.

'See over there,' said Charlie. 'That's Maggie Williams, next to her are sisters Mary and Caroline Bradford. Caroline is talking to Violet Stanley...' and so on. Practically every other woman was called Maggie and it was impossible to keep track.

Nell had met these women, out and about, and knew of them to at least say a greeting to. But there were the core generals that remained aloof: Gert Sculley, Laura Partridge, Nellie Morris and Bertha Tappenden. They all worked with Alice and Maggie.

'You see her over at the table of men? That's Ada Johnstone,' said Charlie, tipping her head in the direction of a glamorous woman in her forties. 'Ada's brother runs the Elephant Gang, and she's a fence for both gangs.'

'Fence?' Nell didn't know why but had assumed the fences were not involved in the gangs themselves.

'Yes, we use the fences we are told, most either have been or are still in the Forties, or are related.'

So that's why they had to use the specific fences – to keep all the profits in the same organisation. But that couldn't be that fair, could it? Not all the time, not if *some* of the Forties were getting additional profit from the onward chain of supply after the girls in the cells had been paid. Also, how did they know they were getting the best price for the risks they were taking on the front line from these fences?

The whole evening was like a stately event for the elites of south-London crime. Foul mouths, smokers, drinkers, bad manners, all dressed up like movie stars, *putting on the posh*. It was true: at a quick glance most looked amazing, but if you were to linger, you might see the evidence of hard living. As soon as any one of them opened their mouths it was a giveaway that they weren't as elegant as their outfits. It was other things too: how they stood, the way they used their hands. So desperate had Nell been to fit in, she'd adopted these ritualistic displays, but now she was struck with the idea that being different could be an asset.

Later in the evening, Maggie Hughes and her entourage came past where Charlie and Nell stood. Both were forced to lean back over the bar to let them through. Maggie stopped at Nell and considered her. Nell was petrified and froze on the spot. Wild Maggie was staring straight at her, and just when Nell thought things couldn't get much worse, Maggie took the cigarette from her mouth.

'Nelly, isn't it?'

Nell nodded. She didn't like being called Nelly, but she

wasn't about to complain to Maggie Hughes about it. She could only dwell on the stories of how too many girls had been scarred up by Maggie and a smashed glass.

'You have a very pretty face.' Her entourage gathered close behind, watching the exchange. Nell was too stricken with fear to do much and could only smile feebly as Charlie watched, wide-eyed. Maggie went on, 'I was the prettiest girl in London once.'

Maggie tapped Nell on the cheek twice – not hard, what you might call an authority tap. Then, drawing on Nell's cigarette, which was now hers, she announced to her entourage and anyone else listening, as if she were Cleopatra, 'I'm off!'

She was hustled out by her herd of loyalists.

Exhaling as soon as Maggie had gone, Nell turned to Charlie.

'What was that about? Have I done something wrong?'

'Probably nothing. Don't worry. She's likely battered. It's Maggie – that's what she does!' said Charlie.

But Nell wasn't so sure even Charlie believed that.

CHAPTER TWENTY-THREE

A FEW DAYS LATER THE CELL WAS AT HOME AND SETTLING in after a day of shopping when there was a bang at the door. Nell opened it – it was a boy from the flats with a message.

'Maggie Hughes is outside. She wants to speak to Nelly.'

'That's me. What about?' she asked him. As if he would know. Of course, all he did was shrug.

'They're waiting in a black car,' he said.

'What? Who?'

'A whole bunch of women. Older.'

Shit. Had Nell done something wrong? When she told the others they were equally bewildered.

'What do you think it means?' she asked.

Lily looked unsettled. 'It's a test. It's about discipline, I reckon. Have you got something to protect yourself?' Nell's mind leapt to her mother's machete stashed in her suitcase at the top of the wardrobe.

'Yes.'

'Take it with you. It'll be about nothing but sniffing you out a bit, I'm sure of it.'

Charlie looked worried, 'Or it could be an initiation thing. I don't like those things but… do what they say, Nell, let it happen.'

'Let what happen?' Nell asked. Charlie shrugged.

Nell ran to the bedroom and retrieved her machete with its leather sheath. Her hands were refusing to work as her nerves needed them to. *God help me.* She had to find her guts. But Maggie was violent, and Nell's guts turned to jelly at the mere threat of anything physical. To hide the machete, she put the sheath strap over her shoulder and her coat over the top. This way it could be reached easily, like the gun holsters they have at the pictures. That would do. Nell was buttoning up her coat and shoving her hat on when Effie came in with a serious expression. That meant it must be terrible.

'Just *do*, don't think. I know what you're like.'

'Why is everybody speaking in riddles – what does that even mean!?'

'This is as hard as you want to make it, Nell. This is Maggie's idea of fun – play along.'

When she stepped outside, sure enough, there was Maggie's midnight-black motor car with the built-in periscope. A top-end car that rubbish police vehicles had not a hope of keeping up with. The back door opened in the dark. Nell couldn't see inside.

Laura Partridge, a senior general, hopped out. Slim with a long face, but attractive. Nell climbed in and found herself sat in between Laura and another general, Gert Sculley.

Maggie was in the front, with Nellie Morris driving. It felt as if she were being taken to Traitor's Gate, and she didn't even know what she'd done. Nell only hoped no one else could hear her heart thumping.

They set off on a short drive of a few minutes and parked in Warwick Street. They all grouped at the back of the car.

Earlier that day, two teenage boys, sons of a petty criminal not affiliated with any gang, robbed a jeweller and took over a thousand pounds' worth of gold jewellery. A big haul for little boys. The shop paid protection on the Forties' territory, and the little sods hadn't paid their tax. This was a side of business Nell knew nothing about.

'They must pay a share to the Forties. It's what's done, and these boys need reminding of their manners,' said Maggie. 'It's about respect.' She looked at Nell, who received the message loud and clear.

The boys had been spotted outside an ironmongery, playing dice. The five women marched up on them, Maggie at the helm. Nell was at the back with Nellie Morris, probably put there to keep an eye on her. *Don't think, just do.* As they walked along the street, people slunk back inside houses. Ratty old curtains were drawn and doors that had been open were slammed shut. The boys didn't even notice the women until they were upon them. Out came Maggie's truncheon; the others drew out sticks and razors. Nell put her hand inside her coat for the machete but didn't take it out.

'Were you the little cunts what did a job on Cheapside today? And don't fucking lie,' said Maggie, pointing her truncheon at them. It was a real policeman's truncheon.

Nell guessed all the boys saw was a bunch of women with the smallest bantam at the front – it must have been laughable. Despite being only stringy bits of piss themselves.

'Don't know what you're talking about, mad cow,' said the oldest. He shook his head and went back to playing dice. The other two boys had more sense, and after a hesitant second, legged it. Pelted it up the street like Olympians.

Maggie didn't bother with another word. Down came the sticks and truncheons, and the boy was on the floor. Crates were kicked away and the five women began kicking, beating and slashing at him. Nell stood there, quivering like a virgin at an orgy, not knowing how to join in. She knew she must do something and shoved her way in and kicked at the boy as he was on the ground, crying, rolling about, bent up to protect himself. Heart pounding. Nerves screaming. *Don't think, just do.* Nell reached inside her coat and took out the machete. As she lifted it high, the blade must have reflected off something. Laura flinched and put her arm up to protect herself.

'Whoa there! What the fuck is that!?' shouted Laura. The beating came to a pause.

Nell held the machete in the air, as if she were about to commit a beheading. Everyone stepped back. Choruses of *Fuck me, what is it? Nell! Is that a sword?* The boy, bruised and bleeding but thankful for the reprieve, tried to get on all fours.

'Where did you get that?' asked Maggie.

'My mum.' Nell shrugged.

There was a second of silence before they all fell about laughing. Proper cackling, doubled over, struggling to breathe, hanging onto each other. Nell slowly brought the machete down.

'Let's have a look at it,' said Gert. 'Bloody hell! It's huge!'

The boy had struggled to his knees and was making to escape. But Nellie Morris clocked what he was doing and kicked him in the stomach, sending him back to the ground.

'Stay there, you little shit.'

Maggie got hold of him by the scruff of the neck and told him he had exactly one day to cough up the entire takings, all of it, or they'd be back. For good measure, she reminded the boy she knew his mother and sisters, and if he cared about them, he'd cough up and watch his manners in future.

'Or my friend here will cut your fucking tongue out with her machete. Now go on, fuck off.' And the boy scarpered, limping and bleeding, as best he could.

His clothes had been slashed to pieces, but his flesh had no more than surface cuts. The boy would recover. He'd be black and blue, with a split lip, but his ego would bear the most damage.

'All right, Arthur, you can put Excalibur away now,' said Gert.

Nell thought she'd really messed up, but it turned out they found it hilarious. Maggie asked Nell how her mum had come by a machete, so she told her the story of how she had been given it by a great aunt, a nun, and she lapped it up.

'Not like any of the nuns I've bloody well met!' Maggie laughed.

Nell was invited back to Gert's for a fish supper and

a few gins. She sat crosslegged on the floor as the others sat in chairs and ate fish and chips from newspaper, quietly listening as they chatted about menfolk and kids, troublesome business and near misses. After about an hour, Nell was dismissed.

'You best get off now, King Arthur,' said Maggie. 'Serious though, don't bring that with you again. You'll get locked up if you get caught with it. Get yourself something small and ladylike, like a screwdriver.'

'Or a razor,' offered Gert.

When Nell got outside, she could finally relax. The women closer to Alice were of a different league. Amiable enough but with the ability to turn nasty, fast as you like. Nell understood why violence was necessary, of course. People took the piss without the threat of it and as women, the only advantage to be taken was the element of surprise and safety in numbers. But, after today, her feeling that she couldn't be violent herself had only intensified.

Nell had a ten-minute walk on her own in the dark to get home. Call it seven with a stomp on.

CHAPTER TWENTY-FOUR

NELL WAS HEADING HOME. HER MORAL CODE HAD adjusted to hoisting without much resistance – it was stealing from big companies who had so much already – but violence to people, especially ordinary ones, didn't come easy. But it made sense that as women, the Forty Elephant girls had to go in hard.

Gone midnight by now, Nell took a shortcut through Lamlash Street, a skinny cut through with allotments where people dumped rubbish that made strange dark shadows. There were no lights, but with a brisk walk it would take less than a minute to get through and Nell would be back on Elliot's Row. Nell bowed her head and let her diminutive frame be swallowed between two tall buildings looming like towers. Ahead was a pitch-black rat run. She took one look behind, saw no one, and picked up the pace and strode fast as the wind picked up. Nell must have been halfway when one of those strange shapes leapt out and a light blinded her. She stumbled backwards, barely stopped herself from screaming, and shielded her eyes with a hand. The other hand was inside her coat reaching for the machete.

'Police! No need to be alarmed, miss.'

Tall, slim, uniformed – it was a policeman. His voice sounded young, and as he lowered the torch to the ground, Nell saw black spots in her eyes. She could see the truncheon dangling from his wrist, the exact same as Maggie had.

'Flipping heck!' Nell panted, instantly relieved she'd not brought out the machete, heartbeat like a drum. 'You gave me such a fright!'

'It's very late to be out alone, miss.'

'Please, tell me you aren't lurking in the dark to inform lone women of the hour,' Nell said, fear turning swiftly to anger.

'Best you get home, this neighbourhood isn't safe,' said the young officer.

'I was trying to go home before you scared me out of my wits! Do you often jump out on women at night?'

He didn't like that. The policeman did a sweep of the lane with his torch. Nell could see even in the dark he was about her age, with sharp features and narrow eyes, but not unattractive. That was until he shone the torch in Nell's face.

'Is that necessary, Mr Constable?' Nell held her hands up.

'I recognise you.'

'That doesn't sound good.'

The policeman diverted the torch to the ground.

'You're a new face around here, but I have seen you. You heed my warning: be mindful of the company you have started to keep.'

Condescending arse. He was pulling rank far beyond the limitations of his ridiculous little uniform. Though it was best not to get into a debate on this.

'I shall be mindful, thank you, and good evening, Constable.'

Pulling her coat about her, Nell made to move on, but the truncheon blocked her path on an extended arm. Well, now her hackles were up. Nell was not about to be bullied by a little boy with a badge.

'You should think carefully before you become involved in their works,' he said. 'It won't end well.'

Nell put a hand on the truncheon and gently pushed it away; the officer didn't resist.

'End well? For me? What other ending shall I choose, Mr Police Constable, sir? Perhaps I should become a policeman: pension, progression through the ranks, a smart uniform, and a torch to shine in women's faces. When they get choppy, I can whip out my truncheon.'

'Now, hang on a minute, I was only trying to… I mean, you're a good-looking girl…'

'Are you saying I should prostitute myself, Constable?'

'What?! No! Hang on! Wait! That's not what I was saying at all. I'm… My… My job is to protect…' It was too dark to see but Nell was sure the constable was blushing.

'Who?'

'What?'

'Protect who?' Nell asked. 'Because it's peelers that sent my dad to the hospital after he served this country and came home in pieces. The police took the side of the shopkeepers when all he was doing was trying to make a wage on the stalls, a barrow boy, at his age.'

'I was merely looking out for your safety. I thought...
These people, they are well known to take advantage of
naïve newcomers.'

'I'm not naïve, Constable.'

'I'm trying to help. A girl like you could meet a nice chap
with prospects, but not around here.'

'You boys, you think you know it all and take the grace
of a woman's silence as proof of our stupidity. Let me let
you in on something: when you lot spout your rubbish, we
keep quiet because we can't be arsed to get into another
row about whatever it is. No doubt, when the next war
comes, we'll suddenly be useful again.'

'There won't be another war, not like that one,' he said,
perhaps to reassure himself.

'I hope not. I'm not sure I could survive the poetry.'

The policeman reluctantly chuckled. 'Look, I didn't mean
to startle you, miss. I don't use the torch unless I have to as
it lights me up like a bloody Christmas tree, but down here
even I get spooked. I didn't mean to frighten or offend you,
but those people... they're not your friends.'

'*Those people* have given me more than anything King
and Country saw fit to. But I'll apologise for biting your
head off. I was scared, is all.'

'Now that we're friends, may I walk you home, miss?'

'Lord no!' Nell laughed, 'I should think I might come
off worse if *those people* were to see me walking with a
policeman. Thank you, but I politely decline.'

'Then I'll light the way until you reach the end. Have a
good evening.'

'Thank you, that's very gentlemanly.' Nell did an

elaborate curtsey. 'And there I was thinking it was another man sticking something hard in my face.'

'All right, all right. Enough of that. I'll have my eye on you.'

'Well, I'll take that as a compliment, Constable...?'

'PC Bevan, miss.'

'What's your off-duty name, PC Bevan?' Nell walked backwards, swinging her handbag. There was something about the young officer that held her intrigue. Such an earnest sort, young and optimistic, polite, and not bad looking neither. The policeman tried not to laugh. Those eyes did have a sparkle when he cracked a smile, even in the dark.

'Horace, if you must.'

'Good evening, Horace!'

'Good night. I'm fairly confident we'll meet again.'

'Ta-ra then!' said Nell, spinning around, waving with her handbag in the air and sauntering home in the light of the policeman's torch, with an extra wiggle.

Nell rushed home to tell the other girls about the policeman, but Lil and Charlie were in bed, and only Effie awake. Effie seemed distinctly underwhelmed, whereas Nell had hurried back as if she were delivering military intelligence straight from the enemy. This was all normal business for these girls; they'd been through it all before, whereas for Nell, it was a seismic event and she'd only recently stopped shaking.

'I wouldn't worry about that,' said Effie, rolling her eyes. 'They know very well what everyone is up to – won't catch us though. Most can't be bothered and are on the take anyway.'

'How can you be so sure?'

'Because... they don't have the time or people to catch us. Besides, we're women. It's too shameful to admit they're being outwitted by a bunch of poor girls, so they simply don't admit it. Works out quite well, I wouldn't complain. It's more exciting to chase men. You know, smash and grab, armed robbers, bond fraudsters. As long as we stay in our delicate little lane, we may get a silly little charge for larceny and a short stint in the Holly, but they aren't interested in us. You worry far too much about all the wrong things.'

'It wasn't long ago you were worrying if Jesus would approve of what we do.'

'That's different, that's Jesus. Jesus is for everyone, whereas the police not so much. If they're not bent, they soon will be. And that's when they're not bullying little people and turning a blind eye to what the rich get up to.'

'But what if I don't ever want to be up on a silly little charge if I can help it?' asked Nell. She couldn't understand this brazen apathy.

'Well, this is where you come unstuck, isn't it? Nice girl like you, you can't imagine what it's like to be in and out of borstal and simply move on to prison. I suppose you think of it as a shameful thing, whereas all our mothers, aunts and sisters have been inside. You must toughen up, Nell, or get out while you can.'

But that wasn't an option now she'd started to make decent money, and send some home. Nell would have to find a way to toughen up.

CHAPTER TWENTY-FIVE

THE DISCIPLINE JOB WITH MAGGIE QUICKLY BECAME known as 'the machete incident' in the gossip mill of Lambeth. Bizarrely it seemed to gift Nell some credibility in the surrounding culture around the Forties. The day after the incident, she'd been walking past the pub when a young man from the Elephant Gang named Bert had called out from across the road.

'Here she comes, it's none other than our *Machete Mack*!' shouted Bert. A stringy young lad who hadn't quite yet grown into his own body, he wore his greased hair in a peak with shaved back and sides. Charlie told her it was obvious to anyone that poor Bert was a little sweet on Nell, hence the endless engagement in what felt like rather witless repartee. Nell chuckled along but didn't know what to make of this new name.

Sure enough, the name stuck, and within weeks it had been bastardised to *Nell the Mack*, *Nelly Mack* or *Mackie*. Any variation, such were the bards of Southwark. It was not unusual for her to see one of the Elephant lads in the street

– *How goes it, Mackie?* Or acknowledge her with a doff of the cap and *Afternoon, Lady Mack.* Always accompanied by a knowing grin. A reputation for violence might have been a good thing, had Nell not known she was a quivering fraud.

Nell's reputation as a colonial skirmisher had more to thank Chinese whispers for, and the machete was back in the suitcase.

'It won't be a short stint you'll get; it'll be years with that thing. That's if you don't kill someone.' Lily had made Nell swear never to take it out again. No more warning required.

Lily instead tried to train Nell how to use a man's cut-throat razor wrapped in a silk handkerchief and keep it in her pocket. It wasn't there to kill, nor a weapon, and therefore the likelihood of killing anyone was low.

'In a panic you need to be fast,' said Lily. 'Slash and tear but never stab. You want to create enough fear and pain, if necessary, to get away. I've no intention of seeing inside the Holly again, and certainly not the scaffold.'

'Have you cut people?' asked Nell.

'Of course,' said Lil, bemused by the question. 'And so will you, at some point.' The mere utterance of the words sent Nell into a jelly-like tremble.

No woman had been executed at Holloway since 1902, when two baby farmers had been hanged at the same time for murdering babies left in their care by desperate mothers. Those hangings had been the first at Holloway in the year it became a women's prison to cope with the number of suffragettes demanding the vote. There had been others condemned. All had seen their sentences commuted to life imprisonment, but the threat of the scaffold was always there. And so was the spectre of violence.

An organic cluster of Forties and Elephants had, on a whim, decided to go drinking up the West End to celebrate the boring days between Christmas and New Year. A large number had congregated in the Melody nightclub. Nell, Effie, Charlie and Lily were near the edge of the dancefloor, when a drunken girl bumped into Lily too many times. Lily had ignored each little bump, but the girl was so drunk she lurched and knocked Lily as she had her glass of champagne to her lips and knocked half of it down her cleavage. Lily closed her eyes, inhaled deeply as if she might let the infringement pass, and then a sharp elbow from the same girl nudged her impudently in the back. Lil handed her glass and handbag to Nell, turned and tapped the girl on the shoulder.

'Excuse me, do you mind? You've knocked me several times now. You must have noticed,' she said.

'I can't help it,' said the girl, swaying, her eyes rolling almost independently of each other as she gave Lily the once over, head to foot and back again. She slurred, 'It's not my fault you take up so much room.' The girl turned her back to Lily and laughed along with three male companions as they sniggered into their drinks.

Lily remained expressionless: dark unblinking eyes on a poker face.

Effie was grinning, tonguing the end of a long glass filter, and Charlie bit her bottom lip. Nell didn't understand what was about to happen. Lily tapped the girl on the shoulder once again, and as soon as she turned around, Lily grabbed the girl by the ruche of her dress and punched her in the face. Nell was horrified and stood open mouthed like an idiot holding Lil's handbag and glass.

The girl fell to the floor, hands shaking wildly, screaming with blood gushing down her dress. One of her male friends put a hand on Lily's shoulder, which was all the baiting it took for anyone watching from the Elephants or Forties to surge forwards.

Then, all hell broke loose. It was like a saloon punch up from the Wild West. Punches were thrown, kicking, screaming, glasses smashed. Even a bar stool flew over Nell's head, and she watched, stuck like a frozen rabbit. So much for Machete Mack. The band stopped playing and ran backstage. Charlie had climbed onto the bar to avoid being dragged into the fray. Effie grabbed Nell and they made a dash for the exit. They were swallowed by the bottle neck of a crowd as it surged towards the door.

Effie and Nell managed to get a taxi, but the driver refused to take them further than Westminster Bridge. Taxis would often do this, taking them only as far as the river and wanting to return north. Despite offering more money, begging and then arguing, the driver refused and kicked them out. They had to roam the streets dressed like a pair of lost starlets. Worse for wear and resigned to walking home, at which point it started to rain. They trudged in silence getting soaked all through Lambeth.

'I'm gutless,' Nell said, after they had been marching a while. 'When it comes to fighting, I don't have it in me.'

'Rubbish! Everyone has it in them,' said Effie. 'We're animals.'

'Machete Mack, they've been calling me! I'm pathetic. I'm a fraud.'

'Do stop with the self-pity, Nell, it's boring, and irritating.'

Effie leapt into Nell's path, hopping about like a boxer. 'Come on, hit me.' Her fists up in front of her face.

She wore a white mink bolero, and her hair was stuck to her face from the rain. Effie looked like a mad march hare shadow boxing with her tiny fists.

'What on earth are you doing?' said Nell, who only wanted to get home.

Disinterested stragglers passed by, but this was London, so no one really noticed two bedraggled women fighting in the street.

'Hit me, you coward!' shouted Effie.

'Don't be ridiculous.'

Effie slapped Nell around the face. Nell clutched her cheek, stunned by the sting as Effie continued to dance.

'That hurt!'

'Good! Come on! Queensbury rules – hit me!' Effie slapped her again, this time harder, across the other cheek.

'Ow!' Nell now clutched both in shock. Her lip trembled.

'Don't you dare cry!' growled Effie, as she put her fists up again. Effie pushed and shoved Nell, occasionally surprising her with a hard slap about the head.

'Fight back!'

'I can't!' said Nell.

Throwing her handbag down on the ground, Effie took off her coat and hung it over a wall.

'Let's have it!' Effie said. 'We're not going home until you hit me and get over… whatever this is.'

'Fine,' said Nell. She took off her coat, dumped her

and Lily's bags by Effie's, and resigned herself to receive a thrashing by lurcher-thin Effie, of all creatures.

'I'm frightened.'

'Of what?'

'I don't know!'

'Didn't you fight at school?'

'Yes, but... not really.'

Effie kept hopping around Nell. She riled herself up and finally slapped Effie, a little tap about the face.

'That didn't even hurt,' said Effie, genuinely disappointed. 'Come on, Nell, think about it. Use that big brain of yours! You've been trained to believe fighting belongs to men. So, you got the cane, and took it. You've been pushed about, by men, by teachers, bosses – and mothers; mine hit me all the time until I hit her back. Fighting belongs to us all. They try and make us girls believe fighting isn't natural for us – it's all rubbish. Men only want to keep violence all for themselves.'

'Why would they do that?' asked Nell.

'Because it feels powerful, and it's good for controlling little women with big mouths.' Effie put her hands on her hips. 'If it felt bad, would men come home and beat their wives?'

'Surely not!'

'Think! If it felt bad, they wouldn't do it. Boys may beg for forgiveness *after* they slap their women about, make boo hoo! *I'm sorry! It hurts me more than it hurts you! It was your fault. You made me do it!* All lies! If it was about punishing themselves, they'd come home and slam their cock in a drawer. But they don't do that, do they? Beating someone into submission feels powerful. Worse, it's what makes the world go round – so do it. Fucking hit me, you lily-livered bitch!'

With that, Nell swung at Effie, making real contact. Effie swayed and stretched her mouth.

'Harder,' said Effie. Then as Nell was preparing herself, Effie punched Nell in the face with a right hook and Nell stumbled backwards.

'You punched me!'

'Damn right I did. Your turn!'

Nell balled up a fist and hit Effie in the face and made good contact. Effie was right, it did feel strangely good, as well as painful. It was raw, and released something dormant, a forbidden rage. Effie groaned and clutched her face, bent over groaning, and then started to laugh like a lunatic. It made no sense, but soon they were laughing in between bouts of slapping and hitting and punching, stumbling towards home. Nell started to feel more at ease with throwing her hands about, a little practice to deaden the fear of hitting or being hit was all that was needed. How often in Nell's life she had been reminded how delicate and frail women were, how *submissive*. But what was natural for men simply must be natural for women too. Naturally submissive animals do not need reminding to behave in a certain way, whereas women for some reason needed endless reminding of what they were capable of. She didn't like it, but at least Nell felt a right to strike out if she had need to.

Nell tore Effie's dress. Effie tore some of Nell's hair out, which made her scream, and that made a woman come to her window and tell them to *clear off!* The journey home dissolved into a farcical scrap, whacking with a swing of the handbag once retrieved, then tackling the other in the middle as if they were playing rugby, sending them both to the filthy ground. When they made it home, they undressed, leaving filthy clothes on the floor, and lay on top of the bed in their underwear. Both were exhausted, sporting bruises, cuts and scratches. It was near two o'clock when Lily and Charlie returned.

'What happened to you two?' asked Charlie, from the doorway.

'We got in a fight,' said Nell, raising her head from the pillow. 'I saved your handbag though, Lily.'

'Thank God! Thanks. Who did you get into a fight with?' asked Lily.

'Some nasty old brasses,' said Effie.

'We won though!' said Nell, raising a fist to the ceiling as Effie giggled.

Lily retrieved her handbag, and both her and Charlie took themselves off to bed.

CHAPTER TWENTY-SIX

1923

IT WAS A QUIETER SHOPPING PERIOD IN JANUARY, BUT Nell had graduated to holding up a dress as a red herring while rolling another with the other hand, bottom to top, letting it slip through the rails into her bloomers. The biggest pain were the coat hangers as they could get stuck or tear something, but leaving them on the rail was an amateurish giveaway. Effie would signal – a stroke of the eyebrow, cough, or even a double blink – to let her know when she was clear to drop, then they would swap.

Nell's progress had been so solid that by only mid-January, the cell was assigned Whiteley's of Bayswater – one of the bigger stores. Lily and Charlie were already inside when Effie and Nell arrived in the ready-to-wear section. Nell had dropped two blouses into her bloomers when she saw Effie signal with a rub of the nose that she had been spotted and Nell iced over, rigid with terror. Stupidly, she even glanced about, only to fix eyes with the glare of a middle-aged male shop walker. Her whole body began to tremble, worst of all her knees, which threatened not to obey when she urged them to walk. Nell struggled to remember training; it was all a jumbled mess. All the voices of Maggie, the Anns and the others in her cell shouted at her until it was a chaos of noise between her own ears. Struggling to retain her composure, Nell pushed dresses around rails, nerves screaming. Her face grew clammy with sweat springing up from her pores, threatening to drip down her chin and give her away.

Nell knew if she was stopped there was a good chance the police would be called and she would be detained until she could be searched by a woman, as was the morally decent thing to do – even to thieves. In instances such as this, all bets were off: bite, punch, kick, spit, lamp them, and slash. Nell's razor wrapped in a handkerchief was in her pocket. If violence was necessary, then she had to find the courage to choose it – but do it fast. Faced with her first real threat, if the choice was between lashing out or going to prison, lashing out it was.

Nell peered up and saw Lil behind the shop walker mouthing, *go*. She abandoned the rack, handbag on arm, and walked towards the exit. As she made her move, the shop walker took strides to thwart her escape. But Charlie fell straight into his path and the man easily knocked such a delicate woman to the floor, dragging clothes off racks with her. Charlie let out a whinny like a horse, for all the attention she could muster, and promptly burst into tears.

'Good heavens!' Lily steamed in, playing a blousy matron in glasses, as two ladies helped Charlie to her feet, loudly voicing their disgust, tutting and disrupting the entire department.

'Did you see that!?' Lily bellowed. 'That man pushed a lady to the floor! Did you see?!'

Nell rushed out of the department, almost running as she fled the doors, leaving the chorus of offended ladies behind.

Once outside, Nell did run, bloomers jiggling, all the way to the drop-off vehicle. She threw the measly two blouses she'd taken with shaky hands, then took herself off down a side street to hide away and try and control her breathing. She felt as if she might be sick or bring up her own heart since it threatened to leap out of her throat. Nell tried to light a cigarette to calm herself but could barely hold the flame still enough.

When the others found her, she was still using the cool brick wall of a building for support. They seemed unbothered. How could they be calm when she thought she might disintegrate into a pile of ashes? How did they ever beat the fear of prison? It had been going so well and this was the first near miss, and probably nothing much compared to what the others had gone through, but it had shaken her to the foundations.

'Nell, are you all right?' asked Lil.

When she opened her mouth to speak, she could barely form the words.

'I thought... I thought that was it... I can't go to prison. I can't.' With that Nell stood clear of the wall, and overcome with dizziness, turned and placed a hand on the brickwork to steady herself. She inhaled deeply in an attempt to calm herself, the other hand on her stomach.

'Nell! You're not going to prison! We got you out,' said Charlie, eyes bone dry. Careful not to crowd her, Charlie put an arm softly on Nell's shoulder. 'You're all right.'

'That's why we stick together, and if that doesn't work,

then we fight our way out,' said Lily, who had come to Nell's other side.

'I don't know if I can,' said Nell.

'Of course you can. Don't be so bloody pathetic,' snapped Effie, arms folded.

'Effie! Have a little patience,' said Lily. 'Nell, we all get scared time to time, but you are in good company. This is why we practise and organise and change routines up. No one is getting caught or having to fight today.'

But what of tomorrow? Nell had never been a fighter, not with her fists anyway. The Forty Elephants went for the face, like men. She'd seen the fights break out. One minute it was laughter, and the next all hell would break loose, like an explosion.

When time caught up with her, as she was sure it would, Nell felt sure she'd be torn to pieces.

CHAPTER TWENTY-SEVEN

COME THE END OF JANUARY, CHRISSIE SAID THAT there was cheap rent on an empty terrace her sister owned on Colnbrook Street. In truly hideous timing, it was the weekend Nell had arranged to go home. But it was the only weekend everyone agreed the move could take place, as there were newer girls in the Forties who Chrissie wanted to put in the flat. Turned out flats and houses were all let or sublet out between the Forty Elephants and their families. Another tidy little earner adding more profit for certain members. Nell didn't resent it; it made perfect sense and she'd surely do the same thing if given half the chance. But it was like being at the bottom of a pecking order, with your betters earning off your rent.

Nell had to send a telegram letting Steph know (she was far too scared to message her mother) she would need to rearrange. Only she received one back with a terrible tone.

Things have changed. Dad's poorly. It's
about time you did the decent thing and

remembered your responsibility to your
family. Yours, Steph.

But it really couldn't be helped, and Nell didn't think
much of Steph laying it on thick about Dad, because that
was the very sort of thing she would do – theatrics to play
on the heartstrings. Dad had always been poorly. What
difference would a couple more weeks make?

Their new house was a three-bed with smart Victorian
steps up to a black front door and an entrance hall they
could all stand in, with plenty of space for hanging furs. It
was far too fancy for the likes of them. The kitchen was on a
lower floor, and it had a courtyard garden at the back. Nell
and Effie took the adjoining rooms on the upper ground
floor. Charlie and Lil took the first-floor bedrooms with a
small balcony terrace. This life was surreal. How far she
had come in a matter of months – Nell had to pinch herself.
If only she could invite her family up to see her new house!
But it would raise too many questions.

All four women agreed it might be a good idea to save
money and found spots outside to hide enamel tins of cash.
Charlie and Lil on their terrace behind bricks in the walls.
Effie and Nell under the paving slabs in the yard.

That first week, in the dead of night, there was a
hammering at the door. All four sprang up like startled cats
and ran to the windows. Nell was already thinking about
the escape route they'd planned should the police raid: out
onto the terrace roof, across the neighbour's terrace, climb
down and make a run for it. It was Lily who spotted him
first.

'Urgh! Nell! It's John – Jesus Christ!'

'You're joking.' Nell ripped up the sash window and leaned out. 'John? What the hell are you doing!?'

John looked around as if he couldn't fathom where the voice was coming from, eventually looking up and breaking into a daft smile.

'Oh, there you are!' he said. He only had one shoe, and his shirt was askew.

'Where's your other shoe?' asked Nell.

John looked down at his feet and from one foot to the other several times before he could reconcile the difference.

'I must have lost it.' He shrugged.

'Are you going to let him in?' hissed Effie, eyelids half closed. 'If you're going to be doing *it*, remember I can hear everything.'

'Does he look capable?' asked Nell.

Effie poked her head out of the window, then back in. 'No.'

Nell did let John in, where he practically fell into the hallway. The others were in foul moods and slipped back to their rooms. Nell took John to the kitchen and tried to sober him up with bread and butter, watching the man eat with arms folded, as he swayed and looked as if he might bite his hand. He passed out on the sofa not too long after, and she kicked him out in the morning. That was the first time.

In February, John turned up unannounced a few times, uninvited and always at random. The cheek of it! He even left his things about the place: newspapers, coats, ties, gloves, a bunch of keys that likely didn't belong to him, empty packs of cigarettes – boys' mess.

In Nell's room, he would leave clothes on the floor. Once

he left his shoes outside in the hall and Effie kicked them into Nell's room. As soon as John had fallen asleep, he would let off like a cart horse. Worse than a balloon – he should, by rights, have flown around the room, then at least Nell could have let him out of the window. He took up too much of her bed, elbowed her in the head, and snored. He left the toilet seat up and blocked it with his inhuman deposits, which Nell would then have to take a plunger to, as whichever of her housemates would stand watching, waiting to use it, glowering. The straw that broke the camel's back was when he put his feet over her legs, and they stank of rotting cheese.

In the resulting epiphany, Nell realised she was very much a honeymoon girlfriend. She liked men when things were fresh and exciting, and they put the proper effort in. After that wore off, much like cocaine, what you're left with seemed even worse than before. Nell had summoned the courage to tell John she wanted to concentrate on work and that she didn't think she'd be able to 'see' him anymore. John shrugged; Nell wasn't even sure if he'd been listening.

While packing up ready to move house, Nell had stumbled across the safe John had given her at Christmas. She thought she may as well ask Lady Jay to have a crack at it, as Chrissie had suggested, and went to look for Jay at a local venue.

The Ring boxing venue was as popular with the working classes as it was with pickpockets. You could spend a few shillings and see three fights, five rounds, or maybe a six-rounder. Have a few ales and, if you had any sense, leave your valuables at home. But it was here that Nell had made an appointment to meet Lady Jay.

A night at the Ring meant wading through dockers, labourers, carpenters and the odd bookie. Because of the war, sport had stopped for four years, so when it all opened up again, illegal gambling flourished. Everyone loved a flutter. You could put a bet on anything these days: growing marrows, dice, pigeons or greyhounds – anything. The Ring crowd was full of woollen coats and flat caps, smoking and spilling ale down your fur coat. The Elephant Gang would be there in a colony, eager young recruits buzzing around them like flies round jam. The Elephant men were easily spotted by their dapper dress, perhaps even a collar and a tie, and the unmistakable swagger of men who make it their business to intimidate.

Alice and her closest associates would often be found at The Ring. Nell arrived and caught sight of John with his mates. Rumours had abounded that John had got into a habit of turning up drunk at the house. Everyone knew about it – pub gossip – but Nell hadn't reckoned on Alice ushering her over as soon as she saw her. Nell's stomach lurched; why would Alice want to speak to *her*?

When Nell approached, Alice put an arm around her and turned her away from the crowd so they could talk privately, in a corner. It was like being hugged by a grizzly bear in Alice's big fur and tight grip. She was so tall that when she wrapped her arm around Nell it fell under her chin. The sparkles from her diamond rings twinkled in Nell's eyes. The affection grip could easily have turned into a choke hold.

'You want to sort all this bad gossip about John out,' said Alice. 'You know he's always chasing younger girls, don't you?'

'We're not together, we're friends. I don't care if he's going with other girls.' Nell shrugged. But that wasn't the right answer.

'You might not care, but I do. It's what it looks like. It says you're weak, and if a man can disrespect you, *that* is my problem as long as you're in the Forty Elephants. Do you want to leave?'

'No! I don't want to leave,' pleaded Nell.

'If people don't respect you, they'll take the piss. I can't have people taking the piss out of my girls. Deal with it and don't make me ask you again.'

Nell nodded and Alice released her grip.

Shit, now she really did have to cast John adrift, like a fucking dead weight by the looks of things.

Nell was shaken by the interaction. Aside from being petrified of Alice, and the woman's forearm around her neck, she didn't want to be thrown out because of John ruining things.

The gossip going round was that Alice was poking her nose into relationships. The code said that all love matches must be approved, and she had begun taking more of an interest in the social lives of the Forty Elephants *to avoid embarrassment*. Nell wasn't stupid – instilling a fear of embarrassment was about conformity. But even Nell had to admit the truth, which is that for some girls it didn't matter what you gave them – a job, money, diamonds, furs – they'd still throw it all away for a wedding, and fuck everything up for everyone else. Those women didn't want independence.

Alice could have given them everything and they would still go looking for a daddy. Nell wasn't one of them and needed to prove it – fast. But now she had to meet Jay and find out what was in this safe.

Nell found Jay playing cards with three fellas, sat on stools at a turned-up barrel in a corner, as quiet as it could possibly be in the Ring. Jay's hair was styled in the Eton crop with a side parting. She wore trousers and a waistcoat, shirt and tie, with sleeves rolled up and a cigarette dangling from her lips. It was obvious Jay was female if you took more than a glance – long eyelashes, slender wrists – but she prided herself on gentlemanly manners. While Jay didn't hide who she was, she didn't explain either.

'Jay,' called Nell.

Jay looked up and stood.

Nell offered her right hand like a lady, and Lady Jay bent and kissed it – she always had been an audacious flirt.

'I have an old safe that needs cracking,' Nell got straight to business.

'Can't your boyfriend sort that for you?'

'What boyfriend? I don't have one,' snapped Nell.

Lady Jay stifled a laugh and looked over at John, who was larking about, pissed as a fart, acting the fool with his friends. They'd all had too much to drink and no sense of each other's space, barging into men who dare not so much as look at them. Nell didn't look, indignant at the insinuation she somehow belonged to someone.

'Me and John are *friends*.'

'All right then, can't your *friend* crack it for you?'

'Turns out he can't, doesn't have the skillset. Chrissie says you are... a person of considerable talents.'

'Always admired Chrissie. I bet that's not the only thing he's incapable of cracking for you?'

'You are terrible, Jay. Now come on, what will it take for you to look at it? I have no idea what's inside, but I'll split whatever it is if it's worth anything, and if it's not...'

'Friday, come round mine, I'll see what I can do. If I do open it, then you have to come to dinner with me.'

'I can buy dinner.'

'No, I'll buy. I'm not a savage.'

'You know I'm not into girls.'

'We'll see,' said Jay, laughing and taking her seat back at the card game.

'I'm not! How many times!'

'They all say that when they're sober, dearie, or not in prison. Friday – I'll cook, you bring a bottle.' Jay offered her hand to shake.

As the deal was struck, the crowd erupted into a deafening roar. The underdog had lost his fight on points, but not before Alice had jumped up and was hanging off the ropes, screaming at the referee. Nell got out sharpish, before the pints of mysterious yellow fluids started flying.

CHAPTER TWENTY-EIGHT

FRIDAY NIGHT CAME AND NELL ARRIVED UP AT LADY Jay's carrying the safe. Jay rented a flat above a hosiery shop off Blackfriars Road and, as promised, Nell brought a bottle of gin.

Dinner was steak, mashed potato and peas. A radio played a live boxing match with commentary at Olympia in London.

Jay had the little safe on a coffee table and fiddled about with various tools – stethoscope, forked tongs, metal files – growing more and more frustrated. Nell lost interest, a little tipsy and drinking gin straight from the bottle. When she was least expecting it, the safe popped open. Both looked at each other and then peered inside. It didn't look as if anything was in there after all.

'Oh, hang on,' said Jay, reaching in and pulling out a yellowing envelope. There was nothing written on it, and it wasn't sealed.

'Go on, what are you waiting for?' said Nell.

Jay opened the envelope and took out black and white

photographs, fifteen in all. Jay passed half to Nell. They both studied the photographs and squinted harder, not quite able to understand what they were looking at. Jay turned hers sideways whereas Nell tried blinking.

'Good grief!' said Lady Jay, who rarely swore – if only men had the same manners. 'Where did you say this came from?'

'John said he won it in a card game off a bloke who'd stolen it from a flat up West, I think.'

They swapped piles and leafed through in bewildered silence. Both felt sober, despite half a bottle of gin being put away. Once they'd finished, each gazed off into the distance, unsure what to say.

'You may want to find out who these belong to. I can't imagine they're comfortable with them missing,' said Jay after a long silence.

'I don't understand,' said Nell. 'Why would someone have such photographs? Why would one, do such... *things*?'

'Ours is not to reason why.' Jay picked up the pile again, shuffling it into one and leafing through as Nell peered over a shoulder. 'Bondage, isn't it? Pain and... what not.'

'Not for me,' grimaced Nell.

'Me neither, but, er... horses for courses, so they say.'

'Yeah, not me.'

'This may sound nuts, but the man in them does seem familiar,' said Jay. 'I mean, it's hard to tell, as they all look the same when they get to a certain age. Round belly, no hair, spectacles – but it's the black moustache. Only I can't place him.'

The first picture was of a woman whipping two naked women, bent over, with a riding crop. Another was of a

woman bent over, no drawers on, and whipping herself. All
the pictures were of women in various states of nakedness.
Grabbing each other or in compromising positions with
handcuffs, whips or a black bodice. One woman wore a
tail sticking up like a phallus from her rear end. But two
of the photographs showed a man – the same man. He was
the only one fully clothed, in a suit and tie. In one, he held
the riding crop above a woman's bare back, and in the
other he was preparing to give a girl a caning across the
buttocks as she bent over a desk with a skirt over her head.

'Infuriating,' said Lady Jay. 'I was going to try my luck
with you as well, but I have to admit, this has really put me
off my stride.'

'I thought you might,' said Nell. 'You are naughty, Jay.'

'Let's finish the gin, if only to dampen the images from
our eyes.'

Nell blamed the gin, but soon she was gabbling
about her fear of getting caught, hoisting from the same
department stores and boutiques over and over. About the
policeman and his foreboding warning, and her near miss at
Whiteley's. Jay was working in a gang targeting warehouses
and distribution houses, taking big hauls under the cover of
night. The return on one job could be more than treble the
cell could take in a week.

'Why don't you try and do a little moonlighting on the
side,' Jay suggested.

'What? Are you mad? Alice would kill us. Wouldn't she?'

Jay laughed. 'Yes, that's the party line, but trust me
when I say you wouldn't be the only Forty who did a little
freelance.' Nell had not considered other work, off the
books, so to speak.

It was intriguing to hear that other Forties got up to off the books work to earn a little extra here and there.

Was it wrong? It felt a little like betrayal, but Nell obviously wasn't the only one who had noted that the system set up benefited a few veteran women in the Forties who had extra profit from their part in the chain, be it acting as fences and taking a bigger share of the sale, or subletting their properties to girls lower down the ranks. And the appeal of exploring other, perhaps less risky work opened up other avenues that Nell could explore. Otherwise they would repeat the same job over and over until exhaustion, or arrest. Nell did not want to betray anyone in the Forties, least of all Chrissie or Alice, but she did want to avoid the shame of prison and a criminal record. Not only for her own reputation, but for her family. She didn't want them to know where her little money parcels were coming from or suffer shame from decisions she herself had made.

'But what if Alice found out?'

'Then don't let her find out. I have a friend, Emma Kershaw, she works at the Savoy. Emma has been looking for women to work with on an idea she has. She's a clever woman, discreet too. I could put you in contact with her if you like. What have you got to lose?'

'My life if Alice finds out! And Chrissie, and I don't know what the others will think.'

'It's not without risk but think on it. One building, no police and no shop walkers. Emma needs women who can pass as housekeeping staff. People who can keep their cool under pressure and play a role. Plan well, prepare, execute, and get the fuck out. You know all the fences you can sell to. Alice won't find out. It's not like anyone would snitch on you because everyone is at it. It certainly helps you keep your face out of the department stores so much if that's what is worrying you. You still work your rota, only not as hard. Still make decent income via the network set up in the Forties, just a little extra on the side. Takes the risk down a notch. Don't you think Alice and Chrissie get up to other things as well? Nice girls like you could easily get away with such a blag.'

Nell had to admit, it was intriguing. 'All right. Maybe it is worth considering, thanks, Jay.'

Lady Jay unsurprisingly didn't want half of the photographs and gave the entire safe and its contents back to Nell.

Only a few days later, Jay was arrested after breaking into a clothing warehouse at night. She had climbed through a window and opened the main doors to let her associate in. They had taken expensive dresses and coats, stolen the cash in the till and driven off. But opposite the warehouse was an animal emporium selling exotic pets. The owner had seen the mystery car and taken down the number and passed it to the police the very next day. In a timely stroke of bad luck, a police officer saw the car and jumped on the footplate, forcing the vehicle to stop with Lady Jay behind the wheel.

Jay made it into the newspapers. They described the well-mannered gentleman as a 'hard-bitten gangster' masquerading in men's attire. The papers blamed loose morals and an undisciplined youth causing homosexuality to rise. The first dangerous step to this was allowing women to act like men: wearing trousers, drinking, smoking, *working*. This was exactly what people had feared would happen with the war and then the vote; where would it end?

On the date Lady Jay was to be sentenced, a group of Christian women handed pamphlets outside the court:

> The woman shall not wear that which
> pertaineth unto a man.
> Neither shall a man put on a woman's garment
> for all that do so are an abomination unto
> the lord thy God.

The pamphlets littered the street. Nell didn't go to the court on Lady Jay's request. Jay didn't want anyone to see her in a dress and would rather suffer humiliation alone. The magistrate said Jay exemplified an extraordinary instance of female depravity. *A mistress in all manner of wickedness as Satan himself could make her.*

Jay was sentenced to two years in the Holly.

CHAPTER TWENTY-NINE

Dearest Nell,

It is quite unacceptable that it's been nearly three months and you have yet to come home to see your family. Aside from your moral duty, you could at least make an appearance, so we know you are quite well. *Maman* said that you had suggested a telephone call, but she has quite the temper regarding this subject now. I do not think a telephone call, even given how exciting she finds the invention, will suffice. Furthermore, it would give Dad tremendous cheer to see you. I urge you to come back as soon as possible, I feel his health has declined since the new year. Thank you for the money. It is appreciated, and I wouldn't want you to think we are ungrateful. The boys are well. Paul is well. I am well. But you must visit home.

Your devoted sister,
Stephanie Mackridge.

P.S.: I hope the move went well. Perhaps in the summer

I could bring the boys before they can't remember their aunt anymore. I do fancy a bit of shopping.

While reading the letter from her sister, the noise of an argument from downstairs reached her room. When Nell traced the noise to the kitchen, she found Lily and Effie in the middle of a blazing row.

'Charlie is sick, Effie – she can't work with a fever. We'll have to call a doctor.'

'I'm not losing money because Charlie has a sniffle!' shouted Effie, still in her nightgown.

'Of course not. You couldn't possibly be affected, and no one would want you as their nurse, would they?! Selfish Effie who only cares about herself. Same old story,' snapped Lily.

'That's not true!' shouted Effie, fists by her side.

It was a little true. Effie was terrific fun but selfish, like a child. If it meant going without in some way, or even sharing, the other person could go to hell.

'I'll call a doctor,' said Lily.

'How noble. Always thought you'd make a good nursemaid. Nell, you're coming shopping with me.' Effie, satisfied she had got her way, stomped out of the kitchen and up the stairs. Lily addressed Nell but made sure it was loud enough for Effie to hear: 'Good! I could do with a day off from *her* myself!'

'Whatever we earn today we split four ways, as always,' stated Nell. 'I'll speak to Effie. She's having a brattish moment.'

'When isn't she?' snapped Lily.

Since the move, Nell had noticed a simmering tension

between the oldest friends of the cell, Effie and Lily. Effie had become slovenlier with more space to abuse, and different philosophies were emerging.

Nell had raised the idea of talking to the chambermaid Jay had mentioned. Effie had immediately scoffed and Charlie was ambivalent. Lil, on the other hand, had been interested. Lily also knew that running the same tricks over and over could only result in being caught, eventually. She had spent six months in Holloway already and had no wish to repeat her experience. It was with Lily's enthusiasm that Nell was stirred to tracking down the chambermaid. Despite her belligerence, Nell suspected Effie was simply terrified of change. Effie fretted about the cell splitting up – all she needed, Nell supposed, was reassurance. It wasn't good to have Lil and Effie bickering while having to rely on each other for work. Effie feared being alone and ongoing tension with Lil would only play into this, although Effie would never admit it. Instead, she would act the brat – it was a vicious circle. Having a day with Effie would allow Nell to convince her no one was going anywhere. But other ideas were worth investigating. Lily was fearful of prison too, and if other work avoided that catastrophe, then there was less chance of the cell breaking up, Effie surely had to understand that. Nell needed to make Effie understand that throwing tantrums wasn't going to make people stay bound together.

Nell dressed in a bottle-green coat with fur cuffs and collar, with a crêpe de Chine dress and a turban. Effie wore a long beige coat with a fur trim and a beige hat with black feathers – and both wore wigs. A respectable French society lady and her English companion.

When they opened the door to leave, Nell saw the sky

was a livid purple with streaks like an old matron's varicose veins. Something was in the air – there would be thunder and lightning today.

The pair hit Selfridges at lunchtime, where respectable women elbowed each other to the discounted rack in the clearance section. Others created an unholy mess, tearing dresses off racks, unfolding blouses and scarfs, unrolling silks to touch the fabric and throwing products everywhere. The scramble to attract an assistant could be a sport itself, with throngs of waving women demanding service.

Nell smuggled clothes into the changing rooms and transferred the trafficked items into her bloomers. She left the changing room with decoy outfits. It was beyond comprehension how fast she had grown accustomed to the tricks. But something was up with Effie – Nell had watched her acting with cavalier abandon, clouting bolts of silk into her bloomers, almost daring someone to catch her. Her black mood threatened them both.

The pair left Selfridges and dropped off goods to the open top Velux motor car with no problems, thankfully. But Nell took an omen when the first bolt of lightning followed immediately by a clap of thunder ripped through the sky. They'd had a good day and she wanted to quit while they were ahead. But when she said as much, Effie stamped her feet.

'The day isn't over! What's wrong with everyone?'

'What's wrong with *you*?' hissed Nell. 'I don't know what's got into you today, but can't you leave it?'

'I'm the same,' shouted Effie. 'It's everyone else who's changed. This talk of other jobs. What's wrong with what we have?! You've all become boring fishwives!'

'It's about being smart and not getting caught, Effie,' said Nell, as Effie pouted with her hands in her pockets.

'What about the Forty Elephants, Alice and Chrissie? It feels disloyal.'

'Oh, come on, Effie. I'd buy that from anyone other than you! *Think*. We're told which fences to use because some make extra profit that way. We all rent flats and houses from inside the Forties, too, because they make extra out of us. I'm not complaining – it makes good sense. But they've all got other things on the go, so why shouldn't we? It's about getting better and staying one step ahead and keeping out of prison! Surely you understand that by doing the same thing over and over we'll run out of luck eventually, however much we switch up routines or tricks. This will keep us together, don't you see? Hotels don't have shop walkers or the police. It's like waitressing. Hear me out: lots of tables means you have to work harder for tips. But host an event and you take away more money from one job, with less risk of getting caught. It would be stupid not to—'

'Fine!'

'What?'

'I'll agree, to entertain this blarney with the maid-to-raid, or whatever she is. But only if we can do one more job today.' Effie pouted. 'You know diamonds cheer me up.'

'Really?' That was easier than Nell anticipated. 'Fine! One more job, then we go home.' Effie really did have the emotional instincts of a child, although she was terrifyingly clever in other ways.

Nell put it down to the instincts Effie had had to rely on in childhood. It hadn't been pleasant from the little she had learned. Often Effie appeared cold, if not calculating.

In reality, poor Effie had simply never experienced anyone else acting in her best interests and found it hard to accept people actually did such a thing in the first place.

Against her instincts, but willing to placate Effie, the pair walked to Cecil Court: an alleyway lined with Victorian shops. Booksellers, antiques, art, and of course, jewellery. The sort of elegant alleyway tourists adore; but don't look too hard or ask where the money comes from, because hiding in theatreland were showgirls and dilly boys for rent. Several brothels operated in the apartments over the quintessentially English shops.

The pair entered Leapman's Jewellers. Nell went straight to beguile the assistant by asking the price of several pieces in a thick French accent, as Effie hovered near the window and door. Trays were placed on the counter and the French lady perused. Nell prepared to swap and stick a ring under the counter when Effie grabbed a whole tray of rings and sprinted out. Nell didn't know who was more shocked – her, or the shop assistant. *What the hell was she doing?*

'Wait! Thief!' The shop assistant reacted faster than Nell, who had no clue Effie was about to pull such a mad stunt. Her first instinct was to let Effie run, escape herself and give Effie a good thrashing later when she got hold of her.

Leaping from behind the counter, the shop assistant gave chase, and Nell had no choice but to follow, if only to make sure Effie got away. Effie had almost reached Charing Cross Road, crammed with pedestrians, motor cars and horse-drawn carts. The assistant was closing in as Nell gained on him. With a final push, she shoved him in the back, and he fell to the ground. Nell ran past him and caught up with Effie at the end of Cecil Court. Nell grabbed Effie and slung a right, pushing shrieking people clear, towards Leicester Square Underground station. The earnest shop assistant wasn't giving up, however, and had made it to his feet again and to the end of the alleyway.

'Police! Stop! Thieves!' Red faced, he waved his arms as if flagging an aeroplane. Nell saw two police offers over the road. 'Police. Help! Those women. Thieves!'

The coppers blew their whistles and headed for Nell and Effie. Thankfully they were blocked by traffic on the road.

'We can't go to the station, we'll be trapped.' Nell grabbed Effie and dragged her into a street on the right, St Martin's Court.

They ran past Wyndham's Theatre, took a left and continued running until they found themselves in a claustrophobic courtyard of shops, bars and restaurants. Patrons on wooden chairs enjoyed a leisurely lunch. They heard the policeman's whistle again, and people started to wonder what was going on. Effie saw a gap between two buildings and the two disappeared down it. Surrounded by filth, stinking rubbish and rotting boxes, they discarded their coats and hats and threw them on the ground. Having both worn wigs, Effie's red and Nell's dark blonde, they swapped, and despite being out of breath and bedraggled, they at least looked different.

'Why did you do that?' spat Nell, panting. 'Get rid of that tray, now!'

Effie clutched the tray to her chest, although a few rings had dropped out of the velvet spacing. She looked at them, unable to let go.

'Dump it!' Nell growled. She pulled the tray from

Effie's grasp and lobbed it down the alley, rings clattering everywhere.

Nell crept to the opening and poked her red head out, looking in each direction, then leaned back.

'We need to split. You go down Cranbourn Street.'

'But the station is right there,' said Effie.

'No! They'll expect us to try the station. You go down Cranbourn and get over Waterloo Bridge.'

'What about you?'

'I'll go along St Martin's Lane, then to the bridge. Meet me at the pub.'

'All right.'

Effie slipped out first, blending into the crowds, her now dark-blonde hair bobbing behind her. Nell went in the other direction, but on the corner of St Martin's, she heard the whistle again.

'Stop! Police!'

Without looking, Nell sprinted through St Martin's Lane. A commercial street, full of crowds, where she could get lost. That's if the policeman didn't catch her first. She could not outrun a fit young man and would have to lose him somehow. She saw an open door to the New Theatre and rushed inside, hoping to hide and let the policeman past.

'You can't come in here!' Up leapt a young man of mixed race, like dark Ann, but tall and lean.

The poor lad looked more frightened than Nell. Nell took in the small room: cabinets, tools, piles of boxes. The boy, flat capped and wearing overalls, had been painting papier mâché heads a lurid gold on the desk. He was a stagehand.

'Help, please, the police are after me. I'll pay you,' she pleaded.

The boy hesitated then, with a tip of his head, gestured to Nell to hide under the desk. She crawled under and he sat back down and pulled the stool in. Her face stuck at his knees. Then came a hard rap at the door, which was still open, and in stepped the unmistakable sound of clodhoppers.

'Good afternoon, son. Have you seen a slim redhead come this way, green dress?'

Nell recognised his voice at once, it was the young policeman who had shone a torch in her face near the old flat. *Horace.* The stagehand didn't speak, and Nell thought he might give her away. All she could do was tremble, hold her breath and pray for a miracle.

'No, sir. I haven't,' said the stagehand. Nell tried not to sigh with relief; the boy wasn't going to grass, thank God.

The policeman stepped closer to the desk. A tall cabinet pushed up against the side hid her.

'Apologies for the interruption. Allow me to introduce myself. I'm PC Bevan, and you might be…?'

'Sam, Constable. I'm a stagehand. If you want to speak to the gaffer, he won't be long.'

'No, it's not him I'm after. Sam, are you absolutely sure the young woman I described didn't pass this way? You know you can get into trouble if you don't tell me the truth.'

Sam sighed. Give him his dues – he half laughed.

'Constable, the thing is – and no offence, sir – I'm going to get into trouble with you lot no matter what. But, for what it's worth, I haven't seen such a woman. I think I'd remember. Slim? Red hair? Green dress? Sounds like someone I would notice.'

'Righto. Then thank you for your time.'

PC Bevan left, but Sam the stagehand stayed sat.

'Don't move... they always double back.' Sam wasn't wrong. In a matter of seconds the door was knocked on again.

'Me again, Sam, forgive me. I forgot to mention, the woman I'm looking for is part of a gang. A violent gang of thieves. She's just robbed a jeweller in Cecil Court. Do you know it?'

'I'm not much for jewellery, sir.'

'Well, if you do see her, or ever need the assistance of the police, you can find me at the station – PC Bevan. We're all equal in the eyes of the law, son.'

'Righto, Constable Bevan.'

For a second time he left. After a few minutes, Sam shut the door, locked it and pulled the stool out. Nell crawled out.

'I'm not one for thieves,' said Sam, 'but I'm no grass. You best go.'

Nell offered Sam two pounds, which he took, even cracking a smile. 'I don't suppose you could get rid of this?' she asked, holding out the red wig.

Sam laughed. 'I'm sure the costume ladies could make use of it.'

'Thank you.'

Nell emerged from the side door, slipped into the crowds and took a taxi to the Duke of Clarence pub. She saw the Two Anns and told them what happened and asked if anyone had seen Effie, but they hadn't. No one had.

Nell knew then that Effie must have been arrested.

CHAPTER THIRTY

EFFIE HAD BEEN ARRESTED IN THE STATION, WAITING for the next tube to Waterloo. The Two Anns had found out after schlepping to the police station on the sniff for information, where the desk sergeant told them Effie was about to leap onto a carriage as a policeman grabbed her and led her out in handcuffs, spitting and cursing. She had been booked in under the name Effie Deets, avoiding her birth name of Ethel Mary Castle. One she despised that also came with a record. Miss Deets was to be kept on remand in Holloway until her day in west London assizes, where she would be judged by a magistrate. Now Effie needed a defence, and that meant telling Queen Alice Diamond. Lil didn't take the news particularly well either.

'Fuck! Alice will go mad! Half of us weren't there, you two should never have been in that district. It wasn't on our rota! What were you thinking?' shouted Lily. 'We must tell Chrissie first.'

'It might have been my fault. I'd convinced Effie to the meeting with the maid on condition we went hoisting one more time. She was in an odd mood; I shouldn't have agreed to the last job.'

'Nell, this was Effie's doing. She's always been rogue when in a sulk. When she gets herself upset, she lashes out and to hell with the consequences, for her or anyone else. I love her to pieces, Nell, but sometimes I could wring her scrawny neck.' Lily was steaming. Charlie had yet to be told, but Nell was worried about Effie.

Being arrested was Nell's perfect hellscape. That day she had come as close to being arrested as she ever wanted to, ever. It could have been her languishing in a cell right now at the station. It very nearly had been. She was beside herself fretting for Effie.

'What can we do?' she asked Lily. 'Poor Effie! I can't bear to think what's she's going through right now.'

'Let me tell you something about Ethel Castle, Nell,' said Lil, sitting down in the kitchen and pointing to the other chair so Nell would join her. 'That girl will always land on her feet. Please do not worry about Effie. She may seem fragile, but she has a knack of always coming out smelling of roses, trust me! I know her. She is like a sister to me, but you can love your little sister and be a little frightened by her at the same time. Right now, we need to tell Chrissie and hope to God she volunteers to tell Alice for us. The sooner the better.' Lily huffed. 'I suppose it should be me...'

'I'll do it,' said Nell. 'I was with her, and you weren't, so that's not fair.' She perked up with an idea. 'What if I raised the idea with Chrissie about other work, without mentioning the hotel exactly? See what she says.'

Lily balked, then to Nell's horror burst out hysterically laughing, only to turn very grave when she'd calmed down with a sigh.

'Oh Nell! Tread carefully, you've been in the gang about two minutes. I wouldn't be too sure of throwing your weight about with Chrissie or Alice yet. You should be careful with that big old brain and little mouth, or is it the other way around? And if you're going to do it, I'd suggest going very softly and as soon as you get a hint of the negative, shut the fuck up.'

Nell nodded that she understood. She slipped her coat back on to go to Chrissie's house, a mere five-minute walk away. With dreaded legs of lead, and a belly of nerves. This was almost like walking to the schoolmistress to receive a caning, only more frightening.

Chrissie was spitting feathers when she heard the news. Cursing and ranting, giving Nell a dressing down in the parlour as Nell stood with her hands in her pockets, head bowed like a schoolgirl.

'And you can bloody well tell Alice!' Chrissie spat when she'd stopped pacing up and down, hands on hips.

'Me?' said Nell, knees turning to jelly. 'But I'm... new. Would it not land better coming from... you?'

'*Land better?* What are you on, my girl? Nice try, and you're not bloody new anymore! And that'll learn you for going off rota,' said Chrissie, a finger in Nell's face. 'I was with her an hour ago at her house in Milverton Street. Effie needs a solicitor, so go and catch her there now. Go on, off you fuck.' So much for Chrissie's aversion to bad language. Nell thoroughly regretted volunteering to be messenger.

★

Unfortunately for Nell, Alice was at home and answered the door at once. The squeak of the door opening sent Nell's stomach down like a guillotine on her own head. She was let into the parlour and they both sat in armchairs with the radio on. When she blurted out the events of the day, Alice banged the arms of her chair and bellowed at her.

'What the fuck were you two doing in Cecil Court!?'

Nell jumped. Alice had answered the door amiably, even offered her a cup of tea, but no sooner had Nell confessed to Effie's arrest, than she exploded. All Nell could do was survive the blast.

'I can't have you fucking about and doing whatever you like. I run this syndicate, do you understand?' Alice gritted her teeth, her fingers like claws digging into the armchair, upholstery puckering under the pressure. Alice leaned towards Nell and came very close to her face. Nell could only look down. 'This only works if you do as you're fucking told!'

'I'm sorry. It will not happen again.'

'I see you got sent to tell me,' said Alice, leaning back again, almost recovered from the volume in a second; she could switch. It put one on edge, unsure of how to navigate the moment.

'I volunteered.' That seemed to count for something with Alice, and she visibly softened.

'Effie needs to behave, or she can fuck off out of it. You tell her that from me.' Alice rubbed her hands together, cracked her finger knuckles and closed her eyes.

Nell was unsure what to say. Was now the time to enquire

innocently about other work, under the guise of avoiding arrest? *Softly now.*

Nell drew a breath and opened her mouth to speak when Alice opened her eyes and pointed towards a side table by Nell.

'Pass me those chocolates,' said Alice.

Nell took a moment, then reached out for the box of chocolates and passed it over. Alice wasn't much of a drinker, but she was partial to chocolates.

'Here, have one.' Alice offered the tray to Nell, who took the first one she saw.

She was far too nervous not to comply and too scared to dither about picking one she liked. It could have been scraped off the pavement and she would have eaten it and said it was lovely.

Sat in silence, both women chewed on gooey chocolates, sucking their teeth. Alice even stuck a finger in between her gums and sucked the chocolate off it. Nell wasn't sure if this was some last ritual before Alice punched her lights out. Or if she was simply a normal woman who enjoyed the odd chocolate in moments of tension.

'First time I got arrested was for stealing chocolates. I was sixteen,' said Alice. 'Me and Mary Austen got caught on the Strand.' Alice giggled to herself. 'The nutty ones are my favourites. You were going to say something? What was it?'

Nell shook her head, still trying to unlock her jaw from chocolate and hazelnut goo. 'Oh. Nothing.'

Lily was right: perhaps she did have a little brain and big mouth after all. Probably best to stop talking at this point.

'I shall make a telephone call to Mr Hardy, the brief. And

you...' Nell straightened up in her chair. '...you make sure Effie keeps her mouth shut in the meantime. That's *your* job,' said Alice, looking squarely at Nell, who gulped and nodded eagerly. 'You can go now.'

Lil had advised her to go softly. Nell had gone in so softly in fact, she had utterly bottled it. Nell decided then and there it was best to explore other avenues under her own steam. Besides, what Alice and Chrissie didn't know wouldn't hurt then, and it was less likely to backfire on Nell and the others.

CHAPTER THIRTY-ONE

IT WAS A WEEK BEFORE FEBRUARY BECAME MARCH AND A Sunday when Nell received another telegram from Steph. *Shit!* Nell still hadn't visited home and kept forgetting to make it a priority since life was so busy in London. A telegram cost one shilling for twelve words, and one penny for each thereafter. Being a Sunday, Steph must have paid an extra sixpence for every word after twelve and then paid on top of that for the message to be delivered as a priority. Nell's arms had goosebumps as she tipped the boy in his pretty little uniform. The poor thing looked exhausted from escaping the wild children running around the streets only too happy to relieve messenger boys of their bags. She slammed the door shut with a foot and tore it open.

```
The game is up, little sister. Mum tried
to find you at the Savoy to tell you Dad
had been taken ill. Please come home.
Lord knows what you are up to. Steph.
```

By the time Nell got to the end of the message she felt sick. At least she was still more frightened of her mother than the police. When Nell read the message to the others, Lil went pale on her behalf. However, Charlie came up with an idea.

'Tell them you hated the Savoy, that you were unfairly treated by a manager. No! A guest! A guest approached you indecently. They'll never want to know the details.'

'You haven't met my mother, or sister. They'll want to know *every* detail.'

'You could tell them you waitress at a nightclub now but were too scared of what they might think so kept it a secret. It's all perfectly above board, and you mix with dukes and duchesses, which isn't a lie, and receive wonderful tips which are bumping up the money you send home. That should dazzle them.' It was good enough.

If her mother had telephoned on Mr Bright's beloved candlestick and horn and the Savoy had said Nell had never worked there, then she would put it down to a miscommunication. Everyone called her Nell now, not Eleanor, and her mother had an accent. Nell would blame the confusion on her being French. That's right, it would be her mother's fault for being French.

Nell made hasty arrangements to go home the following day, Monday. She would come back to London Tuesday, make sure Effie was coping on remand. Everything would be tickety-boo by Wednesday. Well, as much as it could be given the situation,

★

Nell took the late-morning train and arrived in Brighton early afternoon. She took a cab from the station, thinking that the best way to thwart any inquisition would be to dazzle them. She would shower them with gifts, and once they'd seen she was doing well, concerns would resolve themselves. Her father wouldn't care; it was her mother who she needed to manage. Steph might stick her nose in, but... would it be ostentatious to take them out to dinner? They never ate out, ever, unless it was whelks on the pier.

When Nell arrived home, she knocked on the door and her mother answered. The woman's face fell to the floor as soon as she saw Nell, whose own smile faded as her mother looked her up and down. She took in her outfit: the shoes, bold makeup and short hair. The colour drained from the woman's face.

'What have you done?' her mother said, looking as if she'd been winded.

Nell assumed her mother was referring to her hair. Only then did she consider how very different she must look.

'I forgot I cut my hair. Do you like it, *Maman*?' Nell leaned in to kiss her mother but she stepped out of reach into the hallway, muttering to God Almighty in French. Her Catholicism ebbed and flowed, like gout.

Nell had worn an orange and white crêpe dress, with long bell sleeves and flounces around the skirt, and a beige cloche. She'd bought the outfit with her parents in mind. She was still seeking their approval – if only cosmetically. Now she felt hideously brash.

The house smelled strong now, a stranger's home. Ant powder, boiled potatoes and musty shoes. Nell couldn't help but find it depressing as she followed her mother into the scullery, or the kitchen as they called it in Lambeth.

'Your father is in the garden,' her mother whispered in a fragile voice. She looked exhausted; her hair was unkempt, which was most unlike her.

Nell set the bags down and approached the open back door. Her mother hovered by the recess with the sink. Nell knew there was something she had yet to understand as she stepped outside, but saw Steph sat on a blanket with the boys, crawling now. Steph greeted her with a sheepish smile and the boys squealed in excitement. It was unseasonably warm and sunny, so it made sense to find them outside. There was Dad covered in a blanket on a chair.

Nell took one step towards them but stopped when she saw her father's chair had great wheels. The kind she'd seen at the military hospital when he'd been sent back a lice-eaten bag of bones. It was a wheelchair, one of those great cumbersome contraptions made of wood. Her dad looked even more frail, and older than he had been only three months ago. Nell wasn't the only one who had changed.

'Dad! It's Eleanor! I told you she was coming.' *Why was Steph speaking to him as if he were deaf?*

'Stephanie, I'm making coffee, you want to bring in the boys?' said her mother. Steph scooped up the twins and carried them inside. Steph returned to stand beside Nell, who stared transfixed at their father.

'I see you got my telegram,' said Steph. 'Dad had a stroke. He's struggling with his speech but he's all there, aren't you,

Dad? As much as he ever was, anyway.' Steph and their dad shared the joke and the man nodded his head. He tried to say the words *cheeky beggar*, but they came out warped and the fright sent great electric shocks through Nell.

Nell had always been Daddy's favourite. *Daddy's little monster*, her mother had called her. While her mother had been the disciplinarian, and Steph had always been obedient. Her mother swore Nell had been sent to test her on earth to allow her an easy ascent into heaven. But Dad had found Nell's spirited ways amusing. He had laughed at her naughtiness and had never once struck her. *She's too little*, he would say. *I'll hurt her.*

That man… in that chair… was not her dad. It was Mr Spooner from across the road. This must be what Steph's angry message had been insinuating. Nell bit her bottom lip to stop it from wobbling.

'It's good to have you back,' Steph carried on, saying the expected things one should say. 'You cut your hair; it looks… lovely. Different, mind. Might take a bit of getting used to. That's a colourful dress. She looks like one of those flappers, doesn't she, Dad?'

As her dad tried to speak, Nell struggled to understand what he was saying. He was like a slurring drunk. Steph leaned in closer.

'He says you look beautiful,' said Steph, and Nell forced a smile. 'You always were his favourite. He never says that to me! Do you, Dad? Maybe I need to bugger off to London and come back a different person. To be honest, I'd go to sleep for three months – that would do me!' Nell didn't dare retort to Steph's little digs. She didn't care about such quibbles right now. She wanted to help but didn't know how outside of sending more money now she knew what had happened at home.

Steph took the opportunity to whisper into her ear. 'Come on, say something or he'll think you're scared of him.'

Oh, but she was. This was not her father. This was a crippled old man, riddled with artillery and burned-out lungs, who'd aged ten years in the last three months. Nell was aware she should feel guilty about his stroke, but she didn't. Nell went straight to rage eternal – she was angry. This wasn't a medical calamity that unfortunately had to befall someone. In Nell's eyes this had been done to him. By his own government, by his own King who sat cosy-toed upon a golden throne wearing a silly hat. Like every other serviceman, her father had been discharged with twenty-six shillings a week for six months and then nothing. *Thank you for your service, now piss off.*

Nell remembered the presents and ran to fetch the bags; that would cheer everyone up, and then perhaps she could control her emotions enough to talk to Dad. First came the musical bears from Schuco for the boys. The little dancing bears went down a storm and turned somersaults. The boys were mesmerised, and even her mother managed a smile at those. For Paul, who was at work, there was a silk tie and pocket square. For Steph a silk scarf. The gifts briefly conjured excitement and Steph made a big fuss about loving hers, while their mother mumbled in her native tongue about excess. For Dad there was a three-piece smoking box, and this her mother had to comment on in English to ensure all understood.

'He can't smoke. We will sell it.'

When it came to her mother's present, they all watched as she unwrapped a silver fox-fur wrap to a suitably impressed audience with an unimpressed expression.

'Eleanor! That must have cost a fortune!' Steph clapped both hands together. Before Nell could respond, her mother did.

'You can have it, Steph. Where would I wear such a thing? Weighing carrots? *À vous*.' And she tossed the fur at Steph.

The brutality hit Nell in the stomach, and for the second time that day she bit on her lip. She hadn't cried for months, couldn't remember the last time. Yet here she was on the cusp of bursting into tears every minute.

'Then you have it, Steph. I only thought it would make whoever wore it feel pretty. All girls need a little glamour, don't they? Oh, and I go by the name of Nell, now.'

'Bah! Who is this girl? I don't even know who she is,' her mother exclaimed. She threw a tea towel over her shoulder and walked back to the kitchen.

It was clear she didn't belong anymore. Nell had accepted the reality for a girl of her class and tried to better her situation. Her family played by the rules of a game that only the poor played, as the powerful laughed at their obedience.

Dad reached out to touch the silver fur, and Steph wrapped it about his neck, to lighten the mood.

'Why didn't you tell me about this?' Nell hissed at the back of Steph's head.

'I bloody well tried,' Steph spat back, turning her back on their dad. 'You should have come home. Three bloody months, Eleanor, sorry, Nell?! Really? Don't try and blame me for your neglect.' Then switching on a smile to their father, 'Suits you very much, Dad. You'd do all right at quarter to two on a dark night, I reckon.' A welcome relief of glibness.

Steph went to the kitchen to bring out the coffee and Nell took the opportunity to sit by her dad, without the judgemental scrutiny of her mother and sister.

'I'm so sorry, Dad. I had no idea, I know I've been selfish and caught up with myself,' she said with wobbling lips. She was determined not to cry.

The man made great efforts to grab Nell's hand in his own and pull her closer so he could whisper slow, laboured words into her ear.

'As long as you're enjoying yourself. My monster. Always.' He tried to stroke the cheek nearest him with the back of his hand, fingers not as dexterous anymore. 'Why cut your hair? Look what happened to Samson?' He was referring to the Bible story of Samson losing his power when he cut his hair off.

'Only thing is, Dad,' said Nell, sniffing hard and resorting to easy banter, 'I'm not a bloke, so all my strength is in here.' Nell winked and pointed to her temple.

Her dad's head nodded silently as he laughed, and he mustered the strength to speak. 'That's what scares me,' he said.

After coffee, Nell whispered to Steph that she wanted to catch their mother alone in the kitchen.

'Good luck,' whispered Steph. 'I don't know what you're up to, Eleanor, but where is this money coming from? Actually, don't tell me.'

Nell sloped into the kitchen as her mother was tidying and started silently on the washing up as Steph made anxious glances through the gap in the door. Nell made several attempts to start a conversation only to receive monosyllabic answers and no eye contact. Her mother even retrieved the crystal radio set and switched it on to smother the silence. Provoked by her childishness, Nell switched it off.

'Is there any more news of Mr Bright selling the house?'

'Mr Bright has assured me that with your father the way he is now, there will be no rush.'

'Oh.' What was Mr Bright waiting for? Nell had her own idea.

'Is money all right? I can always send more. I have money—'

'Oh, I bet you have.' And her mother put both straightened arms on the table and glared at Nell for the first time since opening the door.

'How very *anglaise* of you, *Maman*, to be so afraid of saying what you mean.' That seemed to move things along.

Her mother stormed to the back door and slammed it shut. Nell saw a glimpse of a wide-eyed Steph as she disappeared from sight.

'Look at you! Dressed like *that*! Throwing presents around paid for by God only knows what!' screamed her mother. In all her years she had never seen her mother like this.

'I know I should have come home sooner. I'm sorry!' That was it. Nell burst into tears, but to her horror, so did her mother. 'I should have been less selfish, but I was working!'

'Stop lying! They'd never heard of you at the Savoy. Never! You never worked there. Why do you lie? You were always a *sauvageonne*, Eleanor, but I never thought you would grow up to become a whore!' Nell gasped as she realised what her mother was accusing her of. It was clear the farfetched story of her leaving the Savoy to work in a nightclub wasn't going to cut the mustard. Worse, the accusation that Nell was a prostitute made her blow like a stick of dynamite.

'You know what you always told me?' Nell snapped back. 'When a person accuses you of something, they are admitting what they do themselves! Mr Bright lurks, waiting for Dad to pass on. It certainly looks like he will be getting his way sooner than thought!'

Nell would forever regret saying that and seeing the pain on her mother's face. It was her mother's turn to gasp, and she slapped Nell once about the face.

'Get out!' she said, and pointed towards the front door. 'Get out. I do not want you here one moment longer. I don't know you anymore!'

'With pleasure,' said Nell, smashing the plate she had been washing on the floor. 'I want to get away from this shithole anyway,' she screamed through tears.

'Take your presents with you!' cried her mother as Nell ran through the house for her bag and coat.

'Oh, keep them! Sell them! *You need the money more than I do.*' At once she recalled the obnoxious youth that had told Nell the same thing at the Grand.

Nell grabbed her things and ran out of the house and down the garden path, which seemed to go on forever. Her mother chased her to the door and threw the fox fur behind her, but it travelled no more than a foot, landing barely past the step.

'Don't forget this! You may need it for your customers!' her mother screamed.

Nell didn't look back, her body racked with feelings she refused to set free. She made it onto a train back to Waterloo and sobbed all the way home.

CHAPTER THIRTY-TWO

THE JOURNEY BACK WAS A PAINFUL METAMORPHOSIS. Eleanor Mackridge died on the way. Machete Mack killed her. She cut the throat of the feeble weakling and threw her from the carriage. Watched as Eleanor tumbled down a bank, rolled into a ditch where she would rot, never to be found.

Long live Nell.

Poor old Eleanor hadn't seen it coming, but it really was for the best. The poor girl was too fragile for this world.

Rest in peace, Eleanor Mackridge. Long live Nell the Mack.

Blood is thicker than water, they say, but Nell begged to differ. It was money that never let you down. And Diamonds? Even better.

The next week she sent four pounds to Steph, who wrote back and said she had made a mistake and sent too much. Keep it, Nell had written back. Don't tell Mum but spend it on the boys, Paul, Dad, even the woman herself behind her back, of course. Only don't tell her where it came from!

Effie languished in Holloway on remand, waiting for her day in court, and as was the custom when a girl was arrested, her cell would keep a low profile. In their case, there was an additional element of punishment since they'd strayed off rota and assigned district too. If they had anything to do, it was intimidating witnesses, but there would be no attempt to do that in Effie's case. The police had physically arrested Effie on the spot, so there was little to gain if the shop assistant was to retract his testimony; the police evidence was enough. They did sneak contraband in to her on occasion, if only to make Effie's stay at His Majesty's pleasure bearable. Effie could use money, tobacco or snuff to trade with inmates, or curry favour with the prison officers who were poorly paid and easy to bribe.

The same week, with Eleanor freshly dead and buried, along with all her irritating mawkish feelings, Nell decided now was the moment to trace the chambermaid Lady Jay had told her about.

'It doesn't hurt to have a little curiosity,' she'd said to Lil.

'I believe curiosity killed the cat,' Lil fired back.

'We are lucky we are not little pussies, don't you think?' Nell grinned.

'What's got into you? A few months ago, you were a terrified kitten of a thing. Now you are suddenly fearless. That being said, I suppose a conversation won't hurt,' said Lil. Wary, but willing.

'I'm trying to think like a man. Effie once told me that was the way to do it. I should ask myself, what would a man do? Well, I'm sure he'd jolly well do what suited him best.'

'I think it's a good idea,' offered Charlie. 'If it goes

nowhere, no harm done. It's not as if we have much else to do, other than persuade Effie to not cause trouble inside.' Alice had taken the unusually punitive decision to take the cell entirely off rota until Effie was sentenced. This only made Nell feel more entitled in her attempt to track down the maid at the Savoy.

As Lily had predicted, Effie was getting on fine in prison. She complained it was cold and the bed hard. She missed her makeup and her hair was a mess, and it was impossible to sleep with the noise. Apart from the superficial, Effie was unaffected. She really was a unique creature but it didn't stop Nell from worrying about her. Pillow talks with Effie's childish questions had made Nell see Effie as vulnerable, even if Effie didn't know it herself.

In terms of the chambermaid, all Nell had was a name: Emma Kershaw. It might have been clumsy, but all they could do was venture down to the Savoy and ask about.

Part of the allure for Nell was to get inside the Savoy. The ultimate symbol of wealth and privilege, where people used words such as 'sublime' and referred to 'devouring' and 'inhaling' art, much like scavengers pick at a carcass. It was so named after Count Peter of Savoy, a friend of Henry III. In 1246 Henry granted him the estate where Peter built the Savoy Palace. During the Peasants' Revolt of 1381, the Savoy Palace was stormed, set ablaze and burned to the ground. Since then, it had been a military hospital, prison and theatre. The Savoy Hotel opened in 1889, a 'new Savoy Palace' with Count Peter commemorated by the golden statue that stood guard over the Strand entrance.

It was March and a sprightly spring day when Charlie, Lily and Nell made sure to put on the posh and made their way under the glare of Count Peter into the Savoy. They went straight to the bar, where Nell left Charlie and Lil to their cocktails and took to wandering the corridors. She took in the luxurious décor and considered approaching staff and asking if they had heard of Emma Kershaw. On the third floor, Nell came across a maid exiting a room. Her backstory was that she was looking for an old school friend to rekindle a friendship from before the war – everyone loved a bit of sentiment. She approached the maid and had no more than uttered the name when they were interrupted.

'Madam, I'm Emma Kershaw. What business do you have with me?' Nell turned to see a stern-faced woman. The other maid took the chance to move on.

The slim young woman was the same age as Nell. She was plain and indistinguishable from all the other staff in their starched and proper uniforms. The only identifiable feature of this face was that it was one of apparent thunder.

'Ah, Emma! So happy to see you!' Nell kept to the story, at least until the other maid was out of earshot. Then whispered, 'Lady Jay told me to find you here? She said you were looking for people to work with.'

The woman's face relaxed upon the mention of Jay. The cogs whirred, eyes narrowed, but the arms folded across her chest. Emma the wary chambermaid looked to see if anyone was about to witness the interaction.

'Are you Nell?' asked Emma. Nell nodded.

'How many people have you asked about me?' Emma looked about again.

'Only the one. I was lucky.'

'I can't be seen with you – not here! You must leave. Now!'

'But—'

'Meet me Thursday at the Prince Albert, under the arches, Waterloo, on the way to the South Bank. Seven o'clock. Now please, go!' With that, Emma, rigid arms still clasped about herself, walked away from Nell.

Well, thought Nell, a little abrasive, but she would have to wait until that evening to find out more. Nell returned to the bar to find that Charlie had mesmerised the barman and was up on the brass footrail, bent over with her round derrière in the air as if waiting to be spanked. Cupping her chin in her hands, elbows on the bar. The barman could barely see through the glaze of his bedazzled expression. Nell groaned inwardly, and resigned herself to ordering a drink and waiting for Lily, who must have gone on the wander. Nell took up a seat at the bar. It wasn't as if she wanted to hang about unnecessarily. It wasn't unheard of for Chrissie, Alice or any of the Forties to take tea at the Savoy. It was explainable – they had come for a drink – although she'd rather not be seen at all. It was like being caught skipping school.

Only last year, she'd have never dared walk into the Savoy alone – certainly not into a bar. Four months seemed a lifetime ago, and she wondered what had taken her so long. Why had she remained so timid when everything she had ever dreamed of was apparently sat waiting for those audacious enough to take it?

A middle-aged man pontificated loudly on her right. He was holding court with another barman, this one less inclined to glaze in bedazzlement, but dutifully maintaining an interested expression at his patron's anecdotes. The man was speaking about a particular legal case he'd presided over. His voice had the bellow of a well-bred man. Nell had no more than given him a flashing glance, but once his face registered in her mind, she nearly snapped her neck with a second look.

It was the moustache. Wiry and black, a slug over an invisible top lip. The square high forehead, spectacles. It was the man in the filthy photographs! Good God! Nell would know that face anywhere.

Nell nearly knocked over her own drink, grabbing it with both hands, and was like a flea on a hot brick in her seat. She tried to get Charlie's attention, but she was busy. Nell was desperate to tell someone! On cue, Lil strolled back into the bar and, having seen Nell's stunned expression, knew that something was up. Lily stopped, brow wrinkled. Nell signalled her interest in the man along the bar, with a tilt of the head and a tap to the right side of her nose. Lil couldn't understand exactly but followed Nell's lead. Nell slunk along the bar to the man on his left side, as Lily crept up on his right. A talent Lily still had was picking pockets, having been trained as a child, like so many.

'Mr Topping?' interrupted Nell, putting an intrusive hand on the man's forearm. Of course, she didn't know his name. 'It's Marjorie, Marjorie Butterworth from Chipping Norton. We met last summer in Marseille, with my aunt and sister. It was in that restaurant on the waterfront. It is you, isn't it?' Nell had adopted her best clipped accent, as Lil was riffling through the man's coat pockets.

The man took a second to react, almost stumbling backwards into Lil, caught out by Nell's directness. Lil shot him a filthy expression. Befuddled, the man turned back to Nell.

'I'm sorry, madam. You have the wrong man. I've never been to Marseille in my life.' The man was curt, bordering on rude. Perhaps he wasn't comfortable with a blunt approach, especially from a lady.

Unwilling to give up so easily, Nell tried again. She had already learned that fear of public humiliation was a useless tool if someone wanted to achieve anything at all, *ever*.

'I'm so sorry. I'm terribly embarrassed. You must think me so ill-mannered. I do promise, I haven't been dragged up.' Nell played the flappity woman. High pitched, irritating. 'I could have sworn it was you. Your name's not Terence? Are you a lawyer or a solicitor? Or was it, oh, I can't recall now. But you live in Chelsea with your wife and two sons.'

'Madam, you are mistaken. I have two daughters, if only to start.'

'Oh. Perhaps I remember it wrong? Could have sworn it was daughters. But you are a solicitor?' she pressed.

'No, madam, I am not. If you wouldn't mind, I shall be leaving. Good day.' The man stepped away, nervously glancing at Lil behind him, who glowered back.

The conversation had disorientated him enough to make him bumble off towards the door. Curious, the effect a confident woman can have on an old-fashioned type of man. As soon as he was gone, Lil and Nell slid together along the bar, back to the barman.

'What did you find?'

'Not a lot.' Lil held out her bounty. 'A lighter, let's see, engraved *to my dearest Alfred, 1912*. Does that help? What's all this about? Did you find the maid?'

'I've got to meet her later this week. That, Lil, is the man from those awful photographs I showed you all. I swear it!'

Nell had shown them the photographs the same evening she'd returned from Jay's, and how they'd all laughed about it.

'Him? Are you sure?'

'You wouldn't have guessed what his proclivities were from the way he practically ran from us, would you?'

'What's up!?' Charlie slid in, and now all three sat in a row. 'Who was that man? I recognise him. I saw you working him as I was chatting to Rodolfo.' As Charlie mentioned the barman's name she gave him a little wave. The barman blushed and waved back. 'Did you find the maid?'

'Think, Charlie, where have you seen that man before?'

'I can't tell, but I think...' Then Charlie's face drained of colour, and she sat at least three inches taller. 'That's him, isn't it!?' Charlie turned to Nell. 'The dirty bastard in those photographs.' Both Lil and Nell shushed Charlie for swearing too loudly.

'Yes! I really think it is!' said Nell. 'We were trying to find out what his name was, but Lil couldn't find anything in his coat.'

'Aside from the fact his name is Alfred,' added Lil.

'Well, that narrows it down,' scoffed Nell. Lil pursed her lips.

Charlie's face lit up, struck by inspiration. She slid back to Rodolfo the barman, cupping a hand over her mouth to his keenly bent ear. Lily and Nell waited, and eventually Charlie came back.

'And?' said Lil.

'His name is Alfred Cottingham, and he's a regular and... he's only the magistrate at west London assizes. By all accounts, quite a talkative fellow. Happy to tell stories of the curious cases he presides over, especially about the plague of common lady hoisters.'

'Did you say magistrate?' asked Nell, the penny dropping as to the significance of the gift that had for some unknown reason been bestowed upon them. Effie was right, Jesus did approve, apparently.

'A magistrate you say...' said Lil, her mind trying to turn this into usefulness, 'hmmm.'

'Hey! That's where Effie will be sentenced,' added Charlie, catching up.

'Yes,' said Nell. 'Seems a pity to look such a gift horse in the mouth – don't you think?'

'Could be very useful indeed,' added Charlie. 'Only, we, er... might have to persuade the man. He is likely to require a significant amount of encouragement to be made... *comfortable* with the idea of helping girls such as us.' The insinuation somehow made more sinister as she raised her glass to suck from a straw.

Yes! A willing ally on the inside of a court might be a great asset as Effie's day approached.

'Would be terribly rude not to take an opportunity when one arises,' said Nell. 'We're going to need muscle.'

'We're going to need Alice,' said Lily. 'But... I think she'll be quite pleased with this development. Get us back into her good books?'

'But we won't be telling her about our little project, will we?' asked Nell.

'Oh God no! There's nothing to tell,' Lil shrugged.

★

A couple of days after her disastrous trip home, after she had tossed Eleanor from the train, Nell found John on her doorstep again.

It was gone midnight, and he was pissed as a fart and banging on the door begging to be let in. Nell had been woken up by Charlie telling her John was outside, again. She'd dragged herself up and opened the sash window at the front of the house over the front door to find him swaying outside. He'd set the neighbour's dog off barking.

'Don't let him in, Nell,' Charlie pleaded, eye mask on her forehead, yawning.

'Not this time, not ever,' Nell told her, and leaned out of the window.

'Go home, John. You're not coming in.'

'Come on, Nelly. Don't be like that. It's freezing. I only want somewhere to sleep.'

'Then pick a park bench. Or knock up one of your other girls – and don't act like you don't have any. I'm taking myself off the list, so go on, go away.'

'I'm only friendly with the other girls, Nell. I'm a friendly guy. I made friends with you, didn't I? Come on, open up.' For good measure he tried the door handle; it was locked.

'I'm not giving in, John. Go home. It's about respect. The neighbours will give me earache, and it's late. People have work in the morning.'

He didn't like being told no and tried rattling the front door, then he kicked it like a spoiled boy. Nell wondered what she'd ever seen in the man. He hadn't changed so much – it was Nell.

John wasn't budging, so Nell stomped downstairs into the kitchen, grabbed a jug and filled it with water. Then she marched back up to the window. Lil and Charlie had both come out of their rooms to observe the spectacle.

'What are you going to do?' asked Lily.

Nell marched up to the window and tipped the water over John's head, who squealed like a guinea pig.

'What d'you do that for!?' he whined.

'I said go home,' hissed Nell in a furious whisper. The dog still barked.

'Who stuck a carrot up your arse!?' shouted John, angry at not getting his own way.

'I did! And it'll be me who decides when and if it comes out. Until then, piss off!'

John wiped the water from his face and flicked his hands. Lily and Charlie shoved their way next to her to mock John in his pitiful state. The worst part was lights had sprung up along the street, yellow blinking eyes opening up here and there.

'I guess I will go home. That's if I don't fall asleep and die from cold, now I'm wet through.'

'You'll be all right, John. You were in the trenches! A bit of water won't hurt you!' shouted Nell, as they all laughed and jeered.

'You could stop at Chrissie's,' added Lily. 'Except she'd batter you for waking her up at this hour.'

'Why don't you write a poem about your existentialist despair?' Even Charlie joined in. 'It might get published!'

'I'm going, I'm going.' John waved away the abuse and staggered down the path.

The jeering and laughing carried on, the girls squeezed in

the window, hanging over the ledge cackling and hollering at John as he had to take a walk of shame after being rejected.

Nell did feel a little guilty, but he never turned up at their house again after that. Standing up for herself felt strange, nerve wracking, especially when she'd always been trained to feel grateful for male attention and frightened of making a man angry. But it was also liberating. Plenty more fish in the sea, as they say.

CHAPTER THIRTY-THREE

THE PRINCE ALBERT, WHEN SHE FOUND IT, WAS A HELL-hole. The sort of drinking den where hope went to die a quiet death, for old boys to ferment in self-pity. The only noise was the grumbling of the trains passing overhead like the bowels of a coal pit about to crumble, and the odd secretion-filled cough. Nell found Emma, but had very nearly missed her sat in a dark corner by an upturned beer barrel for a table. She was looking out of a window impossible to see through. Steamed up on the inside with thick soot on the outside. Emma had an inconspicuous way about her; Nell had almost left without spotting her.

'What a charming little place,' Nell said as she sat opposite Emma, drawing her back from her wistful daydream. She still wore the chambermaid's dress, although the cap had been replaced by a brown hat and she now had a black overcoat and a muff on her lap with her hands hidden inside.

'First things first,' said Emma, skipping pleasantries, 'I want you to know I am not a criminal.'

Nell leaned over the barrel, barely smothering a snigger. 'I'll let you into a little secret: neither am I.'

'Then who and *what* are you?'

'Lady Jay was a friend and helped me with a little favour. It's a crying shame she's inside. Jay said you were seeking other like-minded women to work with, and that you had a particular idea in regard to your employer, the Savoy.'

'How do I know I can trust you?'

'I can't give you a guarantee – I'm a hoister with the Forty Elephants. I work in a cell of four – three others and myself – and we are professionals. By that I mean, we do this for a living with the intention of not getting caught. We are currently considering other projects if you will. I believe enterprises call it diversification. Don't they?'

Emma scoffed. 'I wouldn't know about any of that. But I've heard of you lot. Degenerate women, they call you. I do not like confrontation, and I certainly do not seek it out.'

'Do I look like a boxer to you?'

'No, but… looks can be deceiving.' Emma took to staring towards the opaque window.

'As are yours, I might say. Sweet little chambermaid. No makeup, hair scraped back, dull clothes – I would guess your appearance is as contrived as mine.' Emma turned her head back to Nell at that, almost smirking at the observation.

'I put absolutely no value in attracting male attention. Fat lot of good it has done me in the past. I quite like being invisible, actually. You get away with a lot more, you know.'

'So, what's this idea?' asked Nell.

Emma explained how she had been common-law wife to a screwsman in a band of criminals who specialised in breaking and entering warehouses. This was how she met Lady Jay.

'When my boyfriend beat me to a pulp and I couldn't see out of either eye, so swollen up was my face, it was Jay who took me in. That's how we grew to care for each other.'

'Didn't that put her in a bad spot with your old man?'

'A little, although he didn't care that much. He soon found another punchbag and, as luck would have it, got himself up on a smash-and-grab charge and has been languishing in Wandsworth ever since. I'm safe for now and I don't fancy being around when he gets out. He'll be on his knees and need money and somewhere to stay and that's when he'll come looking. Jay looked after me and asked for nothing, so now she's having her bad fortune I'm going to look after her. I had the idea before she went to prison but I'm even more determined now. Nearly a year ago, I started work as a chambermaid at the Savoy. I know how to get my hands on all sorts now. I have master keys and maps of every floor, every entrance and exit. I know timetables of all staff movements. I've taken my time over this and I'm looking to run a slow job. I've no time for rushing and grabbing, or attention seeking. I value discretion and subtlety.'

'Sounds good to me,' said Nell. 'But I still don't get it.'

'The Savoy has 267 guest rooms, including sixty-two suites, over nine floors. The wealthiest clientele drift in and out on a daily basis and there's a big income in the restaurants and bars for day trippers and businesspeople. I haven't put a foot wrong since I started. I'm trusted and extremely diligent. The job is, I provide you with access, timetables, maps, information, and I keep lookout, but... I need women who can pass off as dowdy little chambermaids, like me. I can get uniforms. I have a plan in a random pattern of which rooms to target and when. You get them in, and make sure your... *friends* get out with jewellery, clothes, cash, small and easy to carry items found in every room. I don't have contacts to shift those goods on, so that will have to be you as well – what do you call them, fences?' Emma asked, struggling with the terminology or perhaps the taste of criminality as it passed her own lips. Nell nodded as Emma carried on. 'We split the takings. I think we should work over the Savoy for six or eight weeks. Then I find another job at another London hotel, and slowly, we do it again. It's going to require a particular restraint and patience so as not to attract attention.'

Emma was essentially proposing she be a 'maid-to-raid', but with a strategy rather than opportunistic abandon. This was about targeting specific rooms and guests, while leaving others untouched. A carefully executed plan that would confuse. Her speciality would be earning the trust of the house as an efficient maid with good, clean references. Nell's cell would set about raiding jewellery boxes, safes and wardrobes over extended periods of time.

'We could also make the most of other opportunities as they arise. There's a passing trade in teas, lunches, dinners and meetings. You could be opportunistic there because by the time the guests have left and discovered something gone from their coat pocket or handbag, they have no idea where they last had sight of it. Become friendly with the staff, eat in the restaurants, drink in the bars, buy staff drinks – even the girls. Chit chat but present a business front. A London hotel is a goldmine, a whole building full of coats, luggage, handbags. A treasure trove. Over time you can find ways of getting your hands on your own keys and hit the rooms if you want, after me and Jay are gone, that is.'

'Where are you going?'

'I'm going to save as much as I can until Jay gets out. Then I'll take her away to somewhere sunny. That's my plan. I don't know the right actors for the job, and Jay suggested you girls might fit the bill. I don't mean to be rude but,' Emma clearly felt uncomfortable saying this, 'she said you weren't as rough as the others can be.'

'I'll take that as a compliment,' chuckled Nell.

'You should,' said Emma curtly.

The plan was a slow, deliberate theft. Death by a thousand cuts, if you will. If the police were called and staff searched, it would be the newer and less-trusted girls who would be suspected. The rooms not touched however might even raise suspicion of the guest who had reported a theft. This was London – no one was to be trusted. The odd room, one day perhaps an entire floor. Random. Unpredictable. The occasional loss of silver from the rooms. That sort of thing. Handbags and fur coats from the bar. Then Emma would find another job at another hotel, wait a couple of months and start again, carrying on until Jay got out. Nell had to admit, it was a clever and orchestrated plan, and the kind Alice would admire as it was strategic. Not that Alice would know about it. Although it did leave Nell with the issue of how to move the goods along via a fence outside of the syndicate, on the sly. That she would have to sort with the others, later.

'You secrete the goods out of the building and split the proceeds with me fifty-fifty,' proposed Emma. Nell couldn't help but laugh out loud; then, feeling the need to impress Emma with discretion, gathered herself.

'There's four of us – those splits don't work.'

'It's me providing the set up!' snapped Emma.

'And it's us carrying the goods if we get caught. And no one would grass on you, so you've got the easiest job. All up front, yes, but less risk in battle.'

'What do you suggest?' huffed Emma.

'What's fair – five-way split. Twenty each.'

Emma balked. 'I don't bloody think so. You wouldn't be able to do this without me.'

'And you without us. What other girls are you going to approach? How long until enquiring brings you attention, male or not?' Nell pushed. She knew Emma was at a disadvantage in terms of choosing her accomplices.

'All right,' puffed Emma. 'Bloody communists.'

Nell wasn't done. 'Let us in on the plans, and you might find we can contribute more than you think.'

'Discuss what you will with your… cell. But I'll only meet with you. It's risky as it is and it'll have to be somewhere discreet. We can't risk being seen together.'

'Agreed. Wise idea. What about here? I think I'm becoming rather fond of the ambience.'

'No, there's a place I know in Soho, a previous life of mine. It's utterly revolting, so no one decent would see us.'

'Sounds delightful, can't wait.'

'And one thing I insist on,' said Emma.

'What?'

'Keep your girls in order.'

'What do you mean by that?'

'I've heard the stories. Diamond Alice, as they call her

in the papers, I've read the stories, punching men's lights out. Maggie Hughes – What do they call her? Babyface? – glassing women in the face. You walk in there with that sort of... style, it'll be over in seconds. You girls, you give yourselves away and you don't know it. Just because you wear the right shoes and clothes... It's the way you handle yourself, the way you stand and use your hands. Manners you haven't been taught. They might be invisible to the likes of us, but to rich people, they can sniff out their own kind. When you come in as ladies, you'll have to be the part. If you are working the bars and restaurants, you must fit in. Chambermaid duty is different, deferential – invisibility is key. Do you understand?'

'Understood and, despite the sting, point taken. Rest assured, I used to be a waitress at the Grand in Brighton, I'm quite familiar with deferential. Leave that with me. So, shall we meet again and start reviewing these plans of yours?'

'Yes, I think so,' said Emma, who, for the first time, cracked the smallest of smiles.

CHAPTER THIRTY-FOUR

Nell volunteered herself to show Alice the photographs and float the idea of using the intelligence to help Effie, still on remand in Holloway. Time was of the essence, so she arranged to visit that Wednesday evening. Alice sat her in the same armchair where they'd both picked chocolate out of their mouth with fingers. Nell passed Alice the photographs and tried to explain how they'd come to be in her possession.

'Good God, what are you showing me these for!?' said Alice, as she threw them down in disgust. The images fanned out across the table as if trying to offend them both. 'Why on earth would John give you these?'

'It's not what you think! John won a safe in a card game and gave it to me as he couldn't crack it himself. It was meant to be funny, I think. He didn't know these were inside. Lady Jay opened it for me, and we found them, before she got sent down.'

'What a godawful present. I hope you gave John what for.'

'That's what Effie said. But we went to the Savoy—'

'Who went to the Savoy?'

'Us three, we went for a drink.'

'At the Savoy? You aren't working until Effie is sentenced, so shouldn't you be a bit more mindful of how you spend your money?'

'Yes, but I swear we only went for one and saw this man there, in the bar. We found out that he's a regular drinker, and a magistrate. A magistrate, Alice! At west London assizes. That's where Effie will be up, and who knows who else soon enough.' Nell pointed to the man in the photos.

Alice was a clever woman; as soon as she heard the word *magistrate*, she picked them back up and studied them harder.

'Magistrate? West London, you think?'

'Yes! His name is Mr Alfred Cottingham, and he's a talker, goes into the bar on the regular and talks about work.'

'I'm assuming he skips over his hobbies. What a filthy man. Hmmm, I doubt he wants these photographs out in the open.' Alice scrutinised the stack again, pursing her lips at the graphic poses. 'How confident are you that it's the same bloke?'

Nell hesitated; she'd been bloody positive until she was faced with Alice and her heavy eyelids, staring her down. 'Very,' she said.

'We need to be surer than that,' said Alice, tidying the stack up as you would a pack of cards. 'I'd like to hang on to these. A magistrate.' Alice set a neat little pile of photographs face down on the table.

'What should we do?' asked Nell.

'We go to court – that's what we do. Call it a reconnaissance mission. Might be quite nice sitting in the public gallery for a change. What a lovely gift it would be if it was the same man – a gift from God, some might say, Nelly. A gift from the Almighty Himself!'

A goofy grin broke out across Alice's face, her mind whirring with the potential scope of what such an ally could do for her organisation, if properly persuaded with the right kind of leverage. Alice was a shrewd woman and not above intimidating a witness, but a magistrate would be an escalation. No one cared about common criminals striking the fear of God into the ordinary working man or woman, but a professional man of the law – that was a step up.

'Oh, this could be fun,' said Alice. She picked up the photographs one last time and flicked through – the smile stayed fixed. 'I think if Mr Cottingham is who you think he is, then I'm rather looking forward to meeting him, and I can't say I've said that about a magistrate.'

When Alice showed Nell out, she had one last question for her on the doorstep.

'I do hope you put John in his place for this little gift? He might think it's funny, I don't.'

'All sorted, Alice. I won't be getting any more presents from John.'

'Good. What changed? You seemed hesitant before.' Alice leaned in the doorway, arms folded, a wry smile on her lips.

Nell thought on what to say and settled on something diplomatic. 'I took your advice on being mindful of what I put up with. Besides, he was pissing the neighbours off.'

'Good for you,' said Alice. 'Why do you think I wear so many diamonds?' She flashed her large hands, a diamond on every finger. 'They never let me down.'

CHAPTER THIRTY-FIVE

ONE WEEK LATER, ALICE WENT ALONG WITH NELL, Lily and Charlie to sit in the gallery at the assizes to study the moustached man up in the magistrate's chair. He appeared to hand out punishment in much the same way he gave out thrashings on naked buttocks: with liberal abandon. The magistrate was the same man, and they were as sure as they could be without fingerprinting.

Having sat through two considerations, they'd seen a middle-class lady married to a civil servant cry her way out of prison. Her defence was she suffered from melancholia caused by her only son's death in the war. The respectable lady was let off with a ten-pound fine. Next came a wisp of a girl, graduate of the famed Dr Barnardo's school for poor and deprived children, and domestic servant. Her mouth dangled in bewilderment and her eyes danced about between the prosecution and her defence, as if she were watching tennis.

The girl had stolen a dress and coins, less than five shillings, from her employer because she planned to meet a boy in the park. She said she had every intention of putting the dress back but confessed to taking the coins, as she didn't think they'd be missed. This girl would see the inside of prison walls for a month. She had a history, you see, having been at industrial school then Barnardo's and so only stringent punishment would halt the path of degeneracy she was on.

'You are telling me John robbed a magistrate and didn't know it?' whispered Alice to Nell as they watched proceedings.

'He won the safe in a card game from some bloke who stole it from a flat in the West End, that's all I know.'

'Ah, that was it. Still can't believe he gave you such a shit present,' said Alice, peering down as if she were mad. Alice tossed her sable fur around her neck, swatting Charlie, sat the other side of her, in the face. They were crushed in on the hard wooden benches, which meant dead bottoms that might very well need thrashing to get the blood back into them.

'It was meant to be funny.'

'They always try and pull rank, boys. Always. They can't help themselves. They find women like us a threat that needs to be put down, even if they do dress it up as a joke,' said Alice. 'The only man a girl can rely on is her daddy, and mine was a slippery fucker with a terrible temper.'

The others wanted to stay and watch proceedings as Nell went outside to smoke – and who should bounce past with his rubber shoes and shiny badge? The irrepressible policeman, PC Bevan.

'Well, if it isn't Hetty Handcuffs,' said Nell as he loped past.

Horace did a double take and back tracked to stand in front of Nell, who had her back to the wall, a foot against it.

'Bit overdressed for court, aren't you?' he said, looking her up and down, taking in bare legs, scarlet lips, heels and a fur stole.

'Always dress like this. I consider it a matter of civic pride.'

'Now let me see, Nell. Or should I say, *Machete Mack, Nell the Mack, Nelly Mack,* or, as I'm sure your mother refers to you, Eleanor Mackridge. Great nicknames though, variations on a theme. But I ask myself, where could a nickname like that possibly come from?' Horace held his arms open wide in theatrical wonder.

'That's because you lot don't have a sense of humour,' said Nell, blowing smoke in his face, Horace did his best not to cough. 'It's my deadly wit, what else could it be?'

'I can only wonder.'

'Do you like arresting your own kind, PC Horace?'

'I'm a DC now, and criminals are not my kind.'

'Interesting, the lies people tell themselves to justify what they do.'

'I could say the same to you.'

'I'm going to guess you had more choices. Your blind loyalty got you a promotion, Detective Constable! That didn't take long, and up West, too.'

'Blind loyalty? Again, from where I'm standing, it's you that's blindly loyal.' Horace leaned in, a hand against the wall close to Nell, who turned her face away.

'Alice doesn't care if you get sent down. You get a record, that's you done for life, and if you keep going that's exactly what will happen.' Horace stepped back, shifting his stance to one less threatening. 'Why are you here anyway? Didn't know any of your lot were up on trial today.'

'They're not,' said Nell. 'I'm thinking about becoming a lawyer.' This, at least, made him smile.

'I don't want to put you away, Nell. I don't enjoy ruining people's lives and seeing them go to prison.'

'Must be shit being a police officer then.'

'My job is to protect the innocent.'

'The only people the police protect are the rich and connected. There's been plenty of times we needed protecting, and you lot were never around.'

'Everyone is equal in the eyes of the law...'

'But we're not though, are we? I've spent a couple of hours in court and can see that's not true with my own eyes, but you keep telling yourself that.'

'I'm not saying it's perfect, far from it, but if more working-class join up, everything can be changed from within by sheer numbers and collective will. Justice should be for everyone, and it isn't there yet, I grant you, but at some point, Nell, us ordinary people have to stop complaining and come to the table.'

'Do you believe in ghosts?' asked Nell.

'What?'

'Let's make a deal – we both meet back here in a hundred years as our ghostly selves and see if anything has changed.'

'All right, you're on.' They shook hands, both looking about, hoping none of their own had seen such a curious interaction.

Horace shook his head in exasperation and put his helmet on. He left Nell and made his way to the entrance only to stop abruptly and turn back, as if he'd remembered something.

'I much prefer you as a brunette,' he said. 'The red wig didn't suit you.' Horace smiled to himself, spun on his heels and disappeared inside.

Nell threw her cigarette on the ground. *Fuck*.

CHAPTER THIRTY-SIX

ALICE PUT THE FEELERS OUT TO FIND PREMISES THAT would provide services as had appeared in the magistrate's photographs. A couple of working girls in Hayles Buildings gave information about a newsagent in Soho with a basement. The high-end girls worked out of the flats upstairs, but downstairs was a 'dungeon for peculiar proclivities'.

'These photographs look like their thing. I don't go in for that funny business,' said one of the women. Hair in pin curls and headscarf, she couldn't look less erotic if she'd tried. The two women worked out of her flat and the building manager turned a blind eye as long as he was looked after. Their kids would be shuffled between flats while the women worked.

'They sell these pictures to clients, though why someone would want a photograph of that is beyond me,' said the first, handing them back.

Turned out the newsagent-come-dungeon was paying protection to the Elephant Gang. It belonged to a Madame

Noir, and a visit was required to find out more about Mr Cottingham.

Nell and Charlie went to visit her in her dungeon, which was merely a black-painted basement with a pink sofa, long mirrors on every wall, and a series of doors leading off to other rooms. 'We take photographs on the premises, sell them to the client only. If they don't want them, they're destroyed,' explained Madame Noir. 'These will be the only copies. I'm not handing out names and addresses, you'll ruin me.'

'We only want to know what he's like. Is he violent? Free with his hands?'

'Lord no! Harmless, this one. He has a flat up West, he stays there during the week and goes home to his family at weekends, like so many. Sometimes he orders a girl to go over there.'

'We're going to need that address,' said Charlie.

The woman rolled her eyes again and sighed. She knew who they worked for, so saying 'no' wasn't really an option.

'He's quite timid. I don't have much to tell you – he seems quite dull.'

'Really?' asked Nell, happy with that little piece of information, as the crack of a whip followed by a man screaming penetrated the air, and they tried to maintain a particularly English trait of turning a blind eye to the bleeding obvious.

'He likes to punish girls and make them cry, but no homosexual stuff, which is rare. I wouldn't call him a sadist. He likes ticking the girls off, bland really. Oh, he does like a thumb up the bum on occasion—'

'Righto, thanks,' said Nell, clapping her hands. 'I think that'll be all. Won't it?' Looking to Charlie.

'I think so.'

'Oh, and his name here is King Broadsword. Not sure what that's about but we can all dream, can't we?'

Nell stifled a snigger and put the photographs in her bag. They'd done as much research as they could. Now came the second stage: execution.

Nell went to see Alice straight away at her house in Milverton Street.

'We get inside that flat and wait for King Broadsword,' said Alice.

'Do we not talk to him first? Tell him we have the photos?'

Alice rolled her eyes. 'Nell, we're women, you go in hard as you can early doors or you've lost your chance. You, me, Charlie and Lily – we get inside that flat and have a reception waiting for him.'

'What about us getting back on the rota?' Effie had been on remand for a while and the cell's reserves of cash were dwindling.

Ideally, Nell wanted to crack on, get Effie sorted, and pick up some rotas. That and get going on the hotel scam, although she still needed to sort out an agreeably secretive fence. Somehow, they would have to find a way to hoist on the rota like normal, and fit in the sporadic shifts at the Savoy, without Alice and Chrissie finding out. Nell was determined to make it all work.

'You are off rota until this is done,' she said, angrily stubbing out a cigarette into an ashtray.

Nell felt the blow of disappointment; she'd thought Alice might be happy at the information on the magistrate and let them back on rota, but clearly not. The date for Effie's case to go up in front of the magistrate was set for April. They had less than two weeks before Effie joined Lady Jay in Holloway.

It is a distinct advantage to be a lady housebreaker. The communal entrance of King Broadsword's Leicester Square apartment was easy to get in. Charlie waited until a man entered the building and slipped in behind him, and he apologised for not holding the door. Charlie let the others in, and they clipped along the empty marble hall, keeping a lookout while Charlie jimmied the lock to his flat with a metal file. Within minutes they were inside and rifling the apartment, but it was a fruitless affair. No chequebooks, mail, nothing – not even a pair of cufflinks. A few spare clothes and a shaving kit in the bathroom. He did have a bottle of whisky however, and they sat sipping from it to pass the time.

'I wonder if his wife knows about his flat?' said Charlie, the four women in spots about the bedroom. It was late Thursday and the day Mr Cottingham would be staying at his city flat, before going home on a Friday afternoon to his wholesome family. It was still daylight, but the windows didn't let much light in, so they sat in dusk.

'Probably says he's off to a gentleman's club. That's what they usually say, isn't it?' offered Lily.

'She probably doesn't care,' said Alice. 'Likely knows what he's up to and relieved he's bothering someone else.'

'I see him,' said Nell, watching from the window. Everyone sprang into position.

The door opened, closed, and footsteps made their way inside. The bedroom door handle twisted, the door opened, and a hand reached for the light switch. All four women leapt on the man as he came inside and pinned him up against the wall. Lily and Alice had him pincered. Nell drew breath and played her part. *Task in hand, girl! Don't think, just do.* She brought up her razor and pressed it to the skin of his throat. Her eyes fixed on his Adam's apple, rippling under the skin as he tried to swallow. Nell shut down any sympathies or weakness trying to manipulate her. Those mawkish feelings trained into her from birth only served others who wished to take advantage, and this was about helping Effie. Charlie smothered his attempts to scream by stuffing a scarf into his mouth as he retched. Mr Cottingham soon stopped struggling, terrified.

'Do you promise to be quiet?' said Alice. He nodded, and Charlie took the scarf out of his mouth.

The magistrate's desperate eyes leapt about. Nell didn't feel good about seeing anyone frightened like that, but it was a necessary evil to help her friends. It wasn't as if he was going to be physically harmed.

'Who are you?' he stuttered.

'You are going to help us,' said Alice.

'Madam, I don't know what you think I—'

'Shush,' said Alice, putting a finger to his moustached lips. 'You look the heroic type to me,' she continued. 'The type who likes to rescue damsels in distress, and we have a couple that need help.'

'I can't! I'm a magistrate! You—'

Alice slapped him about the face and shoved his head against the wall, hard.

'I'm not interested in pathetic excuses. It's your problem, fix it.'

'You could always try pulling yourself up by the bootstraps,' offered Charlie.

Alice continued. 'Effie Deets will be up next week and you are going to let her off with a fine. We will pay the fine – we're good like that – but she won't be going to prison.'

He began stuttering. 'But... what offence are we talking here? Any previous?'

'Larceny and yes,' said Alice.

'Then I can't!' he whined.

'Then there's not much point to you, is there?' said Nell, losing patience. She pressed the razor against his Adam's apple and felt his knees buckle. Effie was right: it was a strange experience seeing a person wilt under your power. *You must think like a man,* Effie had told her. This was what men did all the time.

'After you let Miss Deets off,' Alice carried on, 'we have a friend in Holloway. She's going to appeal and you're going to help get her sentence reduced. That'll do for now.'

Nell glanced at Alice whose eyes were fixed unblinking on this man, sheer intensity forcing him to submit to her. It was clear in this moment how strategic Alice was; she hadn't shared her ambition to push for Lady Jay to benefit as well as Effie. Nell felt herself swell with loyalty in the moment, stood beside a leader who was willing to get her hands dirty and fight for her tribe. No wonder the women were so loyal to Alice. Nell found herself pushing the razor a little harder into the enemy's skin. A little pressure never killed anyone, did it?

The man began to cry, jabbering and muttering that he didn't know how to make such things happen. His legs went and he started to slide down the wall. The four marched him to the bed where Charlie sat beside him and showed him the photographs. Mr Cottingham turned an ashen colour when he saw them.

'We'll be keeping these for insurance,' said Alice. 'If you don't do what we ask, first we'll send them to your wife and daughters, then to the police, and the newspapers. Do you understand?'

The man enthusiastically nodded. His whole face was wet with sweat. 'All right, all right,' he jabbered, nodding up and down. Trembling.

'Charlie?' prompted Alice.

Lily stuffed the rag back into his mouth and they pushed him face down on the bed as Charlie unbuckled his trousers. The man protested through the rag as Lily and Alice pinned his arms. He tried to kick, but Nell grabbed his ankles as Charlie dragged his trousers down and produced a Fisherman's Friend – her old mate.

'This is a little something to make sure you stay motivated,' said Alice.

Charlie jammed the mentholated tablet where the sun wouldn't ever shine.

King Broadsword or not, they hoped he liked fishing, because he'd be doing a fair bit after they'd gone.

When Effie had her day in court, she was led by the handcuffs in a terrible smock, looking slight, pale and young. Her eyes searched the benches, and when she saw them all she beamed. Alice glared as Nell signalled for her to look sad by rubbing her eyes.

Charlie sat as near to the magistrate as she could. The man desperately tried not to look at her as she smiled and winked at him. The flush in his cheeks was visible, and he fumbled through proceedings. The Forties' retained brief, Geoffrey Hardy, gave a theatrical defence of little Miss Deets as Effie tried her best to look depressed.

'Here we have a young woman, born to the worst of mothers: a common prostitute and incorrigible thief! Part of a marauding troop of wild godless women plaguing the city.'

Mr Hardy, operatic baritone with the nose of a committed drinker, took to his role with relish. Despite being in his late fifties, he had a good head of hair and a roguish twinkle in his eye. He was probably handsome before he dedicated himself to the bottle and became the preferred solicitor for London's underworld.

'As a child,' Mr Hardy went on, 'little Effie was born into a life of petty crime without godly instruction. For her mother's wicked influence, Effie became a mistress of wickedness, as Satan himself was forced upon her!'

Growing up, Effie had found God the Almighty, but after suffering the bitter blow of the loss of a marriage suitor, relapsed into melancholy. You get the drift.

'This unfortunate young lady possessed the mania for shoplifting once again, but I assure you, my good sir, she is suffering from a sickness, a malady. One for which there must be a cure, but it is not the harsh stone walls of a prison. For since God's grace, she has become a Christian, and a Christian couldn't possibly be a thief. It is a dreadful mistake.' A bit much but, by rights, the same ridiculous defences did get a better class of woman off.

Effie stood to speak – the most dangerous part of her defence.

'It is true – I do have the kleptomania, the thieving madness! I am repentant. I wish only to be a decent, ordinary citizen and contribute to society and devote myself to being a good wife and mother,' she said between gasping sobs.

'She does know she's not married and doesn't have kids, right?' Lily whispered to Nell. Luckily, Effie remembered this herself.

'I mean... One day! When I get married to a good Christian man.' Then she promptly burst into wailing with her face in her hands.

'Yes, yes, yes,' said the magistrate. 'Given the circumstances and the previous long spell between charges and Miss Deets's... awakening... we'll settle for the mandatory fine.' And the gavel went down.

It worked!

'Sir, this woman is a criminal. She ran from the police!' shouted the prosecution.

But the sentence was passed, and Effie was led away and stopped crying. Alice didn't give much away other than a wry smile. Nell was proud of her part in operations – the gamble had paid off.

DC Horace Bevan had been waiting to give evidence and stood up, outraged. He saw Nell in the gallery, and she couldn't help it – she blew a kiss at his face of thunder. It was a good day in court for the Forty Elephants, and for Alice, who already had more plans for their new friend.

Nell almost felt sorry for him, but... *what would a man do?*

Later that month, Lady Jay's sentence of two years found itself reduced to six months on appeal, a sympathetic review of her maladies of the mind. In exchange, she had to seek treatment, including wearing dresses and growing her hair. Not bloody likely, but it meant that she would be released on licence before Christmas 1923.

Emma cried when Nell told her – she even hugged Nell. But it meant that they only had a few months left to work at the Savoy.

CHAPTER THIRTY-SEVEN

THE FORTIES' ALLIANCE WITH THE WEST LONDON magistrate was already paying dividends. Alice had got herself arrested alongside Gert Sculley in Bon Marché for stealing hats and coats. She received two concurrent terms of twelve months and was sent to prison. Then, mysteriously, the whole case was quashed due to *mistakes in police evidence* and Alice was released. Unfortunately, there was no such luck for Gert Sculley, who received two concurrent nine-month sentences. Sacrifices had to be made in battle. Whatever happened between Alice and the magistrate after that, Nell and the others knew nothing of it.

Word came down that Alice had police on the payroll with information coming that they were to ramp-up efforts to stop the female scourge that was the Forty Elephants. Pressure was piled on the commissioner via loud criticism from powerful factions suffering sustained financial losses in the West End. The commissioner was preparing an official report on West End shoplifters.

It was a cause of shock and some curiosity among the

establishment that the most noteworthy gang was made up of women. Worse, it was embarrassing. Neither the police nor the Home Office were of the mindset to take female crime seriously, which suited the Forty Elephants fine. Old grey men didn't want to accept that there could even be such a thing as a *professional female criminal*. Such creatures could not possibly be female by definition, but moral degenerates: *monsters* and, of course, *prostitutes*. Whores trained by men. A Harley Street specialist believed there was a cell in the brain that controlled honesty, a defect that he believed could and should be solved by operating on the female brain.

This dismissive attitude wasn't new; it was how the Forties thrived. You wanted to think women idiots? Go ahead – makes life easier. But there was moral panic regarding the behaviour of young women since the war. Morals, decency, discipline, all on the decline. Why, one only had to flick through the papers to read all about it. These women had to be dealt with, before England had an epidemic of female degeneracy.

With Jay on a reduced sentence, Nell was keen to crack on with the Savoy, but Emma wanted to consider every single possible aspect, prepare every contingency. Rework plans over and over until exhaustion. They had many a heated debate in a dingy little club full of heroin addicts in Soho called the Pyramid. The other hotels they had discussed included Brown's in Mayfair, Claridge's, the Great Northern and the Grosvenor. Emma was pedantic, but her plans and attention to detail were worthy of an engineer. For a woman who professed not to be a criminal, she was pretty good at it. With Effie out and their plans ready, they were to start in May 1923.

Charlie had found a fence outside of the Forty Elephants happy enough to handle their goods to sell on in the black market. Funnily enough, his name, or the name he used, was Mr Black. He was an elegantly dressed Indian gentleman with an obsession with English aristocracy. All cravats, monocles and crushed-velvet smoking jackets. He ran an underground showroom hidden among market stalls selling exotic furniture and fabrics staffed by Indian ladies who did a good job of intimidating unwelcome visitors. A triple knock and a password gave entry, where Mr Black, his wife, and their young staff of girls would supervise shoppers as they perused stolen clothes, luggage, watches, jewellery, handbags, antiques – you name it. Good old Lady Diana Manners happened to be a reliable customer – the lady Charlie had purchased her first motor car from. It's a small world.

The plan was to complete the rota double speed, usually finishing around twoish, then change and get to the hotel for the afternoon when scheduled. It made sense, since the shops only opened during daytime, but a hotel was always open. It meant they were working long hours but double the takings. Everyone was game and knew it was only for a short while.

But while Effie tried to skip past her reckless behaviour the day of her arrest, Nell was unwilling to ignore what had happened that day. It was a question of trust. She could have got them both arrested and Nell deserved an explanation.

After the welcome reception, hugs and flowers from the cell at home, Nell immediately cornered Effie in her bedroom alone, much like a second trial.

'What the hell were you playing at?' asked Nell as she slammed the door behind her. Stood arms folded.

'What? Oh, you mean the tray. I don't know exactly, it was there.' Effie shrugged. 'It was too tempting not to grab.'

'Not good enough.'

'It's the truth!'

'Don't bullshit me, Effie. If you want in on the Savoy then I have to be able to trust you.'

'Trust me? How dare you!' Effie was enraged. 'Trust me! I could be tortured and I'd never say a word. This is everything to me. How could you not trust me? I thought we were sisters!'

'How do I know you won't get tempted again, hmmm? And mess it up for everyone. You almost got me arrested. Not to mention how worried I was about you! Cow!' With that, Nell shoved Effie, sending her back onto her bed. Effie seemed confused and then softened into a beaming grin.

'You worried about me? Aww! Nelly! I don't think anyone has ever worried about me ever.' Effie leapt up as if to cuddle Nell and came towards her like Frankenstein's monster, with outstretched arms. Nell flinched and turned away to avoid her forced affections.

'I'm not hugging you. You don't deserve it. Petrified I was, thinking of you rotting in a cell; hungry and cold. If you ever pull a stunt like that again, I will...'

'You'll what?' asked Effie, doe eyed, clearly touched by the sentimentality Nell had displayed.

'I'll get over whatever fear I had of being violent and I'll break your neck myself,' Nell spat through gritted teeth. 'Promise! On your life. You won't do that again.'

'All right. I promise. On my life. I'll stick to the plan and do as I'm told, but only because you care!' Effie grabbed a reluctant Nell around the waist and held her tight, as Nell struggled to peel her off.

'Get off me. I'm still cross with you,' said Nell. Effie's head stuck to her chest.

'I promise I'll play by the rules and be a good girl. Now hug me back.'

'No, you don't deserve affection,' said Nell. 'Not yet!'

Nell struggled to free herself from Effie's grasp. She was surprisingly strong given how damn skinny she was. They struggled and fought until Effie tipped her over onto the bed, and the stern reproach descended into a wrestling match. Effie straddled Nell on the bed and was trying to tickle her. Nell was steaming mad, which made the fight and Effie even more maddening because she didn't want to be tickled or laugh. Exhausted, Effie fell onto the bed next to Nell. They both lay, catching their breath.

'I mean it, Effie. Can I trust you?' asked Nell after a few seconds.

Effie rolled over to face Nell. 'Yes, scout's honour.'

'If you have a problem, please speak to me about it. Don't throw a temper tantrum and try and force your own way. Real friends don't do that.'

Effie nodded. The message seemed to land, but... only time would tell.

★

Charlie went into the Savoy first. She would enter in plain clothes carrying travelling bags and a small suitcase, after completing the rota earlier that day. Secreted into a housekeeping cupboard or laundry room by Emma, she changed into a maid's uniform. A large hotel will always suffer from a high turnover of staff – they practically burn through poor girls like coal – so an unfamiliar face was never rare. Once Charlie was underway, in went Effie under strict instructions to keep her mouth closed. She complied, for now, so there were a pair working the floors as housekeeping staff, with Emma feeding them keys and housekeeping schedules, watching the entrances and exits, observing guests. Emma directed Effie and Charlie through the military plan upstairs, relieving hotel safes and rooms of their contents, prioritising cash and jewellery.

Lily and Nell were patrons in the bars, restaurants and tearooms, only this time, they were French. Nell resumed her role as the Duchess – she wasn't really a Duchess, *bien sûr*, but it helped to think of herself that way. Lily was her companion. Nell's name was Marie-Louise Barbeau, and Lily's, Camille Auclair. Their backstory was that Nell had been recently engaged and was travelling with a friend before nuptials next year. Nell even taught Lil some French 'nothing' words, to fill the air. All so Nell didn't appear to be talking by herself to a mute, with Lily's contribution to Nell's prattling an assorted meringue of *Bahh, En fait. Bref! Du coup. Oh la la! Ouais. Grave! Bisous! Bisous!* Kissing each other on both cheeks before one went off to receive filled bags of plunder from upstairs.

Nell might attract a staff member's attention for a question that must be asked in French since her English was so clumsily bad. The question had to be enough to make the experience uncomfortable, but obvious enough to answer. For example, *C'est possible de réserver un taxi?* Or she might gently interrupt another guest and politely enquire, *Excusez-moi, où est la station de métro?* It was important to act *naturelle* and not sit watching everyone. As patrons in the bar, Lily and Nell, or Camille and Marie-Louise, would discreetly lift stoles, furs, purses, even entire handbags – down to lighters, gloves, hats, anything they could pick up and walk off with. It was opportunistic, much like hoisting in the stores, but with no shop walkers or police! Their real role, of course, was to be there for logistics; Charlie and Effie would pass filled bags to Lil or Nell, who would take them back down, often commandeering a bell boy who they would tip generously, creating a strange concoction of heart-stopping terror and ecstasy. At the entrance, they'd have the staff order them a taxi. The audacity! Proving once again, all you need to be a success in London is an icy little heart and big brass balls.

Then after six days, operations stopped, as planned. All went quiet. Things go missing at a big hotel all the time. As long as Charlie and Effie were out, and Emma was clean during searches, it was an efficient operation. The important thing was to not get greedy and lack the discipline to stop. That's why they watched Effie like a hawk. Nell's furnace was ablaze, all fired up and running like a good combustible engine. She was finally doing something she could be proud of, using brains, determination and confidence. Fortunes could change in a heartbeat; wasn't that exciting? A few weeks ago, Effie was banged up and the rest of them were running out of money, but with a bit of hard work and a pinch of audacity, they were taking more money than they'd ever made before!

Things were going so well during May, hotel jobs fitting in nicely with the Forties rota, that Nell was completely blindsided when a big change of tactic came down from Alice Diamond herself. They were to ditch hoisting in London, for the time being. They would be lifting out of town from now on. This was more than an operational glitch.

CHAPTER THIRTY-EIGHT

It was New Year's Eve at the 43 Club with only minutes to go until 1924. The ceiling was made up like a starlit night with navy-blue fabric like sails and hundreds of twinkling lights as stars. The war seemed long ago.

The price of freight was falling, bringing cheaper food and train fares. Finally, a chink of light that the prices would come down, although that depended on businesses playing along, which the government did absolutely nothing to encourage. Crowds gathered outside St Paul's Cathedral to ring in the new year, and to prove things had moved on, people now referred to homeless war veterans as, simply, tramps. *Long live the King!*

Nell swayed among the heaving crowd. The 43 was a monster's ball of the most preposterous associations. Starlets with opium habits, depressed aristocratic nymphomaniacs, gamblers, lords, gangsters and boxers – all counting down to a new dawn. For the first time in history, it would be rung in by wireless, and Kenneth Ellis would sing 'Auld Lang Syne' from the BBC with invisible wires sending his voice into every home, nightclub or pub with a radio. At midnight, when the streamers went off and the navy-blue sails came loose, balloons fell onto the crowd. The band started up and everyone was kissing as confetti covered them and balloons bounced from head to head. Except for Nell, who found herself very much alone and sober despite necking champagne all night.

Days earlier they'd said goodbye to Jay and Emma. In the end, despite their grand plan, they'd only hit two of the hotels on their list, much to Nell's frustration. Being sent out of town to hoist had slowed things down significantly, too. They had technically worked two jobs for months now, all without anyone in the Forty Elephants catching on. It should have been a cause for celebration: the plan had been a great success. While she understood this, conceptually, Nell was thirsty for more. However, the girls were tired and worn out, and wanted to celebrate and enjoy a slower pace, at least for a while. With Jay released on licence, the couple had skipped off from Southampton to the Port of Tangier in Morocco of all places. Nell was gutted. Despite their fractious relationship, the hotel skims had been such fun and running their own con had been more rewarding than she'd anticipated. Being in control, deciding how to set things up, and keeping all the profit in the cell had been more rewarding than simple hoisting. The hotel scam may have been over, for now, but Nell already knew she would take everything she had learned and think up another way of being master of her own destiny; the frustrating part was she didn't know how, yet. By comparison, simple hoisting in the department stores had begun to feel more like waiting on tables: transactional, front-line duty, and repetitive.

Nell had been at this life for only one year, but it already felt like a lifetime. She hated New Year's Eve and its forced reflection. It made her think of family, and she missed them – perhaps she was drunk after all. Nell sometimes imagined arguing with them. Wanting to rant and convince them how they were wrong, and to open their eyes to the true crimes going on.

Nell and Steph had exchanged Christmas cards of best wishes and brief messages about the family. The messages were bland, more from a lack of confidence in how to navigate uncharted seas for Nell, and determination from Steph to keep the lighthouse burning, if Nell should wish to find her way home.

But mostly Nell was angry. Angry at the war. Angry at her father for going to fight in it – for what!? Glory? Could one eat glory? Could one hold it in their hands!? Angry at her mother for accusing her of being a prostitute. Angry at Steph for having absolutely no sense of curiosity for anything of the world – how could she settle for so little when others had so much? She was angry at the old woman who had prompted her to quit the Grand and her repulsed expression when Nell had touched her arm. Angry at her schoolmistress. Angry at the police, the government, the King, everyone – even God. Nell fought her own war. The Forty Elephants, her regiment. Now she needed to channel this rage into a new venture, a bigger, better con. One that would get her enough money to leave all this risk and stress behind someday.

Lily found Nell and told her they had been invited to a private party at the Erskine club on Whitfield Street. The others had been mixing with the clientele of the 43: the young and horrifically wealthy who found flirting with pretty working-class girls a turn on, like slumming but with people. This dangerous fraternising particularly appealed to the *Bright Young Things*, as they termed them. These people liked hanging about, paying for drinks and sharing cocaine, fucking upon occasion, gleaning satisfaction that their parents would disapprove. Up the revolution and all that – all from the comfort of a chaise longue. Nell collected her coat and, with the others, hustled into taxis to make their way to the venue.

Once at the club, Lily was flirting, and Charlie was playing the soft heart that artistic young men seem to fall for. Nell and Effie sat sipping vodka martinis. Then, in walked a man with a confident stride. He instantly caught Nell's attention. The strong jawline and noble profile, the swagger of confidence as he strode in, and the smudged nose of a boxer. He stood out against all the effete whippets with their sunken artistic chests. Effie slouched with one elbow on the back of a sofa, naked feet up. She'd lost her shoes earlier in the evening and a gentleman had carried her from the taxi into the club. Effie prodded her with a long toe in the ribs, making Nell spill her martini.

'Tongue back in, Mackie.'

'Please! He's not even attractive.'

'Oh, I don't know. We've become used to the soft type who bleats about his feelings. I'll bet he doesn't mind shutting the fuck up and getting filthy.'

'You are the one who is filth.'

'It's called boredom. Oh, to be manhandled, if only for a night. Perhaps you should – the well has been dry since Johnny.'

'Men are only fun in the beginning. Then it's all snoring, mess and "*where's my trousers?*".'

'That's boys for you – but what about a man. A manly rogue?'

'What makes a man, Effie? Please share your wisdom.'

'I wouldn't know, I haven't met one. But… I do like the idea of a man who looks like he could chop wood with an axe and not die of a collapsed lung. Imagine what damage he could do to your negligée.'

'Sounds expensive.' Nell knocked back the rest of her drink, shuddered at the strength and put the glass on the table smeared with cocaine. The sentimentality of the time of year, lamenting the end of the hotel scam, along with too much cocaine and champagne made Nell feel restless, and in need of distraction.

'Your man has spotted you, by the way.'

'He's not looking at me,' said Nell, and she pushed her hair behind her ears, trying desperately not to look, only to lock eyes with the man at first glance. She even looked behind to see if he was looking at someone else. 'Christ, he really is staring, isn't he? How rude.'

Nell picked up her glass to take a sip, only to realise it was empty, and place it back down again. The man watched the clumsy affair, smirked and made strides towards them.

'Don't look now,' said Effie. 'He's coming!'

'No, he's not. Is he?'

He was. The man was abruptly upon them, holding a bottle of champagne, which he set down on the table.

'Ladies, if you don't mind my stating the obvious' – an unabashed drawl – 'you look like you could do with a drink.' Without invitation, he sat down beside Nell, forcing her to shuffle unceremoniously as Effie sniggered.

'Budge up,' he said, and Nell flashed an outraged glare at Effie.

'How do you do? Effie, and this is my friend Nell.' Effie leaned across, offering her hand. 'Now where does that accent come from?'

'Belfast,' he said. 'Peter Delaney. Northern Irish, Presbyterian, and from a long line of uptight military arseholes.' He took Effie's hand. Turning to Nell, he said, 'Do you warm up after a drink?' Effie laughed again.

'I'm sorry?' said Nell, affronted.

'Don't apologise, let me pour you one.' He grabbed their empty martini glasses and poured champagne straight from the bottle into them.

'I'll let you in on a secret,' said Effie, who'd shuffled up to make mischief. Nell found herself squeezed in the middle. Her hands clasped over knees like an unwelcome chaperone. The man's thighs pushing against hers. 'My friend Nell here is a little shy, but she has a nickname – *Machete Mack*.'

'Good God!' he said, regarding Nell, who sat awkwardly stiff and gave Effie furious side eye. 'Now how did you get a name like that?'

'I'm funny,' she said, deadpan. 'Surely it's obvious.' There she was – the Duchess. The haughty cold fish who surfaced whenever Nell felt vulnerable.

'Right, you two,' said Effie. 'I'm going to see what the latest opinions are on all things political, as if I give a shit, and powder my nose.' Effie slipped away, glancing back with an impish grin, and was received like Cleopatra by the children of the titled and wealthy. Those who she would happily use and exploit under the façade of being a terribly fun friend.

'Right, Machete Mack, what about you and me finish this bottle,' said Peter.

'I will allow you to call me Miss Mackridge, Mr Delaney, and I think it's safe to assume we're going to need more than one,' she said.

Nell would like to be able to say they spent the evening having a fascinating, soul-searching tête-à-tête. In truth, they finished the first bottle, then the second, and made their excuses while clutching a third. They didn't even make it out of the building. Mr Delaney paid the red-faced clerk in the cloakroom to piss off for half an hour, and together they disappeared among the coats. But at least Nell's dry spell was over.

CHAPTER THIRTY-NINE

NELL HADN'T EXPECTED ANYTHING OTHER THAN A brief affair with Peter; he was a welcome distraction. By sheer coincidence, he was staying at the Savoy. Nell had to laugh.

'I know it very well,' she said. When he asked how come she was so familiar, Nell replied, 'Oh, tea, lunch, dinner, the bar. Lots of interesting people.' It wasn't a lie.

The Forty Elephants were still running cross country, but on the upside, longer breaks in between jobs gave Nell more time to spend with Peter – when he was about, that was.

Then, after a blissful few weeks, Peter had to leave for work – something dull to do with imports. Nell didn't ask because she wasn't interested, and Peter didn't ask where her money came from either. She didn't expect to hear from him again, but then two weeks later, bold as brass and almost on Valentine's Day, he turned up on the doorstep. Not even a telegram – he simply turned up and expected to be entertained. Nell, by rights, should have played harder to get, but she couldn't be bothered. She grabbed her fur coat from the banister and slung it over a shoulder.

'You could have called, it's good manners. You're lucky I'm in. I'm a busy girl, you know.' She walked past him and straight into his car. She couldn't help herself. Peter was good looking, charming and attentive. And not short of a penny or two. He had a calm demeanour about him, soothing, like water. Nell couldn't believe a man like that could be interested in her.

This time Peter had a room at Brown's in Mayfair, a row of Georgian townhouses that had incidentally been on 'the list' Nell had drawn up with Emma. It was a perverse pleasure to stay there. Time spent with Peter was fun. It was the way Nell wanted relationships: intense desire and sensory pleasure. What was the point of pushing past the fever once it had broken? *To make his dinner? To wash his clothes?* Not bloody likely. And what else did she need him for? To be utterly under the spell of passion was the closest thing to the thrill of stealing. Peter was a useful form of medication in between jobs.

Peter travelled constantly, staying in different hotels, and hadn't had a permanent address since the war. In fact, Nell had no way of contacting him when he went away. He would call her from a hotel when he returned to London.

Nell concocted a story should Peter ask about her background. She was an upper-middle-class girl from Brighton living on Daddy's allowance and studying art – ceramics, as no one knew anything about ceramics.

One evening, Peter picked her up and took her for dinner

at the Savoy. By now, months had passed since the scams they'd played there, and Nell was dressed and made up entirely differently from the dowdy Marie-Louise Barbeau – certainly no spectacles. The couple sat at a table for two, and in between courses, a waiter topped up Nell's wine.

She felt eyes examining her, looked up and – *no!* It was one of the barmen from before, one who she had tipped often. He had recognised Nell and in that split second must have sensed that Nell recognised him too; the smallest glimmer had passed across her eyes.

'Miss Barbeau! Why, I haven't seen you here in months. How do you do?' he said, smiling broadly. Nell had to switch on at once.

'I'm sorry, and you are?' she said, leaning in with her coolest and most arrogant clipped tone. 'Do I know you?' It was dripping with the assumption that she couldn't possibly know someone like *him* – a waiter.

The waiter went beetroot with embarrassment. Nell turned to Peter, who was watching the exchange with a curious amusement, and so she laughed, further embarrassing the waiter. Peter reached for his drink as deflection.

'I'm sorry, madam, I do apologise. I thought you were someone else.'

'Yes, indeed.'

The waiter scuttled off.

The exchange was awkward and embarrassing. Made worse by Nell having to control her own temperature as it shot up, threatening to give herself away. She could tell it had piqued a curiosity in Peter.

'Who was that?' he asked.

'The waiter? The boy mistook me for someone else. I thought that was obvious.'

'No, I didn't mean him, I meant you. You became a different person. Where is that accent from?'

She'd been a bit too snappy, calling on the Duchess to give an air of authoritative dismissal to the situation. Nell didn't know what to say.

'Why don't we do a trade,' Peter said, leaning across the table. 'I'll tell you who I really am, if you do the same.'

Nell grew nervous; was he joking?

'All right,' and she leaned over to whisper. 'I'm really a French heiress on the run from an arranged marriage to a count with rotting teeth. I didn't want to upset my mother, so I faked my own death and ran off to London.' She would go with joking. 'And you?'

'Well then, I guess that makes me a British spy.'

They laughed it off, ignoring the incident entirely and, of course, the evening ended with sex.

The visit after that, in March, Peter turned up in Wimbledon village, in an inn overlooking the common. Once Nell appeared, the couple went straight to bed. Afterwards, Peter fixed drinks, as Nell lay on the bed.

'So, when are you going to tell me who you really are?'

'You go first,' Nell said.

'All right. I break into houses. I crack open safes and steal jewellery belonging to the obscenely rich.' He sipped his whisky without a hint of shame. 'And there you have it. Now you.'

Peter had been a beautiful diversion, but now he had become *interesting*. Nell dreaded to think about what that said about her. She drew breath to speak but lost herself in a hysterical fit of giggling until Peter found himself laughing along too.

'Why is that funny? It's the truth,' he protested.

'You told me you worked in imports.'

'I do! I export jewels from rich people's homes and import them into my possession. Also art, among other things... I've stolen millions over the years.'

'Why?' Nell said, becoming serious and reaching out for her drink. He passed the glass and poured himself another, buttocks out to Wimbledon Common.

'Why?' he asked, not comprehending.

'Why do you do it?' Nell leaned up on an elbow, drink in hand.

'Ah, you think I haven't thought about this, but I have. Because I don't *want* to do anything else. My singular purpose in life is to take some of the wealth the rich have stolen from the world and redistribute it, to me,' he said. 'Your turn now.'

Nell drew breath but there were so many answers she could have given. How open did she want to be with Peter, and was that a dangerous risk in itself? Once she'd answered truthfully, would she have handed this man a weapon by which to hurt her, more than if she kept her mouth shut. Was that worth the risk?

'I'm a wicked girl, Peter. I have no interest in husbands, or babies, or picnics on a bank holiday and singing "God Save the King" over sandwiches. I've been wicked since I could walk, my mother said. I found my tribe when I joined the Forty Elephants. We steal for a living, from department stores, boutiques, hotels even… I'm a thief.'

'I know,' he said, smirking. 'I knew the first time we met.'

Nell puffed and threw a pillow at him. It bounced off his arm.

'What a farce you've had me make of myself! You're such a bastard.'

'We seem well matched, though! Proves the theory there is someone for everyone, even the wicked.'

'Such a romantic!' Nell shrieked as Peter put down his glass and leapt on top of her on the bed, as if going in for a tackle.

'Don't! They'll send security!'

'Good! I need rescuing from a very bad man.'

Peter told Nell how he had struggled with school at Belfast Royal Academy and started breaking into mansions along Malone Road while in uniform. Caught at seventeen, he got six months at Crumlin Road, which is where his real education started. After release, he found he was rather good at climbing and picking locks. He prided himself on his ability to break into a building like a ghost and leave nothing disturbed.

'Preparation is everything,' said Peter. 'Even checking the weather forecast – I learned that after scaling a fifteen-storey in a storm. But finding out I'd let a two-hundred-thousand-pound necklace go for thirty grand to a shitty fence, that's when I knew I had to learn about stones.'

Peter declared he despised the rich and was adamant it wasn't jealousy, but disgust.

'Kings, queens, leaders, they're taught to be cruel. How else could they send their own to their deaths and neglect the innocent the way they do? It's the British way, Nell. Has been since William the Conqueror brought his mates over and said, here, have some land. And likely before that.'

'I'm not political,' said Nell.

'But you are, Nell. You can't not be political. The Forty Elephants, by the very nature of its existence, is political. I admire you girls – not sure about some of your more rapacious members, but I admire you for daring to exist.'

Nell had never thought of it that way. She couldn't help but recall how her mother would rant on about such subjects and how her and Steph would roll their eyes, uninterested in boring talk.

'Who decides our stations, huh?' her mother would ask, pointing a knife as she peeled potatoes, letting the peel fall into a bucket between her legs and throwing potatoes into another. '*Les intimidateurs…*'

'What bullies, *Maman*?'

'Scam artists, racketeers – all of them! Walking around with their silly titles. How do you think they got them? They attack, loot and massacre, and give themselves fancy titles. It is all made up, *n'est-ce pas? Nous sommes les idiots.*'

'What would you have us do, Mummy? Start a revolution?'

'Perhaps,' her mother would say, and peel a potato as if it were a scalp.

Nell banished the affectionate daydream of her mother to the past, where it belonged, and snapped back to the present with a shudder, to the hotel room in Wimbledon with Peter, already on his third whiskey.

'Teach me,' she said.

'Politics?'

'No, bloody idiot. Jewellery. I want to learn.'

Peter tilted his head like a dog regarding a statue, then broadened into a grin.

'Why not,' he said. 'They say it's good for couples to have shared hobbies.'

Nell was sure that a little spark was lit when Peter talked about jewellery and gemstones. This could be the start of an evolution – to something bigger.

CHAPTER FORTY

IT WAS PRACTICALLY IMPOSSIBLE TO SWITCH ON THE wireless in April of 1924 and not be bombarded with news about the British Empire Exhibition on every bulletin:

The exhibition of the British Empire is now open. Months, even years of preparation have gone into the event, which was opened by King George V and Queen Mary. To celebrate, a special set of commemorative stamps has been issued by the Post Office. Four new roads were built to relieve the congestion surrounding the stadium. The opening ceremony was attended by an estimated 150,000 people. More than fifty-eight countries will be exhibiting their nation's exports in celebration of the Empire. A five-shilling ticket will buy entry into the 220-acre ground where people can visit stalls from Australia, New Zealand, Canada, South Africa, India, Ceylon, Burma, The West Indies, Bermuda, Sierra Leone, Malta, Hong Kong, British Guiana and Newfoundland. The exhibition is no small inventory of what the Britain has to offer. Some of the more unusual exhibits include a life-sized model of the Prince of Wales moulded out of Canadian butter…

It was the news the Forty Elephants had been waiting for. No, not that a prince had been modelled out of butter, but that practically every policeman would be sent to police Wembley at the event of the century, and it was running for months!

The order came down from Queen Alice: hit the West End. No one needed asking twice.

The Forty Elephants rammed the department stores like a plague of lipsticked locusts. Harrods in Knightsbridge was heaving with tourists, and, at peak times, it made for light work. Part of the fun was being in such beautiful surroundings. The women's bathrooms in Selfridges were a delight: warm, golden and with the softest of tissue paper.

The first week, Nell played the soon-to-be married Duchess of Sussex, fiancée to an Englishman; Charlie, the meek lady in waiting, bending and scraping, following Nell around the departments. Lily and Effie would walk in ahead, and as Nell was perusing, they'd start gossiping, loud enough for the shop assistants to benefit.

'Good heavens! Is that…?' That would be Effie, because she couldn't be trusted to say the names right.

'Yes, I think it is… It's Lady Béatrice de Havilland.' Lily could pronounce them.

'Isn't she engaged to the Duke of Sussex?' And so on. As for the real Duke of Sussex – there wasn't one.

The almost disappointing part was it worked like a dream. People love all that, a bit of pomp and glamour.

You only have to lead them in the direction of what they wish were true; they do the rest themselves. Nell would be demanding, struggling with English on occasion.

'*Comment dit-on en anglais... des colliers?*'

She would have shop assistants running around like industrious ants. Diamond ring after ring taken out to try on, swapping the genuine and sticking on the underside of the counter, replacing with fakes. Remembering to bark at Charlie for some indeterminable slight. Effie and Lily would trail, scooping up rings stuck on the underside. Chin up, shoulders back, gloves on, unsmiling, no inflection.

Then, once that pretence had run its course, a change of wig, makeup and new characters. Lil, the studious bluestocking, bespectacled and earnest. You'd be surprised (or perhaps not) how many male shop assistants are bewitched by a pretty girl with glasses, especially when her blouse buttons threaten to give up the ghost any second. She'd drop a book and as the male shop assistant bent to pick it up for her, she would do the same. They would both grasp it at the same time and Lily would bring it into her chest. For a whisper of a moment his hand would caress her bosom. The brief proximity of the female breast seemed to have a crippling effect on both mind and body, freeing the others to fill their bloomers.

Charlie even dressed-up heavily pregnant one week. A large bump was particularly useful for furs. This trick involved a small balloon of water under a hollow bump made of papier mâché that she could hide goods in; she even snuck a clock in it once. When the time came, Charlie would pop the balloon under her coat and pretend her waters had broken. Innocent bystanders would help the poor woman into a cab to the nearest hospital, as the others cleaned the shop out. The first few weeks of the Exhibition was one long party – it was good to be back.

Nell was sat having tea by herself at the Savoy. She liked to go there as an ordinary patron and relive the days of the con. A well-groomed woman in her thirties walked in wearing a glorious silver fox fur. Like all addicts, Nell's eyes drifted towards the fur as the woman waved away the offer of the cloakroom. Instead, she carelessly slung it over the back of a chair as she sat down to join two other women. Like a seductress, the fur slipped onto the floor. A waiter scooped it up and informed the woman to whom it belonged, distracted by her friends, that he would hang it on the coat hooks by the exit. Nell watched it all play out as a little voice inside was daring her.

Nell looked about, then back at the fur. *Of course she wasn't going to take it.* After she had paid the cheque and left a generous tip, as was the custom, she strolled past the woman who the coat belonged to, up to the coat rack, found her old black fur and hesitated. Before she knew what she was doing she was emptying the pockets and grabbing the silver fur instead. Nell sauntered out, putting the silver fur on as she walked, and hopped straight into a cab. What did she do that for? Like an itch that needed scratching. She told herself she could stop if she wanted to. The desire for a quick thrill hadn't made her act. It had been a choice. An opportunity had presented itself, hadn't it?

On Waterloo Bridge, the cab stopped at traffic lights.

The door swung open and a man hopped in beside Nell, shutting the door behind him.

'Oi!' said the driver, turning around. He soon fell silent when he saw the badge.

'Fancy seeing you here,' said DC Horace Bevan.

'It's all right, driver, I get the feeling the officer is going my way,' said Nell. The lights turned green and cars behind tooted their horns as the driver pulled away.

'I never did tell you my middle name, did I?' said Horace.

'This fairyland you live in, assuming I entertain thoughts about you at all, is one you inhabit quite alone,' said Nell.

'Should I search you?' he asked.

'Go ahead. You'll embarrass yourself and the driver.'

'Perhaps I should take you to the station.'

'Have you not got somewhere to be? Friends? A girlfriend?'

'You'll never guess where I've been.'

Nell sighed.

'Scotland Yard. I was on my way back when I saw you in the taxi and thought, this must be fate. I'm here by divine intervention to let you know, we're coming for you, Nell. Lily, Effie, the other one whose name I can never remember, and of course the mighty Queen Alice. All of you – the Forty Elephants will need a graveyard of their own.'

'That's not very nice, is it, Horace? You've rehearsed that, haven't you? And I'd always thought of you as having manners.'

'The whole damn pack. I've seen photographs of Alice and Maggie at Scotland Yard. It's over. Game's up. Oh, and sorry to hear about your grubby little magistrate.'

'I don't know what you're on about.' Nell rolled her eyes.

'Alfred Cottingham, poor bloke jumped from his apartment building yesterday. Horrible what happens to a body when it lands on pavement from a great height. Like an explosion. Very sad.' Nell lost her guard. *Dead. The man was dead.*

Quickly pulling herself together, she turned to the window. She could not afford to show a slither of anything – even if a man had died vicariously by his connection to her.

'Alice had been working him for a while. Well, he can't help now, and one by one we'll find the rest of the bastards you've been bribing.'

'Do you enjoy this?' she said, unable to control her temper. 'Ambitious, aren't you? Scotland Yard! How impressive! You must be tantalisingly close to having another rank on your epaulet. I have appreciated your rapid rise from afar.'

'And me, yours.'

'Mine doesn't come with an impossible sense of self-righteousness, or a stupid uniform.'

'It will when you're inside, sweetheart. Get out while you can, Nell.'

'I can't.'

'Why?'

'Why are you telling me this? You know I'll tell Alice.'

'Because I like you.'

'You don't know me!'

'But I do. Not very well, admittedly, but over the years I feel like I've come to know you. I admire you in a way.'

'We're all equal in the eyes of the law, do you remember telling me that?'

'I do,' he said. 'I believe it too.'

'It's almost endearing. So, what's your middle name then?'

'I'll tell you mine if you tell me yours.'

'Sidonie.'

'Leviticus.'

It seemed a bizarre moment to lose herself in a fit of giggles, but Nell began slipping down the seat.

'I thought you'd like it,' he said. 'People in glass houses shouldn't throw bricks. Who calls a baby girl Sidney?'

'Sidonie – my mother is French. I'm surprised you didn't find that out.'

'Is that where you get that certain *je ne sais quoi* from? It's a pity. Another lifetime perhaps.'

'Stop flirting and get out of my cab. Go and arrest some real criminals. Ones that hurt people.' Although as soon as she said that, Nell thought of the magistrate falling to his death.

'Fair enough. But next time I see you, there's a strong possibility I'll be putting you in handcuffs.'

'You boys all have your fantasies.'

'Driver! Pull over. I'm getting out.' The cab stopped and Horace leapt out. 'Good luck,' he said.

'*Et vous – bon chance!*' said Nell, as the door slammed.

Now that she was alone in the cab she could release the air trapped in her lungs that she had been holding on to. She saw an image of a man tumbling from a tall building when she closed her eyes. A bird's eye, looking down as he descended, falling in a star shape, as if he had forgotten his parachute. Grey concrete buildings flying past as he fell towards the merciless filth of the hard streets of London. It was an image that would come back to her at the most random of moments.

CHAPTER FORTY-ONE

HORACE CERTAINLY WASN'T JOKING WHEN HE SAID THE police were coming for them. In May, Alice Diamond herself was arrested and given two concurrent sentences of six months. She'd been caught stealing a diamond ring left unattended as a couple shopped for engagement rings. Old habits die hard, and a little thrill to cope with the pressure of leading a thriving enterprise was likely all she was after, but even the best get caught sometimes. Now she would be out of business until November.

But it wasn't only Alice – women were being nicked all over. Four had been caught in Derby, two in Cheltenham, and during the West End bonanza, three were arrested in Oxford Street. Nell was sure the only reason her cell hadn't been hit was because they put so much effort into switching tricks and presenting themselves differently. As Peter had said, *preparation is everything*. But this wouldn't work forever.

Peter would still vanish and then reappear, leading to another weekend away in some hotel under aliases – only now he brought gemstones, and would have Nell guess which were real.

Nell lay naked in another hotel room as he placed a genuine sapphire in her belly button.

'You rarely see genuine stones with fake metal,' he said as he placed a diamond between her breasts. 'Nor the other way, and fake stones always look too good to be true. Diamonds, now a real diamond will have minor impurities, unless it is extremely rare and expensive.' But Peter was adamant there was no point learning how to spot a real stone if you didn't know how to offload it, profitably.

'You need to find buyers, Nell. A small private list, deal directly, negotiate your own prices. Stop getting ripped off by shitty fences.'

The Forties had always dictated the fences for stolen jewellery, often relatives or associates. Nell had long known they were being ripped off, but given the safety they provided and the rules, they didn't have a choice. Even Mr Black, their fence out of the syndicate, would never pay more than he had to. Fences were a safe option, but an inconvenient cost in the chain of supply that really made money out of others' fear of holding onto stolen wares. They took advantage of that fear and could easily be eradicated if one could reduce the risk, somehow.

'How on earth would I find my own buyers?' asked Nell.

'Easy, you socialise with them. Go where they go,' he said. 'Didn't we meet at the Erskine club? You and your friends seemed pally enough.'

'But I don't understand. Those people have the money to buy the normal way.'

'But where would the thrill be in that?'

'Why do they need a thrill? If I had such money, I'd... I don't know.'

'Nell, you really don't know the rich at all, do you? The things they will do to entertain themselves – anything. You have to pity them; they're so spoiled they can't fail, yet their lives are without meaning much of the time. They go slumming in nightclubs to *feel* something.'

Wealthy people, he explained – not rich people, but hideously rich people – resented spending their own money and always wanted more. They were practically schooled to believe they must win all of life's competitions.

It gave Nell something to think on. What if she could convince Charlie, Effie and Lily to sell the odd piece of high value to a private buyer? They could begin to build their own buyers, and if they got better and sourced high-price pieces, increase their profit. This felt like the beginning of something!

Nell needed something to occupy herself and focus on, especially after hearing about what happened to the magistrate. That and, with Alice inside, leadership wasn't exactly firm and even the other girls in her cell had observed that the newer, younger girls coming up were wild and uncontrollable. Nell and the girls of her age had been considered rebels, but these girls, the eighteen-year-olds, were out of control. They barely remembered the war, hadn't worked in any factories and didn't bear the scars of that generation – thankfully. But it made them loud and entitled. They wore their hair short enough to intentionally offend and skirts the same way. Everyone knew who they were, but they basked in the attention: not the brightest idea for a thief to operate successfully.

Peter showed her how to hold a stone up to the sun and see how glass reflected light, but a real gem bounced it in all directions. He gave her an eye scope and a bottle of aqua fortis, a liquid that dissolved all metal except for platinum and gold. Peter could even tell a real gem by holding it close to the skin.

'Glass will warm slowly, but a true rock? That stays ice cold,' he said. 'Like you, Nell, and like me – ice cold forever.'

Nell prayed he was right on that one.

Another place offensively wealthy people liked to gather were the auction houses of London. Bonhams was the oldest, and where Peter liked to hunt for prey.

The first time he took her to Bonhams to show her the roles, he told her, 'Pay attention to *who* is buying the next lot,' Peter whispered to Nell. 'That's why I want you here.'

'Oh? Why should I help you? I need to find my own buyers,' Nell teased.

'It'll be good experience for when we work together.'

'Oh, pray, when will this be?' she asked.

'Think, Nell. We would make a formidable team. What do you say we start in Monaco? Then travel the world, leaving a trail of empty hotel safes and increased insurance premiums.'

Nell stifled a giggle.

Peter may have been joking, but nevertheless, Nell couldn't stop herself daydreaming about some sort of big adventure. What if they did run away? It wasn't as if she could go on hoisting forever. They were bound to get caught eventually. But what of Effie? Nell had sworn never to leave her.

The auctioneer coughed to attract attention and announced the details of the next lot over a microphone to a hushed audience.

'The next piece is set with a brilliant-cut fancy yellow diamond weighing sixteen carats. With brilliant-cut diamonds of yellow tint, ring mount detachable. Can be worn as a pendant, if desired. Size 4¾. Bidding will start at two hundred thousand pounds.'

'Fucking hell!' gasped Nell, not realising the words had slipped out. Old dames tutted their disapproval while clutching inherited pearls, as Peter winced and shook his head.

'I'm sorry,' she whispered. 'Two hundred thousand – that's offensive and... fascinating!'

'I thought you'd like it here,' grinned Peter.

CHAPTER FORTY-TWO

EVEN FROM INSIDE HOLLOWAY, ALICE WAS STILL running things as best she could. Nell's lack of presence socially, due to Peter, had been noted.

'Strictly speaking, Alice is meant to approve of relationships – you knew this,' said Chrissie in the pub one sunny evening in June.

Nell had taken a few digs about not being around and thought it best to show her face in the same old places.

'This Irish fella, how are we meant to know he's not a grass?' asked Chrissie. Nell had to laugh.

'Trust me, Chrissie, he's got more to worry about in that department than me.'

'I don't want to be one to make a fuss, but it would be... helpful... to know you are still committed.'

'Committed?' *What did that mean?*

'Do you want to be in the Forty Elephants?' said Chrissie.

'Yes! Of course I do! What else is there, Chrissie? Don't say things like that.' Simply hearing that made Nell terrified. She couldn't get expelled, could she? What, for having a boyfriend? Nell fast realised she had walked straight into a little trap.

'Good, because there's a job I need you for – Effie too. It's a little thing helping Ma out.'

Ma being Kate Meyrick, the owner of the 43.

'What kind of job?' asked Nell.

'A minor thing.'

The 'minor thing' was a troublesome plain clothes officer from the Metropolitan police Kate needed on the books, but who had so far resisted. The Home Office was obsessed with bringing down the nightclub scene, and they were always being raided, with news of the raids blasted all over the newspapers, stoking fear. The police officer worked on the team that planned the raids but hadn't been turned yet. Ma wanted to manipulate him into a compromising position so he would tip them off about future raids.

Nell didn't know anything about any of that and didn't want to. She knew it was going to involve something *distasteful*. It seemed an obvious solution, to have Nell do the dirty work and, in the process, prove her loyalty.

The distasteful part was that Mr Plain Clothes preferred the less sophisticated woman. When they said woman, they meant *girl*.

Nell's only experience of jobs requiring manipulation started and stopped with the magistrate they'd blackmailed with the photographs. But that had been an exception – to get Effie out of prison. This was different. This was setting someone up, even if he was a pervert, and that meant someone had to be bait. Nell felt sick at the thought of being tasked with procuring a young girl for such a disgusting act. This was not what she'd signed up for. But she felt trapped. She did owe the Forties loyalty – they had given her everything! But she hadn't realised that it was to be at the expense of her having any opinion on how she demonstrated that loyalty.

Effie knew a desperate runaway when she saw one, like a sparrowhawk spotting a shrew in long grass. The girls would be awed by them in the same way Nell had been by Chrissie at the Grand. These girls wanted to be rescued – they wanted hope. That hope would be what they traded on like good little politicians, while delivering absolutely nothing. Nell couldn't get on board with it. There were no moral acrobatics she could run in her head that made this revolting prospect palatable.

Effie had found one little wisp, a recent arrival in Soho, and not the brightest. She had latched on to Effie in a dive of a nightclub where people took heroin and staggered about the dancefloor like the undead, mouths gaping. Effie had plucked the girl practically off the dancefloor and led her to where Nell stewed over a gin at the bar.

'How old are you?' Nell asked her.

'Seventeen.'

'What year were you born? Answer quickly.'

'All right, I'm fifteen.' The girl's shoulders slumped.

'That'll do,' said Effie, holding her cigarette up to shield her whispering to Nell. 'She looks thirteen. Perfect.'

The girl's name was Sarah Gold, unfortunate because that was the only golden thing about her. Not only was the girl plain with mousy hair, but she had a mysterious quality that made her easy to forget. She'd have made a great chambermaid like Emma, except for the fact that she wasn't switched on at all.

Sarah had been sent to borstal after having a baby by a demobbed soldier. The baby was adopted, and Sarah had run away to London to hide among the thousands of others like her. She assumed she would be caught eventually and sent back, but she was free for now. Poor Sarah Gold thought Effie and Nell might be her rescue.

'I can dance,' she would say between sips of brandy. 'I know all the latest steps. Do you think I could get a job as a dance girl in the clubs?' Neither one of them would break it to her that she didn't have the looks – besides, she might yet grow into some.

'We know the people that run all the clubs,' oiled Effie. 'If you do a favour for us, then perhaps we might be able to help you.'

'Really?'

Nell couldn't bring herself to embellish, instead providing cigarettes and alcohol, telling herself this was generosity. Mostly she felt nauseous and chain smoked herself to stem the queasy feeling in her stomach. It felt like a belly full of oil and grease, sluicing about, rising up in waves.

'We are very good friends with the lady that runs the 43. If you do this for us, I'm sure there'd be something for you,' Effie told Sarah.

'You're in the Forty Elephants, aren't you? The other girls said. How do you get in?'

'You have to be invited,' said Effie. 'There's training, and only the best are accepted.'

'You are so pretty; you both look like movie stars. How do you keep your eyeliner so straight? Mine smudges everywhere,' asked Sarah. *It was awful; the girl thought they were friends.*

'Do you like this? Here, have it.' Effie took her stole from her shoulders and handed it over like a tea towel. The girl looked as if all her Christmases had come at once. Nell recalled how Chrissie had handed her the pear-drop diamond from around her own neck and pressed money into her palm.

'Our friend, Charlie, used to work here doing what you do, rolling. She's in the Forty Elephants now, buys her own drinks, furs, diamonds… You never know what can happen in London. But, let me tell you, it's all about the friends you make. There is so much talent and so many pretty girls. It's the relationships that really make the difference between failure and success.'

Nell felt nauseous as she watched Effie spiel and Sarah lap it all up.

'Does anyone want another drink?' asked Nell. She didn't want much to do with it and couldn't believe Effie was so natural, given the role she was being asked to play.

A few weeks later, they had Sarah Gold in makeup, a new dress and with her hair dyed platinum. Somehow, she looked even younger, like a girl let loose on her mother's makeup with over-bouncy curls. Nell and Effie were to take Sarah to the 43 club and coach her on the target. They hid behind a black curtain against the wall and observed the plain clothes officer with Sarah. She was nervous, so they gave her cocaine for a boost.

The policeman, in his fifties, was a cocaine freak, overweight and brash. The private room had been set up with a hidden camera. The man wasn't appealing in the slightest, and Sarah was getting cold feet.

'You can't back out now,' said Effie.

'How do I know he won't arrest me?' asked Sarah – quite a reasonable question.

'Don't be stupid, he won't arrest you,' snapped Effie. 'Wait here with Nell. I'll be back.' Effie slipped out from behind the curtain where Nell and Sarah hid.

'Are you all right?' asked Nell. Sarah shrugged. She tried to keep her mouth shut, not care, be passive and let this plan take shape. But Nell was overwhelmed by a terrible sense of urgency to do something – anything! She couldn't hold her conscience back any longer.

'You don't have to do this,' Nell blurted out.

'Yes, I do. You told me I had to,' said Sarah, understandably confused.

'I know.' Nell grabbed Sarah's shoulders and had to stop herself from shaking her, fingernails digging into her skinny arms. 'But that's not true. No one can tell you to do anything. You get to choose.'

Sarah stared back blankly. 'Why are you saying this now?'

'Because... Look, let's say you had a friend. What would you tell them to do? If you cared for them and worried about what happened to them. Think of it that way.'

'I don't know,' she said, shrugging. 'It's not that easy.'

'Yes, it is. Think, Sarah.'

'I'd want a friend to tell me what to do. Because I don't know. You tell me what I should do.'

'I can't,' said Nell, on the cusp of tears. They didn't have long. Effie would be back any second.

'It's too late now. If I back out then I'll never get into the Forties, will I? You have to do things for people if you want them to like you.'

'What if I gave you money. You could buy a train ticket. Do you have any family that you—'

Effie ripped back the curtain they were hiding behind and glared at Nell. By the expression on Effie's face, she'd been there long enough to hear the gist of the conversation.

'Come on, Sarah. Now, remember you don't have to do a thing. Let him do it to you and it'll be over before you know it.' With that, Sarah Gold was ushered off, curls bouncing behind her. Stick legs in heels.

Nell couldn't watch. She buried her face in her hands and almost cried but wouldn't let herself. She felt disgusted with herself for agreeing to be part of this. Despite not feeling as if she had a choice.

After escorting Sarah to the policeman, Effie came back to Nell and grabbed her by the shoulder, pulling her backwards and forcing her hands away from her face.

'What the hell are you playing at?' she snapped.

'Effie, this is wrong! It's... Stealing is fine, and yes, I'm prepared to do questionable things to stay out of prison but this!? This isn't what I signed up for.'

'Oh please, that girl is no blushing virgin, don't be so holier than thou. We've all had to do our national service for the lads, Nell... And if you haven't, well, count yourself fucking lucky.'

'What's that mean?'

'What do you think it means? Why do you think I ran away at thirteen?'

Nell shook her head.

'My mother used to rent me out by the hour. I ran off with the first man with a bit of money who asked me. I knew exactly what I was doing, too. Better one pervert than, however many. And I got to keep the jewellery and clothes he bought me.'

Nell was horrified. She knew Effie had a bad relationship with her mother, who herself had been a hardened criminal, but had not been aware of such vile exploitation of her own daughter. She struggled to know what to say.

'I... I'm so sorry, Effie, that's shocking, and horrible...'

'Boo hoo! No one cares, Nell. I accepted the shitty hand I was dealt and played it for a better one. If you get something good, then you must be prepared to protect it. Toughen up. It's a big game! For someone to win, someone must lose. Make sure it's not you. And don't be so bloody pious. It doesn't suit you.' Effie stormed off, leaving Nell on her own, hiding behind a curtain.

Nell had to give it to the girl. Sarah had no chest and the hips of a boy, but when she stuck her thumb in her mouth, she knew exactly what she was doing. The private room was ready, and pictures never lie. Except when they do.

A month later, in July, Nell bumped into a hostess at the 43 and asked after Sarah Gold. She hadn't seen the girl since the set up.

'Oh, *her*,' the hostess said, her face falling. 'No one really knows for sure, she disappeared.'

'What?'

'I... I can't, I'm working. We can catch up later, perhaps,' said the hostess. The poor woman was carrying trays of drinks through crowds as Nell followed her like a debt collector.

'What happened? Please, tell me,' begged Nell. She had to know.

The least she could do was face the truth of what transpired with the girl, rather than turn a blind eye. The waitress handed out her drinks and took Nell to one side.

'All I heard is that Sarah didn't do so well with Ma and ended up at Murray's. But she wasn't a showgirl, she simply didn't have *it*, no matter how hard she tried, bless her. I heard she ended up back in Soho. A place called the Pyramid.'

'No!' The Pyramid was the den Emma and Nell had met in for fear of being seen. Nothing had improved – if anything it was now considered downright dangerous.

'I heard she ended up falling for the syringe in a big way. A syringe girl – she stumbled about, sharing the needle with whoever could be persuaded. It was her job. She got paid to get people hooked, and then they get them doing all sorts, horrible stuff. I heard a rumour she ended up overdosing, then disappeared.'

'Disappeared? How?'

'That's all I know. She went missing. The girls all gossip, and some of us started in Soho. They say that if a girl gets herself in a bad way like that, she'll be put out with the rubbish – chucked in the Thames.'

'That can't be true.'

'Can't it? No one really knows, do they? Maybe she went home.'

'She didn't have one,' said Nell.

'I've got to go.' The waitress touched Nell on the arm and left.

She found Effie snorting cocaine off a table, surrounded by men. She had to tell someone about Sarah.

'Who?' said Effie, wiping her powder-filled nostrils with the back of her hand.

Nell couldn't believe Effie didn't remember Sarah. People were laughing, enjoying the music and dancing, but Nell wasn't having fun anymore.

CHAPTER FORTY-THREE

NELL COULDN'T GET SARAH GOLD OUT OF HER HEAD. The girl was practically haunting her. What if she had run away or been caught and sent back to borstal? It was futile, as there was nothing Nell could do. As Effie said, everyone had to look out for themselves, *didn't they?* What Nell couldn't know was that it was the beginning of a terrible summer, a great unravelling.

Nell was at home alone when there was a knock on the door. It was a telegram, for her. She assumed it was from Peter, because it was about time he reappeared, so she stumbled into reading it with the front door open as the messenger sprinted off. She even thought it might cheer her up.

Until she started reading:

Dearest Eleanor

I am sorry to tell you this way that Dad died last night. Unexpected. So sorry.

We are heartbroken as he had been better
of late. Cannot understand. Doctor said
heart stopped in his sleep. V peaceful.
Wanted you to know at the earliest. Will
confirm funeral arrangements shortly - pls
come home. Steph.

No matter how many times she read those words she couldn't believe them. She stood with the front door open, birds singing and traffic passing. People going about as if nothing had happened at all and it seemed, *obscene*. It couldn't be true. It wasn't *fair*. Dad couldn't be dead. It wasn't... Surely there must be some kind of mistake?

Nothing would ever be the same again. Everything was spoiled. It had started with Sarah Gold and now, her father. Nell stood on the doorstep and screamed. How surreal that the world didn't have the decency to stop.

Nell telegrammed Steph telling her she would come and proposing a telephone call at the post office so they could speak. It was a quiet conversation filled with the buzzing of the telephone lines rather than chatter. It was as if they both had a lot to say but neither really knew how to articulate it. As if they should both have a bloody big row about whose fault everything was, but neither wanted to put the other through that. Instead, they muttered through details of the funeral service, which was to be held at St Leonard's. A Church of England service, as Dad was Protestant. Their mother, a Catholic. Nell knew the church – small and quaint, and very old. The cemetery was well-kept and full of tended graves with a war memorial.

When the day of the funeral came, Nell asked Bert from the Elephant Gang if he would drive her and dressed soberly in black, with a hat with netting across her face. She thought it might shield her from the curious gaze of gossips; she could only imagine what rumours bored old housewives had spread about what she got up to in London.

The church was set back in a horseshoe with a single-track road up to the entrance. Nell had Bert stop at the top of the horseshoe. The cemetery was covered by trees with a big bending weeping willow. In the middle of the graveyard was a small, huddled mass of people in black.

Bert sat in the driver's seat with Nell in the back, flowers on her lap. Dad had loved walks in the country and meadow flowers, so she'd spent liberally on a bouquet of blue, white and purple. Delicate flowers with rustic foliage and moss, nothing garish or ostentatious or overtly sombre and plain. Natural wildflowers you'd find in a woodland or near rivers – the sort of beauty he admired. Nell lost herself staring at her lap until Bert turned around.

'Mackie?'

'Huh? Oh, yes, Bert. I'm nearly ready. Shan't be a moment longer.'

'No rush,' said Bert. 'We can sit here as long as you like. It's only, I wouldn't want you to miss the service, and didn't you say two o'clock? It's two now. Dead on. Oops, sorry.'

For good measure Bert showed her his pocket watch. He was very proud of it, bought off a fence for a good price. He turned back and they sat in silence for a few more minutes.

'Bert? I can't do it,' Nell said, eventually.

'Can't what?' he said, turning in his seat again.

'I can't walk over there. They'll all look. They don't want me there.' She was thankful for the net veil as tears spilled out against her consent.

'Course they do! Why would your sister be telling you and all that? They must want you there.'

'Not my mother. There'll be relatives and friends, and neighbours. They'll all stare at me thinking I'm a whore. That's what my mother thought I was, you know. Last time I spoke to her, she threw me out. What if my dad thought that too? It wasn't as if I could say, "don't worry, I'm not a whore, I'm a thief…"'

Nell couldn't hold it back anymore, now came the ugly sobbing. Bert looked suitably petrified and offered Nell his pocket kerchief. She blew her nose into it like a bugle and tried to give it back. Bert shook his head; Nell could keep it.

'Families, huh, Mackie. They're all lunatics.' Bert sighed. 'Why don't we sit here while you have a think. As I said, no rush.' Bert turned back to the front. 'Lovely church though. Looks nice round here, bit quiet, like…'

But Nell had started sobbing and couldn't stop – gasping sobs and blowing her nose several times.

'I think you might have spoiled your makeup, Nell,' offered Bert.

'I'm so sorry to drag you all the way down here.'

'No! Don't be silly. It's what mates do, ain't it? Who gives a shit what other people think anyway. It's your dad. No one else's – well, aside from your sister, but you know what I mean. I'll come with you if you want, then they'll be talking about my ugly arse. What do you say?'

'Thank you, but I think I should go home.'

'What about the flowers?'

'Bugger the flowers... Bert. Can we go? Now. Please?'

'Course we can,' sighed Bert. 'And don't worry about it. Sometimes it's nice to drive.'

The truth was, Nell was worried what someone might do to her flowers should she put them down. Would someone take offence and tear them up? Or throw them with the rubbish? She couldn't bear the thought, and they belonged to her dad. Nell figured his spirit, if they really did exist, would be as much a part of the flowers as he was trapped inside a body in the ground, so she kept them.

Bert pulled away, careful on the gas so as not to make too much noise and disturb the huddled mourners. They passed backs covered in black and she sat up to see if she recognised who was there. A pale face broke uniform and looked up at the car – flashing against dark-clothed bodies like a white flag. Eyes fixed as they passed in the car, like a portrait as one moves about a room. It was Steph. Knowing her sister had likely seen her passing and Nell had been too cowardly to face them was like a knife between the ribs she'd stuck there herself.

Back at home Nell couldn't break out of grief. She took herself to bed and barely said a word for three days. She didn't work and no one asked her to. The others in her cell crept around outside her room. She heard them whispering about her on occasion, like a mad aunt. On the fourth day, Nell emerged, and they gathered in the kitchen, where they held all their meetings.

'I think we should have a break,' said Lily.

'What, like a holiday?' Effie said, perking up.

'Yes,' said Lily. 'We have a holiday and come back and take stock of things in September. Nell can get some rest, and we could all do with a break. I mean, when was the last time anyone had one? I'll straighten it out with Chrissie. She has enough going on with the young girls fighting over rotas and districts with each other, and doing odd jobs with their own fellas – they make us look docile.'

'Or better liars,' chipped in Effie.

'Where would we go?' asked Charlie.

'Oh, I'll make myself disappear,' said Effie. 'I have that writer friend with a boat... yacht... thing that floats... whatever. He's been asking me to join him. I'll do that.'

'I have a cousin with a café in Plymouth. I'll go and visit her,' said Lily.

'Then I might go on a cruise in the Mediterranean or something,' said Charlie. 'They advertise in the papers all the time; tickets are very reasonable.'

'Nell, what about you?' asked Lily.

'I'll wait for Peter,' offered Nell, wan and exhausted.

'How long will he be? I don't like the idea of leaving you on your own, not like this,' said Lily.

'Like what?' said Nell. She sat in a dressing gown with her feet up on the chair, like a child. Arms around her knees. Hair a mess.

'Like you're going to lie down and let moss grow over you,' said Effie, sensitive as ever.

Charlie cringed as Lil shook her head.

'What?' said Effie, oblivious. 'I'm trying to shake her out of this... despair. You girls can pussy foot around, but she hasn't even been washing – look at her! She looks like she has tuberculosis! Nell, don't wait for Peter. Who knows where he is. You have three choices: yacht with me, cruise with Charlie or Plymouth with Lil. I can't believe that's a choice, but there it is… and if you choose Plymouth, we know you need urgent medical help.'

'I'll wait for Peter. I'll be fine. He makes me happy. I promise to pick myself back up. It's not as if I can have him seeing me like this, is it?' said Nell.

No one was really happy with the arrangement, and it would be the first time in two years the women would be apart.

'I suppose that's settled then,' said Lily.

CHAPTER FORTY-FOUR

T HE OTHERS PACKED THEIR BAGS AND STAMPED DOWN
the stairs dragging suitcases, waving goodbye and
disappearing into taxis one by one, off on their holidays.
Until Nell was alone in the house. It was eerily silent. No
laughter, no bickering, no heavy footsteps running up and
down the stairs. No one accusing anyone of taking anything
from their room or smoking the last cigarette. Nell haunted
the house, occasionally joined by the ghost of Sarah Gold.
Nell waited for Peter. And waited.

But after two weeks of that, he still hadn't turned up. All
Nell was consumed with was where he had got to. What had
happened to Sarah Gold? And Steph's face as she drove away
from their dad's funeral came in intermittent stabs. Fear
flooded through her chest at the thoughts she tortured herself
with. What if Peter had got himself arrested in some far-flung
city, interred into a tortuously close town? Nell would have
no way of knowing. *Where the hell could he be?*

If he'd been arrested, surely he'd have got a message to
her by a solicitor or friend, *something*. What if he had grown

bored of her? She went over and over the last conversations they'd had, but could find no evidence to support this theory. But it made sense: Nell was dull, ordinary, working-class stock. What would someone as handsome and charming as Peter want with her?

The fear of this imagined rejection at least forced her into action. At a loss of what else to do, Nell put on makeup, dressed and took herself to the Café de Paris, Peter's favourite nightclub. It might be socially unexpected for a woman to take herself out, but Nell had enough balls and acquaintances to know she'd not suffer without company, and she had a clear objective.

The Café de Paris was a glittering venue with a dancefloor and restaurant. The Prince of Wales could be found there several times a week. This was why Peter went: to hunt, seeking out the next generation of gullible, gilded youth. He would oil his way into their social sphere, like a vulture will lurk, waiting for their next meal to present itself.

Nell thought she might stumble upon Peter with a woman much prettier. *A wealthy educated and charming girl.* One who lit up a fucking room with a smile, wanted marriage and babies and cooked without getting bored. Who had prospects that didn't involve grand larceny. Nell went out braced for impact, lining her stomach with champagne for what she was sure would feel like a bayonetting. They say things come in threes. After Sarah and her dad, Peter dumping her would be the third. *Hurry up and get on with it!*

Only she didn't find Peter. Nell even bumped into Percival Mills, an Oxford graduate who worked in shipping and a casual acquaintance. He had asked if Peter was with her, and he was the sole person to whom she let the mask slip, confessing she didn't know where Peter was. Percival looked as if he'd regretted asking. Nell realised she'd embarrassed herself and went home.

Next, Nell went to Bonhams, knowing Peter could never stay away from the dazzling drama of gavel-wielders and the buzz of the auction room. But nothing, not a peep.

Desperate, Nell found herself loitering in the foyer near the cloakroom, hoping to spot him wandering through between the auctions rooms. There she witnessed a rude little man shouting at the poor girl in the cloakroom who wasn't working fast enough for his liking. Nell wandered closer; the man continued to bellow. *Useless. Worthless. Utterly incompetent. Pathetic.* The girl continued to work, seemingly oblivious to the man's abuse, but Nell knew exactly how that girl felt. You could see the slight rise and fall in her chest. Her eyes cast down to avoid the ones belonging to everyone else. She had the flat face of someone desperately trying to keep it all in while under intense scrutiny. Knowing any small glimmer of her emotions would be held against her. A queue of people stood waiting, concerned with their own coats, as the little man who thought a lot of himself carried on declaring how awful she was. Finally, the man got his coat, but he still continued the diatribe.

'Do you know how often I come here? How much money I spend? By rights, I could have you fired. You're lucky, I don't have the time. Thanks to you!' The man snatched his coat and stomped off.

As the queue dwindled, Nell hovered. It reminded her of how some had treated her as a waitress. Dismissing her or ordering her about as if she were barely human. Some people enjoy lording it over another person as if it proved them a better one.

When the last had retrieved their coat and the girl was alone, Nell approached the desk and could see the girl was drained. Nell practically saw a mirror image of herself two years before. Except now she felt as if she had lived enough to be the girl's bloody mother.

'Don't you worry about silly old sods like that,' said Nell.

'Oh.' The girl expelled a deflating breath. 'You'd think I'd be used to it by now.' She gave an exhausted smile, attempting to make light of it.

'I used to be a waitress. Best to stay angry or else you might end up believing what they say. He's likely a miserable, unhappy person whose only joy in life is making others feel lousy.'

The girl really did grin now. 'Thank you. That man in particular is a nasty one. Mr Paul Wallace. He's always in here, but everyone hates him. He's always barking at the staff. Lord knows where his money comes from. Apparently he's a retired director, something to do with property. They say he lives on his own like a grumpy old hermit in a rickety cottage in Hampshire. But he thinks he's an expert antiques dealer. Has a shop in Wickham, and comes up here all the time thinking he's lord of the manor. We all groan when we see him – even the auctioneers!'

'Well, ignore him, try not to let it get to you.'

'I don't know why rich people have to be so... mean. Always pushing people around.'

'It's not only rich people, trust me,' said Nell.

★

The week after, Nell went to Bonhams again. Still no sign of Peter. It had been more than a month and no word. No telephone call or telegram. He would never stay away from the auction houses for this long, surely?

Nell had sat through hours of bidding – African art, sporting guns, even armour. It all blended into one long torturous mirage of desperately wondering where Peter was, and why he was doing this to her. Sat in a thronging auction room, she would look about for him.

The auctioneer began to blather on about stamps – not in the least bit interesting, but the room pitched itself forward at the mention of a particular kind.

'...*regarded by many philatelists as the rarest of stamps. Issued in limited numbers in British Guiana in 1856, and only one specimen is now known...*'

Quite frankly, who cared? Except when the bidding started, it began a frenzy, and Nell was astounded when the funny-shaped red stamp finally went for ten thousand pounds.

How amusing, but also sickening, to sense the palpable excitement in the room over a single piddly little stamp.

But Nell had to laugh when she saw the buyer was none other than the rude little man from the cloakroom. The supposed antiques dealer, Mr P. Wallace, looking very pleased with himself. *Honestly, the shit people with money will buy.* Something about it chimed with Nell. She kept thinking on it. She wasn't sure why exactly, but Mr Wallace kept intruding into her eyeline, irritatingly, as she was hunting for Peter. But it felt as if there was some significance to it. Nell had felt this before – when Jay had mentioned a certain chambermaid.

CHAPTER FORTY-FIVE

BY AUGUST, NELL HAD GIVEN UP ON BONHAMS AND the Café de Paris. Now she wandered about the house, waiting for someone to put her out of her misery. The phone rang, and Nell leapt on it.

'Why are you still there?' asked Lil. 'Has Peter not come back?'

'No, I'm worried, Lily. What if something has happened?'

'Nell, by rights, if and when he does turn up, you should be steaming.'

'What if he's been arrested?'

'Come to Plymouth, it'll be good for you. If he doesn't turn up in the next week, promise you will come. You shouldn't be alone.'

'I'll think about it.'

The day after, Nell received another telephone call. This time it had to be Peter, but when she answered it was Percival Mills.

'Nelly, my dear, have you seen the newspapers today?'

'No, why?'

'I think our dear friend Peter may be found.'

'Thank God! Where is he?' Expecting to hear how he had been arrested and languished in a cell somewhere.

'It could be my mistake, I don't know. I could be wrong...'

'What is it? Tell me!'

'Are you with friends? It's only there's this piece in that rag, *Reynolds's*, page eight or nine. Call me when you've seen it.' Then Percival hung up.

Nell dashed out to the newsagent, bought a copy of *Reynolds's* and began tearing through the pages. On page nine her heart stopped.

There was an article on the mystery of a man's body having been found stuck up a chimney. The maid only discovered the body by the terrible odour coming from the flue when cleaning the grates. When she looked up, she saw it was blocked and poked about, expecting a dead pigeon to fall out; instead, out dropped a singed shoe onto the hearth.

It had taken four firemen to retrieve the body of a man, who they estimated was in his thirties and could have been stuck for up to a month in the chimney at Barnwell Manor in Northamptonshire. The police believe the man became trapped while hiding after being disturbed during a robbery, as he had jewellery on his person from the house. The fire had been lit a few times, until a smell had been complained of. Police believed he'd died of smoke inhalation. His identity had taken some time to establish, but photographs and particulars of the body had been shared all over the country. Police were fairly confident the man's name was Vincent McNeilly: thief, robber and confidence man from Belfast, Northern Ireland.

Catholic borstal boy McNeilly was born into a criminal family. McNeilly had graduated after numerous prison terms to the illegal theft and trade of gemstones. A fantasist and trickster, he had relieved a string of young women of family heirlooms and money. He had many aliases, including Peter Johnson, Peter Delaney, John Penfold and Stephen Penners. Police had been initially alerted that the body could be that of the career criminal after several women reported him as missing. A serial philanderer, McNeilly leaves behind a wife in Belfast and one son, and at least three fiancées in England.

Purgatory had ended abruptly, and Nell had been sent falling through a trapdoor to hell.

There was a photograph of Peter with one of his fiancées, wearing a fucking army uniform he had no right to wear. There was no denying it was him.

Nell was simply broken. Punishment rained down in the form of merciless blows: Sarah Gold, her father, now Peter. Nell never returned Percival's call, despite the phone ringing repeatedly.

Nell had thought herself better than this. She was too clever to be treated like a fool. Peter had lied and she didn't even get the chance to scream at him. What had she done to deserve this? Nell knew she was wicked, but there was only one deed she felt hideous shame over – her name was Sarah Gold. If the girl really had been dumped in the Thames, then she deserved this. *That would be fair.*

★

Nell took herself to the Pyramid in Soho, down dark stairs into a dingy basement in Endell Street. It was too dark to see properly, but it was dirty, run-down and stank like a blocked lavvie. Full of soldiers on leave and men with no money and insatiable appetites, fuelled by anger.

The Pyramid had had a makeover since she'd been last there with Emma. The Egyptian fashion had passed and so it seemed the Pyramid had been taking the cast-off props from a better class of club and theatres. The makeshift stage was a wooden platform painted black and they had acquired a Golden Buddha, big enough for girls to sit on and rub his belly. The girls painted gold shimmered with glitter, draping themselves over the misshapen plaster statue. There was a vague attempt at a theme, but when a teenage boy walked by with what looked like a badly made Tutankhamun's death mask, she realised she was overthinking things. Nell took a seat and ordered a gin, looking out for Sarah Gold. If she could find Sarah, there was still a way she could redeem herself in her own mind.

'My mummy told me pills can't make you feel better. It's a trick they play to get children to take pills they don't need,' said a girl who had made her way beside Nell. She had the crooked eyes of the drugged or disturbed. 'But it's better than nothing, don't you think? My name's Sally.' Sally unfolded her hand to reveal a little pill. Nell refused.

'Do you know a girl called Sarah Gold?' she asked, but Sally shook her head.

There were so many girls – all made up, painted gold and in costumes – it was difficult to see if any of them were Sarah. Hours passed, but more people kept coming in, which meant there was still a chance of finding Sarah. Nell drank one after the other until the early hours. It came to the point where one drink made her feel better, the next, worse. On the other side of Nell sat an old man with long silver hair sucking on a hookah, which he offered, uninvited, to Nell. She had smoked them before and assumed it was tobacco.

'Give it a try,' he said, so she did. It wasn't as if she could feel worse.

The smoke stung her eyes, so she closed them, and the next time she opened them there was Alice, ten feet tall, looming over her. Nell woke herself up, startled. There was no Alice; she must have been dreaming. Nell tried to stand but stumbled. The man with the silver hair helped to lower her back into her seat.

'Whoa, you nearly took a tumble. Not to worry, I'll look after you.' He clicked his fingers and the girl called Sally appeared.

'Can I get you a drink?' the girl asked, but Nell had lost her purse.

'My bag, it's gone.'

'Don't worry,' said the girl.

When Nell eyed the girl, it was as if her face morphed into that of Sarah Gold's. And she was painted gold, like the dancers. On stage were two bare-chested women in trousers and braces with slicked short black hair dancing to a Spanish guitar. Sarah Gold stroked Nell on the arm, and held in her hands a silver syringe.

'Do you want to know what bliss feels like?' said Sarah. But it wasn't Sarah Gold, it was the other girl, Sally, who took hold of her arm as the Spanish guitar reached a frenzied crescendo.

'They're from Seville,' said the dope girl with the syringe.

'Why come here?' Nell asked.

'Why do any of us come here?'

'Where's Sarah gone?' said Nell. The dope girl was tying a strip of rubber around Nell's arm.

'I don't want to do that,' said Nell, yanking her arm free and tearing off the tourniquet. 'I want to go home. Where the fuck is my bag!'

Nell stood, but her legs wouldn't stay upright. She tumbled over and stopped herself with her hands on the table, knocking glasses onto the floor. Sally tried to calm her as sullen men in dark corners turned their gaze to the sound of smashing glass.

'Sit down, you need a drink,' said the girl, cajoling Nell.

'I… I need to go.'

'Please, sit down.' The girl yanked her with such force she fell back into the chair.

'Nell? Nell! Thank God I've found you.' A slip of a gentleman glided towards her.

'Jay!' said Nell, jubilant to see a friendly face, 'Why are you here?'

'I came back to visit my mother. But Nell, Lily has been calling the house. Effie is back too. She answered one of Lily's calls and went looking for you at the pub, and bumped into me. She said you'd gone missing! Everyone is worried! Effie and I have been looking for you. What were you thinking?' Jay turned to the syringe girl. 'And you can take that shit and fuck off.'

The girl sloped away as Jay hoisted Nell up, one arm over a shoulder. Then Nell felt someone grab the other arm.

'I've done this before,' said Effie.

'Effie! It's you!' said Nell, slurring her words. Both Jay

and Effie were coming in and out of focus. Either her head had got terribly heavy, or her neck weaker and unable to keep it steady.

'Yes, it is, and you'll never guess what? Turns out I hate sailing. Just as well, isn't it? Because you can't be left alone for five minutes. Come on, Jay. Let's get her out of this dive.'

'The dancers are from Seville,' said Nell.

'That's nice,' said Jay.

Nell had left the newspapers all over the table in the kitchen, and Effie had seen the photograph of Peter, or Vincent, or whatever his name was.

'Why didn't you answer the telephone?' Effie asked the next morning.

'I felt stupid.'

'We've seen you look stupid a thousand times.' Then she looked at the newspapers. 'Peter is gone, I see.'

'Vincent, you mean. I'm such an idiot, Effie. I swallowed it all.' Nell was huddled under a blanket on a chair with tear-filled eyes. 'Things keep going wrong, Effie. All that business with Sarah Gold was rotten. I joined the Forty Elephants to escape poor girls like us being bullied and used. Then with Dad dying. And I missed his funeral. I thought he would live forever, I suppose. How ridiculous is that? He's been ill for years. Why didn't I realise? Then Peter, did he even like me? Was it all an act? Urgh, I'm so stupid.' Nell buried her head in her hands. 'I don't know what to do.'

'Stop that, at once,' shouted Effie. 'Don't you know who you are? Yes, you've had a rough time of late and some of it's been... unseemly. But what did you expect? You think

Alice got to be queen by giving out lollipops and being nice to people? Right, this won't do. Bottle it up, sweep it under the carpet, whatever you must do. But don't you dare shed any more tears over a... *boyfriend*. You're in the Forty Elephants for fuck's sake! And clearly in need of diamonds.'

Nell wiped her eyes and tried to smile. 'Or stamps.'

'What?' Effie looked at Nell as if she'd spoken gibberish.

'Nothing, it's a joke.'

'Hmmm. The sooner we get you back to work, the better,' Effie huffed.

The flame inside Nell was barely flickering, but for some reason she could not let it die. Exhausted and battered about, she still wanted to make something of herself. She felt as if she'd come so far, yet ended up back to feeling worthless. She should have taken respite by the sea like a melancholy Victorian, but alas, there is no rest for the wicked.

Having missed her dad's funeral, she really couldn't disappoint anyone any more than she already had. The truth hurt. It had upset her to see how her father suffered after the war. It was too painful; it was better to be angry. But Nell had learned a lot. She had thought herself brave, but was too cowardly to go home. She had thought she was tough, and yet when Nell thought about Sarah, she was racked with guilt – a useless sentiment if ever there was one. Nell was far too clever to be swindled, but Peter had her skipping along in a fantasy like a gullible spinster. How utterly humiliating.

Nell had wanted to be special, but she was the same as every working-class girl in England. The only talent she had was to have no scruples to get what she wanted. Nell had behaved in the same spoiled, entitled way as the rich and wealthy. They were all as bad as each other. But such lessons allowed her to, as John might say, *take the carrot out of her arse*. It's all about tribes. Teams and clubs people sign up to. They pay the subscription, wear the uniform and do what they're fucking well told. To make money, to belong – to be powerful! To feel *worthy*.

Perhaps the trap was not around her after all, nor imagined. Perhaps Nell's trap was inescapable by nature of *what* she was – an ordinary girl. The curse was not put upon her, but of her own making. Nell's creator must have made a mistake by infecting her mind with the desire for more than the world determined she could have. But Nell wasn't done yet. There was more that could be done; it must be in a different direction, that's all. And she already had a spark of an idea.

CHAPTER FORTY-SIX

BEFORE HE'D GONE MISSING, PETER HAD GIVEN NELL another contact outside of the Forties syndicate of fences, with the intention of sourcing her own buyers, the same as Peter, but she hadn't bothered with it. Nell made a telephone call to explain how one Peter Delaney had passed the details on, and it opened the door to a meeting.

Lady Amelia Lawrence was married to a Scottish lord but estranged and living in London. French and Spanish by background, she invited Nell for a meeting to her apartment overlooking Regent's Park. The woman certainly seemed the part. She lived in a white stucco-fronted building; soot was being scrubbed off by workers with brushes as Nell arrived. The apartment had high windows and ceilings, and classical furniture, artfully chosen pieces befitting a Lady of high birth educated in art and culture. Lady Amelia herself was slim and of good height, delicate bone structure, perfectly formed. She had dark hair, green eyes and an olive complexion. Nell found herself spellbound by the exquisite creature who let her in and offered tea.

'I have a staff, but I prefer privacy for meetings. Discretion is everything,' said Lady Amelia.

'Fair enough,' said Nell. Discretion was fine by her.

Lady Amelia launched into an elaborate explanation of her background. How she had boarded at schools in France and Switzerland, and this was why she might forget an English word and asked for forgiveness in advance. She spoke with clipped vowels and *awfs*, the correct nuance and flat inflection. She also carried a grey miniature poodle under her arm that stared at Nell with its weepy eyes and growled constantly.

'This is my little *bébé*.'

'Adorable,' said Nell. She normally liked dogs, but this was hostile.

The dog wasn't house-trained either, and when Lady Amelia let it down and it did its toilet on the floor, Nell was speechless. Lady Amelia chastised the little dog.

'*Tu es un mauvais petite chien, pourquoi dois-tu m'embarrasser? Notre amie ne sera pas impressionnée – elle ne reviendra pas!*'

'What's the dog's name?' Nell enquired, noting the gender of the dog wasn't clear from how Amelia had spoken.

'Anastasia, in honour of the Romanovs. Awful what happened to them.'

This aroused Nell's suspicion. Native speakers do not muddle such things, and certainly not those from French boarding schools. Amelia said she had potential buyers interested in all artefacts and gemstones. In exchange for a small commission, she could manage the transaction.

'Think of me as a diplomat. My friends must remain

anonymous – they value discretion above all else – but they love a good deal, Miss Mackridge.'

'Don't we all, Lady Lawrence.'

'Amelia, please.'

'Amelia, where in France did you attend school?'

Amelia's eyes took a trip to the floor, she smiled, stood and walked to the window, scooping up the pooch as it scratched its ear on the floor.

'*Pourquoi? Paris, bien sûr,*' she said, smiling serenely.

'*Formidable, ma mère vient de Montélimar, vous le saviez?*' Nell wanted to test Amelia's language skills a little, mentioning her mother's hometown of Montélimar and asking if she knew of the place.

'I'm afraid my boarding school days are long ago,' Amelia laughed. 'I haven't seen much of France.' The woman swallowed so hard, it was as if she'd grown an Adam's apple.

'*Ce n'est pas grave, Montélimar est très connu pour son nougat, mais pas grand-chose d'autre, me dit-elle. J'aimerais y aller pour voir d'où elle vient, mais je n'en ai pas encore eu l'occasion. À quel âge avez-vous déménagé en Angleterre?*'

Nell talked at speed as Amelia stiffened. The woman hadn't understood a word, she was sure of it. Nell feared that this was a trap. Perhaps Scotland Yard were behind the bloody curtains. Nell had her razor, wrapped in silk, *bien sûr.*

'Oh, all right, you've got me,' said Amelia. She dropped the poodle onto the carpet, and it ran away. She slumped back in her chair.

Her accent was thick London, and not the upper-class

variety. Amelia threw one leg over the other. 'Fuck!' she exploded. 'I knew this would happen. I should have said Greek! No one ever speaks Greek.'

'What's going on?'

'I'm not French. I was born in India, Barrackpore. My mother was a memsahib and had an affair with an indigo planter. Her husband was in the Indian Civil Service. He had me shipped off to his spinster cousin in Peckham. Peckham! Of all places!' The way she spat out the word as if it may make her retch couldn't fail to amuse.

'My real name is Maud,' she said, a little embarrassed. Nell was worried about her own self-preservation rather than Lady Amelia's mystique. 'I am a courtesan.'

'A courtesan?'

'A whore, but a posh one. My buyers are my boyfriends, benefactors, sponsors, whatever you want to call them. The proposal is genuine, and my persona is the only act here – but I need it.'

'I find it hard to believe you've never been caught out before.'

Maud laughed and took a cigarette for herself, offering one to Nell, who declined.

'My friends tend not to be so interested in conversation. But they do like a bit of razzle dazzle, if you get what I mean. I don't know what you know about the proper stinking rich, but they make marriages to dull, mouse-like dumplings and live like naughty little schoolboys. Which is why they love buying other people's stolen property – it gives them a kick. My act is about reputation. It doesn't have to be real. They wouldn't pay for a mongrel bastard from Barrackpore, would they? But a French lady, and a lord's wife? Rats up a drainpipe. You understand. Maybe you could teach me a bit of French?' she said, perking up.

'*Peut-être,*' said Nell. 'I didn't notice at first. You are a good mimic.'

'I do a great Victoria Monks. Do you want to hear it?'

'Next time,' said Nell.

The women agreed to talk should Nell have any interesting items to offer, and Amelia agreed to consult with her contacts.

'What kind of things do your buyers entertain?'

'Christ, anything really – the more exclusive the better. Anything rare or unusual. Honestly, they've got so much money they'll buy and fill their houses with crap and forget about it. More about owning it than admiring it, but I'm not complaining,' said Amelia, lighting up another cigarette.

'What about stamps?' asked Nell.

'Stamps? Depends.'

'What about rare ones? Like the British Guiana 1c magenta.'

Amelia repeated the name of the stamp back to herself, smoking with one leg swinging over the arm of her chair.

'Leave it with me. I'll find out. Discreetly, of course.'

'Of course,' said Nell.

With the meeting over, Amelia showed Nell to the door.

'Sad to hear about Peter,' said Amelia. 'He was always kind to me. A real gentleman and great to work with. He shall be missed.'

'Peter? I thought his name was Vincent,' spat Nell, a little too bitter for her own comfort. She didn't want to show her feelings.

Amelia half smiled. 'Did he steal from you?'

'I beg your pardon?'

'Did he steal from you? You see,' said Amelia, leaning in the doorway, 'Vincent despised people. He was a pathological thief. He couldn't stop himself even if he'd wanted to, which he didn't. But if he didn't steal from you, that was real affection. Bye, love.'

With that, Amelia closed the door.

CHAPTER FORTY-SEVEN

NELL RETURNED HOME TO THE SOUND OF DOORS slamming and crockery smashing. Charlie was at the top of the stairs. They shared confused looks, then both dashed to the kitchen. Nell opened the door to see Lily and Effie looking wild, standing over a smashed pudding bowl on the floor.

'What's going on?' said Nell, a hand on the door handle, Charlie behind.

'I'm done with her! She's so bloody selfish!' screamed Lil, pointing at Effie. 'She's got my brooch. I bought that for myself, she took it and now she's denying it.'

'I did not take it!' Effie was comparatively calm in a silk dressing gown, hair in pin curls. 'I have my own and even if I did, which I didn't, why doesn't she buy another? I don't see why you have to smash a perfectly good piece of crockery.'

Lil flared up. 'You are always taking my things and never putting them back. Last time I found my shoes in your room, someone had been sick in one of them.'

'I said sorry about the shoes!' Effie shouted. 'You accuse me of everything that goes wrong around here!'

'Because it's usually you!'

'Is it? I didn't know we were keeping a secret score. Talking of secrets, Lil, when were you going to tell us about your *fiancé*?'

Lil's eyes blazed and her chest puffed up. She clearly hadn't wanted that out in the open.

'What?' Charlie and Nell were stunned. It was like watching a tennis match, but now the ball was stuck with Lily.

'Fiancé?' whispered Charlie. 'You're getting married – to a man?'

'Shut up, Effie.'

But Effie didn't stop. 'Lilian here is in love, with a *shoemaker*. A fucking shoemaker!' Effie cackled. 'He's not even in the firm – he's straight.'

'Why do you have to be such a bitch?' said Lily, turning to the others. 'It wasn't a secret; I was going to tell you.'

'I *knew* you had a boyfriend,' said Charlie. 'We all knew she had a boyfriend, right?'

'I didn't know,' said Nell. 'Why didn't I know?'

'Because...' Lily hesitated. 'I didn't want to upset you because of what happened with Peter.'

'Why would that upset me?' asked Nell, looking at each of the others, whose eyes had drifted to anyone's but hers. 'Does everyone think I'm one step away from the asylum?'

'She's going to leave us,' said Effie. 'We were a family! Sisters! We all promised! I only found out as Chrissie was asking if Florrie would be a good fit *if Lily left us*.'

'I never said I was leaving. Florrie will have to hold her horses before she jumps into my grave, won't she? So what, I've got a fiancé. You're only jealous.'

'Jealous!' Effie laughed. 'Of a shoemaker? I don't think so, sweetheart.'

'Stop!' Nell inserted herself before the row escalated to slapped faces. 'I need to talk to you all.' That got their attention. Now everyone thought Nell was going to leave. 'I've been thinking, and... can we sit down?' With ashen faces, all three women scraped chairs and parked arses at the table, nervous what Nell was about to say.

'I've been thinking. I love you all, and if it were up to me it would stay like this forever. But we have to admit, we need to work out how to earn money other ways, because it's simply a matter of time before one of us gets arrested again. Things aren't the same since Alice has been in prison. Chrissie can't keep control like Alice. We are adrift and being part of a gang is great in the beginning. But we take all the risk being on the front line, and leak profit all the way along. Fuck, we even rent from other Forties – they make more profit than us and it's us out there, taking the risks! The police are hell bent on breaking us anyway. We need to graduate onto other ways of keeping more profit within our group, not passing it off to others. Right?'

There were nods of acceptance around the table and shifting in seats. Everyone knew Nell was right; even the police had upscaled their cars now. And the big shops had employed female store detectives who weren't shy about searching women.

'Peter was teaching me about gemstones and jewellery. What if I can find buyers, bypass the fences, and get better prices for the jewellery we get hold of?'

'That's not allowed – we have to use our fences,' said Charlie. 'Aside from Mr Black of course, but I don't know of any others that will keep their traps shut.'

'But we get ripped off left, right and centre,' said Nell. 'Peter gave me a contact – Amelia. She will find a buyer and broker a deal for us.'

'Like a fence,' said Effie, arms folded.

'No, not like a fence. Fences take on the risk of stolen goods and rip us off in the process, but at least we offload fast. Amelia finds a buyer, manages the transaction and helps negotiate a price. The buyer will never know who we are, and we don't know who they are.'

'How do we know they aren't police?' asked Effie.

'We don't deal with them. Amelia does. They can't arrest people they don't know. Besides, she is a prostitute with wealthy clients, she doesn't want the police anywhere near her, bad for her clients. I'd say we can trust her more than your average London fence,' said Nell.

'How much does she get?' asked Lily.

'Ten per cent. She wants a higher price; that means she gets more.'

'Hang on, how does she get more? You said ten,' said Effie. Maths was not her strong point.

Nell rolled her eyes. 'Per cent, dummy. The higher the price, the higher the cash value of ten per cent.' Effie still didn't get it, but shrugged and went along with it anyway.

'I thought the hotel thing was it. I was always petrified

Alice would walk in and see me in a bloody maid's uniform. What if Chrissie finds out...?' said Charlie.

'Oh, come on, she won't! Without Alice, no one can control the younger girls,' stressed Nell.

'Yeah – they're wild too. Have you seen the skirts they wear? Indecent. Nothing shocks me these days,' said Effie. 'They've got no manners either – rude.'

'I say we put ourselves first and figure out a new game,' said Nell. 'It's the only way to survive – learn and move on. I don't want to be disloyal but not looking facts in the face isn't going to help any of us! And I have an idea of where to start: stamps.' Nell had everyone with her up until that point, then it was all wrinkled noses.

'This is what you were on about the other day – I thought you were having a breakdown,' said Effie.

'I'm not having a breakdown. Listen, when I was at the auction house, there was a bidder who paid ten thousand pounds for a single stamp. A British Guiana 1c magenta, and it's the only one in existence. Then I found out a little about the buyer from a girl on the cloakroom. His name is Paul Wallace, and not only is the man an arsehole but he's rich and... lives on his own in the middle of nowhere! That's all I care about.'

'Ten thousand pounds for a stamp,' said Lily, astonished. 'That's morally reprehensible. The world's gone mad.'

'Say what you will. There's money for all sorts of shit, but none for us unless we go and take it – so I say we take it!' said Nell.

'You're talking about breaking and entering, Nell. This is a bit of a turnaround,' said Charlie. 'I thought you were comfortable with lifting but not keen on that sort of thing? I thought you had your morals?'

'Yes, well, look where those got me. I'm a thief, aren't I? May as well try and be a good one. I say fuck it.'

'How much do you reckon, each?' asked Effie.

'That's something I need to work out with Amelia,' explained Nell. 'I mean, supposing she finds a buyer. I say we start high: nine thousand, less ten per cent, then split four ways. That's still a couple of grand each.'

Sharp intakes of breath engulfed the table and each woman drifted off into a bespoke fantasy of what to do with two thousand pounds. It seemed an incredible sum. Awe inspiring.

'I suppose there's no harm in looking into it,' said Lily. If she was on board, the rest would follow.

'We don't have to commit to anything yet, do we?' asked Charlie.

'No. That's it. This man has an antique shop in Wickham in Hampshire. I say we go and take a look and then see how we feel,' said Nell.

'Fuck it,' said Effie, grinning. 'I'm already in the car. One old bloke living in the arsehole of nowhere. And a stamp. How hard could it be?'

CHAPTER FORTY-EIGHT

OVER THE NEXT WEEKS TO OCTOBER, THERE WAS MUCH work to do, researching and finding out what they could to prepare themselves for their first theft to order. Nell's fire was back. She had something to focus on – something to achieve.

Except it almost went wrong from the beginning. They drove down to Wickham in the Meon Valley. A pretty little market town in a bustling village – cottages and classy Georgian houses. They found the antique dealer with P. Wallace emblazoned on the signage. It was all a bit easy. Nell got out of the car with the intention of entering the shop as a customer, to have a nose about. The others were going to scout around the area for thirty minutes or so in the car and take some notes as part of their investigation. They drove off.

Nell reached the shop only to realise it was closed. She checked her watch – closed at eleven o'clock on Tuesday. *Why?* She was deflated; the girls were long gone.

Nell was stuck, so to kill time she ran over the road to a little tearoom. It was irritating, but there was nothing else to do, so she ordered a tea at the counter and might have sighed a bit too heartily.

'You won't find him there on a Tuesday,' said the woman behind the counter. Fifties or more, she wore glasses that made her eyes huge, her hair up in a scarf and a tabard with tea stains.

'I'm sorry?'

'Him, over there,' she said, tipping her head. 'Never in on a Tuesday. Monday from 10–2pm, rain or shine, but odd hours all other days, when he has appointments. I take it you didn't have one?'

'No, I um... I'm looking for something special for my husband for Christmas, you see. Someone gave me Mr Wallace's card and... I... I really should have made an appointment. I'm such a silly goose,' said Nell, playing the scatty klutz.

'He often runs adverts in the local papers for bits and bobs he's trying to shift, like swords or a mahogany secretary.'

'A what?'

'Posh cabinet.'

'Such a shame! I've driven down from London. My own fault. It's for my husband. I was trying to get him something special,' Nell gushed, the story taking shape as she discovered it herself. 'It's our first Christmas together as a married couple.'

'He lives nearby,' said the woman, her eyes dancing up to the ceiling to access her memories. 'It's a little cottage close to Bursledon, along the creek. You could try him there. It's the last house right up before the railway bridge on the creek, lovely spot. Bit out of the way.'

'Oh really, that's so helpful. Thank you!'

'Depends on what your husband wants,' she said, passing Nell her tea. 'There's milk and sugar over there.'

'Stamps, my husband is a collector,' said Nell, busying herself with sugar lumps.

'You want to catch him at his house then. He only keeps furniture and big things – artefacts, I think you call them – in the shop. Stamps at his house. Although… you might be best making an appointment first.'

'Should I?'

'I don't want to speak badly, but…' The woman looked around to make sure no one could hear her, although there was one elderly lady with a Yorkshire terrier. Nell had to lean in. 'He's not the friendliest of chaps if you get my meaning. You might want to take a fella with you. He can be… unpleasant.'

'How unpleasant?'

'Our Mr Wallace used to be a director at a housing association, but now he's owning properties around here, rents them private. Awful properties – neglected, mouldy, leaking – those poor tenants. He's an odd person, doesn't mix. Comes in on occasion, complains a lot and smells too. I thought I should warn you…'

'Is that a Victoria sponge? It looks fabulous!' Nell pointed at a fresh cake on a stand.

'I baked it this morning.' The woman beamed, proud as punch.

'Would be a shame to come all this way and not have a piece of that beautiful cake,' said Nell. Settling in with her new best friend.

You wouldn't believe the things people will tell you of their own accord, if you only listen.

Each member of the cell had a job to do. Maps were studied. Trips to the area – even spying on the house. They had to gather as much information as they could before the day of the actual job. *Preparation is key.* They brought their findings back to the group, where they would sit at the kitchen table and discuss next steps.

'He lives alone on Hamble River in a tiny village near Swanwick, the perfect location. No security, he's a widower, doesn't even have a dog or a charlady. He's so paranoid about being robbed by staff he won't employ a domestic and won't receive visitors without an appointment,' explained Nell, having drained her sponge-making friend in the teashop for as much as she could.

'How do we get in if he's home?' asked Charlie, the lock breaker.

'He's always at the shop on Mondays from 10–2pm. Four hours should be plenty,' added Nell.

'I don't plan on being there four hours,' said Lily.

Charlie pitched in. 'The bad part is there is only one road to his house. I've studied the map, but we'll need to look in person. It's a dead end as far as I can tell, unless you want to leave by rowboat.'

'How do we know the stamps are at the house?' asked Effie.

'That's what the lady in the tearoom said, but also, I had
Bert telephone the shop and ask,' said Nell.

'...and?'

'Bert asked if he could pop down and have a look, but Mr
Wallace confirmed he didn't keep everything at the shop.'

Charlie and Effie sat in the woods by the creek, watching
with binoculars on one trip. Lily went dressed up as a
charlady and knocked on his door on the beg for work and
got told to piss off. But at the same time, Charlie was looking
through the window and sketched what she saw: a scullery,
parlour, mud room, all downstairs. In the parlour, Charlie
saw a big, locked bureau and a set of shallow drawers, for
holding large-scale maps.

'I reckon that's where he keeps the stamps,' she said,
looking satisfied.

The last piece of the puzzle was to finalise the deal. Lady
Amelia found a buyer willing to pay eight thousand pounds,
but wanted the stamp next Monday, hand delivered to
the Imperial Hotel in Southampton. Lady Amelia would
manage the transaction.

That meant Nell's cell had to get the stamp that Monday,
as the buyer would be leaving on the *Olympic* and travelling
back to New York that night. Amelia said she was sure she
would find a second buyer if the timing was off, but not one
so easy with the price. That meant eight thousand, less ten
per cent, split four ways – so each girl would walk away
with one thousand, eight hundred pounds.

This was it! The plan was set for the second week in
October.

CHAPTER FORTY-NINE

THEY SET OFF TO THE SOUTH COAST EARLY AND FOUND the village near a boatyard and a rickety train station. They parked at the station with only each other and a copy of the *Mirror* for company and waited.

'This is boring,' said Effie. 'Can I have the paper after you, Char?'

'I thought you couldn't read?'

'I can read, a bit.'

'We can play I Spy?' Nell was being sarcastic.

'No, you're all right,' said Effie.

They waited for two hours before Mr Wallace walked up the station approach. He had a long stride, quite sprightly for his age. He was lean with a baggy black suit, the collar of the middle class and dusty bowler hat. He carried a briefcase and an umbrella, despite it being a crisp bright day.

'That's him,' said Nell. They watched as he purchased a ticket and walked to the platform.

'Right, here we go,' said Lily, and banged the back of Charlie's seat. Charlie shut the paper and threw it at Effie in the back beside Lily. Nell was in the passenger seat.

'I don't want it now, do I?' protested Effie.

'Shush,' said Nell. 'We get in and get out. It's tight enough on time as it is. We have to get the stamp to the buyer this evening or we're fucked. The fact that there's only one road makes me nervous.'

'There was a river,' said Effie.

'Why? You going to swim out?' asked Lily.

'No one is swimming. We drive away, quietly and calmly.' Nell exhaled, but her breath escaped shakily.

Nell always had butterflies before work, but not like this. Her stomach was a collapsed mess. It was the rural surroundings – so easy to get lost and found by the wrong people. In London the roads helped escape, one way led to another or looped back. The alleyways all led somewhere. But in places like this, you could get stuck quick. Nell had a sudden flashback to how petrified she'd been on her first near miss hoisting in Whiteley's. It seemed laughable now. Besides, they knew it would be four hours now before Mr Wallace returned to the house, so they had time. Nell wanted to crack on and get the job done.

They drove down a long winding road past pretty cottages. They passed the post office with a pub and came to the road and turned left in a loop. They passed a man with a horse and cart and a young boy dangling his legs off the back. Then came to the part where the road turned into a dirty track lined by trees and a railway bridge overhead. The perception was one of a winding track to isolated seclusion. A metal gate signalled the entrance to Mr Wallace's property.

'It's here,' said Charlie, who drove the car through the gate and down the bumpy track. The car was under the cover of bushes and trees lining the property. On the left was an open meadow of lumpen rye grass and wildflowers. The track was uneven with shallow trenches on both sides. As they bumbled along, rabbits fled across the meadow, white tails bobbing. The only sound was bird song and the idling engine. Then Charlie turned the engine off. Silence.

Get in and get out.

The cottage windows were old and easy to jimmy open, and Charlie climbed inside.

'I'm afraid he hasn't tidied,' said Charlie as she opened the door.

They entered a small, tiled space covered with dried mud, bins, coal and mud-covered boots. Horses' reins hung from the ceiling. The parlour was gloomy with a low, uneven ceiling, a coal fireplace and a wooden mantelpiece with a radio on top. The armchairs were threadbare. There were piles of mouldy newspapers, cups with mould and musty clothes left all about. Mould had taken hold, creeping down the walls, and the windows were filthy. There was the locked bureau and the wooden drawer unit.

'How are we meant to find a single stamp?' asked Lily.

'Honestly? I thought you said this bloke was well off? He lives like a pig!' said Effie.

'I saw it at auction. It's distinctive and has a scrawled signature. It's octagonal. The corners are clipped off, and it's, well, magenta,' said Nell. 'We break into that bureau and then the drawers.'

Charlie set to work on the bureau lock with her files.

'What if we find anything else?' asked Effie.

'Only the stamp,' said Nell.

'Don't touch anything. You know what old people are like,' said Lily. 'They notice if you move anything an inch.'

Charlie eventually opened the bureau, and they searched inside but found only paperwork, letters, chequebooks and cash.

'What about the cash?' asked Effie.

'No! Only the stamp.' This time Nell was firmer. Effie huffed and paced.

The drawer unit was a different beast to conquer, with a main mechanism to unlock all the drawers. Charlie set to work again, but it was proving difficult.

'How long have we been here?' asked Lily, peering out of the filthy windows.

'Half an hour.' Effie was keeping time.

Each woman stared at the back of Charlie's head as she chewed her lips and inhaled sharply, feeling the pressure.

'What's taking so long, Charlie?' Lily gave up her spot by the window.

'I'm going as fast as I can,' Charlie snapped, and at that moment, the lock sprang open. 'I think I might have damaged it,' she said, turning to look at the rest, the skin of her pale face glistening.

'It doesn't matter,' said Nell. 'Let's find the stamp.'

Sliding open the first drawer, Nell's stomach dropped through the floor. Inside were rows and rows of laid-out stamps under loose glass on black boards. The next drawer was the same, and the next. Each of the eight drawers was filled with stamps. It was like searching a Roman temple for an individual mosaic.

'You have got to be having a laugh. How do we know which one is a Guianese magenta? Nell?' Effie shouted. All three glared.

Nell went blank, feeling only panic rising. She had to work fast or she would lose control altogether. All she could see was a million little squares leaping out. All different colours, with heads and side profiles. Indignant heads everywhere, laughing.

'Nell!' shouted Effie. 'Tell me you can find it! Or we take the fucking lot!'

'I saw it... I can find it. It's dark red, clipped corners; it's got a postmark and a black signature. Wait!'

Nell had a furious game to spot the stamp in the sea. Then it sprang out at her in the top row of drawer two. Dark red, as she remembered it, octagonal, black scrawl.

'Found it! Let's go.'

They locked the drawer, but the mechanism wasn't gliding into place after Charlie had tampered with it. They raced back to the car and spun the vehicle around by the cottage. There was a collective feeling of nervous anticipation and desperation to get out, compelling Charlie to drive down the track a little too fast, driving deep tyre marks into the ground. But they were leaving, or rather drifting along, when a thunderous crack rang out and the passenger-side front window shattered, spraying glass all over the car.

Someone screamed and they all slid down. The car stopped. Nell thought it might be a tyre blowing out or something falling from a tree and hitting the window.

'That was a gun!' hissed Effie.

They crouched down, blood pumping, ears ringing. The blood drained from Nell's face. The bullet must have been inches from her head.

CHAPTER FIFTY

Ducked down in the car, Charlie had her foot on the brake, but the engine was still running. It was impossible to tell where the gunman was, but a safe assumption was that it was Mr Wallace.

'Charlie! Drive!' Effie hissed from the back.

Charlie rolled the car along the track, trying to peer over the steering wheel without getting her head blown off. She slid up first, then Effie and Lily, scouting in all directions for the shooter. Nell had just raised her head when Mr Wallace jumped onto the footplate and hung on to the car with one arm, the shotgun waving in the other. Voices screamed at Nell to push him off as she tried to grab the barrel of the shotgun. Mr Wallace tried to point it into the car, but it was moving too fast for bumpy ground. Nell's eyes kept finding two gaping holes flashing past her face.

Charlie hit the brakes to stop the car rolling into a trench. Mr Wallace lost his grip and was thrown forward, landing on the ground in front of the motor vehicle. From turmoil to stillness. The sound of frantic breathing filled the car as the women sat up and waited for the man on the ground to move, shotgun inches from him.

'Is he dead?' asked Lily.

'He can't be.' Charlie's voice quivered.

'He's old,' said Lily.

'He's not that fucking old, he leapt onto the car,' said Effie.

'Look! He's moving,' whimpered Charlie.

Mr Wallace groaned and struggled to get up on his elbows. No one moved. Fight or flight. Now would be a good time to fight.

'Charlie,' said Effie. 'Drive.'

'What if I kill him?'

'He's got a gun, Charlie,' said Effie. 'It's him or us!'

'We kill someone, we go to prison forever. We could hang!' said Lily, emotion peaking the pitch in her voice.

'Nell, what do I do?' Charlie looked to Nell.

But Nell was spinning out with a head full of wool as Mr Wallace struggled to all fours.

'I don't know,' said Nell. She hadn't prepared for this. This wasn't in the plan.

Mr Wallace was clearly as tough as a bucketful of nails. His black suit was covered in mud, but he was on his feet, then he grabbed the gun and pointed it at the car.

'Now, Charlie!' shouted Effie. 'Drive! Or we're dead!'

'No! No! No! What if we give him the stamp back?' pleaded Lily.

'Charlie!' shouted Nell. 'Do it now! Go!'

Charlie stamped on the pedal and shut her eyes. He could have leapt out of the way. As Mr Wallace took aim, the car slammed into him before he could pull the trigger. He flew several feet ahead of them, landing hard on his back. Charlie had stopped as she hit him. Gripping the steering wheel, she drove forward, over where he lay on the ground, revving the engine until it traversed the lump beneath the wheels that was Mr Wallace.

Lily gagged and hid her face in her hands. Even Effie whispered prayers and closed her eyes. Nell clasped the dashboard as they manoeuvred over him. Then Charlie drove a few feet forward, stopped the car and they all turned to the rear.

Mr Wallace was on the ground, not moving.

'He has to be dead, right?' asked Charlie, panting.

'I don't know,' said Nell.

'Someone go and check,' said Lily.

'You go and check,' spat Effie.

But Mr Wallace wasn't dead. He let out a loud groan, rolled onto his front and tried to crawl to the shotgun a foot in front of him.

'You have got to be joking,' said Nell.

With that, Effie opened the car door and marched over to Mr Wallace where he groaned, trying to reach the gun.

'What the fuck is she doing?' said Lily.

Effie looked back into the car at three gawping faces, picked up the shotgun as Mr Wallace's fingers reached for it, cocked it, aimed it at the back of Mr Wallace and pulled the trigger.

That did it.

As the shot rang out, a sea of birds left every tree in a great chorus, as if marking the last of Mr Wallace.

What happened immediately after the untimely death

wasn't easy to recall. An unfocused blur of hysteria and shouting. Nell fell catatonic, and then the next thing she remembered was Effie and Lily screaming at each other over the body. As Mr Wallace's blood mixed with mud. Now was very definitely *not* the time to fall apart.

'Charlie,' Nell whispered. They both sat in the car. 'We should get out of the car.' Charlie nodded, her hands locked on the steering wheel, unfocused eyes ahead. Nell had to peel her fingers off the wheel to bring her to.

'It was him or us, right?' Charlie asked.

'Yeah,' Nell agreed. 'We had no choice.'

Nell got out first, followed by Charlie, and the four stood over the bleeding corpse of Mr Wallace.

'We have to move him. What about the garden? Putting him in the car isn't an option, he'll bleed all over it.'

Nell had spotted a wheelbarrow outside the cottage and ran to get it. They lifted the body into it as Charlie reversed the car back to the cottage, out of sight.

'Someone might have heard the shots,' said Lily.

'Could have been shooting rabbits. There were only two shots,' said Charlie.

'We have to get rid of the body,' said Effie.

They were all in agreement. Like it or not.

'Charlie,' said Nell, 'get a bucket of water and wash away the blood on the track.'

'But what if someone—'

'Hurry! It doesn't have to be spotless, only not obvious someone has been shot,' snapped Nell.

'OK.' Charlie ran off. Any blood would run off into the trenches and hopefully sink away.

'We have an obvious place to put him,' said Effie, calmer

and composed. 'The lake.' Effie threw up her arms at Nell and Lil when no one responded.

'Won't he float?' said Lily. 'Think of the floaters they pull out the Thames.'

'Not if we cut him up and weigh him down,' said Effie.

'Oh my God!' Lily's hands went to her forehead.

'But how? And the blood?' Nell asked.

'I saw a tin bath hanging on the wall. I say we use that – to drain him,' said Effie.

'This is insane! Cut him up!?' The enormity of the situation began falling down on Nell's head. 'I don't even know how!'

'Your machete,' said Effie.

'I don't have—'

'I brought it with me.'

'What?' Nell's mind exploded even more. 'I was told never to bring it, so what the fuck are you doing with it?'

'Lucky I did, isn't it?' Effie broke eye contact, marched back to the car and retrieved Nell's machete, still in its sheath, from the boot of the car.

'She's fucking insane!' wailed Lily. Even if Effie was insane, Lily resigned herself to getting the tin bath from the cottage.

'Are we really going to do this?' asked Nell. 'I feel sick.'

All three women now gawped at Effie, who looked from face to face, and promptly exploded.

'What the fuck! Why are you all looking at me like that!? Huh!? Does anyone have a better fucking idea?' she screamed. 'I know, shall we call Alice? Oh no, she's in prison. What about Chrissie? We could ask her to come and give us a hand! Oh, sorry Chrissie, you don't mind helping do you? Only we accidentally had to shoot a man to death! On a job we should never have been on in the first place!'

'You shot him, Effie!' Lily fought back tears.

Effie balked, as if she'd been winded. 'Oh, is that so? Because I could have sworn Charlie drove over him first. Remember? We broke into his house to *steal* from him, which was Nell's brilliant idea. And I believe you were meant to be lookout, Lil. Cracking job! If that's the way you feel about this, Lily, let me tell you, you're lucky there isn't another bullet in that fucking gun!' Effie was wild now, up in Lily's face, gritted teeth and pointing a finger.

Lily grabbed Effie's finger and smacked her about the head. Effie went for Lily's neck with both hands. Nell and Charlie leapt forward and broke them apart. A grappling group of silly, squabbling women, fighting among themselves at the worst moment.

'Please! Stop! God! This isn't going to help!' screamed Charlie.

'Look, we're either all in this or we're fucked. Does anyone have a better idea?' said Charlie. Everyone shook their heads. 'Then we do what Effie says.'

'I don't think I can,' said Lily, ashen faced, shaking her head.

'Nor me, but we have to,' said Nell, looking green at the prospect.

'I'll do it,' said Effie. 'But I'll need help. We start by stripping him.'

'We all do our part. I've got to get the stamp to the buyer tonight. Let's crack on,' said Nell.

Together the four women stripped Mr Wallace's body

free of his musty clothes. Charlie burned them on the site of an old bonfire. Lil found an axe outside the back door of the cottage.

'This will help,' she said, handing it to Effie.

'He's dead, it's just like being a butcher,' Effie said, to herself mostly. She lifted the axe to take the first swing at removing Mr Wallace's head from his body as the others stood and watched.

'Wait, Effie!' said Nell. 'Your clothes will get blood on them.'

'Shit, you're right.' Effie put the axe down.

She stripped naked, throwing her clothes at Charlie, who folded them up into a neat and tidy little pile. Effie braced herself, naked, for the first swing at the man as they all held their breaths.

'Did you know,' said Lily, 'at Newgate prison, they had huge executions with crowds of fifty thousand. Families would take a picnic. It was a big day out...'

Effie brought down the axe, and as the blow hit Mr Wallace's neck, it bored something deep into each of them. Like a huge electric shock rewiring every circuit. Gone, in a moment, was any semblance of innocence. Obliterated in one swing of an axe. But there was no stopping now.

Effie took on the physical strain of turning a cadaver into pieces. Grunts of exertion in between breathlessness, blood sprayed all over her alabaster body. It was a huge task, and Lily, for all her protests, stepped up to help.

'It really isn't so bad,' said Nell, as she lifted a dismembered leg and carried it into the tin bath to drain. 'Worse things happened in the war, and that's all been forgotten.' This is life. Messy and brutal. Unfair. Kill or be killed. *Casualties of war.* This might be true, but it was also a truth that things could never be the same again after a murder. Each woman had blood on her hands, quite literally.

When each jigsaw part of Mr Wallace was in the bath, Nell and Charlie went hunting in the cottage for potato and coal sacks. They wrapped the body parts in old newspapers once the blood had drained. Lily tipped the blood into the lake, where it spread out, floating like oil on water, turning the lake red. They filled sacks with rocks, placed the wrapped parts into the sacks, and tied them up with wire and twine from around the garden. In pairs, they tossed each part into the water. For the torso, they found an old suitcase on top of a wardrobe in a bedroom.

After it was done, Effie walked into the lake to wash the blood away from her naked body, shuddering at the cold. Lily picked up the axe and hurled it into the lake, then did the same with Nell's machete.

'What are you doing!?' Nell screamed, running at her.

'Getting rid of it,' said Lily.

'That's my machete!'

'No one will know that.'

'What if they do? What if someone finds it?'

'They won't! Even if they did, how would they trace it back to you?'

Nell picked up the sheath from the ground. It was the last thing her mother had given to her and now that was lost too. She would burn it. It was all she could do – that and hope and beg some divine entity for mercy.

Way behind schedule, they had to get out as fast as possible.

★

They drove the seven miles to Southampton to meet Lady Amelia and conduct the transaction. They travelled in silence, the wind tearing through the missing window on Nell's side. Then she remembered the stamp.

'Wait! The stamp!' Nell burst out, panic struck. 'Where is it?'

'I have it,' said Lily.

Nell let out a sigh of relief as Lily handed it to her with shaking hands. 'I don't want this anymore, I'm done.' No one was sure what Lily meant, but no one had the energy to engage in a clarification.

The others waited in the car as Nell went to meet Lady Amelia at the Imperial Hotel, a French Renaissance-style building they called the Southampton Ritz on the corner of Terminus Terrace near the docks. It was a surreal moment when Nell walked into the hotel lobby with red-coated men on hand to offer help, but not the kind she needed. Nell made her way up to Lady Amelia's room.

'Bloody hell, what happened to you?' said Amelia on sight. 'You look like the budgie died. Are you all right?'

'I'm tired,' said Nell, utterly drained. 'Can we get this done?'

'Absolutely,' said Amelia, slipping back into a lady's accent. 'This way, no doubt you'll want to count your money before running off.'

The trade was completed, the stamp handed over to a suited man, who inspected it for authenticity wearing white gloves and nodded to the buyer's valet. Then the money was handed over in an underwhelming brown leather bag. Lady

Amelia counted it out and the men left. Nell gave Amelia her commission and then left carrying the rest in the bag.

No one seemed enthused when she returned to the car with it. The drive home was a bleak affair in silence. Even when they reached home, they spilled out of the car in silence and each went to their room. Nell lay in bed, wondering if the others were asleep. Or if they too lay awake with the sound of the axe breaking human bones and horrific sights flashing before their eyelids each time they blinked.

Around seven o'clock the next morning, Nell was woken by the sound of someone walking down the stairs and the front door opening and closing as quietly as possible. Nell peeked out of the drapes to see Lily dragging a suitcase and bags.

Lily left so much of her wardrobe behind it seemed as if she would return, but she never did.

CHAPTER FIFTY-ONE

THREE DAYS LATER, CHARLIE ANNOUNCED SHE WAS off with some fancy-pants man on the *Orient Express*.

'I'll come back,' she said. 'Tell Chrissie I have a sick aunt. I need to be somewhere else for a while – that's all.'

Charlie was picked up by her lover in a posh motor. She cast a free and breezy smile over her shoulder at Effie and Nell on the doorstep.

Now it was only Effie and Nell rattling about the house, so they moved back to where they had started – to a two-bed flat in Hayles Buildings, rented from a brother of one of the veteran Forties.

Each woman had walked away with one thousand, eight hundred pounds. Charlie and Lily had skipped off with theirs, and their squirrelled cash in the tins from the garden at the old house. Effie and Nell kept theirs in the brown leather bag along with their tins of comparatively meagre savings. Sat crossed legged on the floor, they stared at the bag.

'What should we do with it?' asked Effie.

'Hide it, I suppose,' said Nell. 'We can't spend it. Not yet. People will wonder where all our money has come from. It's not like we've been hoisting much.'

'No, what if we pick up work again, properly? If only for a bit. It'll be a good cover.'

'Yes, good idea. Just while we figure out what to do.'

'Agreed,' nodded Effie.

Then they went back to staring at the bag with chins in hands, elbows on knees. They had dreamed of this kind of money. Now it sat presenting itself, it felt like a lead weight. Despair filled the empty spaces where Lily and Charlie should have been. As a four they'd been invincible, but with only two left, things felt broken.

On a chilly morning near the end of October, Nell sat minding her own business at a table in the window of a coffee house on Regent Street. She'd taken to looking at job ads in the newspapers, wondering what she could possibly do. The stamp heist had shaken her to the core. It was impossible to push the events of that day from her mind. Suppress them, yes. Ignore them, sometimes. But sounds, sights, smells – the smallest thing could bring it all back. Nell had become easily startled and withdrawn. She had little appetite for coming up with any plans but reassured herself her spark would return – she only needed time. Besides, she and Effie were sitting on a tidy sum. She could do anything she wanted, finally, if only she had a clue what that might be.

The papers were full of how women these days had lost their femininity – drinking, smoking, swearing, *being promiscuous*. Such were the habits of men, as if that made them acceptable choices.

In among agricultural reports, stocks, costs on corn and beef, were the births, deaths and marriages of the upper classes – people *worthy* of note. The papers also covered exploits of the criminal. Aristocrats and gangsters, extremities of the species that had more in common than either would admit. One set sought to evade the rules but have them apply to everyone else. The other defied the rules and tried to escape the consequences. But which was which?

Some claimed criminal women had the mental development of children. Others claimed men had not changed their view on what a woman was, used to regarding her as only slave or butterfly. Others blamed unemployment – *the peril of idleness*! Of incarcerated women in 1924, eighty-three per cent had been in prison before, compared with sixty-two per cent of men. Women were at least reliable offenders.

And out of all the people in London who should walk past? DC Horace Bevan. Nell lifted her newspaper to cover her face, hoping he hadn't spotted her. When she heard a double tap on the window, she knew he had. Nell lowered the newspaper and there he was, waving with an impish grin. What it would be to punch him right on the nose. Nell braced herself as DC Bevan made his way inside and sat at her table.

'I don't remember extending an invitation,' said Nell.

'You didn't, I made an assumption.'

'How very confident of you.'

'I'm sorry about your father. It's not right how veterans were treated,' he said, shaking his head as if he almost cared.

'Talk is cheap.'

'Yes, it is. Quite right, so I'll spare you the frustration of any subtle insinuations: you are out of your depth, Nell. The walls are closing in.'

'Yes, this is a common theme. How many years has it been now?' Nell took a sip of her tea. 'And yet... nothing has happened, has it? Anyone would think you were all bluster, Horace.'

'The Forty Elephants got too big, Alice is inside, and you girls don't have the scale and reach of men to keep growing. You don't have the connections to keep your girls out of prison. Alice will be out soon. I heard she's been sniffing out other opportunities.'

'Why wouldn't she?'

'I don't blame her, makes sense to find ways of keeping herself out of danger; blackmail, extortion, *hoisting*, as you call it.'

Nell put the paper down. A crumpled mess on her lap.

'Did you hear about that murder down in Swanwick?' Horace leaned over.

'No.'

'So, this old bloke had been missing for a couple of weeks. Anyway, horrible old sod, no friends, no one liked him. Even his sister, who was the one who reported him missing, but only cos he missed his nephew's birthday.'

'Does this story have a point?'

'It does – in fact, a very sharp one – you'll never guess.'

Nell sighed, put down the paper. Inside her heart thumped between her ears.

'They found him – bits of him, that is. They dredged the lake by his house.... Poor bloke ended up in sacks. Strangest thing, there was a machete in the lake, too. Didn't people used to call you Machete Mack?'

'Are you accusing me of murder?'

'No. I know you wouldn't murder someone.'

'Wouldn't I?'

'You haven't got it in you.'

Christ, that hurt, because she did, didn't she? But this man still thought she was better than that. Despite her best attempts at proving to him and herself she was not.

'You are mixing with people who can and will murder, Nell, and they will drag you down with them. Why don't you think about doing something else?'

'Like what? Open up a sewing school?'

'You're still young.'

'I'm glad you think so. It's very different for us. You've basically been the same bloke since you jumped out on me down a dark alley, and it's been promotion nigh on every year. I don't get the same deal, Horace. What am I meant to do? Be a servant? Look after babies? Go insane?'

'You could get an education. Don't tell me you've spent it all on diamonds and furs?'

'And learn to type for some handsy old bastard in an office? My freedom is better than any of the shit on offer. Knowing I can have anything I want because I've got the guts to go and get it for myself.'

'Illegally, I might add. And all these excuses you make up, they're not real. It's all in here.' Horace pointed at his head.

'Of course, I'm a woman, therefore my perceptions are entirely of my own hysterical creation.'

'That's not what I meant.'

'How much?' said Nell.

'What?' Horace seemed confused.

'I said, how much, Horace? What if we change things up a little. What if you work for me? How much would it cost me? What's your price, I wonder?'

Horace looked outraged for a second, then burst out laughing. He took his hat off and set it down on the table. He looked about to ensure no one was in earshot, and leaned in.

'You want to know what my price is?' he asked.

'I'm interested, why not float it past me and we'll see what we can do.'

'My price is you,' said Horace. 'One night. I get you, for one night. If you're sweet about it, I might even buy you dinner first.'

Now it was Nell's turn to look about, before she leaned over the table and hissed in disgust, 'You... pervert! How dare you! I thought you were better than that. How disappointing.'

Horace laughed. 'I'm winding you up, Nell. I haven't got a price – you can't bribe me. Nice try though. I'll see you around.'

Horace put his hat back on. Shaking his head with an amused sigh, he made his exit.

CHAPTER FIFTY-TWO

SELFRIDGES HAD ALWAYS BEEN NELL'S FAVOURITE. BUT now she couldn't summon even a remote interest in hoisting, or anything for that matter. Effie, for her part, seemed her normal self. The way events bounced off that girl baffled Nell. Was there something wrong with her or was it Effie? They had to go back to work, at least for now, so Selfridges it was.

It was an easy target. For one, it was always busy, and secondly, wealthy tourists flocked there. The clientele was full of the most demanding women – native and foreign – which made it easier to operate. Thirdly, it was a theatre: sensuous fabrics, subtle tones and vibrant colours. Sparkle and glamour. A big girl's fairy tale.

Effie and Nell had decided to dress much older. Both wore thick-rimmed spectacles, and Nell had a dowdy grey-haired wig with a low bun at the nape, while Effie hid her hair under a bucket hat. An armour of long skirts, tweed and woollens. Nell had told Effie what Horace had said about Mr Wallace and even the great unmoved Effie seemed shaken.

'I can't go away for murder,' Effie whispered, white faced.

They would go back to being simple hoisters in the short term to not arouse any suspicion of the Forty Elephants nor the community. Lil and Charlie had scarpered. If they did too, it would surely raise eyebrows. They settled back into a simpler routine until they decided on what to do with that great bag of money. Although Nell couldn't bring herself to look at it without feeling anguish.

Alice would be out in the next month on licence, so the Forty Elephants was holding out until the Queen came back to restore law and order. Hoisting was simple: no buyers, no reconnaissance, no planning – much. No... *dismemberment.*

Selfridges has several entrances and exits, like a stage. Effie and Nell would nearly always use the main entrance. It was more difficult to be apprehended as there were several doors, all busy with footfall. Nell signalled to Effie she was ready to leave by removing her spectacles and cleaning them. Effie made her way to the exit as Nell followed. When Effie sauntered out between security at either end of the doors, Nell had no reason to think her exit would be different. Within feet of daylight, she felt a heavy hand on her shoulder pull her backwards.

'Excuse me, madam, you're going to have to come with us.'

Nell turned to see an older man, tall and wiry, accompanied by a short dumpy woman she recognised – a female shop walker from Bourne & Hollingsworth who, it would appear, now worked here. She glared at Nell, one side of her mouth curled in triumph.

'You took your spectacles off. Those old signals won't

work anymore. I'm only sorry I didn't catch who you were signalling,' said the shop walker.

Every part of Nell screamed at herself to run, but she would have to pick her moment. It's never over until you lose all hope and give up. Nell still had hope of escaping. She looked back at the entrance.

'Don't even think about it,' said the man. 'You lot are dropping like flies, aren't you?' For now, she had no choice but to go with them. *Bloody Effie, trust her to get away.*

They marched Nell to what you might call backstage, or the security offices. Selfridges didn't risk upsetting customers; it offended the patrons to see ladies being manhandled. This march of the condemned depended on Nell remaining compliant. The wooden door loomed as large as debtors' gate at Newgate. If Nell were to allow herself to be swallowed into it, her criminal record would begin.

Nell swung at the lady shop walker with her handbag, hitched her skirt and ran. She had full bloomers, so it wasn't easy, but the element of surprise gave her a small head start. The front entrance was marked by the two security guards ready to stop her. Nell turned left, weaving through racks, knocking what she could onto the floor behind her to gasps and shrieks of shoppers as she flew past them. The store detectives followed the trail of destruction. The side exit was a single unmanned door to the street. She had a fighting chance to escape, and hope swelled inside her like a balloon.

A man, not one who worked there, stepped into her path. An elbow went straight into Nell's chest, sending her crashing to the ground as the store detectives and the security guards caught up. The man undertaking the citizen's arrest loomed over where Nell had been winded from hitting the porcelain floor on her back. Like a spider, her fingers crawled to her silk-wrapped razor. Nell leapt up and slashed at the man out of desperation. She caught the merest flicker of his cheek and he leapt backwards. Nell made to run, but the security guards and the store detectives were on her. She was manhandled by four, holding the razor, until a guard squeezed her wrist and she had no choice but to drop it, sending it clattering to the floor, along with her last hope of escape. Nell was dragged, struggling like a cat being drowned in a sack, all the way to the security office.

Once inside, the door was shut and, away from public gaze, the male store detective grabbed her by the front of her coat and slapped Nell hard across the face, splitting her lip. It was as if her face had exploded.

'Mr Bailey! I cannot condone such behaviour!' said the lady store detective. 'There will be no laying of hands on any woman, thief or not. I insist!'

'Settle down, Mrs Jeffries. It's the only language these women understand,' he said.

Within the hour, uniforms arrived to arrest Nell. Mrs Jeffries gave Nell a cold compress for her lip, which was fast swelling.

The oddest element to this was that Nell felt a sense of relief. She had lived in fear of this moment for two years, and there was a sense of peace now the mystery was over. Her unblemished record – not the longest in the Forties by any stretch – was over. Nell could not foresee that this relief would evolve to humiliation, and a despair that would not shift.

And then who should arrive? Of course, Detective Constable Bevan. He took the uniforms aside and told them he was going to take Nell in.

'We're old friends, aren't we, Mack?' he said.

She could not meet his gaze and wore the unfocused stare of the guilty. Although his lingered on her.

'Did someone hit you?' asked Horace.

The two guards had been dismissed back to their posts and the male store detective was giving his version of the pursuit to the uniforms. Only the lady store detective and Horace remained.

'I fell over,' said Nell. She didn't want the fuss, and the lady store detective didn't say anything. What was the point?

'Come on, I'm taking you in.'

'Aren't I a bit beneath you these days?' asked Nell. The lady store detective looked between them, confused by the familiarity.

'I wouldn't want to miss out on this auspicious moment.'

When Nell was in the back of Horace's police car, rather than start the engine he spun round in the driver's seat; she was staring out of the window. Effie would be wondering where she was.

'Don't,' she said. She had an inkling he was going to say *I told you so.*

'All right, I won't,' he huffed, facing back to the steering wheel. He tutted, then turned round again.

Before he could speak Nell interrupted him. 'Please, I can't bear the disapproval.'

'I won't say anything, but I will tut if I want to.'

'Suit yourself.' Nell sighed.

Horace shook his head and let out another attention-seeking sigh.

'For heaven's sake!' she said. 'Say what you must. Anything to stop that huffing and puffing.'

Nell closed her eyes, ready, but Horace remained quiet, so she opened them.

'Nah, I got nothing,' he said, and started the engine.

Nell was charged with grand larceny and assaulting a member of the public. She was to be remanded in custody until she could appear before a magistrate.

So, this was it. Nell was going to prison.

CHAPTER FIFTY-THREE

To SAY SHE WAS TERRIFIED WOULD BE AN understatement. The only solace she had was that there were already Forties where she was going: to Holloway.

But Nell found herself packed off to Aylesbury prison due to overcrowding. Her counsel, Mr Hardy, said it was because they didn't want any more Forty Elephants in the same prison for fear of violent assembly.

Nell was crushed. She would go alone.

Prison was not as hellish as Nell had imagined. She'd conjured up horrors of medieval dungeons, chains and stone-cold rooms of torture. There were chains, though, and an endless clinking of metal with the locking and unlocking of cell doors all day, every day. These were sometimes accompanied by maniacal laughter, wailing, crying, fighting and the odd filthy limerick. The endless noise drove her insane in the beginning and then one day, she stopped noticing.

The torture was being made to live the same day over and over. Alone with her thoughts and all the banished feelings she'd thought she'd discarded. It all came flooding back now she could not busy herself enough to escape. She let herself feel everything, figuring she deserved it. That was what prison was for, wasn't it? To torture the guilty by leaving them so utterly bored they couldn't help but be driven mad by their own internal thoughts.

Nell was visited often by Sarah Gold, who would come to her dripping wet as if she'd crawled out of the Thames to show her what fate she had met, thanks to Nell. Sarah never uttered a word, but Nell was sure she could feel her presence in her cell at night. Sarah had never been heard in life and remained voiceless in death. Poor girls like Sarah, like Nell, existed to be used and consumed. Desired and devoured. They had no need of a voice. Nell thought of the last moments she'd shared with her father. How he had worn the ridiculously decadent silver fox stole she'd bought for her mother. The malformed words he'd mustered at his weakest. Rendered weak and punished by his own country for his loyalty – his contribution dismissed and diminished. The bravest man who had suffered so much but never complained. Instead avoiding the devastation and then humiliation with flippant jokes and agitated silence. Peter, or Vincent, turned up to remind her what desire felt like and to torment her with the unanswerable question of whether he'd felt the same way, or had it been an act. She wanted it to be an act, because then she could hate him, rather than think of his last moments, trapped in a dark hole, unable to breathe, and wonder if he'd thought of her as he slowly suffocated to death. The worst was Mr Wallace: his malevolence lurked and followed her everywhere. The man enjoyed haunting Nell with his hollow-eyed face

– watching her every move. She was sure his ghost was with her, standing in the corner and shouting obscenities from the other side. Every day at sudden moments she would be dragged back to his earthly body being taken apart. A door slamming reminded her of the swing of the axe. Any noise could take on the form of a crack of a bullet across the sky. Birds taking to the air. Blood floating on the lake. The worst part of prison was existing in the parallel worlds between the living and dead. The past and the future only existed to torment, and the present was uninhabitable. The objective for most women on the inside was to remain lucid enough to be considered sane.

Nell had thought there would be more violence among the women, but in the main she found the other inmates pitiful. Many were mothers or had family to care for and were consumed with worry for their relations. They despaired over duties left behind that no one would pick up. *Who would pay the bills? Who would cook dinner?* Nell felt very lucky by comparison.

She slowed down, her mind made dull as she picked at the walls with her nails and wondered how she had ended up here. She knew how... but *how?*

Effie came to visit and snuck in snuff for Nell to trade. Nell asked her to mail a letter she had written to her mother and Steph explaining her arrest. She'd written the letter much like a news report, devoid of emotion. Nell wasn't sure at all how the news would be received and found it easier to write that way. Nell was a bedraggled, frizzy-haired frump in her prison dress and shoes, whereas Effie was luminous, her outfit divine sophistication in black velvet, platinum hair set in a demi wave and magenta lipstick. When Effie's lips moved, Nell saw that fucking stamp. She passed Effie her letter, having been approved by the governor.

'I'll send it right away.'

'Effie, what have you done with the money?' Nell whispered.

Effie waved her hands. 'Shush, it's safe with me. Best not to talk about that here. Anyway, I have news, Nelly! Big news!' There was something in the way Effie wouldn't look her in the eye and waved away her question.

'News?' Nell could barely muster enthusiasm.

Effie thrust her left hand in Nell's face. On her third finger was a diamond ring that blazed like a new star.

'Good God, that's… huge,' said Nell.

'Isn't it! Who would have thought it? Me getting married. Can you see the little heart motifs? And the shoulders have baguettes.' Effie wiggled her fingers.

'Who?'

'A private jeweller in Hatton Garden.' She shoved her hand closer.

'Who are you *marrying*?'

She looked about, although no one was listening. Everyone was absorbed in their own emotional operas, as was Effie.

'His name is Marco. He's a Sabini!' She winced, as if she was confessing to stealing Nell's favourite dress, and not marrying into an Italian mob – the Elephant Gang's violent rivals.

'The Sabinis?! Are you mad?'

'We can't choose who we fall in love with, Nell. Besides, things are different now. The young girls are wild and they don't listen to Chrissie or Alice or anyone. I'm out of the Forties. It's time I settled down.' Nell had no clue what to say. 'Close your mouth, Nell, your tongue will get dry.'

'Congratulations, Effie. I hope you'll be happy.'

It was Effie who was leaving Nell behind. The one who feared abandonment and called her 'sister' was leaving her to rot in prison. Lily was right; Effie always would land on her feet. Nell didn't get the sense she'd be seeing any of her money either. All that work and all that risk for money and now she couldn't find the will to care.

During her time on remand, Nell met a talkative American girl, Tara. Only twenty-one, she had been committing cheque fraud with a boyfriend. Tara had come from New York and knew all about the legend of Queen Alice and the Forty Elephants. The newspapers over there had been printing stories of these wild women as if they were movie stars – the Diamond Queen and the Mighty Elephants. In America, the women were depicted as rogue idols of brawn, beauty and deviousness. Daring beauties who were as bad to the bone as any man. But Nell didn't find much comfort in that. The British papers portrayed them as stupid, feckless, feeble minded and the molls of bad men. The American ones portrayed them as dangerous, beautiful and romantic. Both were disappointing. One version to be fucked, the other burned at the stake. It might be nice to occupy somewhere in the middle on occasion, as if they were the same species as men.

Tara only wanted to hear stories of Queen Alice and Babyface Maggie. All the girls did, so Nell told them what they wanted to hear. Which was, incidentally, what Mr Hardy wanted her to do when her day in court came to be sentenced.

'As this is your first offence, we need to play on this,' he told her. 'Perhaps you could describe how remorseful you are, sad over your father's struggles since the war. How you served your country working with explosives – that will help. Oh, and as your father was away your mother struggled to raise you with decent morals. She's French, they'll understand, discipline was neglected.'

'No, I won't do that to my mother,' said Nell. 'None of this is her fault.'

'Nell, let me speak plainly. The old defences of kleptomania or the melancholy have run their course. If you will not blame your mother, then we will have to find a way of blaming it on jazz, or negro men or homosexuals.'

Mr Hardy persuaded Nell to write down the lessons she had learned from her time in the criminal underworld. To give a demonstration of contrition and remember to stick in bits about being raised by a lone mother with a father at war, and all the other pulls on the heartstrings.

Nell would read this out in court. It was agreed with the governor that Nell could keep a notebook; in fact, he thought it a spiffing idea.

When the day came, Nell dressed as recommended, as demurely and innocently as she could appear at twenty-four years old, without looking like an overgrown child. Her heart fluttered as she searched the public gallery until out popped all the Forties who had come to see her tried.

Lily and Charlie had made it. They were sat behind Effie, who was next to John and Chrissie. Lily gave a wave when she spotted her. Charlie looked as if she had been somewhere sunny, her skin brown. Nell felt her lip tremble. She hadn't expected anyone to appear for her, but here they were and now it threatened to make her lose her composure. She didn't want to cry, despite Mr Hardy saying a good blub never hurt a woman on trial.

Nell listened to the police constables give their statements of the haul of silk, about her special bloomers, how she had slashed violently at a good public citizen, howled and fought like a savage. Then it was Nell's turn to read out what she had learned from her time of reflection. Nell stood and cleared her throat. Having never spoken in front of this many people, her face grew hot. The notebook she held shook, making the words leap about, but she knew what she had written by heart, and it is difficult to forget the truth.

Her voice began shakily:

'My lawyer instructed me to beg and cry for my freedom, but I cannot. For it is as good as asking for unicorns, elves or magic potions, because it does not exist. The only freedom available to a working-class woman in my country is the freedom to serve, steal or starve. I do not believe any fit what I describe as freedom. What I have learned from my time as a criminal is thus.' Nell cleared her throat, glanced up at a sea of perplexed faces, took a deep breath and carried on.

'Lesson one! Those considered criminal are merely aristocrats without title or inherited wealth. Their ancestors weren't best mates with William the Conqueror, or slave owners compensated by the working people for owning human beings. Criminals and aristocrats are one and the same! Both are selfish, greedy, cruel and violent, and believe all others to be inferior. They care only about winning, and for someone to win, others must lose.'

'Stop! What is this?' asked the magistrate.

'Lesson two! The upper classes lecture the working people on morality and compassion, on Christian values, while flouting them at every opportunity. I was told by a policeman once that all are equal in the eyes of the law – this is bollocks—'

'Stop! Stop speaking at once!' The magistrate called Nell to stop, but she would not.

'…sorry, I mean this is bollocks, sir…' said Nell.

Mr Hardy had his head in his arms on his desk. The gallery was a mix of horrified observers, but in the other half a rumble started. The Forties who had infiltrated the gallery began to stamp their feet. A thunderous round of applause was building, making the very courtroom shake. A female warder stepped up to the dock and tried to snatch the notebook from Nell's hands. Nell stretched as high as she could to keep it out of reach. The stomping was soon accompanied by cheering, clapping and whistling. As Nell kept shouting out her words.

'…they train us like dogs! As they carry on blindly doing as they please, looting, starving, bullying…'

'Take her down! Take her down!' the magistrate cried.

A warder leapt up and wrestled the notebook off Nell. She grabbed on to the dock as a male court warder took hold of her legs and lifted her. The female warder was trying to peel Nell's fingers from where she gripped on, as she kept shouting.

'It's a rigged game! We've no bloody chance!'

Nell's hands were prised free, and the male warden threw her over his shoulder. Nell now faced the police on the prosecution.

'And you lot can piss off and all! The police are corrupt! I've met one decent copper in all my years!' Nell shouted and held her arms up to the raucous cheers as she was carried away. 'Here endeth the lesson!'

Nell got twelve months for her performance.

CHAPTER FIFTY-FOUR

NELL WAS SENT TO THE WOMEN'S PRISON IN AYLESBURY. After six months, she was transferred to Holloway in June 1925, to serve the remainder of her sentence. Nell would be joining a few familiar faces, and that made the move less frightening.

Holloway was a tightly run ship. Work in silence, walk in single file. The building was designed so that every cell was visible from the centre. Inmates were always under scrutiny – a castle no princess could escape, so they said.

A month after Nell was moved to Holloway, Steph started to visit her. She hadn't seen anyone in her family since that awful trip home, but the sisters had always exchanged letters. In August of 1925, their mother and Mr Bright, the most patient Romeo on earth, were married. Steph said it was a small, private affair. To escape the ghost of their father they had rented out the house and purchased a three-bedroom cottage in Hove.

By September, Nell was told by the warden that she would likely be released sooner than she thought. She was well-behaved, helped others with their literacy and letter writing, and had on a few occasions translated for French inmates in Holloway. These things had been to occupy herself but nevertheless impressed the governor.

'You'll be coming back home, of course,' said Steph during one of her visits.

Nell balked. 'What do you mean come home? I'll be as welcome as Judas Iscariot.'

'Nonsense! Where else will you go?' asked Steph, then her face clouded over. 'Don't you tell me you're going to go back to what you were doing. Eleanor, it's time to put Nell or Nelly or whoever that was back in the box. Why not resuscitate the person you were going to be before all that funny business? What better way to do that than being with your family?'

'Mum hasn't spoken to me in years.'

'She's stubborn, exactly like you. But she always talks about "when Eleanor is home". Please don't break her heart, I'm begging you! Come home, at least for a bit.'

'With Mum and Mr Bright?'

'We call him Gerald now. He's a little pious, but he has a good heart. He's convinced everybody can be saved by Jesus and is excited about saving you.'

'Oh God.'

'You can entertain Paul with all your prison stories. Is it true what they say women get up to behind bars... with each other?'

Nell remained silent. At least one talent she had acquired from prison was that dumb insolence is effective and often came with less punishment.

★

Two weeks after Steph's visit, Nell had another visitor – her mother.

'What are *you* doing here?' she asked. 'Steph said you would never step inside a prison.'

'Our little episode has gone on long enough, Eleanor. This quest you have – whatever it is – must stop.' Her mother's new life clearly agreed with her. She looked younger than she had in years. Groomed hair, dark grey suit, makeup. *Was that – the silver fur stole?*

'In case you haven't noticed, I'm not chasing anything – I'm in prison.' Nell held her hands up, presenting the four walls around them.

'*Ouais*, I have noticed. Tell me, why you didn't come to your father's funeral? Steph said she saw you in a car. Why come all that way and not come to the service?'

'Because I knew you didn't want me there.' Nell spat the words but kept her voice low, for fear the prison guards would hear raised voices and take her back to her cell.

'What do you think I would have done? Make a great scene? At a church? During a funeral? Of course not! I couldn't believe you didn't come... I thought... I hoped we could move past things, especially with your father passing. It was such a difficult time. I know he would have wanted us altogether again.'

'Just in case you need reminding, you told me to get out and called me a whore.'

'I'm not proud of how I acted that day, I admit. I was so angry you had moved out and forgotten us all! I thought we were closer than that? I was hurt, Eleanor. I have feelings too! And you are not blameless. Did you intend never to speak to me again? Ever?' her mother asked, agony at the mere concept visible in her eyes.

'No! I wanted to be in a better position. To be someone... I don't know, to have proved to you I was better than that. That I could achieve something or be someone...'

'You have nothing to prove, Eleanor. To me, your father, to this Alice woman. You are far too talented to waste your life in here. You are a defiant one, my darling. Too wriggly to pin down. The world does not want such qualities from you. Forgive yourself, as I forgive you, *ma petite fille.*' It was hard to hear such words from her mother. The sting too painful to bear and Nell's eyes threatened to spill over with tears. 'Do you remember your teacher, the one who had the predilection for the cane? How you would receive the cane every week, and how one day it stopped?'

Nell nodded. 'Mrs Williams. I remember.'

'I told that woman that if she ever hit you again I would break that cane in half and beat her with the sticks. She never hit you again. This is the problem with schools, they beat the spark out of people like you. They do not want pioneers – they want serfs.'

'You thought I was a whore,' said Nell.

'And if you were, I'd still love you. Knowing you, you would have been the best whore. A courtesan to the king, like Jeanne du Barry.'

'Wasn't she beheaded?'

'I think so.' Both women giggled at the absurdity of a beheaded woman as something to aspire to.

'Come home. For me. I can keep you like a canary in a

cage, fatten you up and then when the time is right you can fly away again. As is your way. I miss you.'

'I'm a pain in the arse and I bring nothing but trouble.'

'Bah, but you are my trouble, and at least it is never boring.'

'I don't know what I would do,' said Nell.

'Nothing. You don't have to do or be anything. I will take care of you.'

As difficult as it had been at the time, the visit with her mother had released a great pressure from Nell. It was as if her lungs had been set free from being squeezed and she slept without the ghostly visits from the other side for the first time that night.

Nell's release was brought forward to 13th December and then, for no reason known to her or anyone else, she was released two weeks earlier than that. On her twenty-fifth birthday, 29th November 1925.

Before she knew what was going on, Nell was processed and let out of the gate with her old clothes, shoes and money for a bus or train. It wasn't that she wanted to stay, but she was spat out in such a hurry that it was unnerving. Having been watched, supervised, ordered and having every single instruction issued, now she stumbled on the outside like a newborn deer.

Nell's old coat was baggier. She had lost weight, and she felt insipid and unkempt. She walked along the road in search of a bus stop. Holloway was north of the river, and she needed to go south.

'Are you not going to say hello?'

Nell hadn't noticed the man leaning against his car and walked right past him, overcome with sounds, sights and smells. Nell was stunned.

'Well, if it isn't Horace Leviticus Bevan. What are you now? Chief Inspector?' Nell gave the lip, pulling her coat over her old dress; she was sure she looked a fright.

'A little bird told me it's your birthday,' he said.

'How did you know?'

'Your birth date is on your record.'

'No, that I was getting out?'

'I'm in the police, Nell, give me some credit. I thought you might need a drink.'

'You're offering to take me for a drink?'

'Every girl deserves a drink on her birthday – even the naughty ones. I can give you a lift.'

'Oh yes, take me south!'

'You south London girls. It's the same city, you do realise?'

Horace drove to Waterloo, and she followed him on foot to a Georgian pub on the corner where men stood on the pavement, supping pints and smoking. Nell followed Horace and walked between them, eyes nailed to the back of his shoes. Somewhere along the last couple of years, she'd lost her bottle. Before, she'd have strutted in, bold as brass, dripping in jewellery and fur. Now she trod gingerly behind her police escort and sat at a table looking small, and as if it was the first time she'd been in a pub, as Horace went to the bar.

'Never had you down as a stout man,' said Nell as Horace sat down with his pint.

'Why the devil not?'

'You seem too clerical.'

'Ouch!'

'I'm only teasing, I don't mean it. Not sure why I say half the things I do, I'm sorry.'

Nell stared into her drink; the old act didn't feel right anymore.

'I know you're only pulling my leg. Dare I ask if you've had any thoughts about what you'd like to do?'

'I'm going home to my mother in Brighton. Hove now. But other than that, not a clue. I don't know what I'm good at.'

'Nell, I'm sure you could turn your talents to many things.' But she couldn't think of one.

'You know, my teacher told my mother I was impervious to the cane. It's like even if I know of the consequences it doesn't stop me. Is there a word for that?'

Horace chuckled into his pint. 'Impervious? My turn to tease. To new beginnings.' He lifted his class and so did Nell.

'Do you always take the criminals you arrest out for a drink after they're released?'

'Only the pretty ones.'

Afterwards, Horace escorted Nell to the train station and bought her ticket.

'You don't have to do that,' she told him.

'It's my civic duty. You're going to get on that train and out of this city,' he said. 'I realise I can be annoying, but this is for your own good.' As if he were worried she might abscond and return to the glittering lights of the West End, for the thrills and the familiar. If he hadn't, to be fair, she may well have done.

'Stay out of trouble,' he said, as she boarded the train.

'Aye aye, captain.' Nell saluted. The station master whistled; the train was about to depart.

'I'll check in on you with the Brighton boys,' shouted Horace, hands in his pockets.

'Horace! Don't you bloody dare!' Nell called out, but the train pulled away, and she wasn't sure if he heard her.

CHAPTER FIFTY-FIVE

Nell's mother and stepfather were now living in a modest two-bed in Rottingdean, a few miles away from Brighton, near Roedean, the exclusive boarding school for well-bred girls on the Sussex Downs.

The upstairs rooms had eaves and slanted ceilings with windows in them, a novelty Nell had never seen before. Her mother had made up a bedroom ready for her, and left Nell to settle in. She could only sit on the end of the single bed and wonder how she could at once feel old and like a little girl. With a record, you can lift the needle and take it back to an earlier point and force the needle to trip through the tune all over again. This was how Nell felt. She was an ex-convict, a childless spinster of twenty-five living with her mother and stepfather. She had chosen the criminal life and now the other two choices circled, one on each shoulder: serve or starve?

Nell would become Mr Bright's special protégé. He encouraged her to go to church and sit between him and her mother. If there was a fair or fundraising event or jumble sale, Nell would be cajoled into helping out. It was as if they were petrified of leaving her to her own devices for fear of *the peril of idleness* taking hold. This tranquil, predictable life had been her mother's dream. She wouldn't understand even if Nell had explained how the thrill of being a thief had been worth it, even considering the horrific parts. Nell had experienced real adventures, and now it was over, she felt wretched for not finding pleasure in domesticity.

Nell would cry for no reason, but kept her feelings to herself out of gratitude to her family – many would not have had her back.

She had written to Effie at the old address, but her letters had been returned. Nell had even written to Chrissie, who did reply, and told her no one had seen Effie since she'd run off with Marco Sabini. Chrissie also told her how things had gone awry with both Alice and Maggie being sent down for their part in what would become known as the Lambeth Riot in March of 1926. The old regime crumbled, and younger women fought for the title of Queen of the Forty Elephants. Chrissie herself was stepping back from the Forties, she had said in her letter.

Effie had disappeared with the money, but Nell didn't even care about the money that much. It was the excitement she missed. The sense of purpose, the camaraderie – *the thrill*.

But on occasion, glimmers of old Nell would escape. At the summer fayre in June 1926, among the tombola, coconut shy and bric-a-brac, Nell had a stall selling her own jam. Steph and Nell sat with a red and white checked tablecloth as pastel bunting flapped over their straw hats. A man made a bashful approach and Steph looked excited as the man attempted to make Nell's acquaintance.

'I felt compelled to compliment you on your gooseberry jam, Miss Mackridge. I said to my mother, I don't think I've ever tasted anything quite as good. How did you learn such a skill?'

'Prison,' said Nell, as the poor man near choked on a scone.

'Eleanor!' gasped Steph. 'Sorry about my sister, such a funny sense of humour.'

The poor man couldn't escape fast enough. Steph frowned at her sister.

'What? This merry go round gives me the itch,' said Nell.

In August, as hazy summer days threatened to turn grey and bring relentless rain again, Nell walked home from her job as a cleaner.

Mrs Mackenzie was a retired teacher who thought it a Christian thing to do to have an ex-convict clean for her, but she watched Nell like a hawk. As she dusted the old lady's worthless trinkets, Nell fought the urge to tell the woman her glazed ceramic ornaments were quite safe, and how she'd once had a man place sapphires and diamonds, worth thousands, up and down her naked body.

As she walked along, Nell became aware of a car behind her. She glanced over a shoulder and saw a black Ford crawling along the road. It was three o'clock in the afternoon on a residential street. Perhaps they were drumming, or lost, more likely. It could be local police deciding whether to ruin her day or not. She had been harassed several times after having to report to the station on licence.

The car crept up alongside. Nell braced herself. *Chin up, Duchess.*

'Good God! I wasn't sure if it was you! Why are you dressed like that?' It was Effie, regarding Nell with an expression of shock.

'What are you doing here!?' Nell dropped her bag, astonished to see her old friend.

'It's taken us ages to find you, get in,' Effie waved her towards the car.

Nell opened the door, and on the passenger seat was her enamel tin, the one she had assumed lost forever. Effie picked it up and handed it to her as she sat down.

'I thought you'd nicked it,' said Nell.

'Well, that's gratitude, isn't it, Charlie?' Effie spoke to the back seat, and there was Charlie, who leaned forwards.

'I can't believe it's really you two! How did you find me?' squealed Nell.

'With bloody difficulty,' said Effie. 'The rest of your money is in the boot, and I resent the fact you thought I'd run off with it.'

Charlie wore a pistachio silk blouse and skirt. Effie, a cream silk blouse, but otherwise in black, with hair set, scarlet lips and driving gloves. They all had a few cracks around the eyes these days, but Effie and Charlie were made up and beautiful. Nell wasn't even wearing makeup.

'You can't dress like that if you want to come,' said Effie. 'People will think you have a disease, and when did you last brush your hair?'

'Come where? I'm on licence. I can't go anywhere or I'll go back to prison.'

'They've got to catch you first, silly.' Effie brushed off

her concerns. 'I'm running away, Charlie is coming too. We thought you might want to join us. Now you're out, you don't have to, of course, but…'

'Where are you going?' asked Nell. It was all too much; she thought she might be hallucinating.

'We've been arguing about it on the way,' said Charlie. 'I say Berlin, but Effie says Casablanca. But Berlin is the place where all free-thinking people are going! I always thought of Germans as tightly wound, but they're really very kinky.'

'I… But… aren't you married?' Nell asked Effie.

'Urgh. I am, but I'm leaving him. I have a suitcase of his money in the boot, as well as yours and mine. We won't need to worry about funds for a while.'

'But… he's a Sabini. He'll come looking for you!'

'Not with the photographs I have,' snorted Effie.

Nell was all in a flux. She didn't know what to think. If she ran away, she'd be wanted by the police. Potentially, she could never come home. Then there was her family – she would be running out on them too.

'You should see the photographs – they're so disturbing.' Charlie sniggered.

'What are the photographs of?' Nell asked.

'Imagine, if you will,' said Effie, 'a fat old dog eating hot chips, except the dog is my husband and the chips are the arse of a man who worked for him. Gives a new meaning to the title of backup man, doesn't it?'

'Oh… Effie, I'm… sorry,' said Nell. 'That must have been… upsetting.' Charlie tittered along in the back seat. 'Can I see them?'

'No, you cannot, it's humiliating.'

'I'll show you later,' said Charlie.

'Well? Are you coming or not?' asked Effie.

'Where's Lily?'

'She's working for Kate Meyrick now. Funny story, the shoemaker cheated on her. Can you imagine being cheated on by a shoemaker!? Actually, I can't talk. We could swing by and see if she's interested. We wanted to find you first, thought we might have to save you from swinging from the rafters. Going by the state of you, and those shoes, we've arrived in the nick of time.'

'But I don't have a passport,' Nell suddenly remembered.

'Nell, in case you've forgotten, we know people that can sort all that. We buy passports in London.'

'We can get new names! Can I be Angelica?' gasped Charlie. She gripped the front seats. 'Kenya! We should go there. Have we got enough money for that?'

'Trust me, we have enough,' said Effie. To Nell, 'Well?'

'I'd be deserting my mother after everything and... I feel awful because she and Gerald will be disappointed but... Fuck it! Take me with you. I can't live like this!'

Effie and Charlie radiated with glee as Nell leaned back in the passenger seat, horrified by her own wicked choices.

'Drive, before I change my mind,' said Nell.

Effie put the car into gear. The exhaust sputtered and they pulled away. Nell was exhilarated, and frightened. What the hell was she thinking?

'What about Martinique in the Caribbean? What language do they speak?' asked Charlie.

'Do you know,' said Nell, brightening up, 'I think it might be French.'

ACKNOWLEDGEMENTS

THIS WAS A VERY INTERESTING BOOK TO WRITE BUT also challenging because some of the characters are inspired by real people and I wish not to cause their memory any disrespect or misrepresentation. But as ever, I have been blessed to have a wonderful and supportive team at Head of Zeus who have made it a much easier process than it could have been. Firstly, thank you to my commissioning editor, Madeleine O'Shea, who saw potential in the idea. Secondly, to Bethan Jones and Peyton Stableford, who have been the most joyous and exciting collaborators, as well as editors, a writer could hope for. My thanks to the wider team at Head of Zeus, as it takes a tribe as big as the Forty Elephants to bring a book to market.

Many gracious thanks to my agent, David Headley, without whom I would likely never have been published at all. I'm sure I'm most annoying, but I am quietly confident the best people are, on occasion, at least. Also to one of the kindest humans, Emily Glenister, as well as everyone at DHH Literary Agency for their continued support.

I so enjoyed falling down the rabbit hole while researching the real women of The Forty Elephants, and finding out about this period in our history, in between the two wars, which often gets overlooked. I must extend my admiration to Caitlin Davies, who writes the most brilliant books about criminal women, turning them from two dimensional characters to fully complex human beings. I have included several titles in further reading, and I would encourage anyone interested in the authentic stories of these women to read them. A few characters have been inspired by her research, although I rather did get carried away with it all! Also the non-fiction book by Brian McDonald on Alice Diamond and The Forty Elephants helped to bring the character of Alice to life, who then began strolling through my dreams, which, as a writer, I found most helpful, if a little intense!

To the archivists at the National Archives who helped me find the gold dust mug shots and criminal records of the women at the core of The Forty Elephants during 1920-1925. I could lose a lifetime trawling through such precious materials, but it was made easier with such prompt direction and knowledge.

To my friends, who regularly call me out on my own ludicrous tendencies and who I vow to treasure forever. Anna, Ruth, Ewan and Katie. May we all end up in the same home! Even if it is a state-run gulag by that point. To my best friend, Jodie, upon whom I have a relationship based on meme sharing and mutual rage dumping: thank you for being there for me! To Jenny, for laughing at my quirks, mocking them, but accepting them all the same. And to Caitlin, my daughter, who has always had an unwavering belief that I can somehow do and might know everything. I will always be here for you! Much like Nell's mother, you simply cannot stop me from loving you! I must include her friends, Keisha, Charlotte and Maddy, who helped me bring spark and light to the women in the cell. Although only wilful and extremely loud teenagers, they showed true grit, wit, humour and fun, which I took as inspiration for my characters in the story. Although I must stress, I do not want any of you to be influenced by their activities! To my dog, Jose, who has been by my side religiously in devotion through the worst of times. You would never leave me and I will never leave you.

Lastly, I wish to thank the women of The Forty Elephants, especially Alice Diamond. Alice was a force of nature. She came from nothing and nowhere, and by rights should have disappeared in obscurity and nearly did, but somehow, this young woman born to nothing fought her way to become an entrepreneur, leader and criminal. We have much to learn about the reality of human existence during the socio-economic landscape of the time from these women. Their stories are important, authentic, complex and deserve to be heard. All people, regardless of their origin or status, must be considered with empathy and compassion, as well as critique in our collective history.

FURTHER READING

Arscott, D., 2009. *Brighton & Hove, Events, People and Places over the 20th Century.* 2nd ed. Gloucestershire: The History Press.

Davies, C., 2018. *Bad Girls, The Rebels and Renegades of Holloway Prison.* London: John Murray.

Davies, C., 2021. *Queens of the Underworld.* 1st ed. Cheltenham: The History Press.

Ferrero, G. and Lombroso, C., 2004. *Criminal Woman, the Prostitute, and the Normal Woman.* Durham and London: Duke University Press.

Gamman, L., 2013. *Gone Shopping, The Story of Shirley Pitts Queen of Thieves.* 2nd ed. London: Bloomsbury Reader.

Horlock, C., 2019. *Lost Brighton.* Gloucestershire: Amberley Publishing.

McDonald, B., 2015. *Alice Diamond and The Forty Elephants.* London: Milo Books.

Partridge, C., 2020. *Brighton's Past Brought to Life.* 2nd ed. s.l.:s.n.

Pugh, M., 2009. *We Danced All Night – A Social History of Britain Between the Wars.* London: Vintage.

READING GROUP QUESTIONS

1. Consider the Eleanor we meet at the start of the novel. How do you think her personal history shapes her decision to become involved in organised crime? Is there a specific turning point for her transition into Nell, and what do you think it might be? In what ways does Nell differ from Eleanor by the end of the novel?

2. The novel is set against the backdrop of the 'roaring' 20s – a time period known for being a decade of change, post-war discovery and decadence.
   o How does 1920s London contribute to the story's atmosphere? Are there particular historical events or cultural elements that play a significant role in the plot or character development?
   o Consider how the Forties navigate the gender norms of the 1920s. What challenges do they face as women in a criminal world? What do you think about their defence in court: using melancholia or kleptomania to play the system?

3. How does *Poor Girls* portray the intersection of class and crime? In what ways do the Forties' working-class backgrounds influence their choices or their opportunities?

   o Can you draw any parallels between Nell's experiences and modern-day issues of class and gender? How relevant are the book's themes to today?

4. Do the characters justify their criminal actions in any way? If so, how do these justifications reflect their personal values or societal pressures?

   o Do you find yourself empathising with Nell and the others despite their criminal actions? Why or why not?

   o What, if any, moral lessons do you take away from the story? Does the story challenge your own perceptions of what's right and wrong?

5. Consider the title: *Poor Girls*. How did you interpret this when you first picked up the book? How has it changed now? What do you think 'poor' means in this instance?

ABOUT THE AUTHOR

CLARE WHITFIELD is a UK-based writer. While studying for an MA in Creative & Critical Writing at the University of Winchester, her fiction appeared on Spelk, Commuter-Lit, Literary Orphans and in Matt Shaw's *Masters of Horror* anthology. Clare has published two crime fiction novels, *People of Abandoned Character,* which won the Goldsboro Glass Bell Award 2021, and *The Gone and The Forgotten. Poor Girls* is her third novel.